UNSAFE HAVEN

UNSAFE HAVEN

Mayer Abramowitz

gefen publishing house
גפן בית הוצאה לאור
JERUSALEM • NEW YORK

Typesetting: Jerusalem Typesetting, Jerusalem
Cover Design: S. Kim Glassman, Jerusalem

ISBN 965-299-311-1

1 3 5 7 9 8 6 4 2

Gefen Publishing House
6 Hatzvi Street, Jerusalem 94386, Israel
972-2-538-0247 • orders@gefenpublishing.com

Gefen Books
600 Broadway, Lynbrook, NY 11563, USA
1-800-477-5257 • orders@gefenpublishing.com

www.israelbooks.com

Printed in Israel

Preface

THE STORY I RELATE sheds light on a dark period in our history. True, the characters and the names of some of the places are fictitious, but the events are real events, events experienced by real people who survived the real nightmare of the Holocaust and those who brought it on.

I met the remarkable survivors in various DP camps in Germany and Austria, where I was stationed as a Jewish chaplain in the US Army from the winter of 1945 to the spring of 1951. For three years following the cessation of World War II, after their liberation from Hitler's death camps, these people lived behind barbed-wire fences, surviving on only eleven hundred calories per day. At that time, no country was willing to resettle the survivors.

After my demobilization, I was with them in Italy where I served as Chief Emigration Officer for the American Joint Distribution Committee (the Jewish welfare agency) helping to resettle them.

It was in the DP camps that they told me their harrowing tales of incredible suffering and their struggle to survive. Also, during that time, I worked with the Bricha, the organization that was carrying out the illegal immigration to Palestine known in Hebrew as Aliyah Bet. The Bricha shepherded survivors from Eastern Europe and Russia to the US zone of occupation in Germany. From there, these Jews illegally made their way to Palestine. This was all covert, but years later, after the birth of Israel, I was invited to a Bricha reunion in Tel Aviv, where the group's clandestine actions were, at last, publicly discussed.

In writing *Unsafe Haven: A Novel Based on the Holocaust*, I acknowledge my eternal debt to the hundreds or perhaps thousands of survivors who shared their stories with me, and who allowed me a glimpse into their inner selves, forged by torture and pain.

Above all, I am thankful for the lesson the survivors taught me: the lesson of life's renewal. Despite the traumas they endured, they rose above their hideous experiences with tremendous strength and built new lives for themselves both in Israel and the Diaspora, often achieving extraordinary prominence.

So, the story of Jodi is a compilation of hundreds of case histories. I have woven them into one account, in the form of a novel, to tell the story of events before, during, and after the years of the Holocaust in the only way they can begin to be understood: one person at a time.

I owe a large debt of gratitude to my editors, Erica Rauzin and Rachel Feldman, and thanks to Ilan Greenfield of Gefen Publishing – for their unstinting support in producing the novel that was twenty-five years in the making. Above all, to my wife, Rachel, whose constant encouragement made my writing a joy as well as a mission.

Mayer Abramowitz,
Miami Beach, Florida, 2004

Chapter 1

EVERYONE CALLED HER FRANYA, never Franceska, her full name. At fifteen, short, chubby, with jet black hair framing her face, she was not particularly attractive, but she had warmth and premature serenity. She already knew what she wanted: Stasha Wojchiechowski. Despite her youth and ordinary appearance, Franya Novikov was determined to have this handsome stalwart who dominated the young men of Grochov. Like everyone in this farming village, she knew Stasha had an uncontrollable temper, but in her imaginings, it didn't matter. She fantasized about him during her tedious chores, oblivious to his volatility and nasty, abrupt anger. He was tall, ruddy faced, and powerfully built. But, like a steam boiler, he was quite capable of exploding and devastating anyone near him.

Franya's father owned a small farm just up the road from Stasha's. At twelve years old, her widowed father sent her to a convent school ten kilometers away in Warsaw, so she rarely saw Stasha or his farm then. Three years later, his health failing, her father reluctantly brought her back to help with the farm's unending chores. Franya did little work in the fields, but she was busy tending her father, the house, the kitchen, and in the farmers' market. If she felt burdened or anxious, she never said so, fearing that complaints would sap her father's declining strength. Her break came on a market day, when she harnessed the old horse to a rickety wagon and took their produce to the farmers' market on the outskirts of Warsaw.

That is where Stasha began to notice her.

Stasha also brought his farm goods to sell. However, unlike placid Franya, he dashed all over the market, enticing buyers, quarreling with competitors, making sales, and being intrusive and bothersome. Franya was so struck by his bravado that she dismissed his obstreperous antics and his boisterous vulgarity.

One day, as Franya was selling her produce, her wagon was struck by an out-of-control government garbage truck. It rammed her wagon, which buckled and splintered. The impact of the collision killed the horse and felled Franya, sending her crashing to the ground. Amid the chaos of the horse's last snortings, the grinding gears, the squealing tires of the truck, and the vegetables strewn in every direction, the startled people flocked toward her. For a few moments, Franya was semiconscious and as the fog lifted, she saw Stasha coming through the thick gray dust.

True to his nature, he pushed aside the gathering crowd and took charge. Haranguing the shaken truck driver, he ordered him and some of the men to haul away the horse and the wreckage and to dispose of the strewn produce so that the market could return to its normal affairs.

He eased Franya into his produce cart and took her home. She settled down enough during the ride to become aware of what he was trying to tell her – a message he repeated to her father when the three of them sat down at the weathered kitchen table. Stasha, always aggressive, advised the old man to sue the government for the loss of his horse and wagon. The ailing man was daunted at the prospect of undertaking a lawsuit, which would require his traveling back and forth to Warsaw and taking on the practically impenetrable bureaucracy. He admitted he was too weak, too exhausted, to fight the government and pleaded with Stasha to help Franya pursue the case.

As she served glasses of hot tea and then sat by silently, still shaken, Stasha negotiated the commission for himself should he succeed in getting the government to make restitution.

For two months, Stasha and Franya spent almost every day together, driving to and from Warsaw. Like a tornado, Stasha stormed various government offices insisting on fair repayment. Through his unremitting intervention and in order to avoid a drawn-out lawsuit, the officials in the Properties Division settled the case agreeing to compensate Franya's father 75,000 zlotys for the horse and the wagon.

Dr. Vladek Konarski, a minor official in the Properties Division, met with Franya and Stasha to wrap up the case. He told Stasha he admired his belligerent persistence.

"I'm impressed with your ability to cut through government red tape," Konarski said. "If you ever want a job, come see me."

"No, thanks. No government job for me, ever," Stasha brashly replied. "I belong on the farm."

"You act like your father. You even sound like him," Dr. Konarski said, adding, "I'm sorry I couldn't help you when he died. But I'm delighted to give Franceska this check."

When Konarski handed Franya the check, she asked him what help Stasha needed when his father died.

"Stasha was a little boy, a minor, in the eyes of the law," Dr. Konarski explained. "His uncle, Piotr, who was his father's partner in the family's farm, was given full ownership. In the final settlement there was a stipulation that Stasha would be his heir. I thought the judgment was wrong. Stasha should have been given fifty percent ownership of the farm. But I could do nothing."

Franya expressed her sorrow, handed Stasha the check, and thanked Dr. Konarski warmly.

Escorting them out of the building, Konarski asked, "By the way, Stasha, what happened to your uncle?"

Stasha sighed, but didn't hesitate to answer: "Four years ago, he beat me pretty bad. I threatened to kill him if he ever hit me, even once. The next night, he came after me again. I was only fifteen years old but I beat the shit out of him. When I got up the next morning, he was gone. Haven't seen him since. Haven't missed him."

During their bus ride back to Grochov, Franya listened patiently as Stasha enthusiastically described the type of truck she could purchase with her government money, but he stopped his discourse when the bus drew near the market. When it halted to pick up passengers at the market, Stasha hung from the doorway of the bus and triumphantly waved the government check in a victory salute, flaunting the check like a trophy. The crowd cheered and yelled, heartened and surprised to see one of their own beat the government.

Stasha's market cronies crowded around the bus to shake hands with him, but the bus driver honked several times ordering him to get out of the doorway and back into the bus or he would drive off, leaving them at the market place.

"If you interrupt my victory celebration, I'll slash your tires," Stasha yelled at him belligerently. The driver grudgingly waited another fifteen minutes before the bus could get moving again.

When they reached Grochov, several farmers from the village sat around the shabby parlor of Franya's home, drinking home-brewed beer with her father. When Stasha walked in and bragged about winning the settlement, the men raised their glasses and cheered. Stasha handed the check to Franya's father and said, "Now that we have this, you can pay me my commission. Then I'll help you find a truck for your farm."

Everyone was boisterous, a little drunk, and openly happy, glad for the rare occasion to celebrate. Franya watched them quietly for a time, and slipped into her small kitchen. When Stasha and the neighbors left, her father came into the kitchen and asked her, "Why are you so gloomy, so sad? It's our victory day."

She looked at him, trying to decide how to explain, when he rebuked her, "You didn't even thank Stasha for getting our money. Why not?"

Tears running down her face, she fled from her father and curled up in the rocking chair on the small porch. He came out slowly and sat on his usual chair beside her as she dried her eyes on her apron.

"You are in love with him," her father said. "That's why."

She sniveled, and looked at him wide eyed, grateful that he understood and she would not need to unburden herself to him.

"Papa, we've been together almost every day for two months, but only to settle this case. To him, I was just another farm girl. I worked with him and went with him and spent time with him, but now that we've won the case, why would he come back here?"

*

Franya's fears proved correct. Now that his quest for his share of the commission was paid, Stasha paid her little attention. During the next two years, he visited the farm infrequently, and then only to drive the new truck. He rarely approached Franya's stall at the market place.

Her father, whose health had deteriorated, rarely came to the market. The one day he did get there to help his daughter, he suddenly teetered and fell to the ground. Franya cried for help – and Stasha was the first to hear and respond. She was surrounded by people who couldn't figure out what to do. Finally someone ran to the nearby police station and, shortly, an ambulance arrived, siren blasting, and the stricken man was loaded onto a stretcher and sped away. Taking in the situation, Stasha guided Franya onto her truck, quickly got behind the wheel, and followed the ambulance to the hospital.

They waited in the hallway. Franya, for once, was not thinking about Stasha, but frantic about her father. And Stasha, for once, was thinking about Franya, whom he had seen little of since his triumph with the restitution check.

She was now days away from turning seventeen, more adult, rosy, and strong, with a thick braid of black hair and an erect, capable bearing. He was drawn to her shapely body and lovely face. He watched her as she questioned the doctor who emerged to tell her that her father would need weeks of care and rest to get over his heart attack.

During the next couple of days, whenever she was not needed at her father's bedside, Stasha took her for long walks in the leafy park adjacent to the hospital grounds. As they sat on a shady bench, exchanging their experiences, Stasha desired her more and more. To win her over, he would brag about his success in the market or about Dr. Konarski's offer to work in Warsaw. He would also listen attentively when she discussed her religious education or her interest in church matters. And, on the fourth night, Stasha even went with her to a vesper service at a nearby church. When they left the small church, they passed through the park. As they stood under an enormous oak in the fading light, she confided that once, while at school, she had considered becoming a nun, but when she came home and told her father her plans, he was horrified at the idea of losing his daughter to the convent. He begged her not to return to Warsaw at all.

"I'll go to church to please you," Stasha said, reaching to embrace her. "But, Franya, I'll be damned if I could ever get close to a nun."

Franya felt him drawing her closer and did not resist when he put his hand around her waist. As he tenderly held her she at last relaxed, allowing her body to mesh into his.

She whispered, "I love you. I always have."

*

Stasha stayed at Warsaw Hospital to be with Franya and sent a message for his hired hand to look after the two farms in Grochov.

"Do you think I will have to sell my farm?" she asked when he told her that he had also arranged with his workers to tend her farm.

"We're going to go beyond just farming," Stasha replied, again bragging about his grandiose plan. "I have an idea to set up a delivery system that will pick up crops from the farms near us. We can sell our neighbors' produce for them at the market, along with ours. Franya, we'll share the profits."

"Stasha," she smiled, enjoying his assumption that she would be included in his plans, "that's a wonderful idea. You can start by using our new truck to enlist farmers."

Stasha shook his head. "No, the truck is too small. I think this business can be very big, requiring a fleet of trucks, which we can lease from the city's Construction Department. They only begin at eight in the morning and my delivery program would begin at five. By eight o'clock, I'd have their trucks back in the garages. I know it sounds far-fetched, but that's what I've been dreaming of doing."

"You should definitely try it," she said. "Your plan is a sound one. It will work."

"I spoke to my friends about it, even to Konarski," he said with an edge of anger, "and they all think I'm crazy. You're the first one who understands me."

"No one knows you better than me," she replied and, after a long pause, she added, "that's because I love you."

"I don't know what love is," he said, describing his life – a life devoid of affection. "But being with you makes me happy."

On his fifth day in the hospital, Franya's father rallied. He was eating well and speaking with clarity. That evening, he grasped Stasha's muscular arm, thanked him for his help, and begged him to help Franya.

"Don't worry about Franya. I'll be around all the time," Stasha assured him.

When the nurse came to give him his medications and prepare him for sleep, Stasha and Franya returned to a dark, secluded spot in the park. They lay quietly on the still-warm grass, looking up at the stars. She moved closer, resting her head on his chest. As he gently rolled over her, her breath began to deepen.

Franya whispered, "I've never been with a man before."

*

The following afternoon, as she and Stasha sat by her father's bed, the doctor called Franya into his office.

"It doesn't look good," the doctor said. "I'm sorry, we've done all we can. Your father's chance of surviving is dropping. He is slipping fast. I'm afraid he may not last the week."

Totally overwhelmed and dizzy, the room was suddenly shifting around her, and Franya passed out. The doctor revived her, then called Stasha to take her back to her father. They stayed by him most of the day, leaving only when he slept. And that night, he died.

Returning to the farm, Franya moved numbly through the days that followed. Stasha began to work with her on her farm. With time, he moved into her cottage, working both his farm and hers, toiling from early morning to late at night.

One evening, as Franya massaged the muscles in his sore back with hot oil, she pleaded with him. "You can't go on like this. Go to Warsaw. See what you can do about your delivery plan."

"Franya, I have a better idea. Let's sell your farm and with the money I can make my farm more profitable by rotating the crops and adding hired laborers."

She, of course, agreed and began to plan an orderly transfer of her belongings to his farm. But some days later, a bank official appeared at the farm, flashing an official-looking document. The official explained that her father had drastically indebted the farm and that the bank demanded immediate payment. If not made, the farm would be foreclosed.

Stasha argued, cajoled, ranted, and, in a fit of anger, almost strangled the bank messenger. The man managed to escape Stasha's fury but succeeded in leaving the eviction notice on the table with a shouted warning that Franya must vacate by the end of the week.

Barely containing his anger, Stasha drove Franya in the new truck to Konarski's office in Warsaw.

"I'll check with the bank," Konarski said, when Stasha handed him the eviction notice. "But, Franya, you must return to the farm right now. Protect your belongings, because the bank can seize them any time. Pack all you can. Stasha, take her to the bus depot and come right back."

When Stasha returned, he found Dr. Konarski glaring at the notice, murmuring angrily and repeating, "It's kaput, finished." Then, shaking the document in front of Stasha's eyes, he wailed, "The bank has rights to Franya's farm," he explained. "The land. The house. The equipment. Everything. Even the truck. And there's nothing, nothing you can do."

Stasha was strangely quiet.

Picking up the document, as if it were just a piece of worthless paper, he said, "We can sell my farm to pay off this loan."

"Excellent idea," Konarski replied. "Let's go now and see what we can do."

Stasha followed Konarski up two flights to the Land Registry Office. There he requested and received the abstract of Stasha's farm.

"Stasha, I don't know how to tell you this. Try to be calm. You can't sell the farm. You don't own it. I'll have to go back to the original court ruling to find out how he did it, but your uncle, Piotr Wojchiechowski, has transferred legal ownership to his children."

"Son of a bitch! *Psiakrev!*" cursed Stasha. "My uncle always threatened to take the farm from me. Now we have nothing. Not me, not Franya, we have nothing! How am I going to tell her?"

Enraged, Stasha cursed and shouted, swearing he wouldn't work another day on his uncle's farm.

"My promise is still good," Konarski said. "I'll have work for you if you come to Warsaw."

Stasha could not reply. He stormed out of the office and ran wildly through the streets, dodging traffic, bumping into people, rushing blindly. When he passed a familiar bar, he fell inside and drank himself into a stupor. At closing time, Alek, the bartender, asked him to leave.

"Alek, you have known me all my life. I worked hard, never asked anyone for help. I can't stop the bank from taking Franya's farm and my farm is gone. And, now, Alek, I have nothing. I am a nothing."

"Stasha, you're not a nothing," Alek said. "Take Konarski's offer."

"I don't know," Stasha said, reaching for the nearly empty bottle. "Do I return to Grochov to work on somebody's farm, or do I stay in Warsaw, and find work here?"

"Let Konarski advise you – I'm closing," Alek said, lifting the last drink out of Stasha's hand and leading him out of the bar.

Distraught, Stasha walked for hours along the Vistula. The chilly night penetrated his jacket and sobered him again. Finally, he sat down on the grass where he and Franya had first made love, buried his face in his hands, and wept softly.

*

When Stasha stumbled into Dr. Konarski's office early the next morning, the bureaucrat took one look at him and ordered, "Go to my apartment. Here, take my key. Shave. Get yourself cleaned up. I'll be there in three hours."

When Dr. Konarski arrived, exactly three hours later, he found Stasha presentable but deeply troubled about the future.

"Stasha, you must never let yourself get so sloppy. If you want to work in the city, you must maintain a certain look, a good appearance, at all times."

As he lectured on proper appearances, Konarski prepared a light meal, which Stasha ate with a ravenous appetite. They discussed Stasha's problems, including the loss of Franya's farm and his determination not to return to his farm.

While Dr. Konarski spoke, Stasha noticed how often the balding man used the crumpled handkerchief clutched in his tight fist to wipe beads of perspiration from his oval, puffy face. Deep pince-nez indentations scored each side of his bulbous nose.

Konarski paused in his discourse to point a stubby finger at Stasha and asked abruptly, "What will happen to Franya?"

"I like her. I like her very much," Stasha replied. "But as long as I can't help her, I can't go back to Grochov. I can't face her."

"If you like her so much, why don't you think of marriage?"

"I can't think of anything now, certainly not marriage. First we've got to straighten out our problems, hers and mine."

"I always trust a family man much more than a bachelor," Konarski said and launched into a lengthy lecture, extolling family life.

"First things first," Stasha barked, finally cutting off the old man's lecture. "I don't know what to do. Should I go to Grochov to work on somebody else's farm even though I can't help Franya? Should I get a job here as a laborer? How would that help her?"

"In these days of political turmoil, Warsaw is the place to be," Konarski said, "but not as a common laborer."

"What else can I do?"

"What do you know about today's political climate?"

"Not much," Stasha admitted.

Konarski again subjected Stasha to a lengthy dissertation, this time about historic events taking place in Germany.

Unfolding a map on his desk, he said, pointing to various cities on the map, "Hitler's armies are here, in Vienna, finalizing the Anschluss. Chamberlain is here, in Munich, giving in to Hitler's demands to partition Czechoslovakia. Nobody knows who'll be next on Hitler's timetable of conquests. But we, here in Poland, must be ready for any eventuality."

Stasha stood there dumbfounded. He admitted he knew little about those political events.

"Here, read the last line of Hitler's latest speech," Konarski said, handing Stasha a newspaper.

"I can't read," he stammered. "I went up to third grade then was taken out of school to work on the farm. I don't know anything about this Anschluss, or about Chamberlain. I heard of Hitler, but that's all."

Stasha listened, first politely and then avidly, as Dr. Konarski expounded his political opinions and described Hitler's phenomenal rise to power.

"Tonight we will begin your plunge into politics," Dr. Konarski said authoritatively. "Come with me to a meeting of the Sviatova Association. You will meet a group of patriots who could save Poland from her internal enemies."

*

They arrived at the basement of a run-down hotel half an hour before the session was to begin. Konarski shepherded Stasha around the room, introducing him to several Sviatova members. Having never known anyone of any rank whatsoever, except Konarski, Stasha was profoundly impressed, shaking hands with Father Grzybowski, the priest of St. Michael's Church, and meeting two representatives from the Sejm, Poland's parliament. Among the two dozen persons there, he recognized only two: Alek, the bartender, and the doctor who had cared for Franya's father.

Dr. Konarski presided over the meeting and introduced the guest speaker, a university professor who spoke passionately, if in a whispery voice, about "the Jewish Communist Conspiracy." Stasha moved closer to the rostrum to better hear the speaker, because the man's paper-thin voice was almost inaudible.

When the professor paused for a drink of water, Stasha asked Konarski, "He keeps talking about socialist anarchy. What does that mean?"

"That's how the regime is able to use Jewish bankers to rob Franya of her farm," Konarski replied.

"Hitler has the solution," the professor hissed in conclusion. "It's been successfully tried in Germany and it can work here in Poland: put the Jews in their place and this place will belong to you. Get rid of the Jews and you get rid of the poison that infects all of Poland."

The sparse audience burst into applause and when Dr. Konarski asked for volunteers to sign up for Sviatova's campaign against the Jews, Stasha was first in line. He was interviewed and enrolled by Antek Karpov, a younger man, not much older than Stasha, who was the vice president of the Sviatova Association.

"Where do you live?" Karpov asked, filling in Stasha's membership application.

"I live on a farm in Grochov, but here in Warsaw I have no address, not even a place to sleep tonight," Stasha replied.

"Well then," said Karpov, "you can stay with me. I have a small apartment, but new members are welcome."

Stasha remained with Antek for several weeks, learning from him how to stir up street riots, how to harass shopkeepers, and how to evade police roundups. The anger and aggression Stasha had felt all his life was being channeled into violence against the Jews and into other political attacks, but not into sex; that was Antek's department.

Stasha soon discovered Antek's insatiable appetite for women. Quite often Stasha had to sleep on a park bench as Antek's women came and went through the night. Despite this, the two brash young men became not only coworkers but also close friends. For months they ran riot together, generating harassment, assaulting Jews in the streets, and setting fire to Jewish stores.

Stasha Wojchiechowski and Antek Karpov soon headed the Warsaw police department's "Most Wanted" list. They were arrested for disturbing the peace several times, but each time, Dr. Konarski pulled political strings, getting them off with light fines or suspended sentences. Yet they did make headlines and even rated an editorial in Warsaw's leading newspaper, which commented on the "Two Hoodlums – a Blight of Polish Society."

During one of their street brawls in the Jewish Quarter, several Jewish youths routed Stasha's gang, sending Antek to the hospital with a severe head wound. The doctors saved his eye, but a deep scar remained above his crushed right cheek bone. When he was healed enough to return to an association meeting, he was hailed as a hero. His scar became his trademark.

"That's the hard way to get a battlefield medal," Stasha joked with him, as he at last moved out of Antek's apartment.

Because Dr. Konarski was satisfied with Stasha's progress, he set him up in an apartment near the hotel where the association met. Under Konarski's tutelage, Stasha applied himself to his newly discovered mission: to save Poland from the Jewish menace. Dr. Konarski engaged him as secretary of the Sviatova Association for a minimal salary and found him part-time government employment in the Properties Division.

Stasha displayed superb organizational talent and ruthless zeal, forming new youth bands and planning their operations. But his greatest accomplishment was learning to read. Konarski helped him at first, but soon he was voraciously consuming every book, every tract in the doctor's library. At Konarski's suggestion, Stasha also read books on Judaism and even learned a bit of Yiddish so that he would be conversant with Jewish topics if he ever needed to penetrate Jewish circles covertly.

"In just a few months, you have become quite indispensable to me," Konarski told Stasha in his library one evening.

"I'm glad," Stasha said, "and since you're satisfied with my work, I have a request."

"What is it, Stasha?"

"Five months ago, when I first came to your home, you asked what would happen to Franya. At the time, I told you I couldn't face her because I couldn't do anything for her. But now, I have an apartment and two salaries – from the association and the government – so I can help her. I'd like to go back to Grochov and bring her here and maybe soon get married."

At dawn the next day, Stasha took the city bus to Grochov, looking forward to having breakfast with Franya. Getting off the bus, he ran along the dirt road leading to her farm. His excitement grew when, from afar, he saw Franya's bungalow. Without knocking, he burst into the house and called out her name. He was immediately confronted by a stranger who shoved him back through the doorway, shouting, "There's no Franya here. Get out."

He stumbled out of the house, disheartened, overcome with guilt that he had forgotten the eviction notice. He cursed himself for having abandoned Franya when she needed him. Dejectedly, he headed to his farm, hoping to find Franya there. As he walked up the dirt path to the house, through the morning haze, he saw a figure in the distance. He recognized

Franya, and raced toward her, repeatedly shouting her name. She looked up and ran to meet him. They locked in a prolonged embrace, smothering each other with kisses as they hugged and fell and rolled on the grass that was wet with dew. He helped her up and found himself tongue-tied as he mumbled apologies, trying to explain his long absence.

"No need to explain. No need to apologize," she calmly said, leading him to his house.

He didn't recognize the changed appearance of the house. She had cleaned, decorated, and remodeled everything, converting the shabby hovel into a cozy cottage. She expected him to praise the transformation, but he looked dismayed and said nothing.

"Don't you like it?" she asked at last.

"It's all for Piotr, my thieving uncle," he said, explaining what Konarski discovered about the legal ownership of the farm.

"We'll have plenty of time later to discuss our problems," Franya said. "Nothing should disturb our happiness now."

And to prove the point, she led him to the bedroom.

At lunch she said, "I want to hear about your work in Warsaw."

Stasha described the political agenda of the Sviatova Association, ending with, "Now, Konarski says I'm indispensable to them, that I've really helped them grow."

"I always knew you could do it."

"And, Franya, that's not all," he said and, taking a book off the shelf, he began to read out loud.

"Stasha, your reading is perfect!" she exclaimed with surprise. "Still, the work you describe sounds dangerous. I'm happy for you, but, despite your success, I wouldn't trade farm life for that kind of work. My father often told me, 'Clean out the manure in your own barn, that's where you get your milk.' Warsaw and its politics are not your barn."

Stasha began to reply, but she put her finger to his lips and asked, "What happened to your plan to set up a produce delivery system that would keep us in Grochov?"

Stasha waved his hand as though he were chasing away a pesky fly. "I've outgrown Grochov. It's too narrow and confining," he stated bluntly. "Look at the kind of exciting, prosperous life we could have in town, with Konarski as my patron."

By supper time, she had a solution. "I've thought it over," she said.

"We can have the best of both worlds. You can work with Dr. Konarski and then come back here to me as often as you like. I'll remain on the farm, right here, or, every so often, I could come up to Warsaw to be with you as long as you like."

"But," Stasha shot back, "I want to marry you."

Those words had barely passed his lips before tears of joy began trickling down Franya's face. "You proposed! Stasha, you actually proposed," she said. "Yes, yes, I want to be your wife. That's all I've really ever wanted."

"Then come with me to Warsaw. Right now. And don't worry about the association."

"I'll come as soon as I can close the farm," she said.

"Do it fast," he ordered. "The farm doesn't matter. It's only my uncle's now anyway. We'll get married in Warsaw, no later than September 15."

"Why, what's so important about September 15?"

"That's when I leave on my first inspection tour with Dr. Konarski. We're visiting Sviatova chapters I've set up all over Poland."

"If that is when you have to leave," she said, "I'll be ready."

*

Stasha's involvement with the Sviatova Association became more intense because of his unusual ability to get things done. When his friend Antek became president of the association, he took Stasha off the streets and gave him more responsible assignments. In addition, his part-time government job as a Properties Division clerk became a full-time occupation because, at Dr. Konarski's suggestion, Stasha began to accumulate data on all the property held by Jews by pilfering government lists of householders and lists of Polish communists.

One evening, while he was scanning these lists, a name popped out at Stasha: "Antek Karpov." Since Karpov was a common name, Stasha at first thought of sharing this coincidence with Antek. But, as he continued researching government records of communist agents, Stasha noticed several similarities between the Karpov he knew and the Karpov listed in the government files. The birth date and the physical description of Karpov's height, weight, sandy hair, and blue eyes, matched the Antek he knew.

At first, Stasha continued to investigate Antek without disclosing his suspicions to anyone, not even to Dr. Konarski. He worked alone and in secret. After a lengthy investigation, he failed to find concrete, incriminating evidence. Without that, Karpov could claim that someone put his name on the government list to discredit him politically because he headed Sviatova. Perplexed, Stasha finally turned to Konarski, asking his advice on this delicate matter.

The doctor seemed inordinately perturbed and, for a long time, did not reply. Then, he warned Stasha, "Last night Antek asked me why you're working late into the night and why you're away so often without reporting to him. So, if your suspicions are correct, Antek may have discovered that you are onto something. If so, your life is in danger as is the association."

To add to their fears, the following morning Antek suddenly invited Stasha to his apartment to review plans for association activities. The sudden invitation was all the more troublesome because he hadn't been invited to Antek's home since the day Stasha moved out.

Konarski said, "Stasha, you have no choice but to accept his invitation. You have to go."

Antek grilled him throughout the night about his work in the government archives and his unreported travels. Stasha replied that he had been to Grochov to see Franya and had scouted the suburbs surrounding Warsaw to try to find her a government job.

"Please don't tell Konarski," Stasha said, embellishing his story. "I haven't cleared any of this with him."

"Don't hand me that bullshit," Karpov replied menacingly. "You're up to something. You want to be the president. Right? Now that you've become Konarski's right-hand man, you think you can knock me out."

"Never," Stasha shouted. "And, to prove to you about my travels, I'm bringing my girl from Grochov. And we're going to be married. That's what I got out of Konarski. If the presidency were offered to me, I would not even consider it."

Karpov slapped Stasha on the back, "Hey, congratulations. I'm really sorry I suspected you."

Grateful for the turn in the conversation, Stasha sprawled on Antek's bed reminiscing about the many nights he had to sleep outside while Antek was busy with his lovemaking. They both laughed salaciously, sharing lascivious descriptions of women who had succumbed to Karpov's lust.

After he finally left Antek's apartment, Stasha told Konarski that while lying on the bed in Karpov's apartment, he decided on a scheme to trap Antek.

"He still likes women. So we'll use women to entrap him."

He recruited Lara, a beautiful, trustworthy girl, who was passionately involved in the work of the Sviatova branch in Lublin. She had never met Antek, but, based on Stasha's suspicion that he was disloyal, she agreed to sleep with Karpov to ferret out information.

She made contact with Karpov and disappeared with him. Konarski and Stasha heard nothing from either of them for almost a month. They both simply vanished. Then Lara reappeared in the middle of the night, assuring them she could confirm Stasha's suspicions.

"Antek has had clandestine meetings with Communist agents," she reported, "and he has been to Russia several times."

Konarski and Stasha confronted Antek with Lara's incriminating findings. He vehemently denied the allegations.

"She is furious that I dropped her. I told her I never wanted to see her again!" he shouted. "She would say anything. Of course I met with the Communists, in secret, but I was spying on them for the association."

"How about your name appearing on the government's lists?" Konarski asked threateningly.

Antek stood up at his desk. "I'll prove to you that I'm spying on them," he vowed. "I have evidence at home. You'll see what I have learned about them! Wait here. I'll be back in fifteen minutes. You'll see, I'm the best president Sviatova ever had." He stormed out, slamming the door behind him.

They never heard from him again.

Days later, Poland's leading newspaper carried a front-page report that Sviatova Association president Antek Karpov had committed suicide. At the next meeting of the association, Dr. Konarski reported Stasha's role in exposing Karpov and congratulated him on his singular contribution to the association.

Stasha's stature and ruthlessness grew with his credibility.

He went to Grochov, where he disposed of his livestock and abandoned his uncle's farm. He helped Franya pack her belongings into his car, and together they drove to Warsaw. When they entered Stasha's apartment, they found a bouquet of flowers with a note from Dr. Konarski. "Welcome, my dear Franya," he wrote. "I wish you and Stasha well on your forthcoming marriage. When you get this, please come to my apartment as soon as you can."

*

"Welcome, welcome Franya," Dr. Konarski greeted her warmly. "Stasha, you have found a beautiful bride. Franya, I promise I'll do all I can to make your life in Warsaw pleasant and comfortable."

"Thank you for what you've already done for Stasha and for making it possible for us to get married." Franya said, kissing him on both cheeks. "But I don't want any fuss, just a quiet wedding."

"Nonsense," Dr. Konarski summarily replied, "I already arranged with Father Grzybowski that the entire Sviatova membership will celebrate your wedding with an outdoor dinner in the church gardens. And I will have Berlin underwrite all the costs."

He served them coffee and cake and then, looking at his watch, he apologized that he had to leave them.

"I am going to Berlin to attend my cousin's wedding to Colonel Karl Greifler, a high-ranking officer in the Gestapo. A taxi should be here any minute. Come ride with me to the railroad station. We can talk along the way."

In the taxi, Konarski said, "Stasha, when I get back, I'll go with you to visit the association's new branches and Franya, you will come with us."

"Thank you, but no," she said. "Now that I'm in Warsaw, I have to concentrate on our wedding. Truly, I'm not much interested in anything else right now."

"You are going to be Stasha's wife," Konarski scolded, "and you will have to join his work. Your husband is going to be a national leader in the association, and when the Nazi Party takes its rightful place leading Poland's government, no one must doubt your loyalty to our cause."

Somewhat afraid, Franya feigned laughter. "Dr. Konarski, this is all too much for me. I'm just a simple farm girl. I left my home village only today. Please, be patient. I know Stasha is going to be important, but I don't matter, not yet."

The cabdriver dropped Konarski at the train depot and obeyed Stasha's instruction to take them to St. Michael's Church.

In the taxi, Franya begged, "Stasha, please tell me what's going on. Who is this high-ranking Gestapo officer? What's he up to, what are we involved in?"

"Franya, remember what you said to Konarski: the only thing that interests you now is the wedding," Stasha said, giving her a dismissive peck on the cheek. "Don't worry about anything else."

The taxi stopped in front of the church, where Father Grzybowski enthusiastically welcomed Franya. She was deeply touched by his warmth but soon realized he had been her teacher at the convent school. "Come in, come in," he said, "I'll tell you what Dr. Konarski has planned for your wedding."

Chapter 2

KARL GREIFLER, Dr. Konarski's cousin-to-be, was a handsome young man – tall, blond with blue eyes – the perfect specimen of the Nordic ideal in whose image Hitler was fashioning the new Reich.

Karl had come up through the Nazi youth ranks. At nineteen he was the acknowledged Brownshirt leader. That was when he met Heinrich Hummel, father of Hitler's elite armed guard, the SS. Hummel recognized Karl's razor-sharp mind and supervised his training, grooming him to rise in the Nazi hierarchy. Greifler graduated from the University of Heidelberg School of Law the same year Hitler became chancellor of the Third Reich.

Seven months after Karl's graduation, Hummel invited him to lunch. They ate in the magnificent rose garden surrounding Hummel's home on the Wansee. A warm, fall breeze stirred the leaves; the sun shone high in a cloudless Berlin sky, setting the garden ablaze in a burst of yellow, gold, and amber. As they sat overlooking the lake, Karl nervously plucked at his sleeve, like a bird tugging at a worm. Finally, he wondered out loud why he had been invited to the mansion.

"I have been your mentor ever since we met nine or ten years ago," Hummel said, "so don't get apprehensive now. You've always followed my advice to your advantage. You earned your law degree, as I suggested. And now that you have graduated, I am asking you to join the SS as a commissioned officer."

Karl hesitated, "But, I don't like being a soldier and I hate the thought of being a policeman."

"I'm not asking you to do either," Hummel replied. "Joining the SS does not necessarily imply a military career. Come, let's go into the library. I will show you what I mean."

Two walnut bookcases with crystal glass doors flanked a grand piano in the large, exquisitely furnished library. French and Flemish paintings in ornate gilded frames hung on the paneled walls. A carved teak-wood desk with a matching high-backed, leather-covered chair stood at the far end of the room.

"There are only two powers of any consequence in Germany today: the government and the military," Hummel began as they both took their seats at the desk. "In the past seven months, we – that is the party – assumed complete control of the government, but not of the military. Neither the army nor even our own SA, the Sturmabteilung, our elite storm troops, is loyal to the führer."

"I can understand the army," Karl said, as Hummel paused to sip his coffee. "The Wehrmacht has its own tradition, and tradition dies hard. But what's with Röhm?"

"He looks upon the SA as his personal army. He has his own brand of socialism. Does as he pleases. Even omits the '*Heil Hitler*' from his salute."

Hummel snapped a rosebud from the vase on the piano, stuck it into his lapel, and spread a map of Europe over the desk. "Come, Karl," he beckoned, and pointed to the map. "Look at the countries around us. First, right here in Germany, we'll clear out the Jews, the Communists, and all the other undesirables. Then, here, in Austria, in Sudetenland, then Czechoslovakia, later Poland – our armies will enter as liberators to establish Nazi rule. Karl, it's no pipe dream. All of Europe will be Germany's fortress."

"Where does the SS come in?"

"To insure the Wehrmacht's loyalty to our führer both here and in the occupied lands."

"Where do I fit in?"

"As Trustee of all German property."

"Trustee of German property? What for?"

"You mean why not the State Treasury?" Hummel responded, smiling. "Because the properties in question will not be acquired by normal means. They will be seized, captured, sequestered. New directives will have to be established both for the acquisition and the disposition of such holdings. That is where you come in, my dear Karl."

"Sir, what do you mean by 'acquisition'?"

"The old Romans had an expression, 'Shorten your weapons and lengthen your boundaries,'" Hummel said, his finger wiping across the pastel countries of Europe as he spoke. "From the Atlantic to the Urals, there will be no boundary, no borders. As the national borders disappear, so will many people – but not their holdings, mines, factories, banks, buildings, cars, furnishing, gems, paintings, everything of value. We will create a trusteeship department that transfers these assets to the state. The army cannot be trusted with such vast and uncountable riches. From its top-ranking officers to its lowest privates, the military looks upon property of a conquered people as war booty, up for grabs."

"True. I understand; acquiring such properties is a matter of trust."

"A matter of trust," Hummel repeated. "Exactly so. Only the SS can be entrusted with the future wealth of the Third Reich. That will be your mandate. I have selected you over other men, who have far more experience, because I trained you and I know I can trust you."

Visibly touched, Karl sank slowly into the brocade-covered armchair behind him. Then, realizing that he was slumping into Hummel's chair, he quickly sprang to his feet. "I'm sorry, Sir. Your chair…"

"Karl, sit," Hummel said, gently nudging him back into the armchair. "One day, you will sit in my seat. It's your destiny. And I want you to know that Hitler knows about my offer to you. He will personally install you in your new post."

Momentarily speechless, Karl whispered with reverence, "Hitler himself."

When he finally spoke, his voice carried a ring of certainty. "I shall not fail," he said, as though acknowledging his destiny.

"I know," Hummel said, walking over to stand behind Karl and putting his hands on the younger man's shoulders. "And I knew that you would realize it too. But I also have another task that only you and an elite group around the führer will be privy to."

"Just tell me what you want me to do."

"Transferring property to the German state is only one phase," Hummel replied. "Guaranteeing its safety is another."

"I don't understand."

"Why do people invest their money in Swiss banks?" Hummel asked rhetorically, and then answered his own question. "Because of anonymity."

"Of course," Karl added, "the jewelry, the fine paintings, even the sterling coffee services must be owned by the state, but their owners must never learn where they went."

A week later, Karl sat in the second row among various dignitaries as the Nazi Party staged one of its most extravagant parades, designed to demonstrate Nazi strength and German unity. More than a million spectators crowded Berlin's huge plaza, which was awash with red and black banners displaying the swastika. Hitler marched alone down a long, red carpet to the melodramatic rat-a-tat of a single snare drum and slowly mounted the bunting-draped podium. Karl sat on the dais no more than twenty feet from where Adolf Hitler spoke. The führer electrified the huge throng with his frenzied delivery as he demanded abandonment of the Treaty of Versailles. He proclaimed Germany's right to reclaim property that was "stolen from her by the Communists, by the Jews, and by the democracies."

Karl joined a million voices in the synchronized shout, "*Sieg Heil, Sieg Heil, Sieg Heil.*" The masses shrieked in unison like sharp claps of thunder, "*Ein Volk, ein Reich, ein Führer.*" One nation, one land, one führer.

Hitler remained at the podium acknowledging the roaring masses. He then turned to shake hands with the ministers surrounding him.

Hummel introduced Karl to Hitler, "My Führer, this is the new director of your Trusteeship Office."

Hitler cupped Karl's hand and, holding onto it for quite a while, declared, "A man of trust to direct the Trusteeship Office. *Ja*, that is good!"

Karl seized his destiny and for the next three years, he diligently worked directing the new Treuhandstelle – the Trusteeship Office. He supervised the liquidation of properties belonging to Jews and other disenfranchised nationals. In every memorandum, he referred to the seized properties as "the sacred possessions of the German Reich."

*

Colonel Greifler's wedding was the social event of the year in Berlin, a glittering ray of bright festivity amid the gathering storm clouds of war.

Dr. Konarski, the bride's first cousin, was thrilled to be there. The guest list read like a who's who of Berlin society. Konarski introduced himself to everyone as "Wilhelm," forbidding anyone – even his sister – to use his Polish first name, Vladek. At the elaborate wedding feast, Hummel and the new groom engaged Konarski in long conversations about the situation in Warsaw. They were interested in his description of the Sviatova Association's activities, and quizzed him when he bragged about Stasha's list of Jewish properties. Hummel approved all the association's expenditures that Dr. Konarski had requested, including the cost of Stasha's wedding.

As he agreed to the budget, Hummel told Konarski, "I look to your Sviatova members to become the civilian backbone of the Generalgouvernement, the civil administration that we will set up in the territories that our armies occupy. Be ready. In Poland it will be very soon."

*

On the morning of September 1, 1939, one month after Dr. Konarski returned to Warsaw, Stasha and Franya headed for the church to finalize arrangements for their wedding. When they stepped out of their apartment, they saw German fighter planes in formation overhead, dominating Polish skies. Panic was spreading in the city as civilians and soldiers rushed about in the streets. Since public transportation was totally disrupted, Franya and Stasha had to walk all the way to the church, where they found Father Grzybowski highly agitated.

"It's very bad, very bad," the priest told them. "We can't hold out. It's going to be horses against tanks, foot soldiers against planes. Instead of giving up, the government decided to fight the Germans. There will be many dead when they take over Warsaw. God help us."

"Father," Stasha said respectfully, "your analysis of the war isn't our priority right now. We need to know how the war will affect our wedding."

"Who knows where we will be on September 10," Father Grzybowski said. "You'll have to wait and see, Perhaps it would be best to reschedule your wedding."

"Can you marry us now?" Stasha asked, taking Franya by surprise. "The war's changed everything. I'll be drafted and if the Germans do take over Poland, there's no telling what will happen. At least we'll have each other."

Franya did not say a word. She lifted Stasha's hand to her cheek and kissed it.

The priest thought a while and then said, "In view of the war, there would be no religious objection to your getting married without the usual publication of banns."

As Hitler's Panzer Divisions began to tear Poland apart, Stasha Wojchiechowski and Franya Novikov were united as husband and wife.

*

In March, seven months after the blitz invasion of Poland, Colonel Karl Greifler set up the Warsaw Trusteeship Office. Berlin's High Command had every reason to be satisfied with the Wehrmacht's swift occupation of Poland, but they were furious with the military's civil administration. Despite explicit directives regulating the sequestering of property, commanders had failed in the invasion's main mission: the transfer of Polish riches to Germany.

Although the Wehrmacht's military headquarters was in Kraków, Colonel Greifler set up his office in Warsaw. First, he wanted to avoid clashing with the military, since he was about to demand that its inefficiency be investigated. Second, the city's Jewish population of 300,000 souls represented more than ten percent of Poland's total Jewish population. Warsaw was therefore a classic controlled testing area to implement the transferal of Jewish property to the German state. The Bristol Hotel, the headquarters of the German military, now became the headquarters for Greifler's Trusteeship Office.

Shortly after his arrival, SS Colonel Karl Greifler summoned Dr. Konarski. A bitter, cold wind blew hard in his face as he navigated ice-covered sidewalks, making his way into the hotel. He was dressed in the uniform of the Selbstschutz, the special police force made up of the Volksdeutch, ethnic Germans, living in Poland.

"My dear Dr. Konarski, how good of you to come in this terrible weather," the colonel said, calling to an aide for hot coffee. "I'm afraid your dear cousin, my wife, will not be coming to Warsaw for quite a while, because I'll be traveling so much, but I'll ask my adjutant to plan a social evening just for you and me, so we can relax."

"Sir," Konarski replied deferentially, "I know you have more pressing matters on your mind than dinner with a recently acquired relative."

"Tell me then, Wilhelm, what have you done with your Sviatova Association since the liberation of Poland?"

"My dear Colonel…"

"No, no. Call me Karl."

"Very well then," he hesitated, "...Karl. As you see, we've been enlisted in this police unit. Under that authority, we regularly raid and search the Jewish quarters."

"Are you still working in the Polish Properties Division?" Greifler asked.

"No, that's been closed since the occupation nine months ago."

"At my wedding you were quite proud of your detailed records of Jewish properties. Where are they now?"

"We turned those lists over to the military," Konarski stated, "six months ago, October 4 to be exact. I remember the date because I personally transferred all the files under military orders."

"*Donnerwetter!*" the colonel raged, "Damn it! They're probably gathering dust in some warehouse."

"I can find out. I remember exactly where I delivered them."

"You will do more than that," the colonel said. "I am transferring you to my department. You will have the specific assignment of supervising the transfer of Jewish property to the fatherland."

The colonel handed a copy of a formal order, transferring Konarski from the Selbstschutz to the Trusteeship Office.

"Now you are Captain Konarski. Your German military uniform will bear the SS insignia. This gives you a German staff car, and provides you with an office and whatever else you need to get me those lists and seize those properties."

"And when I seize the properties, what do I do with the Jewish owners?" he asked.

"That's for Berlin to decide. My problem is to transfer all Jewish property to the state before it slips through our fingers thanks to crooked German charlatans. And that includes our own generals. They look upon Polish property just as they do Polish prostitutes. It's theirs! No questions asked! Our military personnel have become wholesale black marketeers. I'm here to root them out and impound their illegal gains. And, my dear Wilhelm, you will help me do it."

Greifler gave Konarski a copy of new regulations, under which the German government established severe penalties, including death before a firing squad, for any person dealing on the black market. "Here's a staff list for your new department, Captain Konarski. Now get to work."

"I'm ready to start," Konarski said, "but I must ask you if I can assign one other person to work with me?"

"You have someone in mind. Who?"

"My assistant before the liberation of Poland, Stanislaw Wojchiechowski. We call him Stasha."

"A Pole," Colonel Greifler said, mouthing the name "Wojchiechowski" with disdain. "Remember, Wilhelm, a Pole is one degree, just one degree, higher than a Jew. I prefer you to work with German personnel."

"As do I," Dr. Konarski said, "but this Pole has already completed the search of Jewish properties. If you would meet him, Karl, you would agree to make him an exception."

"Because you say so, Wilhelm, and only because you ask it, I will do that."

Karl picked up the phone and ordered his military aide to trace Stasha. He received a report several weeks later that Stanislaw Wojchiechowski was captured during the invasion and had been put to work with a maintenance crew in a German military installation outside Warsaw. When the unit was transferred, the report continued, the entire team of prisoners was shipped to a Silesian slave labor camp in Germany.

Days after Colonel Greifler's order to trace prisoner Wojchiechowski, a military vehicle brought Stasha directly from the Silesian coal mine to Dr. Konarski's office. Wearing ragged, grimy tatters from the forced labor camp, the sickly Stasha was barely able to stand. He coughed constantly, spitting blood, while trying to answer Konarski's frantic questions. Finally, Konarski gave up.

"Stasha, go recuperate somewhere. Go find Franya to tend to you. We have important things to do, and I can't take a sick Pole to Colonel Greifler."

*

While Stasha was confined to a work crew in Warsaw, he was allowed to visit his wife in the city, but when Stasha's group was suddenly transferred to a Silesian labor camp, Franya could not trace him. She returned to Grochov, hoping to find a haven on Stasha's farm. But all she found was devastation. The entire farm had been trampled by German tanks. The house was in shambles; only two of its walls and part of the roof remained. After a few nights of sleeping in the fields, she used some of the lumber from the wreckage to construct a rough lean-to shack.

With Konarski's help, Stasha received a change of clothing and was driven to the farm in Grochov. Weak and sick he found his wife lying in a pool of blood on the floor of the ruined farmhouse. She was ashen gray, groaning, writhing in pain. Barely able to speak, she whispered hoarsely that she was seven months pregnant and couldn't stop the flow of blood. He rushed her to the hospital in Warsaw where the doctors worked swiftly and carefully to control the hemorrhage, remove the dead fetus, and perform a hysterectomy to save Franya's life.

Over the next few days, she miraculously recovered from the physical trauma, but when a nurse informed her that she could never become pregnant again, Franya was crushed. For a week, she refused to leave the hospital. She cried constantly, brooding and miserable, all her visions of the future destroyed.

"Please, let me go back to the farm," she pleaded with Stasha. "It's the only place where I can find any peace."

She had to get away from Warsaw, from Stasha, from herself. Reluctantly, Stasha took her back to the ruins of his uncle's farm. Working slowly because of his crushing chest pains and coughing spells, he managed to rebuild part of the cottage. The two slowly nursed each other back to health and, after a few short weeks, Konarski summoned Stasha back to Warsaw.

*

"No one can find your original list," Konarski said. "I am meeting with my commanding officer and I must have it. Search for it now, Stasha, Find it. Your life and probably mine depend on that list."

Days later, Stasha was forced to admit failure. "I searched the office where I worked…my old apartment and…even Antek's old apartment," Stasha spoke haltingly, still struggling to breathe normally.

Konarski angrily cut him off, shouting obscenities, "You dumb Pollock. The meeting is Tuesday afternoon, that's only four days away. Get me that list or you'll go back to the mines."

Despite his weakened condition and his astonishment at Konarski's hostility, Stasha searched day and night for scraps of his original papers. Finally, in one corner of a Sviatova warehouse, he found a dusty carton with some of the original work sheets from which he had culled his final list. Poring over them frantically, he created a new list of Jewish-owned businesses. After hasty research, he revised it to include corporations with Jewish directors, the amounts of shares they held, and the balances in their bank accounts.

On Tuesday morning, Stasha appeared with his lists in Colonel Greifler's office, where Konarski introduced him to the colonel. Stasha had not fully recovered from his months of slave labor in the coal mines. His face was gaunt and his reddened eyes were deeply sunk in their sockets. He still had a persistent hacking cough, for which he repeatedly apologized. Annoyed by the constant coughing, Greifler ordered his secretary to bring Stasha a glass of water.

When she returned, she told the colonel, "The leaders of the Judenrat are waiting outside in the corridor."

"Let them wait," the colonel said. "It will be good for them to recognize their own insignificance."

Dr. Konarski showed Stasha's lists,which the colonel reviewed, asking pertinent questions about the entries. An hour later, after studying Stasha's list, he summoned the Jewish representatives. Because this was their first meeting with the colonel, Konarski introduced Dr. David Poliakov, president of the Judenrat, and Dr. Szymon Berson, chairman of its medical committee. The colonel did not invite them to sit.

"You," the colonel asked pointing his riding crop at Dr. Poliakov, "what kind of a doctor are you?"

"Juris Doctor, University of Heidelberg."

"I remind you, according to the Nuremberg Laws of September 15, 1935, Jews are prohibited from practicing law."

The colonel then pointed his stick at Dr. Berson, "You. Berson?"

"I'm a physician, in charge of the Czyste Hospital in Warsaw," replied Dr. Berson.

"I remind you that Jewish doctors are now forbidden to attend to Aryan patients. Now, Poliakov, what do you want?"

Dr. Poliakov, a man in his early fifties with graying hair and a deeply wrinkled face, answered, "I have several vital issues. First, the order requiring us to wear a Jewish Star armband is encouraging Polish ruffians and German soldiers to molest us openly."

Dr. Poliakov stopped talking when Stasha burst into a fit of coughing. Then he continued, "We are being harassed, brutalized, humiliated."

"Wearing the armbands is an order from Berlin," Greifler said, mockingly adding, "There's little we can do to make the local populace love you. I called you here to discuss disposing of Jewish property. I'm in no mood to hear your petty complaints."

Poliakov persisted, "But Dr. Konarski has been transferred to the Trusteeship Office. Before that, he was our liaison. Now there is no one to whom we can bring our concerns. Since there is no one, I must bring some other urgent matters to your attention."

The colonel nodded, "I grant permission for a five-minute discussion of conditions affecting the Jews."

"Yesterday, fifty Jews were picked up at random and shot," Dr. Poliakov protested to the colonel.

"We have orders to kill twenty-five Jews for every German shot at," Dr. Konarski explained to the colonel. "The fifty were killed in reprisal for the murder of a German soldier and another German who was wounded by gunshots coming from a Jewish home."

Dr. Poliakov violently shook his head, "No. No. No. We did not kill them. Our investigation showed that the soldiers were trading on the black market and they shot at one another."

Dr. Konarski began to explain, but Colonel Greifler stopped him and again pointed his riding crop at Dr. Poliakov.

"Poliakov, we're not the least bit interested in your investigations. The military investigates, the military decides, the military acts. Case closed. Discussion closed."

"The families want to claim the bodies to give the dead a decent burial," Dr. Poliakov stated, despite the colonel's growing impatience.

"You must forward that request to the civil authorities," Dr. Konarski replied.

"Stop this now!" the colonel barked. "Konarski, there is to be no more random killing of Jews. I have more important matters to worry about."

Surprised, Poliakov began to thank the colonel, but Stasha's hacking cough interrupted their discussion.

"Poliakov, enough drivel," Greifler said as Stasha covered his face with a blood-drenched cloth. "You have wasted enough of my time. I called you here today to hear the report of the registration of Jewish property that you were ordered to prepare."

Despite the colonel's angry tone, Dr. Poliakov persisted, "There's an urgent matter of health and I beg you to listen to Dr. Berson's report."

"I will listen, but that's it. That will be the last item on your agenda. Make it brief."

An experienced physician even though he was only thirty-six, Dr. Berson handed the colonel a typewritten report. The colonel set it aside without a glance.

Berson explained, "Sir, this report clearly indicates that you may be courting death. The danger of a typhus epidemic now threatens the entire city – Jews, Poles, and Germans. I appeal not only for the hospital, which is short of everything...beds, medications..., but for immediate measures to curb the spread of infection. Disease is everywhere and it will get worse if nothing is..."

"Enough," the colonel interrupted. "That problem, too, will be solved when Berlin decides what to do with the Jews of Warsaw. Perhaps they must be isolated. I don't want to hear any more about this from you."

Greifler then turned to Dr. Poliakov, "Now, give me the Jewish Property Registry that the Judenrat prepared."

Poliakov handed Konarski a forty-two-page file listing 2,750 businesses and 3,517 homes, buildings, and other Jewish real estate holdings. The colonel took the report from Konarski, flung it back into Dr. Poliakov's face, and banged his riding crop on the desk so hard that the crop split in two.

He bristled at Dr. Poliakov, "Is there no end to Jewish chicanery, Mr. President of the Jewish Council? There are more than 350,000 Jews in Warsaw and you dare to tell me that barely two percent own property?"

He flung the broken stick into Poliakov's face. "Stasha, give him your file. Look, more than one hundred pages, more than twenty thousand properties owned by Jews! Do you think I am stupid?"

Greifler paced around the desk and then assumed a condescending, paternalistic tone, "Why can't you Jews be honest? One of the first acts of the General gouvernement was to recognize the Judenrat as the representative body of the Jews of Warsaw. We did not dictate its membership and we do not order its agenda. It's your organization but we, the German military, vested it with responsibility and granted it many privileges. The least you can do is to carry out our requests honestly. Fortunately, Wojchiechowski here supplied us with a full record of Jewish-owned properties."

He paused, allowing Dr. Poliakov to study the huge file. Greifler then took it and laid it in front of Stasha.

"How correct are your figures?" he asked.

Once again Stasha burst into a coughing spell, unable to respond and barely able to catch his breath. Dr. Berson walked over to Stasha and placed his hand on his forehead, lifted his eyelids, and examined his nostrils.

"Have you worked in coal mines or as a stoker? Your cough, your pallor, your eye infection are all symptoms of coal tar poisoning. You'd better see us at the Czyste Hospital for special inhalation therapy. What you have can be cured."

"Go back to your seat, Doctor," Greifler ordered. "We can take care of our men without help from Jews. Now, Stasha, how correct are your figures?"

"Each property was identified," Stasha rasped, wheezing heavily between each phrase, "checked for proper ownership...and rated for assessed value. I even computed back taxes owed to the state."

"How much do these properties owe in delinquent taxes?" the colonel asked.

"There's an addendum here," Stasha said, leafing through the file. "More than two billion zlotys."

"As of today," Colonel Greifler summarily announced, "the Judenrat is assessed two billion zlotys for back taxes. You will begin repayment of all outstanding taxes for the Jewish properties. How you collect this money is your concern, but the first billion is due in two weeks, May 7, 1940."

"We will have our own accountants study these figures," Dr. Poliakov bluntly stated. As Greifler raised his hand to stop him, Dr. Poliakov continued, "Colonel, you stated that the military vested us with responsibilities. These include fiscal responsibilities and we must have our own accountants study these figures. Also, we feel justified apprising you of serious problems facing the Judenrat."

The colonel looked at his watch, then curtly said, "Fine, I will listen, but you must raise this money anyway. What's so important that it requires our attention?"

Dr. Poliakov replied, "The three orphanages we finance need additional space, the cemeteries require constant repair, as do the synagogues, which are falling apart. Four schools are seriously overcrowded, not to mention the problems with the soup kitchens and the hospitals, which are our responsibility. We need construction material, which is available only through the military."

The colonel, apparently surprised by Poliakov's litany of the Judenrat's activities, turned to Konarski, “Doctor, you must serve as liaison again with the Judenrat. Take care of these things.”

He turned back to Poliakov. “Remember, the delinquent tax money is to be deposited in Konarski’s office on the demanded date.” He stood up, indicating that the meeting had ended.

When Berson and Poliakov had left, Konarski asked the colonel, “Why is it necessary to work with the Jewish Council? Why can’t my office simply issue an order and follow it up ourselves? I find it odious to meet with these Jews. Why give them official status?”

The Colonel replied, “Wilhelm, did you hear the scope of activities undertaken by their council? Are you ready to attend to the orphanages, the cemeteries, the synagogues, the schools, the soup kitchens, hospitals, and God knows what else? I don’t like working with Jews any more than you, but remember that working through the Jewish Council also guarantees cooperation of the Jews in the carrying out of German policies.”

“So, what did you mean by ordering that there is to be no more random killing of Jews?”

“Before any Jew is put to death, my Trusteeship Office must ascertain that he has filled out the Personal Property Form, which requires every Jew to list his possessions and their whereabouts. That gives us an accurate record so we can immediately effect a proper transfer of his possessions.” Greifler snorted, “Then kill him.”

“Won’t the Jews eventually realize that filling out the form is a prelude to death? They only have to put two and two together,” Konarski said.

“They won’t,” Greifler smiled chillingly. “You will tell them that this form insures the return of their property when Germany wins the war and civil government is restored. They will believe you. They do not yet understand.”

Chapter 3

SZYMON BERSON was an only child, born to parents in the upper echelon of Warsaw's well-organized Jewish community. His father was a wealthy textile manufacturer and, to maintain his far-flung business connections, he would travel the length and breadth of Poland, often coming home only for the holidays. His mother tended their three stores in Warsaw. Successful and busy, the Bersons denied their son nothing except their presence, often leaving him in the care of a *niania*, a Polish maid. Szymon treasured the rare occasions when his father took him along on business trips to far away cities, just the two of them, riding in first-class train compartments.

On one of these trips, the train derailed, plunging into a ravine. The violent crash fatally wounded a woman passenger. Amidst the turmoil, a passenger rushed through the crowd and called out that he was a doctor. He examined the woman, and announced that she was dead but pregnant. He told the passengers to leave the car because he was going to perform an emergency Caesarian section. Szymon was twelve years old but, unlike the other passengers, he stood by, to watch the doctor throughout the procedure. When the baby was born, Szymon handed the doctor his fur-lined coat to swaddle the infant.

Years later, when Szymon graduated from the gymnasium, his parents had every reason to believe that their son would enter their textile business. They were surprised, and not pleased, when he announced that he had applied to Warsaw University Medical School. When they badgered him to explain why he was spurning a successful future in the textile business, he reminded his father of the train accident, and how moved he had been watching a doctor give life to a dead woman's baby. In contrast to the boy's emotionally charged description of that event, the father said he could hardly remember it.

"Father, for me, that moment was filled with awe. I decided then and there that medicine is what I want to do. I could never do what you do. I don't understand the constant ups and downs of the textile market, and I can't make myself care about it, or spend my life on the road. I care about being a doctor."

His parents had little choice but to accept his decision. Resigned, they promised to help him if they could. Shortly after, Szymon asked for that help.

"Look at this letter from the university," he said, handing the letter to his father. "They've turned me down."

"Rejected?" his father asked.

"Not exactly rejected, but deferred to a waiting list because of the Jewish quota. Can you get me into medical school…anywhere…in France, Germany, Italy, anywhere?"

Szymon's father was able to get his son accepted at Bologna's Medical College, where he graduated three years later with high honors. The State Hospital of Warsaw immediately engaged him as a pathologist and within a short time he was appointed medical director of the famed Czyste Hospital. Because of his brilliance, Warsaw University repeatedly asked him to accept a faculty position. He refused due to his hospital workload, but he agreed to give occasional lectures to the medical students.

Berson was brilliant. He was one of the few Jews in the university, where colleagues called him "the *Yiddishe Kopf*," the Jewish mind, a genius. Just for sport, he could reel off the origins and insertions of every muscle in the body. It took his genius to make Czyste Hospital one of Poland's leading medical facilities.

Like his father, he also assumed leadership in the Jewish community, serving as a member of the Judenrat. Although the hospital's deficit was underwritten by the Judenrat, he rarely attended the council's meetings. He considered the haggling and endless debating a "waste of time" when he could be with patients. Instead, he designated one of his assistants to represent him at the Judenrat.

*

As they left their meeting with Colonel Greifler, Berson congratulated Poliakov on standing up to the colonel.

"It is meaningless," Poliakov responded ruefully, "I have to give in to their demands all too often. Yet, much of the time, the Jewish community often benefits by agreeing to their demands. People do not realize how difficult these Germans can be."

"David, despite the financial burden heaped on us to pay the back taxes, Greifler acquiesced to most of your demands," Berson noted. As they walked in silence, he suddenly asked, "Who is this Wojchiechowski?"

"To us he's Stasha, a local thug, a menace to the Jews," Poliakov replied. "He was Konarski's sidekick, sort of a glorified messenger boy."

"He's no messenger boy. Watch him. I respect a man who is sharp with figures," Berson said, and repeated, "Stasha Wojchiechowski, Wojchiechowski…Our paths have crossed somewhere before. It will come to me."

Neither man realized that Stasha had furtively followed them from the moment they left the Bristol Hotel. He appeared before them stealthily as they passed through a wooded park, hidden from view of the main highway.

"Wait," he said to the startled Berson. "Where can I get the medication you mentioned?"

"Come to my office where I will get you both the medication you need and the inhalation therapy," Berson said before hurrying on with Poliakov.

Over the next month or two, Stasha appeared at the hospital three times each week for inhalation therapy. When he completed the therapy, he stopped by Dr. Berson's office to thank him for curing his infection and ridding him of its persistent cough. "I apologize for bringing up the statistics of Jewish properties at the colonel's office," Stasha added. "I was only following orders."

"I didn't follow orders when I operated on your wife when she hemorrhaged. Maybe following orders is not such a good thing," Berson said softly.

Shocked and stunned, Stasha murmured, "I didn't know that was you. I'll never forget what you did for my wife that day."

"I'll never forget you, either," Dr. Berson replied, answering the phone as Stasha left.

"Szymon, it's David Poliakov. I need you to come to the next Judenrat meeting."

"David, I'm swamped. I can't be at the meeting, but I'll send my assistant to represent me."

"No, Szymon," Dr. Poliakov insisted, "I'm preparing the agenda now and I want you there because we have a rebellion to contend with. You are involved."

"I'm involved? All I want is to not be involved."

"Too late. I can only tell you about it in private," Dr. Poliakov replied. "I'm coming to your office right away."

Sitting in a chair facing the doctor, his body stiff with tension, Poliakov dismissed Berson's small talk about Stasha and refused the customary cup of tea.

"Szymon, this is urgent. Do you remember our meeting with Colonel Greifler a couple of months ago?"

"Yes, of course. What's he up to now?"

"He's about to order us into a ghetto."

"A what!"

"You heard right. A ghetto," Dr. Poliakov responded in a whisper.

"I remember Greifler's response to my warning about a typhus epidemic," Dr. Berson said. "He told us, 'Berlin decides what to do with the Jews of Warsaw.' I thought he was referring to a typhus isolation ward."

"Isolation it is," Poliakov said bitterly. "A ghetto for Jews."

"I can't believe it, David. I can't believe that even the Nazis would resort to the barbarism of the Dark Ages."

"Believe it, believe it, Szymon. I received this from Konarski last week," Dr. Poliakov said, handing him a map of Warsaw. "The city is going to be divided into these two sectors. You see, the areas are marked in heavy red ink: '*Judische*' and '*Aryanische*'."

Berson studied the map and shook his head. Abruptly, he banged his fist on the table with rage. "No! It isn't possible. It can't happen."

"It's possible and it's happening," Poliakov said, and taking a printed sheet out of his pocket, he continued, "Listen to Greifler's published instructions.

'One. A Jewish Ghetto will be established as per the attached area map.

'Two. All Jews presently residing in Warsaw and those to be transferred from outlying districts will be restricted to the Jewish area designated in the map.

'Three. A wall three meters high will enclose the Ghetto. Jews will supply labor battalions for the construction of the wall, which will be financed by the Judenrat.

'Four. Any Jew found outside the Ghetto after a specified date will be shot.

'Five. Housing allocation will be under the supervision of the Judenrat.

'Six. Security during the construction period will be provided by the German military police and the Polish militia.'"

"This is barbaric!" Berson shouted, grabbing the memo.

"There's more. When the orders for the Ghetto are issued, the Germans will say it is being created for medical reasons."

"Medical justification for a ghetto?"

"That's why I am here," Poliakov said. "I need your help to explain to the Judenrat the medical necessity of creating the Ghetto."

"Medical necessity! David, what the hell are you talking about?"

"According to their chief medical officer, Jews carry typhus and are spreading it and other infectious diseases to the military and civilian populations. Therefore, the need for the Ghetto!"

"Chief Medical Officer Lieutenant Colonel Dr. Berthold Wolrauch," Dr. Berson said mockingly. "That fat son of a bitch. He's here practically every day demanding treatment for military patients who are not supposed to be in my hospital in the first place. Look, here's a roster of the German military patients we are caring for here."

"Fine, you're a good doctor, good to the Germans," Poliakov sarcastically said, scanning the list of German patients.

"David, I'm going to have a talk with Chief Medical Officer Wolrauch."

"It's too late," Poliakov said. "Orders for the Ghetto come directly from Berlin. It's only a matter of time. The 'medical necessity' is a smoke screen to hide the real intent of the Ghetto."

"Then the situation is hopeless. So, what do you want from me?"

"Just what I said," Dr. Poliakov repeated. "Help me explain this order to the Judenrat."

"I don't understand."

"Well, after we met with Greifler, the issue of an epidemic was raised at a meeting of the Judenrat. I mentioned your report to Colonel Greifler about the threat of an epidemic. Then, trying to be casual, I repeated what he said to you, that Berlin was considering isolating the Jews."

"You did? What happened?"

"If I had detonated a bomb in that room, I couldn't have created greater pandemonium. Everyone shouted, 'Ghetto! Ghetto!' Accusations came from all sides. First came the hotheads, led by Leon Viner. He insisted that we call a general strike to demonstrate what he termed 'Jewish resistance.' Of course, he was voted down. Then the political hacks wanted to form a committee to deal directly with the Germans because they accuse me of kowtowing."

"Why do you come to me? What can I do? I'm totally opposed to a ghetto."

"Szymon, I need you there when I bring this up," Poliakov said, waving the map in front of Berson's face. "You must be a voice of moderation. Maybe your presence, your explanations, will quiet the tempers."

"Me? Quiet their tempers? You are not hearing me. I agree with Viner."

"You what?" Dr. Poliakov asked in disbelief. "You agree with Viner?"

"Well, I don't agree that a general strike will stop the Germans from going ahead with a ghetto. But I do agree that the Ghetto will be the beginning of our end. You just said it yourself: the medical excuse is a smoke screen to hide their real intent."

"I don't know their intent, or the intent of the Ghetto," Poliakov said wearily. "I just know it is inevitable. But I still want you at the meeting. At least you don't agree with staging a general strike."

"But I think that a little bit of Viner's noncompliance is not altogether wrong. Let's not make it easy for the Germans to destroy us."

"Szymon, you haven't dealt with them," Dr. Poliakov said.

"I practice some of Viner's noncompliance every day," Dr. Berson replied. "I'm not supposed to treat German nationals, but I do. I'm not supposed to buy black market supplies, but I do."

"You're isolated in your sanitized hospital. It has protected you from the reality of German brutality. They need you. They are in awe of your medical expertise."

"David, they threaten me constantly."

"No one shoots doctors in hospitals," Poliakov said. "But Jews they kill everywhere – in the streets, in their homes, in their offices. Remember how they slaughtered the Jewish students who staged a protest against wearing the 'JUDE' arm band."

"Remember? I treated the wounded. But I still believe that Viner is right, that outright acceptance of the Ghetto is wrong. Somehow we must set up some obstacles, some roadblocks that will make the Germans reconsider or, at least, delay this scheme."

"I've already used up all my roadblocks," Poliakov said. "You know, the Lodz Ghetto was built in April, five months ago. I've been stalling since then. Buying time, day after day, week after week, delaying as much as I can."

"David, no one questions your leadership, certainly not me," Dr. Berson said. "I saw you stand up to Greifler and I admire you. That takes courage. But what Viner is saying is, 'Let everyone demonstrate that kind of courage.'"

"You may be a good doctor, Szymon, but you're impractical. Viner is advocating national suicide and by supporting him, you become his accomplice."

Stunned, Berson again tried to explain his stand, but Poliakov slumped down in his chair and raised his hands to silence his friend.

"Szymon, I didn't come here to debate with you and, frankly, I don't want to hear your arguments. I'm dealing with a fact unfolding in front of me, and I need you to head off a catastrophe within the Judenrat. Yes or no?"

"Yes," Berson replied. "I can't abandon you with this disaster. Within my own beliefs, I will try to help. What do you want me to do?"

"I want you to explain any possible health benefits we might achieve when we are forced to live in a ghetto."

"But that's nonsense. There aren't any," the doctor shot back, quietly adding, "But I'll help you another way. I'll meet with Greifler."

"That may take weeks," Dr. Poliakov replied. "Konarski is now in charge. Even to get to Konarski I have to go through Stasha the Satan, who's now strutting about like the chief executioner."

Berson reached for the telephone and dialed Wolrauch's number. Within a few seconds, Dr. Wolrauch was on the phone.

"Berthold, Szymon here. Have you decided what to do with your German patients when the Ghetto is established?"

"When is that?" Wolrauch asked.

"Looks like it's coming soon," replied Dr. Berson. "Do you know if your people will have free access to and from the hospital?"

Wolrauch said nothing.

"Will your sick or wounded German soldiers be enclosed with us in the Ghetto?"

Again, no response.

"Are we still to accept your new patients? Do we discharge the men we have?"

Berson waited for Wolrauch's response and, receiving none, he finally said, "Berthold, I think it's time for you and me to meet with Colonel Greifler."

Slowly Wolrauch replied, "Yes, I believe so. I'll call you right back."

"Fine," Berson said. "But tell him that Dr. Poliakov will come with me."

While waiting for Wolrauch's call, Poliakov and Berson discussed how to negotiate further with Greifler. Since the Ghetto orders came from Berlin, they decided that postponement was the best they could hope for, and to demand two concessions: open gates and a bigger area.

"If we can achieve a larger ghetto with free movement in and out, perhaps it won't be totally impossible," Poliakov was saying when the phone rang.

"Berson, it's Wolrauch. Greifler will meet with us at three this afternoon."

*

A military aide showed them into the Trusteeship's newly decorated office. Wolrauch and Konarski greeted them in the anteroom and escorted them to Colonel Greifler's office, freshly furnished with mahogany furniture and Persian carpets. This time Greifler did not keep the Judenrat representatives waiting. They were convinced that Wolrauch had updated the colonel about the critical medical services Czyste Hospital was providing to the Germans because, as they walked in, Karl Greifler actually greeted them with rare effusiveness.

"Dr. Berson, I've been meaning to congratulate you on your hospital's good work, on your high standards. I'm grateful Dr. Wolrauch brought this matter to my attention. Welcome, welcome. Here, sit down, have some coffee."

"This may be our lucky day," Berson whispered to Poliakov when the colonel paused to answer his telephone.

Hanging up, Greifler called out to his secretary, "No more calls now. We're in an important meeting." He picked up the list containing names of German personnel being cared for at Czyste Hospital and began, "Now, doctors, how long would it take to clear this case load?"

Wolrauch and Berson conferred. "At least four weeks, if we don't refer any more patients there," Wolrauch answered.

"Can the current patients be transferred to our military hospital for treatment?" Greifler asked.

"No, Sir," Wolrauch explained. "We sent them to Czyste in the first place because they have serious conditions or unusual illnesses. Czyste has been very successful in treating such cases. It would benefit our soldiers if we could keep treating them at Czyste. Could some arrangement be made?"

Greifler nodded at Wolrauch, but turned and spoke to Berson. "Doctor, clearly you have maintained a fine medical institution. My congratulations. But now I must ask Dr. Poliakov, did you bring a map of the proposed Ghetto site?"

Somewhat surprised at being called upon so suddenly, Poliakov produced the map. "Colonel," he ventured, "the use of the hospital is not the only problem this raises. In the designated Ghetto there are many problems. There is no place for sewage to drain, a very limited supply of water, and overloaded power lines."

Greifler scanned the map. "Konarski," he ordered, "you investigate these water and engineering problems. Let me know what the situation is there."

Encouraged by the colonel's attitude, Poliakov continued, "According to the map, only two percent of Warsaw's area is being allocated to more than 42 percent of its population. This places a tremendous burden on the people who will have to live there, especially in view of the inadequate facilities. Surely, increasing the space presently allotted for the Ghetto will in no way indicate any opposition to orders from Berlin."

"The allocated area is a potential medical hazard," Berson said, adding weight to Poliakov's arguments.

"These orders are from Berlin," Greifler confirmed, indicating that little could be done.

Dr. Wolrauch spoke up, "With the Colonel's permission, I will contact my superiors in Berlin to urge them to recognize the importance of this hospital."

"And when the Ghetto is established," Dr. Poliakov added, "keeping it open, with free access for its residents, will allow German troops to continue to use this hospital."

The colonel again nodded, encouraging him to continue, so Poliakov plunged in, "Colonel, I cannot stress enough how urgent it is to increase the size allotted for the Ghetto."

Greifler took the map from Poliakov and propped it on an easel in the far corner of his office. He huddled there with Wolrauch and Konarski, whispering. Meanwhile, Berson quietly assured Poliakov, "We've accomplished more than we set out to do. A postponement, an open ghetto, and better physical conditions."

The colonel then placed the map on his desk and drew a line around the neighborhood of the Czyste Hospital.

"The solution is quite simple," the colonel said. "The Czyste Hospital will not be part of the Ghetto. It will be on the Aryan side. Berson, set aside one building in the Ghetto as the hospital annex. Dr. Konarski will redraw the boundaries. By tomorrow you will receive a new map."

Poliakov and Berson were horrified, startled. "But Colonel," Berson began, "how can I make provision for all the people…"

"Stop," the colonel commanded. "Enough. Construction of the Ghetto will begin on schedule. Now, Jews, get out."

"Failure, Szymon, total failure," Dr. Poliakov said when they stood outside the gate. "We accomplished nothing."

"Not even a postponement," Dr. Berson added, unable to find a comforting thought.

"And we have no idea when this diabolical scheme will befall us," said Poliakov, who seemed to have aged suddenly far beyond his fifty-one years.

"Now I see the burden you carry for the Judenrat," Berson said, as Poliakov turned his head away, sobbing softly.

"My God, now you will have to tell the Judenrat that the Ghetto is a reality," Berson said, almost in a whisper.

Poliakov took a few minutes to collect himself and managed to murmur, "It is worse than you imagine. Far worse."

"Why? I realize that the Ghetto is dreadful."

"But I cannot present it that way. To avoid mass panic I'll have to introduce this calamity to the Judenrat in some kind of favorable light. If I don't, there will be chaos. I will have to urge compliance so that our property is transferred in an orderly way and living quarters are assigned fairly."

"David, if you still want me," Dr. Berson said, "I will come to your meeting next Monday night."

"Thank you. I think you understand now what we are facing."

Near the hospital, they crossed a field where Stasha was drilling his troop of civilian militia. He was dressed in the gray uniform. As he approached them, Berson nudged Poliakov and whispered, "Look, the Satan is a sergeant now; he's even allowed to carry a rifle."

When Stasha reached them, Berson asked him, "How is your chest?"

"Still sore, here," he replied, pointing to his rib cage.

Dr. Berson took him aside, away from his men, kneaded his ribs, and quietly asked, "What do you know about the Ghetto?"

"I don't know anything," Stasha said under his voice, "but I have orders to station guards for Jewish labor battalions at Cigalana and Wilcow streets next Wednesday." Louder he added, "I'll come to the hospital this afternoon."

Berson returned to Poliakov, "Well, our trip today was not a total waste. I've learned that the construction of the Ghetto will start Wednesday."

"Wednesday!" Dr. Poliakov said. "We have only six days to prepare for the disaster. I cannot wait until Monday to call the meeting. Can you come to an emergency meeting tonight? About seven?"

*

The rains that had threatened all day came down hard, making the streets almost impassable. But for members of the Judenrat the storm proved a blessing. Because of the downpour, they could walk the streets without the usual harassment from the roving gangs of Polish thugs and militia troops.

Emergencies at the hospital kept Dr. Berson long past seven that evening. Finally, head nurse, Rivka Segal, reminded him of the emergency meeting. He rushed out, but the Judenrat meeting was well underway when he arrived.

"I studied the map, Dr. Poliakov," Faivel Garfunkel was saying when Berson took a seat, "and the statistics are frightening."

Garfunkel was a unique member of the Judenrat. First, he was the only member with no party affiliation, a much sought-after swing vote amid the representatives of the Religious non-Zionists, the Religious Zionists, the Bundists, the Labor non-Zionists, the Labor Zionists, the Revisionists, and many other splintered parties. Second, he was a respected academician, a physics instructor at the University of Warsaw. He rarely spoke at meetings, but when he did, everyone listened.

He walked up to the Ghetto map tacked onto Poliakov's lectern. "Look here. This area, two square kilometers, is intended for roughly 300,000 people. Now look at the rest of the city – more than 85,000 square kilometers – for the rest of Warsaw's population, about 900,000 people. That means that the Jews, more than 42 percent of the population, get about 2 percent of the city's area."

"Did you tell that to the Germans, Poliakov?" a taunting voice called out from the rear.

Dr. Poliakov ignored the gibe and asked, "Professor, do you have anything else to add?"

"This is a fact," Garfunkel said, shaking his head, "not statistics. Three hundred thousand souls cannot survive in two square kilometers."

A babble of voices greeted Garfunkel as he returned to his seat. Hands went up all around the room, seeking recognition. Some shouted their opinions; others yelled, "Over here, David!" "Mr. President!"

"Everyone who wants to speak will be heard," Poliakov assured them. "Even if we have to stay here all night. No need to shout. You go next, Hersh." He nodded at Hersh Mayer, the former city engineer.

"David, I know this area like I know my own backyard. I can tell you that the sewage facilities are inadequate. Especially from the railroad station all the way to the north, alongside the cemetery…raw sewage is spilling into the streets. Some of it already backs up into toilets and sinks of nearby homes."

Once again, someone shouted, "Dr. Poliakov, did you tell this to your German friends!"

Again, Dr. Poliakov did not respond. He kept encouraging everyone to speak. A rabbi warned that Rosh Hashanah would be celebrated soon and that *shul*s, places of worship, would have to be provided for the masses to pray. Menachem Katz, a school principal, asked about providing school space for more than 75,000 children. Yossel Burstyn, the wealthy merchant, wanted to know if provisions would be made for warehousing merchandise for the storekeepers. The nurse, Rivka Segal, a young mother whose husband was part of the group of fifty Jews who were shot in the public square, was pregnant with her third child. She asked, "Why isn't Czyste Hospital part of the Ghetto?"

The famous actress Esther Wishna was almost in tears when she spoke. "What is to become of us in this Ghetto? What's to be the fate of Polish Jewry if we are to be herded and imprisoned like cattle? We must exist for something. Even in the Ghetto, I will sponsor my Yiddish theater group, to lift our spirits, to show we are still alive! Just give me a theater."

Then there was Leon Viner. "Dr. Poliakov, why did you call this emergency meeting? You wanted to announce this Ghetto to us, to prepare us, in your own words, 'for an orderly transfer.' Is that right?"

Poliakov nodded.

"Who the hell wants an orderly transfer!" Viner screamed. "You said that any form of noncompliance or opposition on our part would invite wholesale killings by the Germans. And I say the Ghetto is not only going to be our prison, but our cemetery. No one who goes in will come out alive! We must refuse!"

Some in the angry crowd hooted at him and shouted him down, but just as many shouted back with equal anger, "Let him talk."

Dr. Poliakov banged his gavel, trying to restore order. The more he banged, the noisier the crowd grew. Finally, Viner ripped the Ghetto map off the wall.

"Poliakov," Viner outshouted the hecklers, "you are collaborating with the Germans. Anyone who agrees with this piece of paper is a collaborator. You're all collaborators."

In the stunned silence, Viner shredded the map and stalked back to his seat. He turned and defiantly said, "Poliakov, don't lead them to their deaths. I say, escape. Escape to the woods, escape anywhere, but don't go into the Ghetto."

Catcalls answered him: "Hothead," "Terrorist," "Wild man," "*Meshuggener*."

Struggling to restore order, Poliakov stood at the front of the room and answered firmly, "For the next six days, you are free, we are free, free to make the choice. To transfer our people in an orderly and just fashion into the Ghetto or, as Viner suggests, to flee from the Germans. Each person must decide. But first, you should listen to Dr. Berson."

"Viner may be right," Dr. Berson said, somewhat to Viner's own surprise. "His suspicions could be justified. Perhaps there is some hidden motive behind the Germans' ghetto. You all know that ghettos are being erected in every Polish city. And, yes, we must be suspicious of the Germans' schemes." Viner smiled broadly as people turned to look at him.

"But I don't agree with Viner's solution," Berson continued. "To escape now is plain and simple suicide. They will pick us up one by one. In the Ghetto at least we'll be together; we'll care for each other. Eventually, we might even survive this madness by helping each other. And, as far as being locked up in a closed ghetto, don't forget there's one good thing to be said about that – a closed ghetto will keep out the Poles who harass and hurt us day after day."

Dr. Berson looked about the room. He noticed many heads nodding in assent. No one shouted or taunted him. Only Viner remained opposed, calling out, "Don't be an optimist, Doctor. We'll all die together here!"

"Leon, I have reason to be an optimist. The Germans may have an altogether different motive in setting up the Ghetto."

"You're not an optimist," Viner called out. "You're naive, a simpleton."

"Listen, Leon. When Dr. Poliakov and I visited Colonel Greifler this afternoon, David was as brave as a lion. Courageously he raised every argument you heard here this evening. Given Greifler's first reaction, we hoped, for a moment, that we would get a postponement, a few more kilometers, something. We failed. But I noticed something odd: Greifler is not a military man in the ordinary sense of the word. He's the head of a civilian department called the Treuhandstelle Ost, the Trusteeship Office East. His only function is to confiscate Polish property. This Ghetto may only be a wartime expedient project to facilitate the seizure of our property. Getting Jews out of their homes and out of their factories makes it easier for Greifler to grab everything we own."

Dr. Berson walked up to Viner. "Well, Leon, could I be right?" Viner's silence affected the entire room. People were hushed, listening.

"We must stick together," Berson said urgently. "Not just because we have no choice, but because that may be the only tactic that can insure our survival."

When Poliakov called for a consensus vote, only Viner shouted, "*No!*"

Berson sat down as Poliakov ran through the rest of the agenda as if he were conducting a routine business meeting. He established rules affecting space allocation, and committees to implement these decisions. And, just before dawn, Poliakov adjourned the meeting. People crowded around Dr. Berson as though seeking comfort and protection. He felt unable to accept the role of the comforter of his people. He knew he had only shown up to accommodate Poliakov.

He was haunted by Viner's words: "The Ghetto is not only going to be our prison, but our cemetery."

Mendel Rozen, the newly appointed head of the security committee, the Ghetto police, waited until the crowd drifted away and then spoke to Berson. "In Grochov, before the war, Stasha was my neighbor. Now that I am head of the Jewish police, I'll probably have to work with him. What's your sense of him?"

"Be very careful," Berson answered. "I met him only recently and treated him as best as I could, but he's someone to watch. He can't be trusted."

"Right," Rozen concurred. "He's become Konarski's right-hand man. He not only carries out their orders, he probably plans their operations. Did you know he planned lots of the anti-Jewish violence here, before the invasion?"

"I didn't know," Berson said, "but I am not surprised."

As Dr. Berson put on his raincoat, Viner came up to him, "Doctor, let me walk you back to the hospital." Berson agreed, feeling dwarfed beside the tall, hulking rebel.

"My own party rejected my opposition to the Ghetto," Viner said, as they walked through Warsaw's dark, wet streets.

"That makes you even more extreme than your own party."

"I know that you've been lukewarm to Zionism generally, and violently opposed to my party in particular," Viner said.

"Do you want to debate the issue of a national homeland now?"

"Not at all," Viner replied. "What I mean to say is that even if you and I don't agree on Zionism, we can agree on the danger of surviving in a ghetto."

"That's for the Judenrat to decide."

"They'll replace me at the Judenrat. You'll never see me at another meeting."

"I don't attend any meetings either. I came tonight only because David Poliakov asked me to."

"That's good," Viner said.

"Why?"

"Because you have a way of convincing people," Viner said, "like you did tonight."

"Is that bad?"

"Yes, you did a bad thing tonight. A very bad thing. Your speech swayed them. Tell me, Doctor, do you really believe what you told them?"

"I told them many things."

"Don't hide," Viner said. "You know I'm referring to what you said about the Germans' plans for the Ghetto. About it being only a way to seize Jewish properties."

"Leon Viner, may I ask you, do you really believe that escaping into the woods will guarantee survival? Do you have a right to recommend Jews escape, to create mass hysteria, which could only lead to a wholesale slaughter? And what about the old and the sick, the children who can't escape? Do you have a right to seal their fate?"

"No," Viner replied, subdued, "I don't. I can't tell anyone else to escape to the forest. That awesome responsibility has to be each family's choice, each person's choice. But as for me, I will enter no ghetto. No matter what you say, I am sure that the Germans will use the Ghetto to kill us, not just to seize our properties. I hope you can live with your conscience after what you've done tonight."

They walked in silence. When they reached the hospital, Dr. Berson reached out in the shadows and shook Viner's hand.

"Leon, I promise you one thing. If your theory proves correct, if it ever becomes evident to me that the Ghetto is being used as a staging area for death, I will escape rather than wait for the final blow."

"I will hold you to that," Viner said, and vanished into the darkness.

*

Two weeks after the Judenrat meeting, Colonel Greifler summoned Dr. Konarski, Stasha, and Dr. Wolrauch to his office, where he outlined the plans for managing the Ghetto and asked Konarski, "Will construction of the Ghetto walls be completed as scheduled?"

"Sir, as you ordered, I have assurance from Dr. Poliakov that his work crews will start building the walls next Wednesday," Dr. Konarski stated. "I've also ordered the evacuation of all non-Jews from the designated Ghetto area."

"What about the militia?" the colonel asked.

"Stasha will have guard units at the construction sites to make sure no one interferes with the workers."

"Wolrauch, have you removed all our German patients from the Czyste Hospital?"

"Colonel, all but three. I've asked Berson to continue to care for three men in critical condition. They'll stay in the hospital annex only until their condition is stabilized."

"I told you that every German patient must clear out of the Ghetto area," the colonel bristled.

"With all due respect, Sir, this is a medical necessity," Wolrauch pleaded. "Their lives are at stake. If I move them, they will die."

"Doctor, when I give an order, I want it carried out," Greifler raged.

"These are wounded German soldiers, Sir," Wolrauch ventured.

"Move them!" the colonel glared at Wolrauch, who quickly saluted and retreated to a corner of the office.

"Now, that's taken care of," Greifler continued, "I brought you here to inform you that orders from Berlin command the Jews to register at the Ghetto on the morning of September 23. Stasha will compare names of those registered with his list of Jewish properties, and will immediately inform Dr. Konarski, so that liquidation can commence."

Stasha surprised everyone by stating, "The date should be moved up another week, to September 30."

"You are not being consulted here!" Konarski scolded, but Colonel Greifler turned to Stasha, asking, "Why, what difference does the date make?"

"September 30 is a big day for the Jews. They call it Rosh Hashanah," Stasha replied. "They will all be in their synagogues."

Chapter 4

On September 30, hundreds of thousands of Jews crowded into Warsaw's synagogues for Rosh Hashanah. As they prayed for life in the coming year, helmeted German troops suddenly stormed the synagogues, brandishing guns and bayonets, shouting orders for all Jews to move immediately into the Ghetto.

"Anyone not reporting will be killed on sight," the troopers shouted through their bullhorns, waving wooden clubs and bashing worshipers' heads to herd them out of the synagogues.

Pandemonium broke out throughout the city as men, women, and children spilled into the streets, running toward the Ghetto to avoid being assaulted by Stasha's militia or by the German troops. As the synagogue's Jews were streaming into the ghetto, militiamen, under Stasha's direction, broke into homes where Jews were hiding, ordering them to report to the Ghetto. At the same time, Konarski and his men emptied the homes, carrying off valuable furnishings.

Dr. Poliakov and his committee members hurried to the Ghetto to register the mob fleeing to it. The preparations they had made after the meeting helped maintain a semblance of order amidst the chaos. Most of the committee members, who had been assigned special tasks, stood at the gates to assign living quarters, apartments, rooms, and community and commercial spaces. Despite the near chaos that reigned in the Ghetto over the first few days, several schools were already functioning, soup kitchens were set up for the poor, and two orphanages were established. Although the Czyste Hospital, now called the Annex, was reduced to two bungalows adjacent to the Ghetto wall, Dr. Berson succeeded in providing space for all his patients. His nurse Rivka Segal rushed home and quickly stuffed her family's clothing into a valise. Into another valise, she packed some kitchen equipment and some dinnerware. She piled layers of clothing on her children because they were too small to carry the family's few, now precious belongings.

"But why do I have to wear three dresses and this big coat?" her eldest, Ruthie, aged eight, whined. "It feels stuffy and heavy."

"Because Mommy is putting on four dresses and several sweaters," Rivka replied, pulling and stretching her sweaters to button them over her pregnant abdomen.

Brisk, efficient Menachem Katz was the principal of the Tarbut School – Warsaw's largest elementary school, which held classes in Hebrew and Polish. He met with Poliakov's allocation committee early to acquire space for a school. And, immediately after the Judenrat meeting in which the Ghetto had been bitterly debated, he had sent word to all his students to keep their books ready for the day when they would have to register in the Ghetto. Thereby, when the Ghetto became a reality, he would be assured a fully functioning school with sufficient text books. Thanks to his foresight, when the Ghetto school opened, it even had sports equipment. Katz also encouraged several social and educational organizations to use the school's facilities in the evenings. Among them was the theater troupe formed by Esther Wishna, who announced that a full-length play would be presented only two weeks after the opening of the Ghetto.

After working feverishly to register all the residents, Dr. Poliakov met with his staff one evening to plan for future registrations, knowing that soon the Germans and the militia would force Jews from outlying districts to crowd into the already over-populated Ghetto. Dr. Berson attended the meeting to make sure his hospital, small as it was, would receive its quota of food rations.

Dr. Poliakov and his diligent committee members all believed that it was Stasha who had advised the Germans to round up the Jews on Rosh Hashanah.

"Whoever planned this operation knew the German policy of *Schlagartige* and executed it brilliantly," Police Chief Rozen said.

"*Schlagartige*?" Hersh Mayer asked.

"Creating a riot, instilling fear, terror, while issuing orders to register into the Ghetto," Rozen replied. "That's an old trick the Germans have used in many campaigns."

*

By the end of the Ghetto's first three months, nearly 400,000 Jews, including those transferred from nearby towns, were registered. The Judenrat struggled to find living quarters for each person; families were crammed into tiny spaces, in cellars and hallways. Basic furnishings such as tables, beds, and even cooking utensils were at a premium. The once-famed Czyste Hospital, reduced to its two small buildings, was no longer permitted to order supplies or medications from the German authorities. Dr. Berson and his staff worked around the clock to care for the growing numbers of sick people, already in the hundreds. In addition, Berson raced between the orphanages and the homes for the elderly, making sure that they received the meager daily rations – eleven hundred calories, of bread and potatoes, promised by the German military authorities.

Rivka Segal was lucky. As one of the early registrants in the Ghetto, she was able to get a fairly decent room in an apartment house for herself and her girls. Her small stipend from her job at the hospital was hardly enough to buy food for her family, including half a cup of milk for her four-year-old. By selling her extra clothing in the markets that sprang up along the crowded streets, she was able to buy food for the first couple of months. In addition, wearing her nurse's uniform, which was growing very tight as her pregnancy progressed, she even managed to slip over to the Aryan side of Warsaw to trade her dwindling supply of belongings for vital food and provisions from the Polish stores.

Others in the Ghetto, like the wealthy merchant Yossel Burstyn, brought in money, jewels, and family heirlooms. Like Rivka Segal, he secretly bartered his belongings with non-Jews from the Aryan side to get food and to carry on a brisk business within the Ghetto.

To Dr. Berson's amazement, life in the Ghetto took on an almost normal existence. Children sang and studied in their schools, worshipers packed the synagogues, huge audiences attended the cultural lectures that political parties presented, sports teams played throughout the week, and Esther's theater group was not the only cast performing classical and Yiddish plays.

Before long, however, all this activity and all the attempts to live a normal life dwindled and gradually came to an end. The precious items used for barter were depleted; food sources dried up as the Germans enforced strict laws against Jews contacting non-Jews outside of the Ghetto. Before long, the Germans also drastically reduced the food rations they sold to the Judenrat at exorbitant prices. The winter months brought untold suffering because Dr. Poliakov had no way of providing fuel for the Ghetto residents. Homes, hospitals, and schools were like icehouses – freezing temperatures wreaked havoc on the starving populace. Poliakov was in Konarski's office every day, pleading for food and fuel, but the Germans were deaf to his pleas. Hunger was widespread throughout the Ghetto. People were starving and sickness became rampant. Dr. Berson, who saw death stalking the city, stormed into the Judenrat office, where the council members sat in desperate consultation cramped around a wooden table. He glanced at the assembled men, and then turned to Poliakov, begging for food.

"David, what's going on here? You can't supply me with medicines and you can't supply me with hospital equipment, but give me food. My patients are dying from hunger. I need food for them."

"Szymon, bad news is everywhere. Konarski has become the civil administrator and I'm desperately trying to buy food from him," Poliakov said. "If we can reach a price agreement, I will allot the hospital its share."

"Reach an agreement!" Berson demanded. "Buy all you can."

"If only it were that simple. It is difficult and getting worse," Poliakov said, handing the doctor a list of prices. "Look at the enormous price the Germans are demanding. A loaf of bread – 140 zlotys for us, 37 on the Aryan side. A kilo of fish – 700 zlotys, but 70 on the Aryan side. And we don't need kilos. We need tons of food. There's no money to pay what they're asking."

"If you can't raise that money," Berson called out to the Judenrat members, "there will be an avalanche. An avalanche of dead bodies."

Rozen solemnly shook his head, "Maybe Viner was right. The Ghetto may become our cemetery."

Poliakov buried his head in his hands, "I don't know. I don't know. It is quite apparent that the Germans are intent on creating these conditions."

"People will die in the streets," Berson warned. "The Ghetto will become the City of the Dead."

*

It did. The sick, the old, and the small children began to die. The first to succumb among the men was a former city engineer, Hersh Mayer. His prediction when he had spoken out at the heated Judenrat meeting of the looming health dangers proved a self-fulfilling prophecy. Hersh was in his late forties, robust and hale when he registered in the Ghetto. At first he had managed to feed himself and Sura, his wife, from provisions he had stored and with money he had saved and made by selling plumbing tools. Half a year later, when these were gone, he and Sura would line up at their assigned food-distribution center, with others Jews from their apartment complex, to receive scant rations of bread and soup.

In the fifth month of its operation, the distribution center had curtailed food distribution days to Mondays and Fridays. Sura and Hersh began a starvation diet; fasting became their way of life. He was down sixteen kilos from his weight when he entered the Ghetto, and Sura had, like him, become emaciated. She weakened, and when she could barely breathe, Hersh brought her to the Czyste Annex. Because of its overcrowded condition, the only place they could find for her was on the floor in a corridor. He visited daily, bringing her meager rations. The hospital itself had no food at all. Hersh, who had traded away most of his goods – even his clothing – had only a thin coat against the bitter winter. He lay most of the day in their room, huddled under his straw mattress to warm his weak, frozen body. Although he suffered wrenching stomach pains and dizzy spells, he would stumble to the hospital each day to see his wife.

During one of these visits, Dr. Berson noticed Hersh's ashen pallor and examined him. Hersh was running a high fever, which Berson diagnosed as cholera and forbade him to return to his apartment. But the ailing man refused to remain in the hospital, in fear of losing his food rations. A few days later, as he was groping through the streets to reach Sura, he stumbled, falling on his face, unable to get up. He remained sprawled on the sidewalk, his head resting on the leg of a cadaver, the body of an old man who had collapsed in a doorway. By nightfall both bodies had been hauled away on the death cart and buried in the old cemetery.

"He's better off now," Sura hoarsely whispered, when Berson told her about her husband. She knew her own death would follow soon.

*

Rivka Segal had been the first woman to give birth in the Ghetto, but as soon as she recovered and could get around, Berson asked her to continue her work at the hospital. She agreed when he promised her adequate food rations for her and her three daughters. The promised food was either late in coming or never appeared. She, too, soon succumbed to hunger. She could barely stand on her feet; dizzy spells slowed her down and, although she told no one, she knew she was infected – probably with cholera. Tucking her infant son into a blanket-lined box in Berson's office, she assigned Ruthie, her eight-year-old daughter, to take her little sister and stand in line to receive the family's ration of bread, milk, and a pot of watery soup. She had to rely on the children to procure the food because she could not leave her patients or her newborn infant. Inevitably, the day came when Ruthie returned empty-handed, explaining that by the time the girls got to the head of the line, there was no food left to be distributed.

Rivka begged Dr. Berson for some food from the hospital. There was none. He gave her his own rations – a slice of bread and a scant cup of black coffee – which Rivka doled out to her daughters. Two days later, Rivka trudged to work at the hospital holding her baby and trailed by her daughters. As she entered, she, like Hersh, stumbled and collapsed on the floor. By the time Berson reached her, she was dead. The baby was barely breathing and the girls were sobbing and terrified.

Turning the children over to another emaciated nurse, Berson again stormed the Judenrat office.

"Rivka Segal and Hersh Mayer died from hunger," he harshly announced, pleading for food. "I can cure illness, even cholera. But I can't cure starvation."

Poliakov and his committee members were silent.

*

Colonel Greifler's *Schlagartige* policy produced excellent results for the Trusteeship Office. As Jews streamed into the Ghetto, Stasha compared Dr. Poliakov's daily registration list with his own roster of Jewish-owned enterprises. He then made card files of those properties owned by residents in the Ghetto. He submitted the cards to Dr. Konarski so that the Trusteeship Office could initiate confiscation procedures from the homes and offices listed on the cards. When seizure was not undertaken immediately, Stasha would often lead Konarski to hidden warehouses in abandoned buildings, where they found treasures of furs and textiles, appliances, cars, medical equipment, artwork, and jewels. As a result of this massive supply of Jewish property, Greifler increased Konarski's staff so that Stasha could direct several German units to break into abandoned homes and offices.

They confiscated vast amounts of treasures that the Jews had left behind. For these dazzling results, Colonel Greifler was summoned to Berlin, where his superiors bestowed highest commendations for his startling record. At the special award ceremony, Heinrich Hummel compared Greifler's confiscation style to the *blitzkrieg* method of the German tanks.

In Warsaw, a different kind of award ceremony was held in Stasha's home, where several members of the militia gathered to honor Dr. Konarski. It was a simple affair. Franya served Polish food while the celebrants lauded Konarski, played cards, and listened to Polish music throughout the night. When the group began to leave, Stasha asked Dr. Konarski to remain with him.

"May I ask you about something that troubles me?" Stasha inquired. "I am very proud of my contribution to this campaign, to yours and the colonel's success. But why hasn't Colonel Greifler commended me for the enormous amount of Jewish property I helped uncover?"

Dr. Konarski put down his glass, stood up, and turned to leave.

"You want me to tell our colonel how great you are," he snapped. "Well, just remember that the colonel doesn't like Polacks and neither do I. Yes, I have kept him informed of your successes. That's why you're eating well, living well, and commanding the militia. Count yourself fortunate."

"Dr. Konarski, I'm sorry, but I have been loyal, I've worked..."

Konarski slammed the door in his face, stalking out of the house without saying so much as good-bye.

One month later, Konarski, who remained more distant and cold after the party, called Stasha to his office and announced, "Your assignment in the Trusteeship Office is being terminated."

"I don't understand. You said you informed the colonel about my successful work for the Trusteeship Office. Why am I being terminated?"

"It's because of your outstanding success over the past nine months that you and the Trusteeship Office are being terminated. There is little else left to confiscate. The militia will be transferred to the Ghetto's gates and surrounding walls to guard against fleeing Jews. You will continue to lead the militia."

*

Stasha's new assignment brought him into the Ghetto every day. Zealously, he delved into uncovering plots by Jews who somehow managed to escape the Ghetto. He apprehended many Jews, as well as Poles suspected of abetting escapees, turning them over to the German military authorities for execution.

When Stasha told Franya about the dead and the dying in the Ghetto, she panicked, fearing that Stasha would become infected with the raging cholera there.

"You have to get Dr. Konarski to transfer you from your Ghetto work."

"I'm still considered Konarski's aide," Stasha lamented, "but Konarski never asks me for reports, never even returns my greetings when we meet in the Bristol Hotel."

"Don't wait for Konarski to come to you. Go to him," Franya urged. "Now that he's a ranking German officer, he probably wants to distance himself further from all Poles. Find some excuse to go to his office."

His excuse came sooner than expected. When two of Stasha's militiamen, stationed in the Ghetto, came down with typhoid fever and died, his guards began to grumble about serving so close to the Jews. Later, at the funeral of the two men, the entire unit staged a protest, refusing to report for their assigned duties at the Ghetto. Stasha burst into Konarski's office to report the breakdown of discipline within the militia.

"The men are frightened. Scared to be near that Ghetto," Stasha said. "About four hundred Jews die each day there. It's dangerous to be near that place."

Konarski was annoyed by Stasha's interruption. His face reddening, he stared at Stasha coldly. "You are in charge of their discipline," he stated. "Anyone in your unit who doesn't report to his assigned duty will have his rations cut and will be subject to military discipline."

"Dr. Konarski," Stasha stood up to his mentor, "the men serving in the Ghetto are in real danger. Disease is everywhere. If I keep working in the Ghetto, I will die too, just as surely as the Jews are dying."

Konarski got up, paced the floor, and then scribbled a note and handed it to Stasha.

"Station your Polish guards at a safe distance from the gates," Konarski ordered, "and give more authority to the Jewish police to patrol inside and outside the main gates."

"Is there any chance for me to be transferred back to the Trusteeship Office?"

"I told you your services will no longer be needed because there are no further confiscations to be undertaken," Dr. Konarski stated.

Stasha replied that he cross-referenced his lists of the Jewish residents of Poland with the names of those registered in the Ghetto and discovered that there were many Jews, perhaps several thousand, who were not accounted for. He suggested that they were probably still living illegally outside the Ghetto, in hiding, or with Christian families. He volunteered to find them and recover their property.

"But," Konarski warned, "that means you must also track down your own Poles who are hiding those Jews."

Stasha promised to prosecute the traitors who were hiding the Jews, saying, "Relieve me of my guard duties at the Ghetto and I'll locate any Jews who are hiding on the Aryan side."

Konarski, concerned with his own dismissal, promised to speak to the colonel that very afternoon when he was to meet with him to discuss the closure of the Trusteeship Office. At that meeting, Colonel Greifler spoke somberly, "Wilhelm, I called you here to tell you that Berlin has directed me to close down the Trusteeship Office of Warsaw. After all, confiscation of Jewish properties has dwindled down to practically nothing."

"Colonel, your office can keep going if you order me to search for the property of lawbreaking Jews who are living illegally outside the Ghetto," Konarski said.

"Living outside the Ghetto?" Colonel Greifler asked. "Do you have evidence of this?"

"I have personally cross-referenced the lists of those Jews who lived in Warsaw and those who registered in the Ghetto, and the number of Jews who have not registered is staggering."

"So," Greifler said, "they're still living in Warsaw, right under our noses."

"If it meets with your approval, I will personally direct that operation, without Stasha and without the Polish militia."

"That has possibilities, but why do you want to take over Stasha's work and eliminate him and his Polish militia from their duties? You are the one who persuaded me to trust him. Have you changed your mind?"

"No, it's not a matter of trust," Konarski hastily replied. "I just don't like Poles getting into Jewish homes and warehouses as often as they do. Also, in this operation, Stasha and his gang would have to apprehend their fellow Poles who are hiding those Jews. And I suspect that he won't give it his full attention."

"In other words, you don't trust Stasha?" the colonel asked.

"It's not only trust," Konarski said. "More important, Karl, it's my loyalty to you. If you have to terminate your work in Warsaw, I want to be with you to the very end of this campaign, maybe even go back to Germany with you."

The colonel hesitated, then said, "I appreciate how you feel. But searching for Jews in hiding and apprehending the traitors who are harboring them, that's the kind of work Stasha is more suited for. Bring him to me."

Konarski returned that evening with Stasha, who was neatly dressed in his militia uniform. Konarski slipped back into the chair he had occupied earlier as Greifler looked Stasha up and down.

"Stasha, Dr. Konarski tells me there are Jews living illegally on the Aryan side. Who is hiding them? Do they still have valuables?"

He explained how he had compared names on lists of Jews registered in the Ghetto with his own list of Jews previously residing in the city. He concluded with his estimation that there were thousands of Jews who had not registered into the Ghetto. He also bragged that he got a confession from Rozen, chief of the Jewish police, that ten people or more managed to escape from the Ghetto each week, even though the Jewish police and the militia kept them under constant surveillance.

"Finding those Jews means finding more valuable properties."

The colonel nodded, appreciating the good news Stasha was outlining.

"What are the chances of recovering any meaningful properties if you find the Jews on the Aryan side?" the colonel asked.

"If I were a Jew in the Ghetto today," Stasha replied intoning a Yiddish accent, "and I had hidden jewelry or money or gold before I reported to the Ghetto, I'd be the first one to risk escape. The Jews in the Ghetto are starving. Even if they still had jewels or money in the Ghetto, there is no food to be found anywhere. But on the outside, a person with valuables to trade could get food, could support himself."

The colonel nodded, impressed with Stasha's determination. He challengingly asked, "How would you find the Jews who are still in the Aryan section?"

"I would start with Mendel Rozen, put him through the wringer," Stasha said. "I wouldn't let him go until I got the names of every Jew he helped to get out or the ones he knows have escaped."

"What about the Jews who never entered the Ghetto?" the colonel asked. "They are the ones who really interest me."

"If you saw the card file that I had prepared for you, Sir, listing Jewish properties of those who had reported to the Ghetto..."

"What card file? Which lists?" Colonel Greifler interrupted, turning to Konarski, "Have you ever given me such cards?"

"About a hundred at the beginning of the operation," Dr. Konarski replied, avoiding Stasha's gaze, "but the later ones proved worthless so we didn't bother with them."

"A hundred?" Stasha cried out. "I went into those warehouses, sometimes with Dr. Konarski, and compiled lists of thousands of places with valuable merchandise, which the Trusteeship Office was supposed to confiscate."

"What's he talking about?" the colonel asked Konarski.

"I have no idea."

Stasha began to explain his procedure, but Greifler impatiently cut him short. "You visited those sites? Did you have authority to enter Jewish warehouses?"

"No, Sir. Only, when there was no action..."

"Did you, in fact, enter any warehouse before its contents were confiscated by German authorities?" the colonel interrupted.

"Yes, Sir."

"Who permitted you to even open the doors of those properties?"

"Dr. Konarski," Stasha replied.

"Is that true?"

"Absolutely not," Konarski said flatly.

"Wait," Stasha pleaded, "I kept a list of the entire duplicate card file in my home. Colonel, Dr. Konarski rescued me when I was starving. He's been my mentor, my guide, like a father to me. I don't know what this is about. But we cataloged those warehouses together..."

He sank into a chair without even realizing he had done so, and put his head in his hands. "I feel like an orphan," he muttered in distress.

Colonel Greifler never laughed, rarely even smiled. But he now let out a guffaw that reverberated throughout the compound.

"Stasha, you're either a great actor or a great swindler. I believe you're both. I think you're a clever, conniving Polack who would sell his grandmother for a lousy pfennig. You've now spun yourself into a web and you won't escape so easily. I'm sure you broke into those warehouses and sold the property on the black market."

The colonel stood up and walked around his desk. He smacked Stasha's chest hard with his swagger stick and shouted, "Get up! I'm going to make an example of you and everyone who is in the black market business with you."

Stasha jumped to his feet. He looked at Konarski and then at the colonel, searching for words to defend himself. Suddenly he blurted out, "Give me ten days, I can get proof."

"You have proof? I give you one week to prove your innocence. I'm not interested in your never-ending lists. Just prove to me that you didn't sell property on the black market!"

As Stasha stumbled out of the office, Greifler turned to Konarski. "We have a serious problem with this Polack, this Stasha you highly recommended to me."

Konarski started to apologize, but Greifler stopped him. "I don't blame you. We all make mistakes."

"Thank you, Karl," Konarski said, stating he agreed with the colonel's estimate of Stasha's involvement with the black market. "I'm only sorry, I didn't catch him red-handed."

"Wilhelm, I can trust no one. Only you," the colonel said, now keeping his voice low. "Before I close this office, I have huge amounts of gold and silver that must immediately be shipped out of Poland. I give you one final assignment. I am making you my courier. Tomorrow morning and every morning thereafter, you will fly to Switzerland on a private military plane to deposit gold, jewels, and other valuables in several banks. I'll tell you where to go, and I'll arrange a flight back for you each night."

The colonel embraced Konarski. "Remember, Wilhelm, I trust only you."

The next morning, Greifler himself came to Konarski's dwelling in a staff car to escort him to the airport, where he handed him a sealed briefcase before his boarding the military plane to Zurich.

*

Franya had never been the "I told you so" type. She loved Stasha, despite his violent temper and bullheaded, impulsive decisions. Even when she knew he was wrong, she never belittled or blamed him. But this time, when Stasha told her what had happened in Greifler's office, she quietly said, "You've been betrayed. I told you that you don't belong in politics. That militia uniform doesn't fit you. You were born a farmer, and that's where you belong."

Annoyed, Stasha didn't even reply. Instead, he handed her a few pages of his properties list, asking her to go through it with him.

"I don't understand what you want."

"You've been to Konarski's home. Try to remember what you saw there – a statue, a piece of furniture, anything. Perhaps you can link Konarski with one thing on this list, something you might have noticed even on his person."

He went on to explain that Konarski had his lists and that he probably often went into the warehouses and took what he wanted. He asked her to study the lists, hoping she would recognize something, anything, that Konarski had in his apartment. They studied the lists for hours, but came up with nothing that would implicate Konarski. Finally, Stasha put on his heavy jacket.

"If he did pilfer any movable property," Stasha said, "he had to sell it to someone, somewhere. I'm going about the city, I'll talk to my men, maybe I can find some evidence linking Konarski to the sale of an item on my lists."

Stasha went to each militia post in town and circled the Ghetto's perimeter, asking his men if they had ever seen or heard about Konarski offering anything on the black market, if they knew if he had been to the warehouses or taken anything. None of them had any information for him. One by one, Stasha returned to the now-empty warehouses he had visited with Konarski, inspecting them for items which had been reported but were no longer there. He found nothing. Desperate, Stasha jimmied the padlock and broke into Konarski's apartment, hoping to find some objects he had previously seen in the warehouses. But again he came up empty-handed. As he closed the fire escape door behind him and rebolted it, he had to admit to himself that he was out of ideas.

In six days, Stasha had not found a shred of evidence against Konarski. On the last day of his allotted week, a German sergeant came to Stasha's home to order him to report to Colonel Greifler. Franya told the sergeant that Stasha was not at home, but that she would try to find him. The sergeant warned her if Stasha tried to escape and if she was protecting him, they would face the firing squad. She breathlessly ran around the city but found no trace of him. She visited some of the addresses on Stasha's lists – old buildings and offices. Increasingly upset, she even checked the hillside caves outside the city.

She could not find Stasha, so she decided to go somewhere she had never been…inside the year-old Ghetto.

Like other Poles and Germans, she never ventured near it because of the warning signs that the German military posted around the Ghetto walls: "Jews-Lice-Typhus." Specific orders prohibited civilians and military personnel from entering the Ghetto or even straying within three meters of its walls. When she approached the outer gate on Zamenhof Plac, a Polish militiaman stopped her. She asked if Stasha was in the Ghetto.

"I don't know," he told her, "I just came on duty. Talk to the Jewish guard, over there, by the inner gate."

Franya entered the Ghetto and asked the gaunt Jewish officer, "Do you know where captain Stasha Wojchiechowski is?"

Frightened at the very mention of Stasha's name, the guard stammered, "Why, why are you here? I've done nothing wrong. What would the militia captain want with me?"

When Franya assured the man that she was Stasha's wife and meant no harm to him, the guard replied, "Come, I'll take you to Rozen. He might know."

Franya told him she was amazed at the fear Stasha's name evoked. He did not respond, but she followed the guard through the Ghetto.

As she walked those few blocks, she was appalled by the skeletal people with emaciated faces who approached her from every side, begging for food. She was terrified as wizened women reached out and tried to grasp her, to take her scarf, her coat, to beseech her for a piece of bread. With difficulty, she maneuvered through the streets avoiding the piles of garbage and the stinking streams of human waste flowing freely, flooding the open sewers. She almost fainted at the ghastly sight of dead bodies – some fully exposed, others covered with rags or newspapers – lying in the street and on the sidewalk. The stench of death was everywhere. To avoid slipping because of her unsure steps, she clutched at the arm of the guardsman. The Jewish policeman steadied her gait.

"The bodies won't be here long. The cart comes every day to haul away the bodies," he explained. Then, reaching the police station, he said, "Here, you can go in now, Rozen's office is on the right just inside this alleyway."

She ran toward Rozen's office, frantic to flee the wretched street.

"You, are you Rozen?" she asked the thin, grave-faced man bent over a scratched-up desk. She sat down to catch her breath, then she berated him, "How can you let people live like this? It's horrible here, wretched. Don't you Jews even care?"

"I don't know who you are," Rozen replied dourly, "but the Poles and the Germans created this Ghetto and jailed us here to starve and die."

Franya did not like his comparing the Poles to the Germans and told him so. She was on the verge of letting him know that not all Poles shared the German's extreme racist views. Wearily, she decided not to bother, not to get into an argument in this dreadful place.

"I'm Franya Wojchiechowski. I'm looking for my husband. I need to find him. Do you know if he is here?"

"No, no, he's not here now," Rozen said. "He was in the Ghetto earlier today. He came to investigate some of the residents, but then he left."

"If he comes back, tell him to report to Colonel Greifler," Franya said.

"I'll tell him. They're two of a kind," Rozen replied and murmured a phrase in Yiddish, which she understood to mean "A curse on both of them."

When Franya got home, she couldn't wait to undress and shower, anxious to wash the Ghetto and its smells out of her hair, off her body. When darkness fell, Stasha returned. Looking at his haggard face, she knew he had found no evidence against Konarski.

"I looked for you all day," she told him. "Greifler wanted to see you."

Stasha picked up the phone and called the German military office. The duty officer told him to report to the colonel in the morning.

Early the next day, the last day for Stasha to prove his innocence, a military police car halted in front of the Wojchiechowski's apartment building. A German officer ran up to the apartment, banged on the door, and stomped into the apartment when Stasha opened it.

"You! In the car, now!" he ordered, not even giving Stasha a moment to say good-bye to his wife.

Aghast, Franya stood by the window, helplessly watching as the police vehicle sped off, sirens screeching, with Stasha inside as a virtual prisoner. She remained motionless by the window for most of the morning, staring out into the street, terrified that she would never see her husband again.

*

When the officer marched Stasha into Greifler's office, the colonel was at his desk with a revolver placed on the green felt blotter in front of him.

He did not look up. For a full minute, which seemed like an hour to Stasha, Greifler said nothing. The only sound Stasha recognized was the occasional burst of rifle fire as a firing squad in the quadrangle below went through its paces. Stasha was stricken with fear. He knew he would soon stand in the plaza, facing those guns. His heart beat so rapidly, he was certain the colonel could hear its thumping. The room began to swirl about him. He heard the colonel's voice as though it echoed out of a deep barrel.

"Come," Greifler grunted loudly, "I want you to see the firing squad."

As Greifler pulled open the curtain, Stasha turned white when he saw Konarski standing blindfolded before the firing squad. He grasped the arms of a chair for support.

"Look, now!" the colonel ordered. Stasha saw the firing squad stationed in the courtyard. Their captain looked up at the window as Greifler signaled, raising his hand. Within seconds, Stasha heard the order, "Fire," and saw Konarski's bullet-ridden body crumple to the ground.

"Sit," Greifler said in a commanding tone. "Konarski's body will be on display in the courtyard today. I want you to bring all your militiamen to see it. That's what will happen to black marketers who steal from the fatherland."

Stasha showed no remorse over Konarski's death. He went to the window to look again at the pelleted corpse of the man who plotted against him. Eagerly he asked how and why Konarski was brought before the firing squad.

"At ease, Stasha," Greifler finally said, in a more conversational tone. "Even before your last confrontation with Konarski, I suspected something, but I could not prove it. I decided to investigate him. I set a trap and

Konarski took the bait. We sent him out of Poland and found evidence of his black market activities on a grand scale – exporting hundreds of thousands of items. Nothing was sold locally, only worldwide. We followed up his contacts while he was on a mission for me in Switzerland. Yesterday, at a special court-martial where you were to testify that you have supplied him with lists of Jewish properties, he was sentenced to be shot."

"That's why I couldn't find any incriminating evidence against him."

The colonel callously spoke of Konarski's death as a victory for the Trusteeship Office, and then recalled Stasha's plan to find Jews living illegally on the Aryan side of Warsaw and confiscate their property. He ordered Stasha to proceed with that plan, and, to facilitate his work, the colonel appointed him commandant of Warsaw's police department.

"Your orders and your commission are all in this file," the colonel said, commanding him to begin his work immediately.

In the weeks that followed, Stasha did his job well for Greifler. First, he organized a spy network of Poles who ferreted out information from apartment house owners, janitors, repairmen, and anyone who had access to private homes. He hired a crew of construction workers to investigate suspicious-looking houses for newly built walls or freshly dug trenches or cellars where Jews could be hiding. He offered staggering rewards to any Polish civilian who exposed hidden Jews. Under his command, several dozen Jewish families were apprehended. The colonel had them lined up – men, women, and children – and shot in a public square outside the Ghetto. He promptly transferred their property to the Trusteeship Office.

For his diligence, Stasha was given an elegant apartment on Chmielna Street and a staff car. Franya regarded her lovely new home with an equal mix of appreciation and fear. She worried that one day Stasha would meet the same fate as Konarski. But she kept her thoughts to herself, knowing that Stasha could explode if she shared her fears with him.

Chapter 5

ONE YEAR LATER, in the summer of 1942, the Germans transferred Stasha to the Resettlement Program. He was charged with rounding up the Jews remaining in the Ghetto and putting them on the Ostbahn, the train traveling east to Poland's interior. Stasha commanded the militia units to herd the Jews onto the train and guard the packed boxcars so no one could escape. His units continued to patrol the streets, ferreting out hidden Jews.

"It's supposed to be a big secret," Stasha explained when Franya asked about his work at the train station. "Anyone getting on that train will never come back alive."

Franya pressed him for details, but he refused to discuss his work. "I can only tell you what one of the professors said many years ago at a Sviatova meeting: 'Get rid of the Jews and you rid Poland of the poison that infects it.'"

When Dr. Berson initially heard the German announcement of the Resettlement Program, he hurried to the Judenrat to find David Poliakov. Two years had passed since the Judenrat was ordered to construct the Ghetto walls. In that time, both men, Poliakov and Berson, had aged terribly, emaciated by hunger and beaten down by responsibility. Berson haltingly walked into Poliakov's office and immediately sat down to catch his breath. "Szymon, when did you cat last?" Poliakov asked.

"I don't remember," Dr. Berson replied, pressing his palms against his abdomen to ease the hunger pains. Poliakov reached into the bottom drawer of his desk, brought out a can with a few left-over sardines, and offered it to the doctor, who hesitated.

"Here, take it. You can't die on us," Poliakov said, placing the can in front of him.

Berson reached into the can, put the sardines in his mouth, and munched on them slowly. He then sucked the remaining drops of oil from the can and from his fingers.

"Now what is to become of us?" he asked Poliakov. "What do these orders mean – the orders to get on to the Resettlement Program?"

"Szymon, before I tell you what I know about the Resettlement procedures, I have to tell you that the Germans are ordering me to turn the Annex back over to them. With no hospital here, you understand there will be no hospital rations and no hospital work permits. So I am sending a carpenter to salvage whatever we can from the building before the Germans take it."

He called the carpenter who was waiting at the door, introduced him to Dr. Berson, and asked them to set a time they can start dismantling the hospital. Berson asked the carpenter to wait until he finished talking with Dr. Poliakov.

"David, that's not what I came to talk to you about," Berson said when they were alone. "The hospital is a bad joke anyway. There's no equipment, no supplies, and no medications. At this point, we're one step away from being a burial society."

"There's little I can do to help," Poliakov admitted. "We are at the end of our rope."

Berson continued, "Everybody knows about our medical bankruptcy. Even Haskel Kornblit, the forger, offered to sell me forged medical supply cards so that I could procure medication and equipment from the Germans."

"Stay away from Haskel," Poliakov warned. "He'll get caught and anyone who's done any business with him will be in trouble."

"Haskel has done more to save Jews than we have, with all our contacts with the German officials," Berson countered.

"I tell you again," Poliakov said, "stay away from him."

"That's not what I came to discuss with you," Berson repeated, with a note of defiance. "I'll decide for myself about doing business with Kornblit."

"So what did you come about? What's on your mind?"

"Tell me about the Resettlement Program."

Dr. Poliakov handed Dr. Berson the Judenrat's printed announcement that described the Resettlement initiative launched by the German authorities. It announced in Yiddish and Polish that the Germans intended to move all the Ghetto's Jews to jobs in German factories.

The doctor waved it off, saying, "That isn't news, David. I've seen it posted on almost every building in the Ghetto. But there are rumors. The rumors worry me."

"Szymon," Poliakov said, slowly emphasizing every word, "this project is finally helping people. Since launching the program two months ago, we've sent more than 200,000 Jews to start a new life outside the Ghetto…"

"Dr. Poliakov," Berson interrupted, as though he were speaking to a stranger, "don't lecture me about how many Jews you sent. I don't want statistics. What do you personally know about the program?"

"The Germans tell me that they will relocate the Jews of the Ghetto into work camps where they will be trained in specific crafts and that it will help relieve the German's acute labor shortage. For us this is a blessing because, as you well know, the entire Ghetto is now one big death house. We're up to six hundred people dying from hunger and disease each week."

"I know, I know," Berson said. "I'm interested in the labor camps. What have the Germans told you about those camps? Can you trust them?"

"Szymon, don't start that debate with me. I've had it up to here," Dr. Poliakov said, raising his hand to his chin. "If the Germans want us to work in their war factories, we have no choice. I'm no philosopher and I don't care about the moral imperatives of Jews helping the German war machine. I know only one thing: it will keep us alive."

"David, I'm not here to debate or to talk philosophy either. It's far too late for that. What I want to know is: do you know for sure where the Jews are working – those already sent for Resettlement?"

"The German high command doesn't clear the locations or the specific work of their secret war factories with me," Dr. Poliakov replied with scorn. "But they did admit to me that Jewish labor is now vital to them. So vital that they insist on getting five thousand Jews out of the Ghetto every day to meet their production quotas. This Resettlement is good for them and it's good for us. It's the only way we can survive the war."

"There are rumors that there are no work camps. That the whole thing is a lie, a cover-up for mass murder."

Annoyed, Poliakov walked over to the window to overcome his pique. He looked down on the crowd of people seeking rations, milling outside his office. He turned around, saying, "Szymon, I plead with you, don't contribute to the rumor campaign. It'll lead to mass hysteria. And that's one thing I can't cope with. It is not as if we have a choice. This afternoon I am negotiating with the Resettlement Program people to exempt the children in the orphanages until the Judenrat can be assured of proper care for them in the new labor camps."

"David, that's not what I asked. What do you know about those labor camps? Do they really exist as Resettlement centers for Jews?"

Poliakov replied, "In the beginning, when the Resettlement was first announced, everyone wanted to get on the list for the Ostbahn. Now, the hotheads are stirring up trouble, spreading fear throughout the Ghetto that the trains are 'death trains.' Because of this rumor, our Jews are no longer reporting at the Umschlagg Plac to board the trains. When their names are listed for a transport, they go into hiding."

"You're still not answering my question. Is there a true Resettlement area?"

Dr. Poliakov paid no attention to the interruption and continued, "Now I have to get Rozen's police to round them up, to meet the quota. The Germans are also using our old nemesis, Stasha, to work with Rozen. He and his men are routing Jews from their hiding places. And when the Germans set a 5,000-person quota, they won't settle for 4,999."

"And when the Germans say 'Resettlement', it may mean extermination," Berson retorted. "Yes or no?"

"When the rumors started, I took it up with the German military and they gave me pictures of Jews at work in the factories. These pictures have been authenticated by relatives who are still living in the Ghetto and who recognize the people in the pictures."

Dr. Berson rebutted, "Pictures can be retouched. Right now I have to rely on your judgment. If I find any shred of evidence that death camps do exist, I will be the first to escape."

"And I will come with you," Poliakov said. "If the rumors are true, I would be responsible for the deaths of hundreds of thousands of Jews."

Dr. Berson did not reply. He left Poliakov's office and was immediately besieged by starving people begging for food. Suddenly he heard his name called as someone tapped him on his shoulder.

"I'm the carpenter who has to dismantle the hospital tomorrow morning," the man said. "Please, come with me."

The carpenter led Berson to a nearby apartment house where they descended into the cellar. "Doctor, I must talk with you privately," the carpenter explained. "I am working with the secret JCO, our Jewish Combat Organization. We are planning an uprising against the Germans."

Berson gasped and stared at the man. He was speechless.

"Through outside contacts, more than fifty guns have already been smuggled into the Ghetto," the carpenter said with obvious pride. "We're also making and stacking hundreds of homemade Molotov cocktails."

"How did you get the guns?"

"Some we get by dealing with Haskel, but I'm not really familiar with that part of the operation," the carpenter said. "My job is to repair the guns. Most of the stuff we get is defective and needs to be scraped and cleaned. Parts have to be rebuilt and tested."

Berson tried to respond reasonably, "What you're telling me is impressive, but terribly dangerous. Open rebellion against the Germans will result in mass murder of Jews."

"I can't reply to that." He lifted a trap door beneath a layer of sand, and asked Dr. Berson to follow him, sliding down a water-logged ramp. After they crawled a few paces in total darkness, they reached an area where, in the faint light of a lantern, Dr. Berson saw a young man, and a young girl standing next to him.

"Doctor, I am the commander of the JCO. This is Rachel, one of our leaders. I know about you. Rivka Segal was my sister. She thought very highly of you. You were kind to her and to her children. We miss them terribly."

"We all do, son," said Berson. "She was a real hero. You can't imagine how much she did for our patients. But now the hospital is closing. In the event of an uprising, we would have no way to take care of the wounded. I admire your courage, but the women and children, the sick and elderly – they're totally defenseless. If you attack the Germans, they'll savagely murder the rest of the Jews."

"Dr. Berson, death is the lot of all of us. The young, old, sick, and infirm. The uprising will take place and we'll face the reality of death. But we'll die fighting."

"But a rebellion – that will hasten death," Dr. Berson challenged.

"Rachel is our contact with Poles outside who supply much of our ammunition," the young leader replied. "She knows the ins and outs of this sewer system and we're now considering a plan to transfer our children and elderly to the Aryan side. She thinks many decent Poles with whom she's in contact will be willing to hide them if we can get them out of the Ghetto."

Dr. Berson dampened her hopes, explaining that decent Poles will not endanger their lives to abet the escaping Jews. Rachel was about to reply but the young commander put an end to the debate saying, "Dr. Berson, we only want you to know this area because when the rebellion starts, the wounded will be brought here."

Berson asked, "If this Resettlement Program is legitimate, and Warsaw's Jews are going east to work, why risk the lives of innocent people in an uprising?"

"There's no evidence of any work in these supposed labor camps," the young commander flatly stated. "The longer we wait, the more people will be taken to the death trains. I have to ask you again, Doctor, when the attack begins, will you come here and tend the wounded?"

"Yes, on one condition," Berson answered. "If the Resettlement is proven to be legitimate, to be real, I don't want to hear any further talk of a rebellion."

"I only wish that the Resettlement is real," the commander said gravely, turning to the carpenter. "Please take the doctor back to the hospital."

As they walked back toward the hospital, the carpenter told Berson, "My assignment was only to take you to the commander, but I have to tell you that I won't be working at the hospital tomorrow. I'm not waiting for proof about the Resettlement. I'm leaving without telling anyone, including Dr. Poliakov."

"I'll ask Dr. Poliakov to send someone else to dismantle the hospital," Berson said, "and I won't betray your secrets. But aren't you willing to wait for more information about the Resettlement?"

"My infant daughter can't survive in the Ghetto," the carpenter said, then asked, "What about you, Doctor? Are you going to wait for the death trains to take you?"

"I'm willing to wait for more concrete evidence about the Resettlement Program before giving any credence to the rumors about the final destination of the Ostbahn," Dr. Berson said with finality.

He was among the few who were willing to wait, who held any hope that the trains represented more than a fast trip to death. Daily, the Judenrat struggled to get its quota of five thousand Jews to line up in the *plac* for shipment aboard the Resettlement trains. About two weeks after the meeting with the JCO leader, a tall, husky man with a thick beard stealthily entered Berson's clinic, now held in his small apartment.

"I have to see you now," the man said quietly.

Studying the face of the bearded stranger, he motioned to the man to join him in a small antechamber, where Dr. Berson hesitatingly asked, "Leon Viner?"

"Yes, Dr. Berson, it's me," Viner replied, stroking his long beard. "I need you and I have come to get you."

"Where were you? How are you managing to keep alive?"

"Never mind," Viner replied. "I have come to make you keep a promise you made me two years ago."

"I made you a promise?"

"Right after the meeting of the Judenrat when the issue of the Ghetto was first debated. I walked you home that night."

"Yes, yes, I remember that. I even remember that you proposed that Jews should escape – but I don't recall promising you anything."

"Doctor, you said that if you discover that the Ghetto is being used as a staging center for death, you would escape before the final blow. Those were your exact words."

"Yes, I also remember saying that."

"I have the proof."

"What proof?"

"That there are no labor camps. There's no Resettlement. The Ostbahn, which pulls out of here with boxcars loaded with Jews, ends up in a place called Treblinka, a death camp." Viner handed Dr. Berson two letters, both signed by credible men – men he remembered. The letters described the camp's killing machines, and one included a sketch of Treblinka's special shower rooms and ovens. Viner then gave Berson a train schedule and a map from the Reich's Department of Transportation, which listed Treblinka as the end destination of the Ostbahn. As Berson tried to absorb what he was seeing, Viner handed him a photograph that had been smuggled out of Treblinka.

"This is Yossel Burstyn," Viner said. "Remember him?"

"Of course."

"Look what's written, drawn in code in the leaves of a tree sketched on the back of this photograph."

Dr. Berson could not read the flower-like message, signed by Burstyn. Viner held up a small mirror, allowing the doctor to read the inverted letters in Yiddish: "Jews are being burned in ovens."

"Come with me to Poliakov," Dr. Berson said after reading the documents. "He must know about this."

"I can't, Doctor. That's not why I came to you," he said.

"Why did you come?"

"To take you with me," Viner said. "Where I will take you, Herr Doktor, you can help Jews to live again and you will not be deceiving them as they wait for death."

"Where will you take me?"

"Since the day I left, on the Rosh Hashanah day of panic, I've been in the forests with the Partizans. We have been surviving in the woods and attacking the Germans wherever we can. But after every sortie, we have casualties. The fighters have neither a medic nor medication, but they are not waiting for death. They are fighting for life."

"Why won't you come with me to Poliakov? Please, he must be told."

"There's no time for debate and I can't take the chance of being discovered."

"Wait for me. Just wait. I'll be back in a few minutes."

Berson hurried to Poliakov with his evidence. Poliakov scanned the papers and looked at Burstyn's photograph. "Szymon, you must come with me to the German authorities. This is what I needed. Burstyn's signature and crypted message is just the kind of evidence I need to face the Germans with."

"David, no. You have some 200,000 Jews left. I don't know if they can still be saved, but sending them to the trains is sending them to their deaths. I'm leaving with Viner. It's your responsibility to deal with the realities he uncovered."

"Szymon, wait, wait, please," Poliakov begged. "This is serious, it's horrible. I'll take it up with the German authorities. Maybe we can still negotiate to put a stop to Resettlement, at least until this matter is cleared up. Please, wait till I come back."

"Do you really think that the German authorities here can do anything?

The Ostbahn, the whole Resettlement charade, is controlled by Berlin. No one in Warsaw can change one whit of this scheme."

"I am duty bound to face the Germans with this critical evidence. I have to save the rest of us, the rest of my Jews. I'll win over the Germans."

Berson got up and turned to leave, but Poliakov, trying to forestall him, held onto his arm like a drowning man holding onto a lifeguard.

"Stop it, David. Stop! The Germans have reason to deceive us. But you must stop deceiving yourself. The Germans will not help you. I have to go. I have to go now."

*

The carpenter who had taken Dr. Berson to the JCO commander took his wife and baby girl to Haskel Kornblit's secret print shop to pay for their new, forged identity cards. Days earlier, after they had agreed on a price, Haskel had taken pictures of each of them.

"With the documents I will make for you, you'll be able to leave the Ghetto and live safely on the Aryan side," Haskel had promised.

True to his word, he now produced a set of identity cards showing them to be the Rynek family. He handed them the German identity and ration cards he had made.

As they were studying the identity cards, Haskel explained, "The Rynek family from Krakow were all killed in a train that was bombed by the British. No one survived. None of the deaths have been recorded, because Polish communications are so broken down. These identities are totally secure. So study these Rynek documents. Do they suit you? You will be Tomasz, the husband. Your wife will be Irena and your baby is Jadwiga. All of you are from Krakow."

The carpenter looked at his wife and they both nodded. Deftly, Haskel attached their photographs to the forged documents.

"I wish you well on the outside," he said. "You may have difficulty finding a home or work on the Aryan side, but you'll never have to worry about these papers. You will now be accepted by everyone as Tomasz and Irena Rynek and your baby, little Jadzia."

As the husband was about to pay with two gold bracelets and three gold rings, he noticed that Kornblit was writing their names in a notebook.

"What are you doing?" the carpenter asked abruptly.

"I keep a record of how many Jews I have saved," Haskel bragged.

"Not for us, you don't. If you put our names in that pad, the deal's off," the carpenter said, shoving the forged documents back at Haskel. "I want no record of this transaction to appear anywhere. Is that clear?"

"Sure, sure," Kornblit agreed hastily, and erased their names from the pad. That very afternoon, the young couple made their way out of the Ghetto aided by Haskel's bribing several police, both Jewish and Polish.

*

On the Aryan side of Warsaw, the young father searched out Stefan Casimir, a one-time poverty-stricken teacher who rose to become a municipal judge and remained in that position for as long as anyone could remember. He was a lovable character whom everyone called Dziadzia Stefan, Uncle Stefan. People would come to him for advice on civic and family problems. But, after the German invasion of Poland, he was removed from the bench. Officially, it was announced that he was retired at age seventy-five. But everyone knew the real story: Judge Stefan was removed from the court when he sent a Polish militiaman to jail for setting fire to the one remaining synagogue in the old Jewish section of Warsaw.

When he learned that the Germans were about to arrest him, Judge Stefan publicly rescinded his sentence, apologized for his ruling, and blamed his poor judgment on old age. And, to avoid being sent to a concentration camp, he heaped praises on the occupying forces, urging the Poles to abide by the new laws the Germans had enacted.

Tomasz knew Judge Stefan's plight and waited for him in a park quite a distance from the judge's home, hoping that the judge continued his habit of taking his walks in that park to be available to people seeking help.

"Dziadzia Stefan," the young father whispered when the judge passed him.

The judge embraced him, calling Tomasz by his real name.

"You must never call me by my name. It's now Tomasz, and this is Irena, my wife."

Judge Stefan was shocked hearing about conditions in the Ghetto and the deathly destination of the trains. Tomasz asked whether his family could stay in his home until a secure dwelling could be found in Warsaw for them.

"I can't have you in my house even for one night," Judge Stefan said. "I'm virtually under house arrest. The militia and sometimes German soldiers are keeping watch on my house. I have it on good authority that they want to make an example of me. But I can give you some addresses where you will find people to help you."

He wrote down names and addresses of people to be contacted and handed the slip of paper to Tomasz. He studied the names and said, "I will remember the addresses you've given me. They're my lifeline." He then tore up the slip of paper, explaining that if he were caught by the Germans, the piece of paper will incriminate innocent people.

"Yes, they are innocent people," Judge Stefan said. "They are not like Stasha and his hoodlums. The names I gave you have been saving Jews in their homes and in their factories for almost two years."

When they heard a rustle in the park, the judge kissed Irena and stroked the baby sleeping in her arms. Quickly he made his way out.

A mile or so inside the Aryan sector, they saw a ramshackle house which bore an address that Judge Stefan had written down. That night they moved in with an elderly couple who warmly welcomed them but warned the family that they would have to leave the following day because of an area-wide search for escaped Jews.

"When the search is over, come back to us," the aged woman told them as Tomasz and Irena were leaving the next morning.

They had trouble finding a second home because the judge's next address, which Tomasz had memorized, was occupied by a burly man who said he had only recently moved in and could not accommodate them.

Fortunately, not far from that address, on a building down the same street, they saw a sign, "Room to Rent." The landlady was happy to rent the room not only for the gold bracelet Irena gave them, but because of the high rent they were willing to pay for one room in the tiny attic. From their first day, the young mother was happy with her new freedom. She went on shopping excursions, took long walks with the baby in the park, and rode the city buses. Wherever she went, she introduced herself as Irena. She felt free, from the Germans, from danger.

"No one suspected me and no one questioned me," she would proudly announce to her husband as she recounted her adventures each evening.

The carpenter did not share his wife's sense of security. In their first week on the Aryan side, he heard reports about Stasha's hunt for escaped or hidden Jews. And, what was worse – the fear of meeting someone who had actually known the Ryneks from Krakow would not leave him.

Despite his wife's assurances, the carpenter categorically ordered her, "Don't make friends. We can't let anyone get to know us too well. The fewer the people who know of us, the safer we'll be."

He began to study information about Krakow, learning about its streets and its people, studying city maps and reading old newspapers. Through intensive research, he corroborated Haskel Kornblit's story. There was an item about the train wreck but no record nor mention of the death of the Rynek family. The young father insisted that they practice, every day, calling each other by their newly adopted names – Tomasz, Irena, and Jadwiga, whom they called Jadzia. Before long, they became so accustomed to their new names that they used them even when they were alone with each other.

They found a third home in the fashionable district of Novy Swiat, where a Swedish embassy official sublet his apartment to them when he was ordered to return to Sweden for a ministerial conference. When he returned, they moved into a fourth home and then a fifth, so that during their first year on the Aryan side, they resided in no less than five different homes – as Tomasz and Irena Rynek.

The first shock to their sense of security came when Jadzia fell ill and was taken to the hospital. The mother learned that the attending physician had practiced in Krakow. She made certain to avoid him by leaving the baby in her crib whenever he was due to check on the child. One day, the doctor summoned both parents to his office to instruct them on special care for the baby before discharging her. Tomasz warned his wife to remain calm even if the doctor should ask about the "Ryneks from Krakow."

Irena acted her part splendidly and Tomasz replied to all the doctor's queries. They were elated that he never questioned their identity. When they returned home, Irena gleefully cited the hospital experience as proof of their safety. Tomasz, however, remained layered in secrecy. He reminded her that he was not a carpenter, that before the invasion he had practiced law in a nearby town, and that he may be recognized by others just as Judge Stefan had recognized him. One evening, after much thought, he told his wife, "If we are caught, we'll have to make sure Jadwiga has a chance to live."

"What do you mean?" the young mother asked, challengingly. "We not only survived, no one has ever even suspected us."

"If we are discovered, they'll put us on the death trains," Tomasz said, asking his wife to hear him out. "If that happens, we should leave Jadzia with some Polish family so that she'll survive."

"After a whole year living safely among the Poles," the young mother scoffed at his insecurity, "what's this paranoia that's got you trapped in your own fears? I can't believe that we'll have to give up Jadzia."

Her sense of safety was put to the test once again when Tomasz was suddenly summoned to appear with his family before Police Commandant Stasha Wojchiechowski, known throughout the city as the "Jew hunter."

As a precaution, Tomasz thoroughly researched Stasha's background to learn about his interests and activities. He coached Irena how to reply to any questions that Stasha might ask her. He even coached three-year-old Jadzia until he was finally satisfied with her answers as well. At the interrogation, Stasha closely examined their identity cards and even attempted to peel off their photographs to determine the documents' authenticity. Tomasz feigned mild surprise at Stasha's attempts to unmask them.

"Commandant, you will find nothing in our papers. Why have you even called us in?" he asked.

"You have acted suspiciously," Stasha said menacingly. "Explain to me why you change apartments so often. Are you trying to hide? We checked with your previous landlords. Five of them, in one year!"

"It's money," Tomasz replied, as if he was ashamed. "Every time I move from one place to another, I don't pay the final month's rent. They can't evict me. I'm leaving anyway."

Stasha was not convinced. "Something is strange here. Why did you leave Krakow? Why didn't the doctor who treated your daughter even know you, since you are natives of the same town?"

Tomasz answered every question calmly. He told Stasha bluntly that he could not get work in Krakow so he left the city. And, as to the physician who attended to Jadzia, Tomasz explained, he was an older doctor, from a different neighborhood and a different generation. Stasha quizzed them separately, even little Jadwiga. But, to his disappointment, the interrogations came up with nothing.

However, there was a moment during the questioning when Tomasz thought his end had come. It was when Stasha suddenly asked about Tomasz's involvement with the Sviatova movement in Krakow. Tomasz reeled off the names of the movement's members in Krakow that he recalled through his readings, but when Stasha asked in what specific activity Tomasz took part, his replies did not satisfy the interrogator.

Tomasz did not flinch. He leaned forward, looked squarely into Stasha's eyes, grasped his arm, and said with reverence, "Are you the famous Stasha Wojchiechowski of the Sviatova Association in Warsaw? I'm delighted, actually honored, finally to meet you as the wonder-worker of the association."

Tomasz continued heaping praise on Stasha, reminding Irena that they were in the presence of a great man, and repeating what an honor it was for him to be close to such a famous personality. Ordinarily, Stasha would pay no attention to such tributes but, fortunately, Tomasz quickly changed the subject, asking what happened to Dr. Konarski who took pride in discovering Stasha.

Stasha related his terrifying experiences when Konarski attempted to implicate him in a black market operation.

"Commandant, congratulations on escaping his trap," Tomasz said. "What a traitor he was! You were quite a hero. Listen, if you need any help in your work, I'm a writer. I've written about political intrigue. Someday, I will show you my articles. I can help if you will ever need me."

*

Warmed by Tomasz's regard for him, Stasha ordered an aide to bring coffee for them, and cookies for the little girl. For the rest of the meeting, he reminisced about his work in the Sviatova Association and his visits to chapters in other cities.

"Tomasz, I'm sorry I did not meet you during my visit to Krakow but I'm glad to know you now," he said, reaching into his desk for a small Nazi flag and handing it to Jadzia to play with. When she waved it and giggled delightedly, Stasha said, "You know, I have always loved children, and so has my wife, but she nearly died when a pregnancy went wrong, so it is just the two of us. I'd like you to meet her."

Both of them replied that they would be delighted to meet his wife.

"You, too, must visit me," Stasha said to little Jadzia. "My wife will love you and give you lots of cookies and toys to play with."

As he was seeing them to the door, Stasha said, "Truthfully, since coming here from Grochov we have made no friends. We'd be delighted to have you join us one evening."

"Neither have we," Tomasz answered, telling the truth at last.

Returning home from the interrogation, satisfied but shaken, Tomasz decided that getting close to Stasha and his wife was important because it could guarantee their daughter's survival.

"They're going to be the safe haven for her," Tomasz said, trying to convince his wife that there was always the possibility that they could be sent off on the trains.

Irena rebuked him for his inability to rid himself of his incessant fears. But, to satisfy her husband's abnormal feelings of insecurity, which she considered extreme paranoia, Irena arranged to spend several afternoons with her new friend Franya, always bringing the baby with her. Every Sunday, Irena brought the baby to church and sat beside Franya, and very often, after the service, the two families would have lunch together. At times, Franya would stay with the child for an evening while Tomasz and Irena allegedly went to visit his former clients in another part of the city.

On Jadzia's birthday, Irena threw a party and invited Stasha and Franya, who came laden with gifts. When the precocious birthday girl opened the bright packages brimming with dolls and toys, she happily chirped, "Thank you, Mama Franya."

Both Tomasz and Irena laughed at the child's response, but they could not hide their surprise when the child called her "Mama Franya." She explained that on one occasion when she babysat for the child, Jadzia awakened and began to cry, calling for her mother.

"So to calm her, I hugged her and said quietly, 'Mama Franya is here.' She called me that several times when I would babysit and I never thought of correcting her."

Chapter 6

LEAVING POLIAKOV'S OFFICE agitated and distressed, Dr. Berson returned to his own office where Viner waited impatiently, urging the doctor to pack immediately so that they could get on their way.

"Wait another few minutes while I get supplies from Haskel's black market cache," Dr. Berson said. "Without medication, I'll be useless in the forest."

Searching all over the Ghetto, Haskel was nowhere to be found. Viner angrily said he refused to wait for the elusive forger.

"Follow me and don't say anything," Viner ordered Berson, leading him to a vacant alleyway, where he removed the cover on a handcart, exposing three dead bodies. "There, Doctor, give me your shoes and lie down next to the cadavers, face down, and don't move."

Viner pushed the heavy handcart along the street to the gate, where the guards stopped him. He pointed to the bodies in the cart. Grimacing in disgust at the stink emanating from the handcart, the guards waved him through to the Aryan side. As soon as the cart was a distance away from the gate, Dr. Berson slipped off and walked beside it. They pushed it to the cemetery, where they buried the bodies, and then the two lay among the ancient tombstones, hiding until nightfall. When the moonless night offered complete concealment, the two men continued their flight from the city. They walked several kilometers in total darkness, turning onto a dirt road leading to Wyszkov, a city on the Bug River. By morning, they reached the outskirts of town.

"Come, let me show you how we procure medical equipment," Viner said. "There's a medical installation not far from here and if we're lucky, we'll soon see ambulances heading toward it."

Berson followed Viner deep into a wooded area. Finding a tree he had previously marked, Viner paced five meters eastward from it and dug a shallow hole, where he unearthed two German uniforms wrapped in a bundle of rags. They smoothed the uniforms, dressed, and returned to the road.

"Here, put this on," he said, handing Berson a white smock that bore medical insignias and military rank.

They waited at the roadside and when an ambulance finally came down the road Viner flagged it to stop. In a flash, he forced the driver out of the vehicle and strangled him. After he dropped the body in the dense forest, he drove the ambulance to the hospital.

"My job is to get you into the hospital," Viner said, pulling into the grounds of the medical installation. "Your job is to get the supplies you need. Remember, you're a German officer."

Dr. Berson briskly marched down the hospital's main corridor, stopped at a nursing station, and eyed the young woman who was sitting at the desk. A cabinet stocked with medicines and equipment stood behind her. "Nurse," he ordered, "load up those supplies in a canvas bag and get it into my ambulance, and be quick about it!"

The nurse summoned two orderlies who then filled a large canvas bag with the drugs and surgical equipment Dr. Berson had selected. Then they lugged the bag to the waiting ambulance. Soon, the ambulance was speeding down the road with its siren wailing. When they left the outskirts of town, Viner killed the siren. He drove into the wooded forest, and about ten kilometers in he abandoned the vehicle to unload the medical supplies into a secluded glen.

"Stay here, Doctor, I'm going to organize transport," Viner said and disappeared behind a hill overlooking a nearby farm.

Thirty minutes later he returned with a slightly spavined horse. Slinging the canvas bag over the animal's back, they continued their trek into the thick forest. Fifteen minutes further into the woods, Viner took the bag off the horse and slapped the creature's hindquarters, sending it loping off toward home.

"Where the Partizans are operating, a horse is a hindrance," Viner said, dividing the contents of the canvas bag between himself and the doctor. "Here, you carry this."

Berson, who had been exhausted when they started out, hefted the bag onto his shoulders and staggered under its weight. Viner watched him try to get his balance for a few paces and shook his head.

"Put it down, Doctor, we still have hours to go. Let me take some of that stuff."

As they trekked through the forest, up and down its narrow gullies and steep banks throughout the long afternoon, even Viner showed signs of tiring. They plodded deeper into the forest, where the undergrowth became so heavy it was almost impossible to keep moving. Berson lagged behind most of the time, no longer able to think of anything but putting one foot in front of the other and totally unable to keep up with Viner. Finally, Viner let out a piercing whistle and two heads popped up over a huge boulder. Two Partizans ran down a mossy embankment to help carry the medical supplies into a well-disguised cave with a small entrance hidden by a huge boulder.

*

Berson recognized none of the three women and eight men, two of whom were severely bruised. Although fatigued and still out of breath, the doctor immediately tended to the wounded. Then he stretched out to rest on the ground, with a pile of rags for a pillow, and fell into a heavy sleep.

He slept soundly on the rocky cave floor and was groggy when Viner shook him awake before dawn, handing him a mug full of hot black liquid.

"Here, Szymon, have some PK?"

"What's that?"

"Depends how long you've been with the Partizans," Viner replied. "If you're an old-timer, it's Partizan Kaffe. But if you just joined, it's Pish Kaffe."

Berson took a sip and immediately spat out the foul-smelling, foul-tasting coffee. "It's Pish Kaffe!"

"My dear Dr. Berson, let's hope you'll live long enough to develop a taste for our special brew," Viner said. "Now get ready. Soon there'll be a meeting of unit commanders to plan a coordinated action to be undertaken by the several units active in the forests."

"Unit commanders?"

Leon Viner explained, "We have five units operating in these woods.

Each unit works independently, but today, for the first time, we're undertaking a joint operation and the four other unit commanders are coming here."

As he was speaking, Tevye Krochmalnik arrived and was introduced to the doctor. Tevye greeted the doctor with a bear hug, bemoaning the fact that there have been too many deaths that could have been avoided had there been a doctor in the forest. Over a cup of the bitter coffee and a chunk of crusty, stale bread, Viner related Tevye's story, which had become legendary among the Partizans.

*

The day the Germans ordered the Jews into the Vilna Ghetto in April, 1940, Tevye did not report. He kept his little shoe repair shop open an extra day. It was not a rebellious act on his part. Tevye was an unlikely rebel. He kept his shop open that morning only to finish repairing several pairs of children's shoes he had promised to his customers. The Germans, true to their *Schlagartige* policy, stormed into his shop and arrested him. They dragged him to the market place, tied him to a post, and paraded his entire family before him. The Germans shot his wife, his three children, four brothers, and aged mother, one by one, in front of him.

Like Leon Viner, Tevye Krochmalnik spent less than one day in the Ghetto before he escaped to the woods and organized the first Partizan outfit.

*

"Tevye," Dr. Berson inquired while they were waiting for the group to arrive, "what gave you the idea of starting a Partizan unit operating in a forest?"

"Doctor, do you know that every good Jew knew the forest, the woods in his town very well?"

"Honestly, no. I didn't know."

"Every Shabbat, for example, Jews would go for their Sabbath walk into the woods. Entire families would spend the afternoon enjoying the world of nature."

Dr. Berson admitted that he had never experienced this with his family.

"You never went with your school for an outing into the forest on Lag B'Omer?"

"Yes, I now recall my school's outings," Berson said. "But I'm ashamed to confess that I thought they were a waste of time."

"Lag B'Omer? A waste of time?" Tevye asked almost in disbelief. "In our shtetl, our woods were like our backyard. It was the social meeting place for us."

Tevye smiled as he reached to shake the doctor's hand, "Welcome to the forest, my dear Doctor. You will soon learn the beauty and the mystery of these woods. Now that you have joined our family, we will make up to you what you've missed with your family."

When the unit commanders gathered, Viner introduced Dr. Berson as the "Partizan doctor." Every one of the four immediately pleaded with the doctor to visit his area first. Viner assured them that the doctor will visit every hideout.

"But first we've got to listen to Tevye's plans for a united assault on the Germans," Leon Viner said. "Each of us, every man and woman serving as a Partizan, can become a Tevye, like Samson in the Bible."

To Dr. Berson, Tevye didn't look like a Samson. He was a soft-spoken, mild-mannered, placid person, slightly bald with graying hair. He was very tall but, like the friendly giant, he appeared unintimidating. He spoke to the group in simple terms, first thanking them for their work in the forest and wishing them good fortune in their battles.

Tevye then unfolded a heavily creased map of the area. "I have received information from the Polish underground, the AK, that the Germans are preparing a full-scale invasion of the woods. They estimate that some fifteen hundred soldiers have been moved into Grovnetz, that small village near Lublin. They are poised to strike against us."

Gravely, he continued, "We can either wait for them to move into the forest to destroy us or we can move out to destroy them. There'll be about fifty-eight of us – the biggest force we've ever mounted."

"Well, sitting around is not the answer," someone called from the edge of the group. Everyone nodded in assent; someone else exhorted, "Let's go." Another called out, "Just tell us what we're supposed to do."

And so Tevye did. He outlined the plan of attack and assigned a specific strategic task to each unit.

"We'll be outnumbered almost thirty to one," said Yossi Rochlin. "What about help from the AK? Can't we convince the Polish underground to come in with us? Could they at least supply weapons?"

"No, to both questions," Tevye replied. "No joint attack and no arms. They still think we Jews can't fight. We're fighting the same enemy but they keep repeating their anti-Semitic bullshit about Jews being cowards or Communists."

"But they're getting weapon drops from British flyers," Yossi said. "Is there no way to get word to London that we Jews are getting nothing from these drops?"

Tevye replied resolutely, "Our job now is to kill Germans, not to fight the Polish *goyim*. But be assured, when the Grovnetz operation succeeds, London will hear about the Jewish Partizans, whether the AK wants it or not."

He then turned to Dr. Berson. "The Germans' plan to annihilate the Partizan movement proves that we're no longer just a nuisance. First, there are hundreds of us throughout the forests in Poland and, second, we're not here to just keep ourselves alive. We're inflicting heavy damage on the mighty German military forces – derailing trains, bombing bridges, and disrupting military installations. And, Doctor, every operation brings successes and also terrible casualties. That's why your coming to us today is a good omen and excellent timing."

Tevye concluded the meeting calmly telling his fighters, "For the first time, we now have a chance to kill hundreds, perhaps close to a thousand German soldiers, and it will be a long time before such an opportunity will again present itself."

"Revenge!" Viner called out. "It's our chance for massive revenge!"

"No, not revenge, Leon," Tevye snapped back and then paraphrased a couplet from a poem that he said he learned as a boy:

Revenge? Revenge for killing a little innocent child?
Such revenge, even Satan himself has yet not devised.

"We are to kill the Germans because every German we kill will shorten the war against the Jews."

*

The meeting disbanded as stealthily as it began. People hurried off to their respective hideouts with only a nod of farewell. When they were gone, Dr. Berson asked Viner, "What's the AK? Does Poland have its own underground?"

"AK stands for Armia Krajowa, the Homeland Army, and it's the official Polish underground, sponsored by the Polish government-in-exile and financed by Great Britain," Viner explained. "The Russians established their own underground. And the two aren't working together because Stalin wants to install his own leaders as the postwar government in Warsaw."

"So why doesn't the AK support the Jewish Partizans?"

"Who the hell knows," Viner replied. "The Poles were anti-Semites before the war and despite the fact that we're fighting against the same enemy, they will not start loving us. We'll suffer from any government established in Poland. Palestine is the only answer."

"I see you haven't lost your zeal for Zionism," Dr. Berson said half in jest.

"If anything, life in the woods has made my Zionism stronger than ever," Viner replied. "If we're to survive, we can only do so in Palestine."

"Talking about survival," Dr. Berson asked, "how will I get around these woods to help wounded Partizans?"

Viner went to a crevice behind a boulder in a far corner of the cave, where he awakened a boy sleeping there.

"This is your guide," Viner announced.

Dr. Berson greeted the boy. But when the youngster left the cave to urinate, the doctor protested, "He's only a kid, ten or eleven years old. I'm supposed to trust my life to him?"

"He's seventeen," Viner said. "He knows this forest like no one else and can slither through a whole brigade of German troops without being seen. We call him Ketzalleh, which means 'Kitten.' He'll get you through safe and sound."

Ketzalleh returned and gulped down his breakfast ration, downing a cup of PK in a few quick slurps. After receiving instructions from Viner, the wiry youngster threw the doctor's backpack over one narrow shoulder and, wordlessly, led the doctor out of the cave. Viner followed them down the steep incline out of the hideout.

"Leon, just for curiosity's sake," Dr. Berson asked, "what would you have done if I had refused to join you when you came for me in the Ghetto?"

"I would have beaten you unconscious, put you on the death cart, and dragged you here," Viner replied, grinning humorlessly, wishing them well as he turned back, and leaving the doctor with the skinny youngster.

Dr. Berson attempted to engage the boy in a conversation, but

Ketzalleh paid little attention, often replying with a terse "yes" or "no" without elaboration. The doctor's immediate reaction was to feel skeptical, unsure of the lad's capacity to sense danger and avoid capture. He was also concerned about the youngster's general health; Ketzalleh's scrawny legs and slim build made him look ten, not seventeen.

At about noon, Ketzalleh spotted German troops blocking a clearing they had to cross to get to the first group of Partizans. He circled around to a feeder stream where he tied the backpack to a log and ordered Dr. Berson to follow him into the water. They crouched beside the floating log, eluding the Germans, who were no more than forty-five meters away. When Ketzalleh neared the first hideout, on a hill surrounded by craggy rocks, the Partizans spotted him from their lookouts and came out of hiding to welcome him. The unit, a considerably larger one than the squad at Viner's cave, had several severely wounded men. Berson spent the rest of the day tending to them. Two needed amputations and several others needed to have shrapnel removed from their wounds. While Berson cared for the wounded, Ketzalleh told the Partizan leader the location of German troops they had passed along the way. Slipping through the boulders, he led the small band of Partizans to the entrenched soldiers.

Dr. Berson was still working on his patients when Ketzalleh returned with the Partizans, who were carrying the booty of weapons and food they had seized after they routed out of the Germans. No one shouted for joy. The total silence that pervaded the Partizan community – no shouting of orders, no victory yells, not even cries of pain from the patients – impressed Dr. Berson.

"The basis of Partizan warfare is secrecy, and that's why I didn't answer your questions when we started out," Ketzalleh explained as they threaded their way through the trees to the next hideout. "First, for some reason that I can't explain, sound travels faster in the woods than in the city. Second, you can never tell when a German troop will be waiting, ready to swoop down on you. We could never win a face-to-face confrontation."

Ketzalleh whispered the basic rules of Partizan fighting to Dr. Berson as they plodded through the forest the next morning. Every so often, he reminded the doctor that in the forest, a human voice can be detected from quite a distance. As the day wore on, the youngster showed no sign of fatigue, and kept pushing on to the next hideout. Dr. Berson pleaded with him to stop for a rest, but Ketzalleh refused.

"This area is too exposed," he said, as a chilly rain began to fall. "We could be detected by Germans patrolling inside the forest."

When the rain started to come down in earnest, Berson, looking forward to a rest period, hoped Ketzalleh would find some shelter. Not only did Ketzalleh refuse to stop but as the rain pelted down, he began to run faster, across open fields.

As Berson labored to keep up, Ketzalleh panted, "While it's raining is the safest time to travel. Even if soldiers are in the area, they're probably in their shelters, keeping out of the rain, so they'll never see us."

Dr. Berson recognized the commander at the next hideout. He was Yossi Rochlin, the one who had asked about help from the AK. His unit of seven men, one of whom was wounded from their last engagement, was gathered in a narrow ravine fringed by a thick wooded glen that obscured their camp, which only Ketzalleh could have spotted. When they entered, Yossi was describing the group's assigned task for the attack against the military installation in Grovnetz.

"We start out tonight on a tough three-day march to get there," Yossi said. "We'll be skirting towns to avoid detection. Our assignment is to create obstacles on the eastern approaches to Grovnetz, to make sure that German reinforcements from Lublin can't get through while the main attack is taking place."

"That's marginal," one of the men grumbled. "Why aren't we assigned to the attacking force?"

"This assault isn't focused on individual men or individual units," Yossi replied. "You are not to act on your own! This is a combined, coordinated attack, a planned battle. Now, get some sleep. Tonight we set out on a forty-two-kilometer hike."

As Dr. Berson was stitching up the wounded man's lacerated leg, he listened to Yossi's final instructions to his men.

"Remember, if you're captured, be prepared to suffer torture, even to die, but never reveal the secret positions of the Partizans."

"I wonder if I could endure much pain if I'm captured," Dr. Berson whispered to Ketzalleh.

"You'll never get captured, if I can help it," Ketzalleh said.

Before going to sleep, Dr. Berson slid over to Yossi, telling him that he and Ketzalleh will follow the group to set up a field hospital somewhere in the rear of the battle area.

"Sorry, Doctor, Tevye ordered us to keep you away from any battle zone. Anyone who's wounded will be hauled back to his hideout."

"It's dangerous for the wounded to wait days for medical attention. That's what leads to amputation and death. They must be treated on the spot."

They debated back and forth. Ultimately, Yossi had no alternative but to allow Dr. Berson to join.

Ketzalleh was delighted. "Doctor, I'll stay with you. I can protect you and you can teach me to be your medical aide," he crowed, showing his youth for just a moment.

*

As he plodded through the forest with Ketzalleh, Dr. Berson realized that his initial estimate of the boy's physical and mental ability had been wrong. The boy's capacity to learn amazed Berson. Whenever the lad watched a medical procedure, he grasped the basic practice involved, even delicate surgical methods. Now, as they wound through the forests, they alternated in their roldes as teacher and student. Ketzalleh continued to show Berson how to protect himself, and Berson took pleasure in teaching him medical principles. When Berson showed him how to stitch up a wound, the boy proved as agile with his hands when he sewed an incision as he was with his feet when he scampered up the rocky cliffs.

The long hike to Grovnetz took altogether thirty-six hours because they walked only at night, covering a little more than ten kilometers each night, in total darkness. Yossi's men reached the eastern approaches to the Grovnetz road barely two hours before midnight, when the attack was scheduled to begin. The men worked feverishly to set up a series of obstacles, dragging fallen trees to the middle of the road and digging potholes along a road leading to a narrow bridge over a deep chasm. Satisfied that the obstacles would slow or stop any approaching vehicle, the unit retreated to the woods to await the main attack.

Ketzalleh and Berson contacted all the Partizan units to inform them where to send the wounded – a remote abandoned hut behind the lines. While circling the area, they met Viner, who pointed out their primary target – a three-story school building the Germans had converted into barracks and a barn-like structure that housed Ukrainian guards. Viner pointed to several Partizan fighters at a distance who were stealthily crawling to the buildings. In almost total darkness, they strategically placed several jerricans of gasoline, commandeered from an earlier mission, along the skirts of the buildings.

In a perfectly synchronized attack, the Partizans opened fire on the buildings, exploding the jerricans, and igniting the buildings. Armed Partizans surrounded both flaming buildings so that as the German soldiers and Ukrainian guards ran through the doors or leaped from the windows to escape the fire, they were mowed down by Partizan bullets. Smoke billowed heavenward as the skies lit up with raging flames, creating a giant aura of light that could certainly be seen as far as Lublin. Soon, a column of trucks came speeding toward the narrow bridge that Yossi's men defended. When the trucks screeched to a halt, held up by the Partizans' obstacles, Yossi's men set upon them with a sustained burst of firepower, killing the drivers and soldiers before they could get out of the trucks. The Partizans swiftly carried off weapons and ammo from the dead soldiers.

In less than fifteen minutes, the Grovnetz victory was complete. The fighters swiftly dispersed into the woods, swallowed up by darkness. They knew their attack was a total success because, unlike other assaults, no dogs or handheld lights pursued them. Berson patched up the few men who came to the medical hut, mostly with burns, and they too melted into the pitch-black woods. The next day, Tevye sent Ketzalleh to warn each unit to be alert for severe reprisals by the Germans, who were sure to increase their anti-Partizan attacks.

Dr. Berson and Ketzalleh returned to Viner's cave, where he greeted them warmly and jokingly reprimanded Dr. Berson for participating in the raid, disobeying Tevye's orders.

"Doctors don't take orders. They give them," Ketzalleh said cheekily, looking up at Viner's towering figure.

*

Berson had neither a watch nor a calendar. He calculated time by the seasons. As winter ended and the snow melted into muddy puddles, he realized that he and Ketzalleh had been living in the woods and taking care of the Partizans for almost an entire year. As Tevye predicted, Dr. Berson learned much about the beauty of the forest and far more about its mystery.

But during that year, Tevye's other prediction, that the Germans would retaliate heavily after their defeat at Grovnetz, proved to be true.

As Dr. Berson and Ketzalleh trekked through the forest from unit to unit, they learned the bitter truth: almost every hideout had been hit. As they considered the devastation in each camp, they realized that they had personally escaped death only because Berson had become a doctor-in-motion, always on the go, sleeping outdoors, perpetually in transit from one installation to the next.

"Let's go back to Viner's," Dr. Berson suggested to Ketzalleh as they woke up in a copse of trees one morning. "I'd like to rest a few days. I'm exhausted."

To Berson's surprise, Ketzalleh nodded and confessed, "Dr. Berson, I need a rest too. Let's go."

Berson had not seen Viner for many months. The moment he and Ketzalleh crawled into the cave, Viner warmly welcomed them and when Berson reported on the devastation of the Partizan installations he had visited, he wondered, "Viner, are you safe here? Do the Germans know about this bunker?"

"I'm sure they know and you came just in time. We're moving out tomorrow," Viner answered. "But right now, I have a surprise for you. There's someone here you might remember from your days in the Warsaw Ghetto."

A bearded man, slightly stooped, entered the main part of the cave.

"Faivel! Faivel Garfunkel!" Dr. Berson shouted and embraced him. "Professor Garfunkel, I remember you from that critical meeting we had just before the Ghetto was established. You are the one who warned us, the first one, who said that 300,000 Jews could not survive in the measly two kilometers the Germans allotted for the Ghetto."

"Unfortunately I was right," Garfunkel said. "Neither the Jews nor the Ghetto survived."

"What happened to you?" Dr. Berson asked. And Faivel told his story.

*

"The day I arrived in Treblinka was the darkest day of my life," Faivel said. "I already knew about the smoke stacks, the showers, and the ovens. But a miracle happened."

"Miracle in a death camp?" Viner asked.

"I was on my way to the showers. Three of us men were at the end of the line, and the doors closed before the German guard could push us inside."

"That's really a miracle," Berson said.

"No, there's more," he continued. "We walked back into the barracks and other inmates told us to prepare for an escape, set for that night – a plan that had been in the works for months."

"Escape from Treblinka?" Viner gasped.

"This is what happened," Faivel said. "The leader of the uprising slept in the bunk above me. As I was about to fall asleep, he jumped down from his perch, woke me, and grabbed me by the collar, pulling me out of the slot assigned to me. At that moment, I heard grenades exploding, guns shooting. It sounded like a battlefield you'd see in a movie. I followed him out of the barracks, and it was a full scale rebellion."

"A rebellion in Treblinka?" Dr. Berson asked.

"A complete rebellion," Faivel replied.

"Prisoners had been stealing guns and grenades from storehouses and the first thing they did that night was to blow out the camp's floodlights with their guns, so the area was totally dark. Also, a few weeks before, some prisoners had stolen wire cutters so they could cut through the camp's fence, and ladders so we could go over the top.

"As we came out, about a dozen leaders roamed the camp, shouting, '*Yidden, Yidden loift zum zahm!* Jews, Jews, run to the fence!' I ran, or more correctly, I was pushed toward a certain part of the gate where hundreds of us managed to escape into the woods."

"Amazing, amazing!" Dr. Berson cried out, shaking Faivel's hand. "You survived – it's miraculous. Congratulations! Congratulations!"

"Hundreds escaped," Faivel said, shaking his head, "but many were mowed down by the guards who ran after us with their guns blazing."

"An uprising in Treblinka, ending in slaughter," Berson repeated sadly several times.

Faivel tried to reply but could say nothing. He bit his lower lip and for a long time stared blankly at the floor of the cave.

"Enough, enough," Viner said. "You are alive, and we must all talk about how we will stay alive in this forest. Ketzalleh, you had news for us."

Ketzalleh nodded. "I discovered a long, large tunnel near the edge of the forest. The water company dug the tunnel and laid new pipes before the war broke out. When the war started, they abandoned it. The pipes are very big, bigger than you, Viner."

"That's our new home," Viner announced. "Tomorrow we'll set up an outpost in Ketzalleh's tunnel."

That evening, as they ate their meager rations and packed up their belongings, Viner quite seriously pleaded with Dr. Berson, "Szymon, next time don't stay away so long. I need you around me."

When night fell, Dr. Berson found he could not sleep. He lay down next to Ketzalleh, who looked up and smiled. The doctor patted the boy's face, and the boy grasped his arm and dozed off. When Ketzalleh was sleeping deeply, Berson walked out of the cave and headed down to the valley toward the stream about a kilometer away. In the starlight, he took off his shoes and dipped his feet in the cold, refreshing waters. He was so comfortable he soon fell asleep.

A shattering blast awakened him with a startle. Following the initial explosive burst, he heard grenades detonating and the rapid rat-a-tat of gunfire coming from the direction of the cave's entrance. His first instinct was to run up the embankment to the cave. But he instantly recalled a lesson Ketzalleh had taught him: "Never walk in the direction of gunfire. Always, always move away from it."

Horrified, but unable to do anything but remain frozen in his place, Berson waited in the bushes, hidden from view, listening to the sporadic bursts of mortars and small firearms. When the gunfire stopped, he began to crawl toward the cave. He could hear German soldiers shouting orders and quickly realized it was not safe to approach any closer. He faded back into the underbrush, using all the stealth of his experience in the woods, waiting for the Germans to withdraw. He could see nothing, except bursts of fire, like fire flies darting in the night air. He recalled another of Ketzalleh's lessons: "Trust your hearing – footsteps, the rustle of leaves, muffled commands – heed the clues." These sounds ceased with the first streaks of daylight.

When it had been quiet for a long time, Berson stealthily crawled up the hill, sneaking up to the boulder that had once protected the cave. It was pulverized. The nitrous smell of dynamite permeated the air. Dense smoke still hung over the cave, like a thick black curtain, obscuring his vision. When he made sure the Germans were gone, he slid down into the cave. The carnage stunned him: mangled bodies, pools of blood, limbs strewn all about the cave. Not a single body was left whole. He recognized Viner's and Faivel's bodies or rather their clothing, because their bodies were unrecognizable. He covered them with his coat.

He then found Ketzalleh, lying in his sleeping nook, the crevice behind the inner boulder in the back of the cave. The boy was still breathing. Berson cradled his bloodied head. The boy's feet were sheared off, his hand crushed. He opened his eyes when Berson caressed his blood-spattered face.

"We were a good team," Ketzalleh whispered. They were his last words. He died holding on to Dr. Berson's finger.

Szymon Berson never cried. But now he wept bitterly, holding Ketzalleh's body, unable to put him down. Hours later, exhausted and drained, he laid Ketzalleh in one of the craters carved out by a shell, together with the mangled flesh and bone fragments of the other members of what was once Viner's Partizan group. He covered the grave with a layer of sand heavily tinged with blood and sat beside it, fingering the soil. He had seen death before, but never had he reacted with such deep sorrow, with the kind of grief that now overwhelmed him.

Dr. Berson was not an observant Jew; he had rarely attended religious services. But with tears freely flowing, he recited the kaddish, the prayer for the deceased, "*Yisgadal veyiskadash Shemay rabo*...," words he recalled from his boyhood. He remained at Ketzalleh's grave inside the cave for quite a long time, unable to leave. Suddenly he heard the rustle of leaves at the cave's opening. He crouched beside the mound of the grave, peering cautiously over it. Two chipmunks were sniffing the ground. He made a marker of twigs and stones over the grave, and then walked away.

*

Winter was losing its grip on the forest. Tiny pale buds burst out of the once-frozen branches, converting the somber grays of winter into the promising greens of spring. Everywhere, rippling brooks and gurgling streamlets broke the wintry silence of the forest, orchestrating it with the call of mating birds, heralding a renewal of life.

But not for Dr. Berson. Blinded by grief, he took no notice of nature's beauty unfolding about him. He knew that his work with the Partizans was at an end. Without Ketzalleh, he couldn't find his way in the forest. He stumbled through the dense woodland to the nearest Partizan encampment, the only one he knew he could find without Ketzalleh's help. It too had suffered the same catastrophe. He was at a loss, unable to plan his next move. Somehow, he managed to elude the Germans, foraging in the forest, utilizing Ketzalleh's many lessons. But he knew that sooner or later catastrophe would overtake him too.

It was time to leave the forest.

But getting out of the forest was no easy matter. The woods still bristled with German troops, intent on uprooting any surviving Partizans. Berson had to be vigilant, constantly aware that danger lurked behind every tree. He had no idea what direction to follow. He wandered through the forest, surviving an entire month, feeding himself on the berries, branches, and roots Ketzalleh had shown him.

One night, at the edge of the forest, he came upon a single railroad track paralleling a stream. He hid in a thicket and saw in the distance a shack silhouetted against the faint glow of the moon. When he was certain it was abandoned, he ventured inside, lying there in total darkness. He dozed off, but soon he was awakened by the sound of a scratching on the shack's wooden floor. Thinking it was someone close by ready to pounce on him, he rushed to the door and bumped into someone. They grappled with each other, falling, wrestling on the ground outside the shack. Berson rolled down an embankment with his attacker and they both lay motionless next to the stream. In the faint moonlight, Berson finally took a look at his assailant.

"Tevye!" he shrieked. "Tevye Krochmalnik, what are you doing here?"

"Szymon," Tevye whimpered, "thank Heaven it's you. I'm bleeding, here under my belly."

Dr. Berson saw the deep gash across Tevye's abdomen. He clamped his hand over the wound for almost an hour until he was certain that the flow of blood stopped. He then held both sides of the torn flesh together, hoping for healing to begin. Throughout this manipulation, Tevye was silent, either from faintness or being too weak to speak. Hours later, while Dr. Berson worked over the man's stomach, Tevye opened his eyes. He began to say a few words. Berson asked him what had happened.

"I escaped the Germans' attack on our Partizan hideouts because I was in between installations, conveying orders," he gasped, speaking slowly. "I stumbled into a farmer's home, where some peasants took me in. I thought they were the AK, but soon I heard them planning to hand me over to the Germans. As I was escaping from the hut, one of them swung a scythe and caught me in the stomach. That was this morning."

Berson tore his own shirt to bandage the wound but he frankly told him, "Tevye, you've lost a good deal of blood. I'm seriously concerned that infection could have already set in."

"Szymon, if I survived the Nazis, a little loss of blood is nothing," he said, even managing to smile.

"It's not a little loss of blood. It's very serious. We'll stay here to avoid any strain on your body, which would open the wound again."

They lay at the riverside until the morning sun awakened them. Berson helped Tevye walk up to the shack and made him comfortable. Around noontime, Tevye felt a bit stronger. He reached into his pocket and produced a slab of *babke* and a loaf of bread.

"Here, Herr Doktor, I know you don't work without a fee, so take a piece of this."

With his mouth full of the sweet cake, Berson asked, "Where did you get this? All I've eaten in weeks is berries and tubers."

"When I escape," Tevye said jokingly, "I don't escape only with my life, but also with a good piece of *babke* and freshly baked bread."

The next day, the two men reviewed the events leading to the Germans' near-total destruction of the Partizan fighters in the forest. Tevye suggested that the Germans took their time, finding and destroying each hideout individually, so as not to alert the Partizans with a massive campaign against all the hideouts, which would have given them a chance to escape from the forest. Berson then related in detail the attack on Viner's cave, describing how he buried Viner, Ketzalleh, and the others. Neither Berson nor Tevye could report on any other survivors.

"So what did we accomplish?" Berson moaned. "We killed a few Germans, derailed a few trains. But we're all dead."

"Szymon, we were Partizans. We were victorious."

"I'd call that a Pyrrhic victory."

"You're still mourning Ketzalleh and Viner. Yet, I say we are victorious. First, those who died, died as heroes. Second, we inflicted huge losses on the Germans. Third, they drove us out of this forest, but Partizans are still fighting in many other places, in Poland and elsewhere."

"Maybe you're right, Tevye, but I wanted this to end, 'And they all lived happily ever after.'"

"Then I'll make you happy," Tevye said. "When I was with the Poles, I heard reports of a strong Russian counteroffensive."

"Are the Russians anywhere near us?"

"We're about forty kilometers from Grodno," Tevye replied. "This railroad is a spur, part of the great rail network of Grodno."

"What's so important about Grodno?"

"That's where the Russian counteroffensive was three days ago," Tevye said, trying to get up. "Let's go there, right now."

"Tevye, be realistic," Berson answered, nudging him back. "Your wound needs to heal, at least for another two days. We can't go yet, but we will."

They survived in the shack by rationing Tevye's bread and drinking water Berson would bring up from the stream. On the third day, they saw columns of German soldiers being marched past the shack. That afternoon, they heard a train's whistle coming from the east. Minutes later, the train, packed with German troops, sped by.

"The Germans are in retreat!" Tevye howled with glee. "That's why none of the Germans we saw even bothered with our shack."

That night, Tevye and Szymon began to walk east, toward Grodno.

Three days later, they reached the small village, near Pinsk, about three hundred kilometers east of Warsaw. They found themselves in the midst of a raging tank battle. German tanks fired from entrenched positions in the village as Russian tanks were preparing to storm into the village to dislodge the Germans.

Anxious to get into the battle, Tevye started to run to join the Russian troops. Berson tackled him, brought him to his knees, and held him. "Stop! It's suicidal to get near the Russians without proper identification. They don't take any chances. You run up to them and, first thing, they'll shoot you as a collaborator."

Deflated, Tevye nodded. They looked around for refuge and ducked into an abandoned mill, where, crouching behind the huge millstones, they avoided being hit by bursting shells as tanks crossed the fields shooting intense barrages of artillery. Finally, the Germans retreated as hordes of Russian infantrymen followed the tanks and marched into the village. When the battle was over, Tevye danced with some of the villagers, wildly cheering and welcoming the troops. He introduced himself and Dr. Berson to a Russian officer, eager to describe their experiences in the forest.

At gunpoint, the officer marched them to his brigade's commanding officer, Captain Anatole Dworin, a tough, battle-hardened soldier, who interrogated each of them separately, trying to ferret out information about

German troop movements. Although they insisted they were Partizans who had been battling the Germans, the villagers claimed that the two were strangers. Under Russian questioning, the village elder stated that there had never been any Partizans in the area.

"Enough," Dworin said. "You are collaborators. Men, take these two and have them shot."

"We are innocent – we are Partizans," Tevye shouted in Yiddish, but to no avail.

Dramatically, Berson reached over and yanked down Tevye's pants, exposing the still livid wound on his stomach.

"Look!" he shouted. "I am a doctor with the Partizans. I healed this man's wound. Call in any doctor and he will know what this entails."

The captain looked at the wound and called in his medical officer, who grilled Berson and inspected Tevye's wound. He turned to Dworin. "This man is a doctor, a good one," he said. "Draft him into my medical unit; I can use him."

Berson was assigned to the Third Brigade of Russia's Seventh Infantry Division. Dworin tried to assign Tevye as well, but the Partizan refused to be mobilized.

"I want to fight with the troops. I'll volunteer for that, but no enlistment for me," he said.

After much haggling, the captain agreed, and for almost a year, Tevye fought with the Russian troops as the Red Army rumbled westward toward Warsaw. He demonstrated leonine courage and uncanny fighting wisdom.

On one occasion, in the thick of a tank battle, Tevye was crouching behind a Russian tank that took a direct hit and burst into flames. He swiftly climbed up to the turret, pulled out the unconscious young lieutenant, laid him on the ground at a safe distance from the tank, and extinguished the flames burning the man's uniform. Berson rushed to the victim, covering his blistered body with snow. Seconds later, the tank blew up.

Tevye rejoined his unit as Dr. Berson commandeered a vehicle and brought the unconscious man to a medical facility in the rear, all the while tending to his third-degree burns. Six days later, when the stricken lieutenant recovered, a wounded soldier lying in the bed next to him told the lieutenant about the two men from the Third Brigade who had saved him from certain death. From his bedside, Lieutenant Mieczyslav Kolcharski sent word to Captain Dworin, recommending field commissions for Dr. Berson and Tevye Krochmalnik. When the brigade commander read the account of their heroic courage, he held a special ceremony before the entire Third Brigade, promoting Dr. Berson and Tevye as captains. He also presented both men the Stalin Gold Medal for bravery and handed them citations signed by Marshal Zhukov. Tevye accepted the awards – the Gold Medal and the citations – but refused the commission.

Concluding the award ceremony, Captain Dworin read a letter from Lieutenant Kolcharski. "To Dr. Szymon Berson and Tevye Krochmalnik, I owe my life to you because you saved me from a burning death. If we ever survive this war, I will be at your beck and call."

*

"Why did you turn down a commission?" Berson asked Tevye one evening as he came to share Berson's meal. "You'd have a much more comfortable life in the army as an officer."

"Accepting the commission would be tantamount to enlisting in the Russian Army. They'd keep me in Europe forever."

"Not forever," Berson countered, "until the end of the war."

"And that may be a very long time," Tevye replied. "In the forests, Viner infected me with his Zionism. Personally, when the fighting subsides, I will make my way to Palestine."

"Tevye, be realistic," Berson urged. "You can't get to Palestine while war is still raging. But as a hero of the Soviet Union, especially with the Stalin Gold Medal, you'll have a better chance of getting to Palestine after the war."

"You don't know the Russians," Tevye laughed. "They will never let you go. Their symbol is a bear and their embrace is as deadly as a bear hug."

A month later, the Third Brigade camped ten kilometers east of the Vistula River. Warsaw was in sight. The nine divisions of Marshal Zhukov's First Front came to a complete standstill. He assured his military commanders that in a few days they could begin the attack on Warsaw. But days turned into weeks, and weeks into months, and still the victorious Russians were motionless, as though the entire line was atrophied in place. Forward units reported smoke rising from Warsaw and heavy bombardment could be heard from within the city. Dworin was anxious and did not know what the shelling was about. He and his staff wanted to get on with the battle because, as everyone knew, when Warsaw fell, the war in Poland would be over.

"This is the moment I've been waiting for – to get back to Warsaw," Dr. Berson said to the two men, Tevye and Dworin. "Why aren't they moving in?"

"It's the same problem we had with the AK in the forest," Tevye said. "The Russians will not let Warsaw fall until they know into whose hands she'll fall. Right now in Warsaw, there's an internal war going on between the pro-Russian and pro-British underground units for the control of the city. When Moscow is satisfied that the AK has been destroyed, the Red Army will march in to establish its rule in Warsaw."

*

During a lull in the fighting, Tevye asked Dworin to let him take leave to search for surviving relatives in his native Vilna. Armed with an official pass, Tevye said his good-byes and left the brigade. However, instead of going north, toward Vilna, he headed south. His citation from Marshal Zhukov and his Stalin Gold Medal allowed him to pass through and requisition food from Russian units along the way. Hitching rides with Russian transports when he could, Tevye traveled south, eventually passing through the Alps to Italy. His goal was to reach an Italian port where he hoped to board a ship to Palestine. But his ecstasy was short lived.

He made it to the port of Trieste. As he entered the port, a British military police corporal ordered him to halt. When Tevye was unable to provide orders authorizing him to be in the port, the corporal handcuffed him and put him in the back of his jeep.

As the jeep drove from the port to the center of the city, winding amid columns of soldiers, Tevye saw a squad of British soldiers, each of whom wore a Jewish star patch on his uniform.

"*Shalom aleichem*," Tevye screamed out, attracting the attention of the squad's leader. The lieutenant motioned to the military police to stop.

"You, show me your identity card," the officer said to Tevye.

No one in the outfit could read the Cyrillic writing on the card nor could anyone recognize the name, Zhukov, on the citation. But when Tevye spoke a few words of Hebrew to the group, the squad leader asked the MP what he intended to do with Tevye.

"I'm taking him in for questioning." the corporal explained. "He's wearing a Russian uniform. There aren't any Russian troops within five hundred kilometers."

"He's a Jewish survivor. I'll take charge of him," the lieutenant stated.

With a snappy salute, the corporal took the handcuffs off Tevye. "Go with him," he ordered, "and consider yourself lucky."

"Get in the truck," the lieutenant said to Tevye, speaking in Hebrew. "My name is Daniel Kolodny. I'm part of the Palestine Brigade."

"A Palestine Brigade!" Tevye gasped.

"Yep," Kolodny said. "The British authorized the formation of a Palestine Brigade. Our unit is made up of Jews from Palestine who fought alongside the British. We've been fighting as part of the allied troops since September, 1944, right here in Italy. We even stormed into Austria and Germany."

"And the patches?" Tevye asked.

"The British authorized the Shield of David as the brigade's insignia. At our peak, we had more than thirty thousand men."

"You mean, thirty thousand Jews served in the Jewish Brigade?" Tevye asked, incredulous.

"We are the Palestine Brigade, not the Jewish Brigade," Kolodny explained.

"Do Arabs serve in your units?"

"No, it's the Palestine Brigade, but only Palestinian Jews serve, no Arabs."

"Why?" Tevye started to explore the issue, but Kolodny cut him off.

"I'll fill you in later," he promised, "but I need to know what you can tell me about the Jews in Europe, the Jews under Hitler."

Tevye sighed, "I can't give you accurate figures but in every city, Jews were driven into ghettos, then slaughtered in special camps, concentration camps. From the Warsaw Ghetto, where there was an uprising, we heard about some survivors. But I don't know how many actual survivors there are in Europe."

"And you? How did you survive?"

"Me, I was a Partizan…"

"Partizan?"

"We hid and fought in the woods, derailing trains, blowing up bridges, and doing whatever we could to harass the German war machine. After they killed all the Partizans in my band, I ended up fighting against the Germans as a volunteer with the Russian army."

Kolodny stopped the jeep, turned to Tevye, and said, "You have to tell your story to the world."

"If I have to tell the story, I'll tell it from Jerusalem," Tevye said. "I left the Russian army so I could go to Palestine."

"You're with the right people," Daniel Kolodny assured him. "We're all going to Palestine. Come meet some of my boys."

At their headquarters in Bari, the Palestinian Jews gathered around Tevye, avidly listening as he told them about life in the ghettos, the killing factories in the concentration camps, his exploits with Partizans, and his battles alongside the Red Army. They stood in awe as he flashed his Stalin Gold Medal and read them the citation from Marshal Zhukov. The men passed around beer and refreshments, making it quite an event for both Tevye and the Jewish soldiers from Palestine. Sitting next to Kolodny, Tevye fingered the brocaded Magen David on the lieutenant's uniform and fondly embraced many of the soldiers who came to join them in the mess hall and to shake his hand.

When the long row of admirers had all been acknowledged, he accepted Kolodny's invitation to have dinner with his men. Tevye ate little, although this was his first decent meal in four months. He bombarded them with questions about Palestine and joined them, in his rusty, monotone voice, singing Zionist songs. The dinner lasted most of the evening and ended with an impromptu ceremony when Kolodny presented Tevye with a Palestine Brigade patch.

"I hereby declare you an honorary captain in the Palestine Brigade," the lieutenant said with a grin.

"I don't know how to thank you," Tevye said softly, tears of joy flowing into his ragged beard. He held the Jewish Brigade's patch above his head. "To me, this means a million times more than the Stalin Gold Medal!"

Kolodny embraced Tevye and then made a surprise announcement to his troops. "Men, I can tell you the Brigade is being demobilized. Within a month we will be going home."

The men leaped to their feet with joy, cheering wildly.

"When you go back to Palestine, I'm coming along," Tevye shouted to Kolodny who called out, "That's enough for tonight. Tevye needs to rest, and so do we."

After the men filed out, with much backslapping and many handshakes, Kolodny waited until he and Tevye were alone in the room. "We have already sent several hundred survivors to Palestine," he said to Tevye.

"Who's 'we'?" Tevye asked.

"Have you ever heard of the Mossad?" Daniel asked.

"No. Never."

"The Mossad is the intelligence arm of the Jewish Agency. It organized the Aliyah Bet, the illegal immigration to Palestine."

"I'm still confused," Tevye said. "Why an illegal immigration? Is there no legal immigration to Palestine?"

"The British allow only fifteen hundred Jews to immigrate into Palestine a month."

"Fifteen hundred Jews! That's crazy," Tevye responded. "Thousands, maybe hundreds of thousands survived the Nazi hell. And only fifteen hundred a month!"

"That's why the Mossad organized the illegal *aliyah* beyond the fifteen hundred," Kolodny explained to the disgruntled Tevye.

"That's Aliyah Bet?" Tevye asked. "How does it work?"

"We bring survivors to European ports and transport them illegally to Palestine."

Tevye interrupted, "Some survivors are still trapped in Russia and Poland. They can't get to your port cities."

"Exactly," Daniel Kolodny stated. "That is why we're setting up an organization to feed into the Aliyah Bet system, to bring Jews out of Poland, out of Europe."

"Great," Tevye said, "I'm a Jewish survivor. So, when the Brigade goes to Palestine, that's when I go."

Daniel nodded. "But, Tevye, first you have a job to do here, in Europe."

"What the hell are you talking about? I'm headed for Palestine," Tevye sat up indignantly. "You want me to stay in Poland? Go back to Russia!"

"Tevye, you will get to Palestine when your work in Europe is done," he quietly assured him. But Tevye wasn't assuaged.

"I refuse to stay in Europe even one extra day!" he protested. "I'll have nothing to do with your Mossad, or Aliyah Bet."

He refused to listen to any assignment that would keep him out of Palestine.

"Okay. First you have to accept the fact that you can't return with the Palestine Brigade to Palestine. But you have a choice. If we take you illegally now to Palestine with Aliyah Bet, we have to try to break through the British blockade."

"What British blockade?"

"Blockade – as in barricade – as in barrier," Daniel stated. "The British navy is blockading our ships, boarding them, and stopping us from landing Jewish survivors in any part of Palestine."

"And?"

"And, what?"

"Do you get any Jews into Palestine?"

"Some yes, some no," Daniel replied.

"That's how I get to go to Palestine? Run a blockade?" Tevye grumbled. "What about getting a certificate for legal entry to Palestine? Can I do that?"

"Your chance is as good as about 150,000 other Jews' who are waiting for the same thing."

"That's a pretty dim prospect," Tevye said with dismay.

"There's no other way, except working with us. For now, if we succeed with your illegal transport, you get there. If not, the British send you back to the camps in Europe or to some British detention camp in Greece."

"What's the other choice?" Tevye asked, calming down somewhat. "What do you want me to do?"

"Stay with us in Europe for a while, maybe a couple of months, maybe a year or two. Then I'll be sure that you get one of the precious certificates guaranteeing your legal entry to Palestine."

"Who's 'us'?"

"When the brigade receives demobilization orders, about twenty-five men will remain in Europe. We'll take off our uniforms and live as war refugees to stay in contact with the survivors. That's the Bricha."

"Bricha?"

"Rescue. That's the group that will penetrate into Poland to guide survivors, Jewish survivors, to some port of embarkation for Aliyah Bet," Daniel said. "But we need your help. You know Polish, probably Russian, and you can be one of our Bricha leaders."

Tevye sat silently for some time, considering his options. Then he slowly said with some resignation, "If you can guarantee me a certificate, you can count me in. But I'd rather go now."

"Soon, Tevye, first you are truly needed," Daniel promised, opening two last bottles of beer and raising his in a toast to Tevye, who tipped his bottle back toward the captain before taking a long swig.

"One more thing," Daniel said. "This is all secret, clandestine. All of us, including you, will operate under assumed names."

"By the way, why me?" Tevye asked. "You have lots of men, why do you really want me?"

"Because none of us speak a word of Russian or Polish or, for that matter, even Yiddish," Daniel said. "After hearing about your exploits, we know you're perfectly suited to helping us."

Chapter 7

Haskel, the forger, remained in the Ghetto even as the death trains were being filled with its Jews. As conditions worsened, his forgery business flourished. People sought him out for fake identity cards so they could escape, or for falsified labor certificates so they could be exempt from the Resettlement lists. However, his lucrative business abruptly closed when German troops discovered his forgery operations and raided his print shop. The very next day he was brought, under guard, to the Ostbahn for Resettlement. But he was enterprising enough to extricate himself from even that crisis.

Haskel was not merely a petty forger. He had an uncanny instinct for survival. When the Germans began ordering Judenrat members to the Ostbahn and no longer excused persons holding legal exemptions, Haskel realized he must prepare for the moment when he would also be placed on the dreaded trains. He established close connections with the German guards and the railway officials, lavishly bribing them. Then he found a place in Warsaw to store his own forged identity documents as well as his enormous fortune of gold he had made in the Ghetto.

When his turn came to board the Ostbahn, he was marched along with others to the train. But, at some distance from Warsaw, train officials whisked him out of his boxcar during an emergency stop and helped him make his way back to Warsaw. No one ever found out how or where he managed to secrete his treasured personal documents and the huge amount of gold he reclaimed upon his return to the city.

With the enormous cache of gold and his excellent personal forged documents, including fraudulent commendation letters from high Berlin officials, Haskel, now Friedrich Funkel, not only survived, but lived quite comfortably among unsuspecting German officials and Polish gentry. To his credit, he was captured a year later when he tried to help another survivor, a girl who had participated in the Ghetto uprising in the spring of 1943.

It happened one evening while sitting in an outdoor café, sipping tea, when he noticed a girl crawling out of a sewer whose lid had been left open for repairs. He recognized Rachel, the survivor of the Ghetto uprising. He motioned to her to follow him to his lavish home. When he entered his apartment house, the concierge stared at the shabbily dressed, filthy girl.

"Who is this woman, this slut, Herr Funkel?" he asked.

"Just a friend," Haskel said, winking at the man, whom he knew to be one of the guards Stasha had stationed in every apartment building in Warsaw. Haskel slipped him a gold coin, asking him not to report the girl's presence. When Haskel led Rachel into his apartment, she waited until he locked the door.

"I have to tell you about the rebellion," she said urgently. "We started this uprising to let the world know what was happening in the Ghetto and especially how we rebelled against the mighty Germans. You have to help me get this message out to the world."

"No, wait until you've had a chance to clean up," he said, handing her towels and a cake of soap.

Rachel bathed and got into a simple, long, white dress that Haskel brought her from the wardrobe. Looking painfully thin, but still beautiful in the softly draped dress, she sat with Haskel to share his supper. She tried not to wolf down the soft bread, potatoes, and baked chicken after weeks of starving in the sewers and forests. The meal over, Haskel said she could now relate her story.

"For months we secretly prepared for the uprising and were able to keep it secret, even though hundreds of us were involved. We caught the Germans by complete surprise. In the first few days, we slaughtered hundreds of troopers with our sudden burst of firepower. They actually marched into a hail of bullets. When they retreated, we took the battle to them. Not in a face-to-face engagement but through stealth and deception, we stopped them cold."

"What was your assignment?" Haskel asked.

"I knew all the twists and turns of the sewers," she said with some pride, "so I was the runner bringing arms, even while the battle was going on, or leading people in and out of the sewers. I also prepared a possible rescue operation that would get fighters out through the sewers in the event that the commander ordered us to leave the Ghetto. I regret that order never came. The fighters stayed at their posts till the end.

"We were outnumbered and outgunned," she said, "but we fought off the German infantry for seven weeks. Finally, they sent in their crack armored tanks to dislodge us. The bombardment was unbelievable. They did not know where our fighters were, so they bombed and burned down all the buildings in the Ghetto. There wasn't a single house left after the bombardment. In the end the Ghetto was burned down; many were incinerated in their cellars."

Rachel stopped to dry her tears. Waiting for her to collect herself again, Haskel asked, "Do you know what happened to Dr. Poliakov? Was he at all involved in the rebellion?"

"I saw him one week before the rebellion started. We owed him the courtesy of informing him about our plans. I was surprised when he told us that he knew the truth about the Ostbahn's destination and about the ovens in Treblinka. He said he had taken that information, with proof and evidence, to the Germans. They assured him they would investigate and make plans.

"Dr. Poliakov realized that this was only a delaying tactic. So he decided to call a general strike, a demonstration, where he would disclose his findings to the remnant of Jews who had survived. But before he had a chance to make his findings public, a group of German officers stormed into his office and ordered him to follow them to the Ostbahn."

"What happened then?" Haskel asked.

"Dr. Poliakov asked the Germans to wait outside his office, explaining that he had to collect his personal belongings. When they walked out, he committed suicide. It was in the afternoon, on July 23, 1943, that he committed suicide. We informed…"

A loud banging on the door interrupted her account.

"Stasha will be here right away," the concierge warned Haskel.

Haskel gave him a few gold coins, thanked him for his warning, and locked the door after he left.

Haskel turned to Rachel. "You are not safe here, and I'm not safe while you're here. You have to leave. Here's an address of some Poles who'll take you in. But you have to go right away. It'll be a safe haven for you."

He began to fill a backpack with food for her, but again there was a pounding on his door. Breaking down the door, Stasha rushed in and, pushing Haskel aside, ordered his two accompanying militiamen to seize the girl and bring her to his office.

Rachel may have been a courageous heroine fighting in the Ghetto uprising, but she was no match for Stasha's interrogation. She identified Haskel as the Ghetto forger.

Confronted with the girl's testimony, Haskel tried to save himself. "Commandant, Commandant," he pleaded, "leave me alone and I'll give you a list of all the Jews who got forged documents from me. With that list, you'll find everyone who is living on the Aryan side."

"Shut up, Jew!" Stasha bellowed. "I can get that from you easily enough. You'll tell me everything when my men persuade you to talk."

"If I have to choose my place of death, I'd rather you kill me here than in the concentration camps. What will you gain by sending me off to the trains? Another Jew sent to die at Treblinka? My notebook bearing a complete record of all my forgeries will provide you with names of dozens of Jews living right here under your nose. I guarantee you, without me you'll never find that list, even if a dozen of your men search the entire city of Warsaw. Just think it over. The list can be yours any time you guarantee my safety and the safety of the girl."

Stasha ordered Haskel's arrest.

*

Stasha rarely bothered Colonel Greifler with details of his operations, but this time he discussed Haskel's proposition with him because it would involve tangling with the Gestapo, which had jurisdiction over Jews on the Aryan side.

"Promise the Jew whatever he wants," the colonel said.

"And the girl?"

"I said, whatever he wants. Just get the list."

Stasha had his men bring Haskel and Rachel to his office. He handed them bona fide identity documents, guaranteeing their safety.

"Now the notebook," Stasha said.

"May I use your phone?" Haskel replied, and when Stasha nodded, Haskel dialed a number, spoke three words and hung up the receiver.

"The notebook will be in my apartment in three hours."

Three hours later, a messenger from a Swiss bank appeared with a package, which he handed to Haskel. Stasha grabbed the package, tore the wrapping, and proudly held up the notebook.

"Now, stay here, Jew, and keep the girl with you. Don't go anywhere until I find these people," Stasha commanded.

After a week of intensive searches, Stasha's men were able to round up only three people from Haskel's list. Stasha had no choice but to report his failure to Greifler.

"What do I do with the forger?" he asked.

"Let him be," the colonel said. "He doesn't matter anymore. He may be of use to you sometime in the future. The Trusteeship Office is officially closed."

"Closed?"

"I am leaving for Berlin this afternoon to head the Trusteeship Headquarters there."

"What about me?" Stasha asked, fear clutching his heart.

"You are transferred to the Gestapo," the colonel said. "Here are your orders. Report to Colonel Zahn immediately."

*

"Very impressive," Colonel Rudolf Zahn said as he read Colonel Greifler's report on Stasha, who was standing at attention, watching the colonel – a short, chubby man with bushy eyebrows – as he was paging through the lengthy report.

"Be seated," Zahn finally said, motioning Stasha to a carved armchair. "This is quite impressive, but your work here will be entirely different. With Colonel Greifler, you dealt with Jews. Here you will deal with your Polish compatriots."

The colonel opened another folder and extracted a document detailing Stasha's new assignment. He handed it to Stasha, who glanced through it, relieved to see that he retained his position as police commandant. But he was baffled with his new responsibility, which required him to organize a network of citizens to penetrate the Russian-backed Polish underground.

"Sir, I don't quite understand the scope of this assignment. What is the Wehrmacht's interest in this matter?"

"In the event that the Red Army marches on Warsaw, the Russian-backed underground will be its fifth column," Colonel Zahn explained.

"They will help the Russian troops conquer the city, but, far more important, they will also set up a Communist regime, a Communist Polish government, under Russia's control. The Gestapo's job is to destroy this underground. Your assignment is to discover all you can about its members and leaders. Give us the names and we'll do the rest."

"I did that sort of work before the war," Stasha replied, "and I'm eager to continue working against Communists."

As with everything else, Stasha attacked his new assignment with unbounded energy, if not finesse. His first job would be to explain to his militiamen how important it was to save Warsaw from being taken over by the Communists. Remembering that Tomasz Rynek had offered to help, and recalling that Rynek had told him he had written an article on political intrigue, Stasha turned to Tomasz to enlist him in this primary task.

"Could you write an educational tract?" Stasha asked Tomasz as they shared a cup of whiskey-laced tea. "Write something moving, something persuasive. Something that clearly details the Communist threat on Poland if she is conquered by the Russians."

Tomasz thought a while, then reeled off several ideas that excited their imagination and which they discussed late into the night. Several days later, Tomasz brought him his propaganda tract written in both German and Polish, which Stasha submitted to Colonel Zahn for his approval.

"This is an excellent propaganda tract Rynek has produced," Colonel Zahn said enthusiastically. "I'm making copies for you to distribute to your militia people and am also sending it to Berlin."

He congratulated Stasha on recruiting such a bright man for the new assignment, adding that he looked forward to great accomplishments, as the two will be working together.

With the tract in hand, Stasha recruited several men from his militia whom he began to indoctrinate and who could be trusted to infiltrate the Communist cells. Stasha's weekly reports to Colonel Zahn indicated that most of the pro-Russian cells had been uncovered and would soon be penetrated by his special squad, which was indoctrinated with that mission. Before the month was over, he submitted over a hundred names of Poles active in the underground organizations.

They were summarily executed by Colonel Zahn's death squads.

However, because of these killings, many suspects managed to avoid capture by changing their names and their residences, moving from house to house. To solve that problem, Stasha conceived of a scheme to entrap those Communist Poles who were living in hiding. His first step was to order Haskel to open a new print shop and resort to his old forgery business.

"Now, Haskel, if you value your life, spread the word that you can secretly provide forged identification papers," Stasha commanded.

Haskel opened his print shop in a storefront, and the results were astounding. Hundreds of Poles applied for false documents with which they planned to safely carry on their work as members of the Polish underground supported by Russia. Stasha was able to turn over hundreds of names of Polish Communists to the Gestapo.

*

Unlike Greifler, who had rarely complimented Stasha, Colonel Zahn publicly acknowledged Stasha's outstanding achievements. The colonel hosted a special ceremony in his office to officially commend Stasha for his exceptional work. His wife, Franya, and their friends, the Ryneks, were invited, along with high-ranking officers, to attend the ceremony. Stasha was presented with a scroll recognizing his service to the Gestapo, to which Zahn attached a document, promoting Stasha to the rank of major.

"But don't rest on your laurels," Colonel Zahn said. "There must be hundreds more who need to be discovered and eliminated."

Several days later, Stasha came to Haskel's print shop to launch the second phase of his investigations. While Haskel was busy setting up the press, Stasha rummaged through a packet of old files he found lying around the print shop. Poking amidst these old records, Stasha noticed a financial ledger containing entries of the forger's earnings. Interested in learning of Haskel's accumulated wealth, Stasha paged through the ledgers and was aghast to find an entry that read, "Tomasz Rynek – 3 documents: 2 gold bracelets + 3 gold rings."

Stasha could not believe his eyes. He snatched Haskel out of his chair, holding him by the collar, and shaking the ledger in his face.

"What is this! Did you make this up?"

"No, no, commandant, I did not make it up," Haskel gasped for breath. "This transaction really took place."

When Stasha released his stranglehold, Haskel spoke slowly and succinctly. "In the Ghetto, I made documents for three people in the name of

Rynek – a man, a woman, and a baby girl. The real Ryneks from Krakow died in some train accident."

With fury, Stasha burst into Tomasz's home, where he found Tomasz relaxing and his wife, Irena, holding the child in her arms. She was trembling as Stasha raged wildly.

"Tomasz, you lied. You paraded like my friend. I now discover you're an escaped Jew! Haskel confessed he sold you forged documents."

Tomasz calmly stated, "We have never been to the Ghetto and I have never met this man, Haskel."

Stasha cut him short, "I found your names on the forger's list from the Ghetto."

Little Jadzia, frightened by Stasha's ranting, began to cry hysterically. She was quickly taken out by her mother to the bedroom.

"You've taken advantage of Franya and me," Stasha snarled. "Now, don't take me for a bigger fool. Make it easier on yourselves by confessing and telling me about other Jews who are living on the Aryan side."

Tomasz repeated his denials over and over.

Exasperated, Stasha called his men to arrest the family and, as they were being led out of their lavish home, he called out, "I don't need your confession. I have Haskel's evidence and his testimony that he made the documents for you."

But what he did not tell Tomasz was that he could not use either the evidence or Haskel's testimony. He could not report this to Colonel Zahn nor even seek his advice. Stasha knew that he had to end the Ryneks' deception quickly without it being made public, or the colonel would – at best – ridicule him for his gullibility in having a hidden Jew write his propaganda pamphlet. More likely, Stasha reasoned, the colonel might take action against him for involving the Gestapo in this "Jewish deception."

He therefore decided not to report the incident to Colonel Zahn and immediately ordered Tomasz, Irena, and Jadzia to be shipped off to Treblinka. In the report to the Gestapo, he would merely include the phrase, "Two adults and one child shipped on the Ostbahn," without citing any names.

He had the militia arrest them and personally followed the jail transport, handing them over to Janek, the warden.

"Put them on the first train to Treblinka," Stasha ordered. "This is top secret and no one, I mean no one, in the militia or in the German military, is to know of it. If anyone discovers this shipment, it will be your head that rolls!"

"Yes, Sir…Yes, Sir," Janek said meekly. "There's a 5 A.M. train tomorrow. We have other adults going on it. I can add these people as well."

*

In their cell, Irena clutched Jadzia to her bosom, rocking back and forth and sobbing to the child's utter bewilderment.

To console his wife, Tomasz kept assuring her, "Irena, there's still the possibility that we will soon be free. The war is almost over. I heard a report on the underground radio that Russian army units are close to the Vistula and will move on to Warsaw to liberate the city within days."

However, when Janek made his midnight rounds, he dashed their hopes. "War or no war," he grunted, "you got on the commandant's bad side and you're leaving on the 5 A.M. train."

Irena handed the baby over to the father and crouched in the corner of the cell, crying hysterically. Tomasz could do or say nothing to calm his wife. At about midnight, with the sleeping baby still in his arms, he walked over to his sobbing wife and quietly said, "There is still hope. We can save Jadzia."

"What are you talking about?" she asked.

Tomasz reminded her. "We still have Franya, Stasha's wife. We befriended her for just this purpose, so we could give Jadzia a safe haven."

Irena stared at him in disbelief. "Safe haven? Give up Jadzia? Are you crazy?"

"Now is the time," Tomasz insisted, "and who could be better, or provide better safety for our daughter than someone who already loves her, someone whom she calls 'Mama Franya'?"

Together they wept silently in the dark prison cell, taking turns to hold the child.

"It's not right. I tell you, it's not right," the young mother said quietly, cradling their sleeping three-year-old.

"It's our only chance," her husband replied. "We can't take her with us."

"But maybe we'll survive there, I mean in Treblinka," she said slowly, rising from the damp cell floor.

Tomasz reminded her, "We decided that if we were caught, we'd give her up so she'll have a chance to live."

"We decided? We decided? You decided!" Irena bristled, speaking under her breath so as not to awaken the child.

"If we take her with us, we'll be taking her to die."

"And if she's discovered here, they'll kill her. That's her safe haven?"

"No, that's not true," Tomasz assured her. "This *is* her safe haven. Here she *will* live. Here is her only chance to survive."

"Don't do it! You're throwing away your child. Don't do it. You are killing her," the young mother protested angrily and shouted, "Her blood is on your head."

"There's no other way out," he replied, reaching for the child.

She glared at him, her faced reddened, and hissed angrily, "I can't fight you anymore. Do what you want. Go ahead! Give up your only child!"

The father called out to the prison guard, "Hey, you! Tell Stasha that I'm ready to give him names of Jews living on the Aryan side."

"Shut up, you bastard. It's too late," Janek replied. "The commandant doesn't work at three o'clock in the morning."

"In two hours, we are being sent off to die," the prisoner shouted so the other prisoners would be certain to hear, "and you'll get your ass chewed off for not telling him my offer to give him names of Jews in hiding."

"The commandant is in his private quarters," the warden said derisively.

"That's where we want to go, only there. Just to his house, nowhere else," Tomasz shouted even louder.

Other prisoners, overhearing, jeered at the guard, "Yeah, if you don't let them go to Stasha, we'll tell him this guy's offer – so you'll be behind bars with us," shouted one.

"That's right, we'll tell him," another called out. "Janek, we want to see you fry."

The guard returned to his station, where he reluctantly dialed a number. He knew the commandant would skin him for waking him up. "Commandant, it's Janek. Sorry to disturb you, but the prisoner, this Rynek, wants to come to your home to give you names of other Jews in the…"

"You woke me for this!" Stasha bellowed. "Carry out the transfer! Put those people on the train!"

"Sir, you told me to keep it in confidence. Other prisoners heard the man offer to give you names of Jews. I'm afraid Colonel Zahn will hear about this too."

Janek listened for a minute, then said, "Yes, Sir. Yes, I will, Sir."

Janek hung up the phone and went to the prisoners' cell, where he shackled Tomasz and Irena's ankles in leg irons.

"Stasha will give you exactly two minutes," he said. "Follow me."

Staggering and shuffling with the weight of the chains, they followed the warden through the prison passageways. He shoved them onto the backseat of a police vehicle, the mother cradling the sleeping child on her lap. They were silent during the ride through the dark streets, aware they might never see the outside world again. They arrived at a gabled home in the elegant section of Warsaw, where Stasha, standing astride, awaited them in front of his open door, blocking their entrance.

"My wife's sleeping," Stasha growled. "Start talking and then get the hell out of here."

The prisoners sidestepped him and pushed their way into the foyer, where Tomasz called out, "Franya! Franya!" and at the same time, rattled his iron shackles on the wooden floor. The ruckus he created echoed throughout the house. The baby opened her eyes but Tomasz took the child to quiet her. Almost instantly, Stasha's wife appeared at the head of the staircase.

"What is going on? Irena! Tomasz!" Franya called out, her fingers fumbling to tie her robe.

"They're not Irena and Tomasz!" Stasha said scornfully. "They're Jews who escaped from the Ghetto and betrayed us! Go back to sleep, Franya. I have to talk to this scum."

Tomasz looked at Franya and held her gaze as he placed the tousled, whimpering child on the sofa.

"Franya, we know what the Germans will do to us tomorrow," he said, holding back tears. "She's yours. Don't let her die."

Without waiting for Franya's reply or Stasha's retaliation, Tomasz hurried his wife back out the door, past the dumbfounded Stasha, to the waiting prison vehicle. Stasha made a move to go after them, but Franya ran toward him, held his arm, and pulled him back into the house.

"She's such a pretty little girl," his wife said tenderly, bending down to pick up the child.

"Don't touch her, Franya," Stasha said, clutching his wife. "She's a Jew-child."

Franya gently freed herself from Stasha's grasp and softly said, "She's beautiful, and look at her…"

"She's a Jew! And besides, I sent the list to the Gestapo. I already reported two more adults and one child on tomorrow's Resettlement Transport."

"So? A child can be reported to have died in transit," Franya said, cradling the little girl.

"I know how important a baby is to you," Stasha pleaded, "but this baby can mean death for both of us."

"Look, she's waking up," Franya said, disregarding his angry pleas.

"Franya, we will end up on those trains ourselves if that Jew-baby is discovered in our home."

She turned away from him and calmly walked back up the staircase to their bedroom. She went in and closed the door.

Stasha followed her, knocked on the door, and pleaded, "Franya, give me that child!"

Franya opened the door, placed the baby in the center of their large brocade-covered bed, and sat down on the divan. She spoke to Stasha with a firmness she never thought she could possess. "Stasha," she said, sitting him down on the corner of the bed, looking down at him, "I don't need this elegant home and I don't need your fancy foods. I don't need your car. I need this child. If Tomasz and Irena are going to die, she will need a mother. I will become Jadzia's mother. I am her savior. I don't have to stay here. You do what you have to here with the Germans. I'm going back to Grochov with her. I'll work the farm."

Hurriedly, she wrapped Jadzia in a soft shawl and packed a few things in a suitcase, which she handed to Stasha. He helped her into his military sedan and drove her to their small farm in Grochov. Before dawn, he was back in the gabled house, alone.

That morning, Stasha submitted a list of two unnamed adults sent to Treblinka and a child who died in transit. He handed the list to Janek, the warden, and glared at him, saying with deadly calm, "If you ever happen to wonder what happened to that Jew-child, I suggest you think enough of your own skin that you shut up about it."

The Gestapo accepted Stasha's report and he accepted Jadwiga, as his daughter.

*

Franya had never been as happy as she was the day she returned to the farm with her new daughter. She saw herself not only as Jadzia's mother, but since Tomasz and Irena were going to die in the concentration camp, also as the child's rescuer. Everything she did for the little girl was an act of love – dressing her, bathing her, feeding her, singing to her.

For the first few weeks, the child cried incessantly, asking for her mother and father. Many nights, when nightmares shook little Jadzia awake and the little girl wept inconsolably for her parents, Franya would hold her and rock her to sleep.

"Tell her that her parents will be back," Stasha once advised, but that upset the child even more. She cried hysterically, demanding to be with her mother, "Now. Want Mama. Want my Mama!"

They never mentioned the parents again.

It took several months for Franya to calm little Jadzia by showering her with love. Gradually, as their first year on the farm came to a close, the four-year-old accepted "Mama Franya," and rarely mentioned her parents.

During that year, Stasha would drive from Warsaw to visit his wife once a week. But as time passed, he began spending more and more time in Grochov, because, to Franya's joy, his attachment to Jadzia grew with each visit. He relegated much of his police duties to his subordinates, allowing him time to leave Warsaw in order to be in Grochov. Consciously, whenever he would visit the farm, he would be wearing civilian clothing, so that the child would not associate him with the German soldiers, who frightened her.

At first, the child called him *dziadzia*, "uncle." As time went on, Stasha began spending entire weeks in Grochov. When he picked her up, she would happily poke into his pockets looking for the peppermints he usually carried for her. Jadzia soon called him Papa.

*

While Stasha divided his time between Grochov and Warsaw, dramatic changes were taking place in the German HQ at the Bristol Hotel. German intelligence reported that the Red Army had been ordered to move forward and assault Warsaw. Most of the high-ranking, civil administrative officers had been ordered back to Germany and were replaced by minor functionaries. All the remaining old hands were busy packing. The military pullback became a tidal wave. Stasha stormed into the Gestapo and confronted Sergeant Heinrich Glaubmann, Zahn's replacement.

"What have you arranged in order to protect me and the Polish militiamen, when the Russians take the city?"

"Calm down, Stasha," Glaubmann said. "I assure you, Germany will stand by those who helped in the occupation. Give me a list of all the Polish civilians who have worked with you. We will resettle your people in Germany before Russia conquers Warsaw."

When Stasha told Franya of the military plans to resettle him and the militiamen in Germany, Franya bristled at the thought of leaving Poland, of leaving the farm she loved.

"We have no choice but to go to Germany," Stasha consoled his wife. "When the Russians get here, they'll kill us, if our own Polish compatriots don't do it first."

"You brought this on us," she wept. "You are forcing us into exile because of your work for the Gestapo."

"Now, Franya," he whispered, picking up Jadzia, "if it wasn't for my work, we wouldn't have her."

As they spoke, a police officer from Warsaw knocked on the farmhouse door. "Commandant," he said, "Sergeant Glaubmann needs you back in Warsaw immediately. I think there is news of the Russian army!"

"As soon as my wife finishes packing, bring her and our daughter with you to Warsaw," Stasha commanded the police officer. "I'm going now."

"Stasha, order your group of select Poles to report immediately to the train station and await their turn to leave," Sergeant Glaubmann told Stasha.

"I have the names right here," Stasha replied, handing him the list of his militia personnel. "The officer you sent to get me will bring my family to Warsaw. When they get here, keep them in this office. I'll be back soon."

Stasha left to round up his militiamen and provide for their transportation to the train station. He soon returned to Gestapo HQ, where he changed into his civilian clothing.

"You know, we all wish you well when you get settled in Germany," Glaubmann said. "You can always look to Colonel Zahn, to me, and to the Gestapo if you need any help."

"I need some help, some assurance, now," Stasha said. "I want to make certain that the record of my service with the German army and the Gestapo will not be disclosed to any unauthorized people. It must be confidential."

"That's been taken care of."

"Has the record been destroyed?"

"No. Why destroy such a valuable file?" Sergeant Glaubmann asked. "Sometime in the future, you might need proof of your service to the Reich. Your file has been marked 'Top Secret'. It is labeled only with a code name."

"What name?"

The sergeant burst out laughing as he handed the file to Stasha. "Here, it's the 'Rynek File'."

Stunned, Stasha stared at the folder. "I don't understand," he said.

"Of course, we knew about the Ryneks," Sergeant Glaubmann said. "We are, after all, the Gestapo, and Janek is our agent. It is our business to know everything. Colonel Zahn knew you had a problem with the Rynek couple and with their transport to Treblinka, but he decided not to take action against you because of your splendid service record."

Stasha was too shocked to reply.

"That is why, I repeat, if you need any help in the future, contact him or me. We'll be stationed at the security office of the Frankfurt airport."

"Thank you, Heinrich," Stasha mumbled, still in shock.

"Come, come, Stasha, you are in no danger from us. You have been more than loyal. I'll escort you to the station so I can say good-bye to your wife and to…what's her name, the little one?"

"Jadwiga," he reminded the sergeant.

"Ah, yes, Jadzia, your fringe benefit of the war."

Amid the bustle of the train station, Stasha took Franya aside and whispered so that their daughter would not hear, "He knows all about Jadzia."

Franya gave him a startled look as a military courier approached Stasha and gave him an envelope containing the official passenger list for his group. Enclosed were the group's German identification cards, train tickets, and letters authorizing their resettlement in Germany.

"Commandant, you're in charge of the transport of your Polish group," the courier said, "but German troops will escort the train."

As a train pulled into the station, a voice over the public address system announced that only German military personnel were allowed to board. Stasha looked on nervously as Sergeant Glaubmann boarded the train together with the remnant of the Gestapo's personnel. German guards ordered the Polish group to wait. Despite his fear, Stasha was able to avoid panic as a rumor quickly spread that the Russians were invading the city.

It was not just a rumor. Already, they could see Russian planes strafing the outskirts of Warsaw. Stasha called to the stationmaster, "Are we on the next train? The attack has started!"

"Yes, yes, you'll be on the next one," the man assured him. But just as the train arrived, so did a convoy of German soldiers who all piled aboard. Once again, the Poles were barred from the train.

Fortunately for Stasha, at the very last moment, a group of railway workers, themselves eager to flee, attached several more cars to the train and the Poles were allowed to board. Planes strafed the station as the train pulled away, quickly building speed, heading toward Germany. Relieved, 157 Polish collaborators sank into their seats, escaping their native land to seek sanctuary in Germany.

Later that afternoon, when the train was a safe distance from Warsaw, Franya arranged for a spontaneous party to celebrate Jadzia's fifth birthday. The Polish passengers and the railway crew members joined in the merriment as Franya urged Jadzia to sing and dance in the crowded aisle. Someone soon brought out an accordion and everyone joined in, singing Polish folk songs. When a conductor called out that the train was crossing the Polish border, the group broke into the Polish national anthem, singing heartily until a German officer held up his gun and ordered, "Stop! Singing the Polish national anthem is a political activity. You are in Germany now and your Polish anthem is verboten. Stop!"

A silence fell over the new refugees, who slipped back into their seats. Tired from the excitement, and not really understanding what was going on, Jadzia soon fell asleep, bundled up on the seat. Stasha and Franya leaned in the corner of the swaying car, watching over her.

"Jadzia must never know who her parents were," Franya said. "If Sergeant Glaubmann knows, what are the chances that others will know too?"

"I have no control over the Gestapo," Stasha replied, stooping to pull the blanket up to cover his daughter. "Zahn surely knows. I don't know who else, but I will kill anyone who threatens to tell her."

When they finally arrived at their destination, a small border town in Germany, Stasha heard his name paged on a loudspeaker. Poles were ordered to remain on the train, but a German official boarded and saluted Stasha. "Major, will you please follow me?"

He led Stasha to a small table inside the train station and gave him a list of specific resettlement areas for each Polish refugee family. As they were individually called off the train, Stasha apprised the husband where his assigned area was to be and described the scope of the work to which he was assigned. Thanks to the German's disciplined attention to the minutest detail, the entire procedure took only two hours. Stasha was impressed with the fine reception the Germans were giving to the Poles who had cooperated and worked with him during the German occupation. He returned to Franya and escorted her to a table in the corner of the station, where they were served coffee and Jadzia a glass of milk and a few butter cookies. Away from the hustle and bustle of the station, he glowingly described the Germans' processing procedure.

"They are a marvel," he laughed. "They are as disciplined about this as they are about everything else, down to the last detail."

"Enough about the Germans. Don't work with them anymore," Franya insisted, with an edge of anger in her voice.

"What're you upset about? Look at my assignment," he said, showing her their resettlement card. "I'm assigned to the post office – a safe civil service job in Berlin."

"I don't want you to work for the Nazis anymore," she softly whispered, so as not to attract attention.

"But, Franya, being on good terms with the Germans enabled me to land the best job and the best housing. I don't understand your annoyance."

"Stasha," she said, "I beg you, stay away from the authorities. I want to live without stress, without the dangers of politics."

"Franya, I'll do anything you say, but…"

"No buts," Franya said. "Let's move to a farm. Anywhere but in Berlin. Do it for Jadzia. I want her to grow up as a healthy, normal child without fear, without connivance, without uniforms. Do it for her."

"What's wrong with sorting the mail?"

"It's still the government and it is still close to their headquarters, right in Berlin. I know you. You'll get involved with them again."

"But I have already been assigned to a job there," Stasha protested.

"The man who gave you that assignment was deferential to you. He saluted you. He called you 'Major.' You're a big shot," Franya said. "You can get any resettlement you want. Please, Stasha, please. Get assigned to a farm. Live quietly with me and Jadzia. I'm not asking for too much. It is the only way we can live in peace."

Stasha got up and walked back toward the German officer's table. Reluctantly, he gave up his resettlement to Berlin and returned to Franya five minutes later, handing her his new assignment – a laborer on a farm near Kassel, just over three hundred kilometers south of Berlin.

Franya said with a smile, "Now promise me, as long as we're in Germany, no army, no Gestapo, no politics."

Stasha took his daughter in his arms, kissed his wife, and said, "I promise. No army, no Gestapo, no politics."

*

The Russian army was on the move. No one was happier than Dr. Szymon Berson when the Seventh Division of Marshal Zhukov's First Front began to march forward. Like an awakening giant, the entire Red Army stirred with a mighty rumble. The powerful army reached the Vistula. A steady stream of military vehicles, followed by infantrymen, surged like a tidal wave over the river. Dr. Berson marched into the city with the brigade, proudly liberating his beloved Warsaw. When the fighting was winding down, Major Anatole Dworin, Dr. Berson's commanding officer, called him in.

"Dr. Berson, you have been helpful to us, necessary to us, and I am grateful," Dworin said. "But now, I'm detaching you from my command. You will stay in Warsaw, responsible for setting up a division hospital, as part of Warsaw's general hospital. Let's go see what shape the facilities are in."

Major Dworin, Berson, and a few military staff members drove to the heart of the city in an ambulance. Berson was amazed by the devastation the Germans had wrought on the city. Many of the buildings were heaps of rubble. His own Czyste Hospital had escaped total destruction but it was severely damaged.

Dworin trailed Berson into the hospital, listening as Dr. Berson gave running commentary on every aspect of the institution, even mentioning, in passing, his own role in its expansion. He recalled that he had been appointed to direct the once-famous medical facility shortly after he graduated from medical school.

"Major, I have great plans for restoring the Czyste Hospital to its former glory," he told Dworin.

"Szymon, you make it sound as though it's become your mission to start all over again, as though nothing happened."

"Warsaw is my home and the hospital was my life. I'm free. I'm alone in the world. What else is there to do now that the nightmare is over?"

However, both men knew that Dr. Berson was not really free as long as he was officially in the Russian army and subject to its discipline. Berson therefore asked Major Dworin about possible separation from military service. Dworin informed him that until the Russian forces were demobilized, he would be subject to Russian authority.

"Anatole, I'm not a Russian citizen. I'm a Pole," Berson protested.

"Technically you are a Russian citizen," the captain explained. "When you were commissioned an officer in the Russian army, that made you a Russian citizen. Don't do anything rash. You're still under strict Russian military discipline."

A few days later, Major Dworin called Berson back in. "Doctor, I suggest that you submit a request to be transferred to the Polish army," he said. "That would make you free of direct Russian control."

"I would still be subject to military service," Berson said. "And I imagine that Russia will continue to control the Polish army."

Dworin replied, "I get your point. I'll see what I can do."

The next day, he telephoned Dr. Berson, notifying him that he had arranged for Berson to meet with a Russian major, Gregor Golinkin, the military liaison to the newly established Polish civil government. Eager to get started on his demobilization, he met with the major that very day.

"If you could get a civil service appointment such as a hospital administrator," Major Golinkin said, "you could then be mustered out of the military and be automatically transferred to your new civil service position."

Berson was ecstatic. The Public Health Department controlled the Czyste Hospital, and its directors knew of his work. He was certain he would be getting a civil service assignment and that would be his ticket to freedom. He met with Dr. Marek Swiatowski, administrator of the department and a renowned physician who knew of Dr. Berson's prewar accomplishments.

After sharing wartime experiences with him, the director asked, "What can I do for you, Szymon?"

"I want to rebuild my Czyste Hospital and restore its greatness."

"Sounds good," Director Swiatowski said, "but it can't be done."

"Can't be done? Why not?"

"Because it's not yours anymore," the director said.

"Well, I didn't mean mine personally," Berson said, apologizing for his choice of words. "I meant it was my job."

"It now belongs to someone else," Swiatowski said.

"But it's been mine for almost ten years."

"The war's created a lot of changes," Swiatowski said. "The hospital has changed hands."

"I know it's been run by the Germans since 1940, but I'm back and it's only fair that I get back the hospital."

"A new director was appointed," Swiatowski said.

"I don't mean to be critical," Berson responded, "but that hospital is now an eyesore."

"That's not the problem," Swiatowski replied. "I know you could do a good job for the Czyste."

"Then, what's the problem?"

"I don't want to sound blunt, but you leave me no choice," Director Marek Swiatowski said. "I'm not going to fire the present director of Czyste just because you came back."

"But you've appropriated it from me."

"The Germans did that."

"And you're continuing their criminal acts?"

"Szymon, I know Jews suffered, but the Poles suffered too. To displace them now would bring further rifts between Jews and Poles and justify their hatred for the Jews."

"Justify their hatred for the Jews," he repeated the director's words. His year with the Partizans trained him to hit back, not to take anything lying down, and yet, there he was, standing as though paralyzed, unable to respond. For a long, agonizing moment, he stared at Swiatowski, saying nothing, remembering only what Tevye said about the AK – "This is no time to fight the *goyim*."

"Marek," he finally said, "can you get me just a staff appointment at Czyste?"

"Szymon, you know that's impossible. If you come back, even as a lab technician, you'll upset the whole staff. You'll be a threat to the director, to the governing board, to every doctor on the staff, even to me."

"How about with any other hospital? I need a government civil service job so that I can get out of this uniform."

"I don't make appointments," Swiatowski said. "The new regime does."

"What does that mean?"

"The party, the Russian Komisars, who are running the country today," he replied. "Nothing is done without their approval. But I have a better suggestion. Why don't you try your friends at the university? They might have something."

Berson thanked him for his advice and walked out to the tram to see Professor Myetek Koslowski, dean of the Medical School at the University of Warsaw. He recalled how, before the German invasion, Professor Koslowski had offered him a lectureship, an invitation he repeatedly turned down. At the time, Berson was busy building the Czyste Hospital and could not commit himself to specific class hours.

Dr. Berson approached the university grounds and saw the enormous damage its buildings had sustained. The administration building, where he met Professor Koslowski, felt like the inside of an icebox. Cold winter winds howled through its corridors because part of its roof had been blown off during the bombing of Warsaw and had not yet been repaired.

"It's going to take a long time to get things into shape," Dr. Koslowski said, after greeting Berson as his old colleague and leading him to a small classroom that had been converted to a dean's office.

"I'd like to help get it into shape," Berson said.

They talked at great length about the university, about its needs, and about its future. Professor Koslowski said he liked many of Berson's ideas, asking him to write a memorandum detailing his suggestions.

"Do you have a teaching or administrative post for me here?" he asked. Receiving no reply, he asked again, "Is there a place here for me?"

"We make no appointments," Dr. Koslowski said. "You have to apply to our Russian overlords. They've been running the country for the past three months."

"Even a teaching post?"

"I can't even order a set of reference books for the library without approval from them."

When Berson left the university, he reported to Major Golinkin, informing him that nothing could be done without approval of the Russian military government or the Russian Komisars.

The major asked him to wait while he leafed through some pages. Then, when he found the name he was searching for, he said, "There, Yuri Andreyev. Go see Yuri Andreyev. He's chief of Civilian Personnel. I'm calling him right now so that he'll expect you."

Dr. Berson rushed off to the Komandatura in Pilsudski Square, which was a veritable beehive. Hundreds of people were milling about, trying to get inside the building. He was only able to get inside thanks to his Russian military uniform. When he finally found the Civilian Personnel section, it was as crowded as the outside square.

"My name is Dr. Berson," he said, pushing his way to the secretary's desk after waiting three hours. "I have an appointment with Yuri Andreyev. Major Golinkin called to set up the appointment."

The secretary disappeared and soon returned, announcing in her shrill voice, "Comrade Andreyev is not seeing anyone today. He has important meetings with the Komisariat. Those with appointments, please return tomorrow."

The following day, Berson was back bright and early at the same office. So were hundreds of others. At about noon, he heard someone in the crowded room calling his name. He did not recognize the voice or the smiling face that greeted him.

"I'm Haskel Kornblit," the man said.

The past three years had completely changed Haskel. His boyish appearance was gone, his face was fleshy, and his body corpulent. He regaled Dr. Berson with his wartime exploits, describing how he had saved many Jews of the Ghetto with forged documents. At first, Berson was not interested in the man's bragging. However, his interest was aroused when Haskel Kornblit mentioned he was waiting to see Andreyev on official matters for the Jewish Committee.

"The Jewish Committee?" Berson asked. "Is it still functioning?"

"Yes, this committee was formed a few weeks ago by the Russians to help Jewish survivors," Haskel said.

While Haskel was speaking, the secretary called, "Dr. Szymon Berson, Comrade Andreyev will see you now."

Haskel quickly scribbled the Jewish Committee's address and placed it in Berson's pocket as he turned to go into the office.

Yuri Andreyev apologized for keeping the doctor waiting, explaining he was overworked because everyone was seeking a government job since there were no jobs in the labor market. Dr. Berson got right to the point and asked for a civil service appointment in the medical field so that he could get out of the army and return to his medical profession.

Andreyev also got right to the point. He asked, "What is your political affiliation? Have you ever belonged to the Communist Party?"

"I've never been involved in politics. My interests were and are solely in medicine and I consider myself an expert in that field."

"Dr. Berson," Andreyev said, "you are an expert in your field. I'm an expert in mine, civil administration. We did not liberate Poland only to return her to the Fascists who controlled her before the war. We intend to create a Communist society here in Poland, and our administrative appointments will be made based solely on these political considerations."

"As a doctor, I never had any political affiliation," Berson began to argue.

"I'm sorry, Doctor," Andreyev abruptly cut him off. "Debate is useless. I can't keep others waiting."

Dr. Berson returned to his military quarters in the division's hospital, where he stayed up all night trying to analyze his dilemma. He could understand the plight of Poland's civil leaders who had to contend with the postwar problems. He could even understand Russia's insistence on determining Poland's Communist future. But he could not understand why he was automatically cut off, not worthy of any consideration as compensation for the service he had rendered to the Russian military. He decided that the only option left for him was to get help from the Jewish Committee.

*

"I knew you would come," Haskel said, meeting Berson outside the office of the Jewish Committee, "because I knew what Andreyev would tell you. It's the same he tells every office-seeker."

Dr. Berson was surprised to find Haskel, and even more surprised when Haskel offered to introduce him to the president of the Jewish Committee. He accepted the offer, hoping that he would tell the president about his work in the Warsaw Ghetto. Haskel led him up a winding staircase, into a sparsely furnished room, where Haskel introduced Dr. Berson, praising him lavishly for his accomplishments in the Ghetto.

"I'm grateful to Haskel for bringing me to you," Berson said. "He's given to exaggeration, but my work at the Czyste Jewish Hospital speaks for itself."

"What can we do for you, Doctor?" the president asked.

"Haskel tells me that this committee is a recognized agency by the new Polish civil government," he said. "I would appreciate it if you could get me an appointment in the Jewish Hospital so that I could get out of this uniform."

"There's no need for a Jewish Hospital, Dr. Berson. Jews no longer need special hospitals, special orphanages, special homes for the aged, or even special attention. We have to strip ourselves of our medieval mentality, which has plagued us for centuries. We Jews must now help create a new Communist order in Poland."

Dr. Berson was surprised by the president's remarks but decided against making an issue of it. Instead, he innocently repeated his request, "All I want is to get a position in a hospital or any institution that is recognized as a civil service post so that I can get out of this uniform."

"Doctor, this uniform is a Russian uniform. It's your badge of honor. You disgrace Russia by your desire to discard your uniform."

The president persisted in vilifying Jews for adhering to timeworn traditions. He closed his tirade by blaming Jews for helping Hitler's ascension to power.

Dr. Berson stalked out of the office, bristling with rage.

Haskel followed the doctor out of the building, trying to calm him. They sat down on a partially destroyed brick wall, where Berson related his series of failures with officers of the new civil government.

"You can't get anything from them, but if you ever need my services," Haskel said, "remember, I can always be contacted at my home."

"Out of sheer curiosity, Haskel, what kind of service would I need you for?"

"I can get any document you need, even a certificate of military discharge."

He was about to ask Haskel how much such a certificate would cost, but recalled Dr. Poliakov's warning: "Stay away from Haskel. He's dangerous."

However, to be polite, Dr. Berson thanked Haskel for his offer to help, asked for his home address, and promised to contact him should he decide to use his services.

Dr. Berson returned to his old commanding officer, Major Dworin. "I tried everything you suggested and failed everywhere. I guess the best thing for me is to take up your first option. Transfer to the Polish army."

The major gave him the proper forms to fill out, promising to expedite Dr. Berson's separation from the Russian army.

Chapter 8

AT THE SAME TIME that Dr. Berson was maneuvering to get himself settled in Warsaw, Stasha and Franya arrived in Germany and found their way to the Reichfurt farm as their resettlement assignment. "Welcome, welcome," old Fritz Reichfurt greeted them enthusiastically on his twelve-acre farm. "It's good that you've come. There's plenty of work, but the war's taken all the young men, and I can't get laborers. I can't do it alone anymore." He showed them the main house and suggested, "Why don't you rest a bit."

Despite the long train ride and the uncomfortable bus ride to the farm, they said they did not need rest. However, Stasha eagerly accepted the old farmer's offer to show them around the farm. Franya was delighted as the little one romped on the littered bales of hay and scampered up and down the rolling hills with abandon. She was like a bird freed from its cage. While Franya entertained her daughter, Reichfurt apologized to Stasha for the run-down condition of the farm.

"It's a bit dilapidated," the farmer said, without realizing his own understatement.

Stasha listened to Reichfurt's jeremiad about his difficulties: his children, who were living up in Kassel, were no help; and most serious was the cost of seed, which had gone through the roof. To encourage the old man, Stasha suggested several changes to restore the farm, increase its productivity, and renovate the weathered buildings. Reichfurt scoffed, shaking his head.

"You do as you think best with the farm." he said dejectedly. "I'm moving to Kassel to stay with my children and look after my real estate investments there. You and your family can stay in the big house. I'm only going to come back from time to time to pay you."

They struck a deal whereby Stasha would receive a monthly salary in addition to a fifteen percent share of produce sales from the farm. The farmer then said he was eager to leave because the bus to Kassel would soon be passing by. Stasha helped to load his luggage onto the rickety, horse-drawn wagon and drove him to the main highway to the bus stop. The moment Stasha returned, Franya clasped his hand and flitted about the big house with him, going from room to room, exhilarated to be the mistress of the crumbling but spacious home.

"It's Jadzia's birthday present," she said, hugging the child. "Now aren't you glad you're not in Berlin working with German officials?"

He led her out of the house to the veranda and quietly said, "The farm has enormous potential. But I have to call Colonel Zahn."

She was aghast, demanding to know what connections he still maintained with the Gestapo. Without giving her any details, he simply said he had a plan whereby Zahn would help build up the farm. He called the number Sergeant Glaubmann had given him.

"Zahn left town, destination unknown," Glaubmann said when Stasha asked to speak to the colonel. "That means he's out of the country and not returning. But maybe I can help."

"Can you introduce me to the quartermaster in Kassel?" Stasha asked. "If you can, you and I can do business provided the military can buy my produce. I'm working on a farm near Kassel and can get there anytime you set the appointment."

Glaubmann replied, "I'll do better. I'll come out to the farm and introduce him to you personally."

A week later, Glaubmann arrived with the quartermaster, a German army captain who, after listening to Stasha's plan, agreed to purchase all the grain and vegetables Stasha could produce. The meeting was brief; the three men concluded a profitable deal, providing the captain and Glaubmann with a percentage of all sales.

With several hired hands working the farm, which the captain was able to supply, the first harvest showed a dramatic increase and the farm's income skyrocketed. Stasha sent Reichfurt the profits from the sale of the produce, keeping his fifteen percent share. Reichfurt hurried to the farm to see with his own eyes "the miracle Stasha created."

Stasha led him around the farm, showing him the renovated storage shed, the main house – repaired and freshly painted – and the barn doors that had been rebuilt. Above all, the fields were seeded for rotating crops. Back in the main house, Franya laid out platters of cakes and fruit, and prepared a pot of steaming coffee.

Reichfurt handed him a wad of German marks, saying, "Stasha, this is the best day I've had in many years. I thank you and if you count the money I just gave you, you'll find the salary I promised you and a hefty bonus I added for all your work."

"You're very kind," Stasha said. "But the farm can still be improved by digging a freshwater well, building new silos, and getting a vehicle to deliver our produce."

"That's quite costly," the old farmer said.

"It won't cost you at all if you grant me the right to pay for these things by mortgaging the land."

Without questioning Stasha's integrity, the old man gladly signed the document.

When Reichfurt left, Stasha gave Franya the wad of money, which she counted, and she joyously announced, "I'm putting aside this money for our future."

Stasha laughed. "That's my blood and sweat money."

"Yes, you earned every groszen of it," Franya said.

"Pfennig," Stasha corrected her. "Remember, you're in the mighty German Reich, not in conquered Poland."

He then called Glaubmann and quietly said, "We now own the farm and the land."

Franya prepared a special evening dinner to celebrate the good news. At the dinner table, Jadzia sang in German, and surprised Stasha with a dramatic reading of a German storybook. Franya explained that she had taught the child to read German by teaching her German songs.

"Jadzia, you're a born actress," Stasha said.

"No, if you're an actress you have to change your name," Jadzia replied, saying she heard German actresses speaking on the radio. "Every one of them said she had a different name before she started acting."

"It's called a stage name," her mother said, proud of her precocious daughter's insight. "And, one day, you'll have one, too."

When supper was over, Franya announced bedtime. Stasha led the child to her room and sat next to her on the bed as Franya sang her to sleep.

*

Despite Franya's contentment with farm life, she was inwardly concerned about the outcome of the war and questioned their future in Germany. She never spoke of it to Stasha. One night, when she could not sleep, she forced herself to ask a question that had been worrying her deeply since the first day they arrived on the farm.

"Stasha," she asked hesitantly, "what will happen to us if the Americans defeat Germany?"

"This farm will soon belong to us," Stasha cryptically replied, startling Franya. "And we'll always have enough food to eat and a roof over our head. In war, farmers always eat best."

"That's not what I mean," Franya said. "What will the Americans do to us? Don't forget you were an officer in the Gestapo."

With his characteristic devil-may-care attitude, Stasha brushed away her fears. "Remember, the Rynek File is top secret. No one can have access to it. So stop worrying. Let's enjoy what we have now."

But only a few weeks later, as news of the total destruction of Kassel reached them, even he had to consider Franya's concerns, especially when the sound of exploding bombs reached their farm.

"There must be big Allied bombardments going on there," Stasha told Franya, as they stood on the porch, catching the faint whiff of smoke. He wondered whether it was the Germans counterattacking or the Americans performing a rapid assault.

They found out the next day, when Fritz Reichfurt returned to the farm accompanied by his son and daughter and their large families.

"Kassel is reduced to ashes and the Americans aren't slowing their progress," he explained. "The Allied bombs leveled the city. My real estate investments are kaput. I'm sorry, Franya, but I have nowhere for my family to live. They're coming back here in the next few days."

Franya packed their belongings and moved into the storage shed, where Stasha installed a small cast-iron stove. They brought in three narrow cots to make it livable.

"Mama, don't cry," Jadzia said, cuddling up to Franya as they went to bed that night. "You always told me that as long as we have each other, we can be happy."

"The child is right, Franya," Stasha said, consoling her. "We have a roof over our heads and farm-fresh food to eat."

That, too, did not last long.

On May 8, 1945, Germany surrendered to the Allies. It was a sad and bitter day for Stasha.

*

The United States Third Infantry Division requisitioned the main house for its headquarters and bulldozed the storage shed where Stasha and Franya were living. The army also converted the rest of the farm into a military motor pool and a salvage depot.

Stasha and his family were dispossessed and for four days he, Franya, and the child were homeless, sleeping in open fields or in shacks. Fortunately for the family, Stasha found an abandoned ramshackle house on the outskirts of Fritzlar, where the US Air Force established an air base. He boarded up what was left of the building to make a one-room dwelling. Poverty added to their misery because the German marks Franya had so niggardly saved were now worthless. Had she not found work as a chambermaid in the officers' quarters on the American air base, the family would have literally starved. Her pay was minimal, but she was able to trade the candy bars and cigarettes the soldiers gave her as tips for staples with which to feed her family.

About a month later, Stasha found a job as a night shift driver in the army's motor pool. Franya worked days and he worked nights, so they had little time for each other or for Jadzia. The child was living like a waif, growing up without a decent home or school, or even a family. Yet, she was their only source of joy, always affectionate, often entertaining them with little dramatic recitations or dances.

Winter came early in 1945 and Franya and Stasha worried that the child's health would suffer because their unstable house was like an icebox. Yet, another danger loomed on the horizon: Stasha's security.

He was assigned as a driver for Lieutenant John Kemeris, head of the division's Central Intelligence Corps – the CIC – the unit that hunted down Nazis and collaborators guilty of war crimes. Stasha's fears became real one evening when he came to work early and noticed a thick folder marked "Collaborators" on Kemeris's desk. He opened the folder, searching for his name. When he heard footsteps, he quickly closed it and took his seat outside the office railing, where he would normally sit each day, waiting for his driving assignments. That file ws the bane of his existence and, to add to his stress, he knew he could not share his fears with Franya.

He conceived of a plan to ingratiate himself to Lieutenant Kemeris by doing special favors for him, hoping that thereby the lieutenant would be lenient if he discovered Stasha's record as a collaborator. Therefore, when the lieutenant sent him to purchase cigarettes, chocolate bars, and tins of coffee at the PX, he managed to buy more than the officer ordered and traded the extras on the black market to procure a Leica camera and expensive binoculars, which he presented to Kemeris. Also, he often drove Kemeris to Homberg, an outlying village, where Stasha waited through the night while the young officer was with his fräulein. Kemeris appreciated Stasha's special favors and showed it by giving him some of his PX rations, which Stasha used to buy food and clothing for his family.

The PX rations helped support his family, but they did not diminish his dread of being discovered as a collaborator, a dread he continued to bear alone.

When Franya demanded to know why he volunteered to be away so many nights and why he was so anxiety-ridden, Stasha finally told her about the Collaborators File. Franya, overcome with fear, also confessed that she had hidden from him a copy of *Stars and Stripes*, the US Army newspaper she had picked up at the officers' club.

"I didn't want to worry you," she said, handing Stasha the paper.

Stasha could not read the entire article, written in English, but his face turned white as he read the headline, "Russians Demand US Return Polish Collaborators."

From that day on, Stasha and Franya lived in dread of being sent back to Poland, or worse, of being turned over to the Russians. Their fear of exposure grew with each passing day.

Stasha added to their anxiety by bitterly confessing, "That Collaborators File is not my only fear. I could be exposed by anybody. One of the Poles working for the army might recognize me. They keep marching in and out of Kemeris's office every day, trying to ingratiate themselves with him by giving him information on Poles' wartime activities. I have to hide when they come into the office."

"I'm sorry I didn't let you take that post office job in Berlin," Franya said.

"The Americans there would also have the Collaborators File and there are probably Poles working in Berlin as well," Stasha replied. "I'd be no better off there."

"What would happen to us if we returned to Poland?" Franya asked, astonishing Stasha. "I mean, as part of the United Nations repatriation scheme. They're announcing it on the radio all day long. They're urging all Poles to register for repatriation."

Stasha did not reply.

"I mean it, Stasha. You were originally captured by the German army. You were brought to Germany as a forced laborer to work in a coal mine. What would happen to us if we went home?"

"At best, I would be shipped off to Siberia, if the Poles didn't shoot me first," he said, storming out of the house.

"I know you're hurt," she said, trailing after him. "I know that you're blaming yourself for our suffering, for having worked with Greifler and Zahn. Don't. It's the war. It's not you."

"There's only one way out. I've thought about it all week." Stasha said, interrupting her obvious attempt to console him. "We're going to apply to UNRRA for help, but not for repatriation."

"What are you talking about?"

"We're homeless, right? We're stateless, right? We've got no passports, neither Polish nor German. That makes us stateless, refugees, Displaced Persons. So we're going to an UNRRA DP camp for help as refugees, war refugees."

"What is an UNRRA DP camp?" she asked.

"A United Nations Relief and Rehabilitation Administration Displaced Persons camp," he recited dutifully, like a child answering a teacher's question. "That's the organization that helps refugees."

"You can't be serious," she scoffed. "We weren't brought to Germany as prisoners of war, but as Polish collaborators."

"You don't understand, Franya. I talked to some guys at the motor pool, some Ukrainians whose UNRRA transports stopped there for repairs. They admitted to me that they worked with the Germans during the war. But to UNRRA they all tell the same story: 'We're anti-Communists, escaping from the Russians,'" Stasha explained. "And that makes them war refugees qualifying for relief, and what's more important, they're free from deportation."

"That's our future?" Franya moaned. "Life in a refugee camp?"

"The future of all of Europe is in the DP camps," Stasha said. "That's what they tell me. There's more than a million refugees right here in Germany. They get priority feeding, priority housing, and priority resettlement."

"But what is life like in those camps? Are they like prison camps? What do you know about them?"

"Nothing," Stasha replied. "That's why I'm going to find out."

*

The next day, Stasha called in sick and headed for Eschwege, a small town bordering the Russian occupation zone, the site of a recently opened Displaced Persons camp. Walking most of the fifteen kilometers, he arrived at the camp's gate late at night. The civilian guards told him the administrative offices were closed and they could not admit him.

"Please," Stasha begged, speaking Polish, "let me stay the night. I have nowhere else to go."

The watchman called over to his chief and, after a long whispered conversation, they returned to Stasha.

"*Fun vanent kumt ir?*" the chief asked in Yiddish, taking Stasha by surprise. He hadn't realized Eschwege was a DP camp for Jews.

He quickly recovered and replied in Yiddish, "*Fun Varsheh.*"

"Ah, many of our residents are also from Warsaw," the chief said. "I'll let you sleep in a dormitory tonight but you have to report to the Intake Office and register in the morning."

The guard at the gate brought out an admission sheet on a clipboard and asked for his name. Stasha was about to reply, "Wojchiechowski," but, having just been told there were many Jews from Warsaw in the camp, he replied, "It's Warshawski. Yossel Warshawski."

He spent a restless night in a large dormitory that was already filled to capacity. He fretted through the early dawn, worrying about being recognized as the infamous Stasha of Warsaw. He remained under the covers to avoid recognition. When the morning sun burst through the large dormitory windows, he was startled by shouts from a rioting mob outside.

"Kapo! Collaborator! Nazi!" they were shouting.

Standing on a toilet seat to look out of the small ceiling-high window, Stasha saw people running after a man who was trying to escape their fury. The riot soon spread to the entire camp and the handful of UNRRA officials were unable to restore order. The more they tried to shield the harassed man, the more enraged the rioters became. They cornered him and pelted him with clenched fists. Finally, the sirens of the arriving MP jeeps dispersed the rioters and the protesting victim was whisked out of the camp.

Stasha's concern about his own safety now grew. His fear of being exposed bordered on hysteria. He remained in a toilet cubicle at one end of the dormitory, trying to figure out how to get out of the camp undetected. Suddenly, he heard a voice he recognized from his early years in Warsaw.

"I, Avrum Cohen, accuse the Americans of complicity with the Germans," the voice called out, speaking Polish. "Did you see how the UNRRA people protected the kapo? And how the American MPs actually saved that kapo! They're protecting collaborators. I say, the Russians would know how to take care of him."

Stasha climbed back onto the toilet seat to peer through the window. He saw the stranger huddling with a group of men, urging them to continue the rioting.

"Avrum Cohen? That's Antek Karpov, the Russian spy," Stasha whispered to himself.

From where he was standing, he could see that Antek had changed. He had graying hair, a fuller face, a new mustache, and a trimmed beard. But, much as he tried, he could not see the identifying scar on Antek's cheekbone. Stasha slipped out of the dormitory, staying out of Antek's line of vision, furtively edging closer to him. Although the scar was well hidden under a clump of the scruffy beard, Stasha could now clearly see the distinguishing mark under Antek's right eye. He quickly retreated to the toilet, where he considered the new dangers now facing him. First, he would have to get out of the camp without being recognized. Second, he could no longer bank on becoming a Displaced Person, certainly not in the all-Jewish Eschwege camp. That option was now closed to him. He stealthily walked out of the toilet and, shielding his face with his hat, threaded his way through the mob, making sure Antek would not spot him.

When he approached the gate, someone called out, "Yossel, Yossel Warshawski, where are your registration papers? Where are you going?"

Stasha was startled. He was certain that a new guard would be on duty at the gate, not the one who had admitted him the night before.

"Wait here while I get the chief," the guard demanded.

"No, please," Stasha said, "I can't register without my wife because she'll want to select the dormitory that we're going to live in."

"In this camp no one selects their living quarters. You eat what they give you and sleep where they put you," the guard jeered. But Stasha just kept walking toward the gate anxious to get onto the main road.

The suspicious guard began to chase after him but was restrained by his chief. The guard shrugged and returned to the gatehouse.

Once on the main road, Stasha ran full speed to get away from the camp. A passing farmer gave him a lift in his horse-drawn wagon. When they passed a US military prison, Stasha jumped off, thanking the farmer for his help. He was halted by a military guard who asked to see his identity papers. Stasha showed his civilian employee pass and headed for the prison's motor pool, where he asked the corporal in charge if he could hitch a ride to Divisional Headquarters.

"There's a group of prisoners about to be transported for work at the Fritzlar air base," the corporal said. "If you don't mind sitting with the prisoners, you can ride in their truck."

Sitting in the open two-and-a-half-ton truck, Stasha listened as the prisoners discussed their plight. Their greatest fear, they all agreed, was being interrogated by Lieutenant Kemeris. One prisoner stood up and said, "Remember, we're all anti-Communists running away from the Russians. Kemeris could set us free, lock us up for life, or, worse, hand us over to the Russians. And there's no appeal once he decides."

When the truck passed his hovel, Stasha jumped off and gave the driver a wave. He was eager to tell Franya about discovering Antek Karpov. But she had already left for work. He was delighted when little Jadzia greeted him with a hug and a kiss. All his problems dissolved. He lay down on the rickety cot and fell asleep while she sang her mother's lullaby to him.

He was wakened by Franya and Jadzia, standing over him, calling out, "sleepyhead, sleepyhead," and teasing that he had slept all day. He ravenously ate the sparse meal Franya served and as soon as Jadzia was tucked in bed,

Stasha told Franya about the riot in the DP camp, excitedly describing how he recognized Antek Karpov.

"Why are you so happy about finding Antek?" she asked.

"Antek Karpov is the answer to our dilemma."

Franya told him she did not know whether to laugh or cry at his "stupid announcement."

"Simple! I tell Kemeris about a Russian spy in the DP camp and for that information the CIC erases my name from their Collaborators File."

"It's all right to drive for the military," Franya said, ridiculing his plan, "but don't get involved with intelligence agents again, like you did with the Germans."

"Kemeris holds the power of life and death in his hands," Stasha said, recalling the words of the prisoners he had met on the truck. "When I offer to help the CIC get Antek, the CIC will..."

"Go ahead, work for the CIC," Franya angrily interrupted, "just like you did for the Gestapo. But I hope I'll never have to tell you, 'I told you so.'"

Stasha walked off alone in the darkness. When he returned an hour or so later, she apologized for her temper. As he got into bed, she whispered, "Do what you think is best to get us out of this shack, out of this misery, out of Germany."

He felt her wet tears on his bare chest.

When he reported to Kemeris's office, the lieutenant harshly ordered Stasha to explain his two-day absence and demanded an explanation why he had visited the US military prison. Stasha replied that he went to the Eschwege camp to search for relatives.

"Stasha, you were lying yesterday when you called in sick and you're lying now. Eschwege is a Jewish camp and you have no relatives there," Kemeris scolded him. "I know all about you, but we'll go into that later. Right now, drive me to the regimental HQ in Fulda."

Stasha quickly ran to the motor pool to gas up the lieutenant's jeep. He was so worried about his eventual, dreaded interrogation by Kemeris that he fumbled with the gas tank cap, spilling some of the gas onto the jeep. Kemeris's menacing threat, "I know all about you," kept ringing in his ears.

His fears grew when the thought suddenly occurred to him that the CIC probably possessed the Rynek File. Stasha managed to keep his composure when the lieutenant, still in an angry mood, got into the vehicle, again reprimanding him for lying about his visit to the Eschwege camp. As Stasha drove onto the autobahn, Kemeris was busy with his files. The lieutenant continued making voluminous notes as Stasha sped south in silence for the next hour.

"I can help the CIC," Stasha suddenly spoke up.

"Shut up and drive," Kemeris ordered.

"If the CIC is interested in trapping a Russian spy in Eschwege," Stasha talked rapidly without looking at Kemeris, "I can name the man and take you to him."

"What the hell are you talking about?" Lieutenant Kemeris snapped.

"I can lead you to Antek Karpov," Stasha replied.

"Pull over," Kemeris ordered.

Stasha swerved off the autobahn, stopping the jeep with a jerk. Without waiting for Kemeris to question him, Stasha described how, before the war, he had exposed Karpov as a Russian spy and that Karpov was later reported to have committed suicide.

Kemeris did not reply, but it was quite evident to Stasha that Kemeris was interested.

"Yesterday, I saw Karpov in the Eschwege DP camp," Stasha said and repeated emphatically, "I saw Karpov."

"Turn around," Kemeris ordered. "Back to my office."

Kemeris interrogated Stasha about his relationship with Karpov. "Are you still lying to me, Stasha?" he demanded. "Why did you go to the DP camp? Did you have any contact with Karpov? You'll be severely punished if you keep lying, especially if you are lying about Karpov."

Outwardly, Stasha retained his composure. He succeeded in hiding his fears despite the fact that Kemeris's threat reminded him of Colonel Greifler's accusing him of dealing on the black market. Stasha was terror-stricken when Kemeris opened the Collaborators File, made some notes, and then turned his back on Stasha.

"Lieutenant," Stasha pleaded, "I swear on my daughter's life that I did not contact Karpov in the camp. Before the war, I exposed him as a spy. If he sees me, he'll kill me."

"But you lied to me, Stasha," Kemeris said again, "Why, tell me, once and for all – tell me the truth – why did you go to Eschwege?"

Stasha took a deep breath. "I went to apply for UNRRA Resettlement like all the other Poles and Ukrainians who are fleeing from the Russians," Stasha said. "But I had to get out of the camp once I heard Karpov. There was a riot in the camp, nearly an uprising, which ended only when the MPs took charge of the kapo. The riot was Karpov's doing. I heard his voice. He was stirring up the people in the camp to continue their opposition to the Americans."

Stasha stopped talking as Kemeris picked up the phone, dialed a number, and announced into the receiver, "Redbird is chirping."

He hung up the phone, which minutes later rang.

Kemeris answered it and handed the receiver to Stasha, saying, "Just state one distinguishing feature that will identify Antek Karpov."

Stasha said into the mouthpiece, "A ten- or twelve-centimeter deep scar under his right eye."

Lieutenant Kemeris took the receiver, listened for a moment, and placed it back on its cradle. Then he said to Stasha, "We want that man, but it's not going to be easy to get him. Officially, the CIC can't enter the DP camp to arrest any bona fide refugee. All we can do is interrogate a suspect on the camp premises."

"In that case, Lieutenant," Stasha said immediately, "let me help you nab him."

Disregarding Stasha's offer as if he had never spoken, Kemeris continued, "We can go in there to question him, but when Karpov learns that we sent our man into the camp, he'll probably slip right through our fingers. He can smell a CIC man a mile away."

"Suppose I could get him to leave the camp, could you take him then?"

"It would be a lot easier."

"Then let me be of service to the CIC," Stasha said. "I can lure Antek out of the camp and your men can pick him up."

"You have already been of service to us," Kemeris said. "Without you we wouldn't even know that Antek is alive, much less in the camp. The CIC will pay you well for your information."

"I don't want your money," Stasha bluntly stated.

"What do you want?" Kemeris asked.

"You said you know all about me," Stasha blurted out. "I want you to clear me, to clear my name."

"Report to me tomorrow. I have to see if the proper authorities will accept your offer." As Stasha got up to leave, the lieutenant asked, "By the way, how do you plan to get Antek to leave the camp?"

"The CIC's got its secrets; I've got mine," Stasha replied, with a hint of the old militia commandant still about him.

In truth, he had no plan, not even a shred of an idea how to get Antek out of the camp. Later that night, when Franya asked him how he would deliver Antek to the Americans, he still had no plan.

"I don't need a plan yet. Kemeris may reject my offer, especially after I asked him for something in return for my services."

"What did you ask for?"

"Franya, we need security clearance with the CIC. That's what I asked for."

"You worked for the Germans and they repaid you," she sneered. "Look what we got from them."

"Don't compare Kemeris with Greifler," he retorted.

"They're all the same – Gestapo, NKVD, CIC."

"You just have to meet Kemeris and you'll see that they're not all the same."

"I don't ever want to meet any of them," she pleaded. "We paid dearly for your working with the Germans and we'll pay dearly for your working with the Americans."

"I don't want to argue with you," Stasha said. "Right now we have one problem. Kemeris asked if I had a plan to entrap Antek. That's what I need now, a plan."

Franya brought a cup of coffee and a few cookies she had taken from the Fritzlar officers' club. Sipping the coffee, she asked, "You've trapped Antek before, eight years ago. How did you do it then?"

"I was living with him and I saw his habits. He was a lecher, with an insatiable lust for women. All I had to do then was get one of my Sviatova girls to lure him to her bed," Stasha said. "She did it all."

"Why can't we do the same?" Franya interrupted him.

"Do you think I still have girls around me?" Stasha replied.

"I mean me. I can entice him to follow me, and I'll lead him some place Kemeris can nab him."

Stasha looked at his wife's smooth dark hair, fine eyes, and soft body.

"You could entice any man to do anything you want," he said, "but forget it."

"Thanks for the compliment. So why can't I help?"

"Because you're my wife. That's all."

"No, it's not all."

"Franya, let's not argue. It's premature. I don't even know if the CIC will accept my offer to help them track down Karpov. More important, I don't even know if they will accept my request for security clearance."

That morning, Franya went to the Fritzlar air force base, rushed through her work, and hurried home early, eager to learn of the CIC's decision. But it was only hours later, long after Franya had sung Jadwiga to sleep, that Stasha returned, driven in a civilian car bearing US military license plates.

Bursting into the room, he announced triumphantly, "I got everything I wanted. The CIC accepted my offer. I will get them to Karpov."

"How did you manage to get yourself involved?"

"Because Kemeris knew that the minute he sent a regular agent into the camp, Karpov would go back into hiding."

"Never mind all that," Franya said. "Will they help us?"

"The only thing Kemeris could say was, 'If you get Antek Karpov out of the camp, you'll be in the pipeline.'"

"And what does that mean?"

"According to Kemeris, it means, 'Good-bye, Germany. Hello, America.'"

"Even if they know you collaborated with the Germans?"

"Even if they have the Rynek File."

"Good-bye, Germany, forever," Franya repeated in a grateful whisper, crossing herself.

Then she dabbed her moistened eyes and confronted Stasha. "I'm going to get Antek to follow me out of the camp."

"No, you're not," Stasha replied.

"And why not?"

"Because Antek is a seasoned killer and because Kemeris has been working on an alternate scheme."

"And what is that?"

"The same scheme I used in Warsaw when I trapped Antek," he said. "The CIC will train a female operative to do the job."

Franya grasped him by the sleeve, "No, Stasha, no! If they can trap Antek without you, there goes your 'pipeline'. And, what's worse, if their female agent fails to attract Antek, you fail, too."

"I can't tell the CIC what to do," he said. "I can only rely on their assurances to help me."

She begged him, pleaded with him, shouted at him, "Don't let some other woman take away our last chance to get out of Germany!"

Stasha, with his quick temper, was soon shouting, "Franya, I can't order the CIC to do my bidding! The Americans barely even talk to me!"

Franya began to cry, repeating through her tears, "Go ahead, give up our last chance to get out of this mess."

Jadzia, awakened by the quarrel, came running to her parents, frightened at the sight of her mother weeping. Franya calmed herself and hugged the child to quiet her. "Now, now," she said softly, "it was only make-believe crying, just like I taught you."

Franya looked up at Stasha. "I taught Jadzia to sing a gypsy song and to cry while acting it out."

"I see. We have a little actress as well as a singer," he said, joining Franya in feigned weeping. Then she took the child back to bed.

They resumed their argument in whispers. Stasha adamantly refused to allow her to get involved in entrapping Antek, and Franya just as adamantly insisted on being part of the plan in order to keep the CIC in his debt.

"Good-bye, Germany, forever," she sobbed softly. "Remember, it's our only chance."

"Franya," he said, embracing her, "Antek is a killer."

She pulled away from his embrace, threatening with quiet resolve, "Stasha, I can go into the camp with or without you. I can find your Avrum Cohen and bring him right to Kemeris's door. As a matter of fact, I'm not going to work tomorrow morning – I'm going to the camp. I'll see what's what with Antek."

Frightened by his wife's threat, Stasha offered a reluctant compromise. "Tomorrow, we'll both go to Kemeris and try to convince him about your participation. But if he rejects your plan, you must promise not to go near the Eschwege camp."

Stasha considered her promise a major victory. He was quite certain Kemeris would not agree to Franya's role. The lieutenant might not even want to discuss the CIC's plan of action in Franya's presence.

In the morning, they took Jadzia along. Stasha realized that if, contrary to his expectations, Kemeris accepted Franya's offer to be the female operative, he would also have to understand that the child had to come with her parents into the camp. Without telling Franya, Stasha hoped that the child's presence would be another stumbling block to her plan.

When they appeared at Kemeris's office, they introduced Jadzia, who immediately tried to impress the lieutenant with her fluent German.

"No, no, darling," Franya said, "here they all speak English."

"Why?"

"Because it's an American military compound, and that is their language."

Franya then said, "Jadzia, I taught you an American song. Why don't you sing it now?"

The little girl reached out for the lieutenant's big hands and began to sing, "Ring around the Rosy." Kemeris chuckled and rummaged in his desk. He pulled out a picture book with the American flag on its cover, and gave it to Jadzia.

"Here, cutie-pie," he said. "Now, would you take the book and wait for us just in the next room?"

When she obediently went to the lobby outside his office, Kemeris said, "I congratulate you on such a charming and well-behaved child, but I want to know why you brought her, and why both of you are here."

"Lieutenant, we have a plan to suggest," Stasha began hesitantly. "We will go into the camp as a family to entrap Antek. I will grow my beard, wear glasses, change my entire appearance. As a Jewish family arriving in the camp, using an assumed name, it will be another cover for my presence there. We will not arouse Karpov's suspicion. Franya would be able to befriend him and eventually entice him to follow her out of the camp."

"Forget about participating in this," Kemeris said commandingly. "As Stasha's wife, you couldn't fill the role."

She began to argue, but he put her off, "I'm sure you can entice anyone. Back home, we'd call you a regular pinup girl, but you'd have to go to bed with Karpov to win his confidence. And, I can't see Stasha's wife doing that."

"Lieutenant, how do you feel after you sleep with a woman?" Franya asked, astonishing both her husband and the young lieutenant. Without waiting for his reply, she continued, "After your lovemaking, you feel spent, right? You want to be left alone, right? But before having sex, you feel the enticement. The arousal. The desire to possess? Isn't that as powerful, if not more powerful, than the actual sex act? Don't you even know that?"

Kemeris laughed at Franya's outburst and said, "I guess I hadn't really thought of it that way, but as Stasha knows, this secret operation has already been planned by my superiors."

"Then you aren't accepting Franya's offer?" Stasha asked, convinced that Franya's plan could not be considered.

"I know Antek," she lied. "How would some other woman, a new woman, how could she even know how to find him? And, worse, if she failed and Antek fled, she'd simply come back telling you, 'Well, I tried.'"

Both the lieutenant and Stasha were quiet for quite a long time. Stasha spoke up first, "Sir, you yourself said that Antek could smell a CIC agent a mile away."

"I'm no mere agent," Franya firmly said, pointing her finger at him, "I have the motivation to succeed. I need to get us out of Germany. I promise to bring Antek to you."

"OK, I get the picture," Kemeris said. "Now why don't you two go visit your daughter outside while I talk to my commanding officer. If you ask Sergeant Ross at the desk out there, he'll get her a soda pop."

Jadzia was sipping the fizzy, orange drink when Kemeris called Stasha and Franya back into his office.

"We're going to let Franya try this," he said, "but if at any moment you suspect that you are failing, you're to leave the camp immediately and let us try it. And, I have to warn you, be very careful. I can't guarantee your safety if something goes wrong inside the camp. I have no jurisdiction there."

They thanked him and turned to leave.

"Wait," Lieutenant Kemeris called, "you have to remember that you have two problems."

"Two?" Stasha asked.

"One, Antek is a killer. You won't get a second chance. And two, your little Shirley Temple there, Jadzia. Children can botch up the most carefully laid plans."

That evening, Franya and Stasha sat outside their shack, drinking hot tea and speaking in hushed tones about how to handle Jadzia so that she would not "botch up" their plans in the camp. How could they guarantee that she wouldn't chatter about her singing for the Germans or of her meeting an American officer?

"How do you tell a five-year-old to lie about her identity?" Stasha wondered. "How do you get her to use whatever fake name we give when we register as Displaced Persons? She's just a child; she can't keep a secret."

"The solution is simple," Franya said, suddenly inspired. "Make Jadzia an actress. Remember, we promised we'd help her do just that, become an actress with a real stage name."

"Looks like fate has been preparing this plan for us," Stasha said, with rare optimism. "It's got to succeed."

At breakfast, Franya said to Jadzia, "We're getting out of this dreadful room and moving into a large camp where there'll be lots of other people living there."

"What's a camp?"

"It's like the military compound we visited yesterday, but there will be no soldiers there," Franya said.

"Do they speak English there too?"

"No, mostly Yiddish," her father answered.

"Yiddish?" she asked. "I remember, I think I remember. Did I ever speak Yiddish?"

They did not know what to reply. Obviously, somewhere in the child's mind were memories of the Ghetto.

"Never mind," Franya said. "Here's the thing. In that camp you get to do just what you've always wanted. You will be an actress, just like we promised."

The child was distracted. She not only asked about Yiddish several times, but recalled words like *vasser* and *milch* while sitting at their table. They were worried: Would the memories recur? Would she botch up their plans?

Over the next several weeks, Stasha did not have to report to his driving assignment. Kemeris ordered him to utilize the time to prepare all the necessary details for his registration in the camp, and assigned a Jewish CIC sergeant to teach Franya rudimentary Yiddish and to build on the few words Stasha knew.

Franya found a phonograph record of "Hava Nagila" and other Jewish songs, which she taught Jadzia. Stasha grew his beard and his hair and got accustomed to wearing a pair of thick-rimmed glasses.

As part of her preparations, Franya tailored an enticing dress with a provocative, deep V-shaped neckline.

"What's that for?" Stasha asked, though he had a suspicion.

With a coquettish smile, she replied, "To attract Antek's attention."

"Be careful he doesn't get too attracted. He may grab you."

As they worked on the details of their mission, they considered several names for the family and decided on "Sonnenschein."

One afternoon Franya told Jadzia, "You are ready to be an actress now."

"Really, Mama? Am I? Can I start now?"

"Yes, Jadzia, and the very first thing is to learn your stage name."

Every day, Franya rehearsed with the child, repeatedly reminding her, "Once we get to the camp, everything is a big play, every minute. You can only use your stage name. You must never tell your real name to anyone there because then you would not be a great actress anymore."

When Stasha finally presented himself at Lieutenant Kemeris's office to tell him they were ready to begin, Sergeant Ross barred his entry. He did not recognize the tall, hairy stranger with thick glasses and a bushy beard.

Stasha and the lieutenant were both pleased; his disguise fooled even the sergeant. But Franya did not share their happiness. She feared that the gate officer at the DP camp would recognize Stasha as the man who came one night to register and then ran away the next day.

Chapter 9

When they arrived at the Eschwege DP camp, Stasha registered his family under the name "Sonnenschein."

"Papa, why did you change your name and Mama's name?" Jadzia asked, tugging at his jacket. "Do you and Mama need a stage name too?"

The registrar looked at the child and asked sharply, "What is she talking about?"

Franya and Stasha laughed and whispered so the child would not hear, "We're just playing a game with her, so she won't be frightened."

Unconvinced, the registrar said that they will be required to write down their personal histories both before the war and during. Franya wrote a few lines for both, mentioning towns in Russia as their places of birth and cities where they lived in Poland.

"We were in hiding throughout the war, so that's basically our personal histories," she said, but as she handed over the registration form, Jadzia giggled, telling her father that he looked funny in that beard.

The registrar heard the child's remark and quickly said, "I have to confer with my superiors before we can admit you."

She went to the next booth with their histories in hand and talked at length to her superiors. They were shaking their heads every so often, pointing to Jadzia.

The registrar returned, looking somberly at the three, "They will admit you, but this is just a temporary registration. You've got ten days to find people in the camp who may know you."

"That may be difficult," Stasha said. "We didn't stay anywhere for any length of time."

The registrar explained that there were over three thousand residents in the camp, so there may be someone who would recognize them and could vouch for their identity. She handed them an admission card with their barrack's number.

"If you decide to enroll your daughter in our kindergarten, take this admission slip to present to the school's principal."

They quickly made their way to their assigned barracks, where they unpacked their meager belongings. Soon they heard voices of children playing on the porch. Jadzia made her way to the door to go outside. But, acting quickly, Franya went with the child to introduce her daughter to the group, using the child's stage name.

While the little girl was playing with her newly found friends, Stasha and Franya discussed the various problems now facing them. They realized they would be unable to prove their statelessness and that they certainly could not undertake to find anyone in the camp to vouch for their identity as the registrar suggested. That meant they had only ten days to find Antek. Jadzia's behavior at the registration desk troubled them greatly. They decided that the child must never be allowed to be in the presence of the camp's officials without them. They also had to decide whether to enroll Jadzia in the kindergarten for the ten days or to keep her close to them.

That decision was made for them when Jadzia returned.

"Mama! Papa!" Jadzia squealed, running in with another little girl. "This is Esther. She was outside. She goes to school here. Can I go with her? Can I?"

When Franya nodded, Jadzia hugged her new friend and the two children jumped up and down in their excitement, curls bouncing, before dashing back outside.

That evening, when Franya put Jadzia to bed, she cautioned, "Remember, you must use your stage name, even with Esther, even in school."

The following morning, little Esther was waiting for Jadzia outside their room. Franya followed the children to a barrack at the far end of the camp where a classroom was set aside for new students. She introduced Jadzia to the principal.

"Don't worry, she'll be fine," said the principal, writing Jadzia's name on a piece of paper and pinning it to the child's blouse.

Franya bent down to kiss Jadzia good-bye and whispered, "Remember, your stage name only."

Freed from Jadzia's presence, Stasha and Franya began their search for Antek. He again described Antek's appearance to Franya, even making a rough sketch for her. They both spent the entire day wandering about the huge camp, a converted military base with a drill field surrounded by about fifty two-storied barracks.

Antek was nowhere to be seen.

The following day, Stasha went back to the registrar's office. "Please," he asked the officious-looking woman, "could I search through the list of the camp's residents? Maybe I can find someone who will vouch for us."

With some reluctance, she led him to a warehouse in the rear of the building, where she showed him a cardboard crate containing several hundred pages with names of the camp's residents. There were others in the room, also leafing through the lists, probably searching for relatives or *landsleit* – persons from their home towns.

"Who are you looking for?" an elderly man asked.

"Chaim Cohen or Yitzchok Cohen," Stasha replied, hoping to avoid being exposed.

The elderly man snickered, telling him that there were "hundreds of residents with such names." He asked a lady sitting next to him to give him the list with the *C*s.

She handed it to him and he searched it carefully, writing down the barracks' numbers of thirty-seven Avrohom and Avrum Cohens listed – the name Karpov had used while stirring up the crowd. A few minutes later, he returned the list to the crate.

"Did you find what you need?" the administrator asked as he passed her desk on his way out of the office.

"Well, perhaps," Stasha said evasively.

Stasha furtively circled the barracks on his list and actually espied several Avrum Cohens. But none even remotely resembled Antek. He kept watch, loitering in front of the central dining hall, where hundreds of people ate each day. But there was no sign of Antek.

"Is Antek Karpov Jewish? Is he really a Displaced Person?" Franya asked Stasha on the fifth day of their stay in Eschwege.

"No, of course not," Stasha answered. "Why do you ask?"

"If he's not, what's he doing in this camp?"

"He's probably still working for the Russians, searching for people like me to get them sent back to Russia," Stasha said. "Remember that headline you showed me about the Russians demanding the return of Polish collaborators? Well, the Russians have their Karpovs feeding information to the NKVD."

Stasha spent the next morning lingering around the administration building, watching people come and go. His patrol yielded no results but, aroused suspicion in the camp officials, putting him at risk of exposure.

"Antek would not search the lists in public," Franya whispered as they shared lunch in the main dining room. "He's working somewhere that won't attract attention, like a storage room or a library, or some other place where he wouldn't be observed."

"Is there a library here?" Stasha asked.

"Well, yes," Franya recalled. "In the school building I saw a library room next to the principal's office. But you can't go into a small place like that. Remember, if you recognized Antek despite his beard and long hair, he could just as easily recognize you with your beard and overgrown hair."

"Nobody has recognized me so far, with all my roaming around," Stasha countered.

"No, don't chance it. We can't afford any more scares. When I take Jadzia to school tomorrow morning, I'll peek into the library," she suggested. "If Karpov is there, I can strike up a conversation on Judaism and Zionism."

They sat up most of the night as he briefed her on both subjects, having studied them during his stay with Konarski.

"Remember, you can fake the conversation only to an extent," he said, "but your first concern is to be careful. Karpov is cunning and ruthless."

With only four days left, Franya walked Jadzia to school. She stopped at the library, whose door was closed. She tapped on the door. No one replied. She was about to leave, when someone opened from the inside.

It was Antek Karpov. With difficulty, she contained her excitement. He was exactly as Stasha had described – his fleshy face, his beard, especially the scar over his eye.

"We keep this door locked in the morning hours because the room is reserved for children. Their teacher will bring them soon," Antek said.

"I'm sorry, I didn't know," Franya said, looking at him with wide-open, brown eyes and a dimply smile. "I only wanted to know if there was a book I could borrow to learn English. I can come back later, when the library is open."

"No, no, come right in, Miss…" he said.

"My name is Franceska," she said. "I'm looking for an English reader."

"And I am Avrum," Karpov lied, "Avrum Cohen. It seems to me that we all have to make that choice, English or Hebrew. Will we go to Palestine or some English-speaking country? While we're here, the whole question comes down to which language to study, where to go."

"How right you are," Franya said. "I don't want to disturb the incoming class, but I would be grateful if you could find me a good English book, and I'll be on my way."

"There's plenty of time before the children arrive," he said. "Here, sit at this desk and tell me, why have you chosen to study English instead of Hebrew?"

She chatted back and forth with him, offering opinions and asking questions to keep him engaged. After several minutes of warm conversation, she was most pleased when Karpov quipped, "I'm enjoying talking to you, Franceska. You are as intelligent as you are beautiful."

Just then, two teachers marched a group of children into the room.

"Come, Franceska," Karpov said, offering his arm, "I'll show you around the school. Then, when the children leave, we can come back for your book."

Resting her fingertips in the crook of his arm, she felt a surge of confidence. Surely, he was already interested in her, an insight that was confirmed during the tour, when she felt his arm at her waist.

Knowing her fish had taken the bait, she suddenly looked at her watch. "Oh, Avrum, I am sorry, but I have to go back to the barracks now."

"Shall I walk you there?" he asked.

"Oh, no, don't," she said. "I must not arouse my husband's anger. He's jealous whenever I even speak with another man."

Karpov winked conspiratorially and said, "Well, Franceska, I'll be at the library again tomorrow."

"Call me Franya," she said, squeezing his arm. "I'll come by."

She returned to Stasha who was nervously waiting in their barracks room.

"I met, he saw, and I conquered!" she called out as she pirouetted around him. "The best news is, he asked me to meet him at the library again tomorrow!"

When she calmed down, she asked whether to continue meeting him in the library.

"You have no choice. You're getting there," Stasha said. "But let's devise a plan to get Karpov outside the camp. The library is just the first step."

"On Sunday, the children in the school are being taken out of the camp to go to a circus in Kassel," Franya said. "Parents were asked to volunteer as chaperones. I'll volunteer and ask him to follow me to Kassel."

"Excellent. That's our target date. Sunday. Three days from now – our last day in the camp," Stasha replied, sternly adding, "Remember, you're married to a madman. You're frightened. You arouse Antek's sympathy as well as his lust."

But at supper time, Stasha and Franya were faced with yet another problem: Jadzia wanted to know when she would begin her acting career. During the past week, she told her parents, she had already told everyone at school she was a singer and had proudly added that her name was a stage name. She moaned that her friends teased her because she had never performed.

"If I'm not an actress, then I don't need a stage name."

They looked around the huge mess hall, hoping no one overheard the child's complaint. They recalled Kemeris's warning about the problem with Jadzia and fully realized the danger they would face if she disclosed their real names. It would not only ruin their chance of trapping Antek, but it would expose Stasha as a collaborator.

"Why don't we try to get her a chance to sing somewhere in school?" he suggested.

The following morning, Franya and Jadzia met the principal in his office, where Franya told him that the child was an aspiring singer and asked if he would allow her to sing at some school or class function. The principal was quite pleased with the suggestion and, after he listened to the child singing a few bars, he decided to take her right away to a classroom where she could sing to some children who, he explained, were practicing for a school play. He led Franya to the library, where she noticed Antek Karpov sitting in his usual place. The principal left the door ajar so that she could hear Jadzia's singing.

Jadzia's voice came through loud and clear.

"You have a very talented child," Antek said.

"Thank you," she responded, looking away from him, paying no attention to him.

"And pretty too," Antek said.

"Shhh, don't interrupt," she whispered softly. "Right now, I want to hear my child's performance."

When the child's voice could no longer be heard, Franya sat down next to him, allowing her dress to roll up slightly above her knees.

"I'm sorry. I was rude to you while my daughter was singing," Franya said, reaching for his arm.

"No, no, I understand and I'm sorry. I should have remembered, a mother *kvelling* to hear her daughter performing."

"Are you the librarian here?" she asked, thanking him for understanding her so well.

"Just helping," he responded.

"You seem so knowledgeable," Franya said, "so cultured. So, let me ask your opinion. Would all this attention, singing at a school play, spoil a five- almost six-year-old?"

"It all depends on what the child wants," Antek replied.

"You may be right," she said. "She's a good girl, but she does love attention. And sometimes what a child wants is not always what's best for her. I'm worried and I'm really interested in your opinion."

Just then, the principal returned with a glowing report about Jadzia's singing. "She was just lovely," he said. "Could you bring her to the Community Hall tonight? We're holding a celebration of a Jewish event. The audience will be delighted with your daughter's singing."

"She's only five. Maybe I shouldn't keep her up too late," Franya replied, hesitant.

"We'll put her on first in the program," the principal said. "You can leave with her as soon as she finishes her part."

"I'll think it over and let you know in an hour or two."

Franya again reached for Antek's arm, as though seeking his approval.

"I think you should do what the principal asks," Antek ventured his opinion. "I'll be there, and we can discuss your problem after her performance."

"Fine then," she said to the principal. "But on one condition. I have to introduce my daughter, to give her support. Otherwise the child won't sing."

The principal agreed, "I'll reserve a seat for you near the stage. Thanks very much. I'll see you and little Jadwiga tonight."

She told the principal that Jadzia and Esther had become good friends in the past few days and asked whether Esther would be going on the school outing to Kassel.

"Esther will be coming with us and her mother volunteered to be a chaperone for this outing. I would appreciate it if you could be a chaperone too," the principal said. "I'm trying to recruit as many parents as possible."

"Yes, of course," Franya replied. "I want to be with my daughter."

The principal thanked her and returned to his office. His departure left Franya alone with Antek. When she extended her hand to thank him for his advice, he caressed her arm and she, in turn, firmly squeezed his hand.

"I'm so glad you were here. I needed your advice," she breathed quickly, like a helpless girl. "But now I must hurry back to my husband. I'll be at the concert and afterward, well...perhaps we can, oh, we'll see what fate has in store for us." She giggled and hurried off.

Franya hurried to Stasha to report Jadzia's successful audition and her role at the school's assembly. "Antek will be there and that's where I'll begin my real enticement."

"How?" he asked.

"With this," she said, holding up the tight-fitting dress with the revealing neckline.

"Franya, I've faced danger before," he said. "But just the thought of your being vulnerable to Antek scares the hell out of me. I can't think straight."

"So, for once, let me do the thinking."

Later that evening, Franya pulled a cape over her shoulders and walked with Jadzia to the Community Hall. A huge audience had already gathered when she entered. She and Jadwiga found Esther and her parents in the lobby.

"I'm Moishe Gruenwald and this is my wife, Reva. It seems that our children have become good friends. Where's your husband?"

"He had letters to write, but I'm sure he'll be here when he finishes."

"By the way," Moishe said, "we have a drama club, the Eschwege Drama Circle. Perhaps you and your husband would like to join?"

"My husband isn't really interested in drama," she confessed, "but I'll ask him."

"We meet tomorrow at four, right here in the Community Hall," Gruenwald said. "Come give us a try."

"We'll think about it, certainly."

"One more thing," Gruenwald added. "The parents who volunteered to be chaperones for the Sunday outing will get their instructions after the Drama Circle meeting. So please be there."

The principal interrupted their conversation. "We're ready. Come, let me take you to the seat we've reserved for you."

When the lights in the auditorium were dimmed, Stasha entered the hall and walked down the side aisle searching for Antek. He spotted him sitting in the first seat of the first row. Stasha then took a seat several rows behind him.

The principal opened the program, describing Balfour Day, which, he said, marked Great Britain's promise to establish the Jewish homeland in Palestine. He then called on Franya to introduce her daughter. She took off her cape, and walked up to the platform, where her shapely body in the tight dress with its provocative neckline drew everyone's attention.

She faced the audience. "I would like to introduce you to our daughter, Jadwiga Sonnenschein who, with her singing, will bring a bit of sunshine into our miserable lives."

Jadzia began to sing "Hava Nagila" in honor of the Zionist occasion. She was an instant success. The audience was thrilled by her lilting voice, joining in with her, and clapping their hands in rhythmic cadence. When she finished singing, Jadzia curtseyed to the audience. Franya acknowledged their applause, bowing deeply from her position at the end of the stage, only a few feet from Antek.

Jadzia was thrilled by the thunderous ovation. But Franya, leaving the stage with the child, was even more thrilled when she saw Antek waiting for her at the foot of the stairs, offering his hand to help her down the three steps. She paused in front of him to put on her cape, brushing her body against his. "I have to go, to put the child to bed," she whispered.

"Can you come back?"

"Wait for me," she said and proceeded up the long aisle with Jadzia to leave the hall, as the sustained ovation continued.

Within minutes, Stasha joined them in their room. He picked up Jadzia and held her over his head, shouting his congratulations.

"Here's to the new singing sensation," he cheered, then embraced Franya and whispered, "but your acting was even better!"

They waited until Jadzia went out to play with Esther to plan their next step.

"He wants me to come back tonight."

Stasha laughed and reached over to stroke her breasts, recalling how he too had been enticed by her when they first made love alongside the Vistula. She playfully slapped his hand. "Look, don't touch."

He laughed. She giggled. Then very seriously, she asked, "What do I do now?"

"Let him look, but not touch," Stasha replied still smiling.

"Do I go back now?" she asked.

"Absolutely. You've got him on a string," Stasha said. "You can't let him go now. This is the time to snare him."

She returned to the Community Hall just as the evening's program was concluding. Antek was waiting in the foyer.

"You were so kind to wait, but I can only stay a moment. I told my husband that I left my cape on the stage."

"Come, I'll help you find it."

She giggled softly and showed him the cape tucked under her coat. "I wanted to see you," she said coquettishly, "so I used it as an excuse to get out."

He walked with her to a nearby barracks where an enterprising refugee operated a makeshift coffee house. She took off her coat in the dim room and, in comparative privacy, she sat down close to him. As he ordered coffee, she sidled closer.

Antek stroked her arm, "You are so lovely," he said, "and you have stage presence."

They sipped the bitter coffee and nibbled at the cake the waiter brought.

"I'm so glad you asked me to come back," she said. "You're such an interesting person. You excite me…I mean, my imagination."

"Nothing wrong in being excited physically, not only intellectually," Antek said, stroking her arm.

When she felt his hand on her thigh, she resumed her acting, pulling at her dress about her chest, brushing her hair off her forehead, then tightly grasping his arm and pressing it closer to her body.

"Avrum, I've never experienced such excitement before," she panted. "But I have to go, otherwise..."

"Otherwise, what?"

"My husband will kill me," she said, clutching his arm even tighter, feigning fright.

Nervously, she gathered her coat and got up to leave.

He asked when they could meet again. She repeated the story she and Stasha had rehearsed. "I want to see you so much. But this is our second camp. I'm afraid to take any chances. My husband, that mad Hungarian, almost killed a man in the last camp because he thought the man made a pass at me."

She took a deep breath, exposing her cleavage, leaned over and quickly kissed him on the lips, pressing her body close, lingering a while, and then she drew back.

"I must go. It's late. He may even be out looking for me. Please don't follow me. I don't want him to see you, or hurt you, and get us thrown out of another camp," she said, as if flustered. "If you're free tomorrow, meet me at four at the Community Hall's side entrance, behind the stage. I'll sign up for the Drama Circle, so I can tell him I'm there. Then we can plan something."

She slipped away before he could answer.

Stasha greeted her when she once again marched triumphantly into their room, and before he could say anything she blurted out, teasing him, "He looked and he touched!"

"Where is he so I can kill him?" Stasha said mockingly.

"Not yet, we need him alive," she said.

"You've completed the first two stages of our plan flawlessly."

"And step three is almost assured. He's meeting me at the Community Hall tomorrow afternoon and that's where I will tell him that I am going to chaperone on the trip to Kassel where we can have our tryst."

Despite the excitement of entrapping Antek, they both slept soundly. In the morning, they noticed that Jadzia was not outside playing with Esther. Since they moved into the camp, the child got up early every morning and ate breakfast with Esther in the central dining hall. Then the two girls always came back and played on the veranda. That morning Jadzia had not returned from the central dining room.

Franya went about the compound looking for her and was shocked to find Jadzia on the football field, sitting on Antek's lap, laughing playfully. Franya walked over to Antek, smiled at him warmly, and said to her daughter, "Time to go back to our room now. Esther's waiting to go to school with you."

Back in their room, Franya and Stasha asked the child to tell them everything she said to the strange man. After half a dozen "whys" from Jadzia and repeated reassurances that it was another game they were playing, the mother said, "I'm glad you liked the man. He must be wonderful…singing, telling stories, and playing games with you." Without arousing the child's suspicion, she said, "Now, Jadzia, please tell me everything you told him."

Innocently, Jadzia answered, "I said we took rides, and went on a long train trip with soldiers who spoke German but didn't let us sing Polish songs, and lived on a farm, and then in a terrible barn, and then we visited soldiers who didn't talk any German, but only English. I showed him the coloring book the man gave me. He liked the picture of the American flag on the cover."

"That sounds like fun," Franya said, trying to keep from crying. "Now run along, but don't bother adults any more. Go play with Esther until it's time for school."

When Jadzia skipped outside, Franya and Stasha looked at each other bleakly. They knew Antek had ferreted damaging information from the child, especially about their train ride from Poland and their visit to the encampment of the US Army. They were certain he "smelled a CIC agent" and would take off, escape into thin air.

"There goes our dream of freedom," Franya cried out. "I'm so upset I can't think clearly."

"It's not the end," Stasha said. "Not unless you want to end it now."

"Of course not," she said. "But what do we do?"

"The first thing is to think this through," he said. He took out a piece of paper and began writing down their options. "We have only two choices. We can call it a failure and get word to Kemeris to get his people here before Antek disappears again. Or we can go on as though nothing happened."

"Suppose he's already escaped the camp? What do we tell Kemeris?" she asked.

"I don't know. The test will be if he meets you this afternoon at the Drama Circle."

*

Later that day, when Franya took Jadzia to school, she peeked into the library. Antek was not there. And that afternoon, when she arrived at the Community Hall for the Drama Circle meeting, Antek was not at the side entrance either. Her immediate reaction was to return to Stasha to discuss their next move. But Gruenwald met her as she was about to leave.

"Ah, there you are," he called out to her. "Thanks for coming. We're about to start."

He opened the meeting by listing the club's goals, but Franya couldn't make herself listen. Then, members of the group carried out a reading of a script. Nervous and distracted, Franya repeatedly glanced at her watch. It was already nearly a quarter to five. She kept looking through the window, hoping to see Antek.

As the session dragged on, she worried that even if he came, he wouldn't wait for her. Suddenly, Gruenwald's voice penetrated her foggy thoughts.

"Mrs. Sonnenschein, would you take charge of costumes and cosmetics?" he asked.

"No, I'm sorry, I just can't," she stammered.

"Well, then, could you just make an inventory for us of the supplies we have on hand, then I'll know what to order in Kassel?"

"Sure, I can do that right now," she said, relieved to head backstage, hoping to find Antek outside. She left in the direction of the dressing rooms, but veered off to the exit door, intending to run back to Stasha. But there was Antek, waiting at the side entrance. She smilingly walked up and warmly greeted him.

"OK, who's your husband? What's his real identity?" he barked at her.

"Never mind about him. He's nuts, just a crazy man," she said blithely. "Come with me. I have to make an inventory in the supply room. Then we can make plans."

He followed her into the back room, where she slipped off her heavy sweater, pulled Stasha's loose shirt around her and tied the shirt tails at her waist. She began to lay out the costumes and neatly stack the tubes and jars of make-up creams.

"Stop now," he demanded. "We have things to straighten out between us."

She smiled, paying no attention to him.

"I want to talk to you," he said angrily.

"Let me first list all these supplies, as I promised to," she said, climbing to an upper shelf, deliberately exposing her thighs.

"Franya, tell me now," he demanded, his voice becoming louder. "I want to know where your husband is from. Was he in the war? What did he do for a living?"

"Now, now. If you are going to grill me, do it quietly," she teased. "There's a meeting going on – they'll hear you. Soon they will leave and we can be together, right here, alone."

He grasped her hands and drew her down the stepladder. "I'm asking you now about your husband, about the train rides, the farm, and especially about the American military camp. I know you visited one, just recently. Your cute little birdie told me all about it."

She looked at him, trying to keep her face placid.

"Who are you? Tell me now," he ordered, with new menace in his voice.

"My husband was in a US military prison," she spoke in a crisp monotone, supposedly hiding her anger. "He was arrested for murder. The Americans called him 'The Mad Hungarian'. When we visited him in their prison, I told my daughter that he was in a camp. I never used the word 'prison', because it would frighten her. After his escape from a military jail in Bad Neuheim, we lived on trains. We finally registered in this camp under an assumed name."

"What's your real name?" he asked.

"If I tell you, my husband will kill me," she said. "Right now it's Sonnenschein."

"I want to know more about your husband," he said threateningly, grabbing her hand and twisting it so hard that she winced from pain.

She turned to him, buttoned up her shirt, and said sharply, "Avrum, you want to call the whole thing off? That's fine by me. I can't take this pressure. No one can. You're the first man who has appealed to me, but I can't face the threat of dying again, not by my husband's hand."

"What's this with your husband?" he asked.

"He's mad," she said, wiping tears from her eyes. "Living with him is hell. But he saved my life in Treblinka. Took me out of the showers. I swore then that I would be his wife. I am and will be. But I'm living with a murderer, a madman murderer."

She turned away from him, weeping softly. Antek tried to embrace her but she pulled away from his grasp, begging him to leave her alone. She repeated her story, this time stressing how meeting him was like a balm to her bitter existence.

He apologized for suspecting her and asked forgiveness. He reached out to her and she embraced and kissed him. His hands fondled her beneath her shirt. She did not withdraw. She knew the time had now come for her to implement the final and most important step – to get him out of the camp.

She held onto his hand, speaking with a tremor in her voice, "I didn't sleep all night. I thought of you and what we could do together. I thought of every position, every movement, everything. But not here, not where he's around. I have a plan where we can be together, miles away, practically all day."

"Let's just go to my room," he said.

"My husband will kill you," she said.

"When can we be alone?" he asked.

"Tomorrow."

"Where?"

"I've thought it all out," she spoke rapidly, unbuttoning several top buttons of her shirt. "Sit down and listen."

In a matter-of-fact voice, she said, "You remember, I volunteered to chaperone the children on their excursion to Kassel. I asked my husband's permission. He said I could take Jadwiga. I will now accept Gruenwald's request to tend to the cosmetics in Kassel. Everyone will think I left to buy make-up and other stage equipment – but I will be yours all day."

"You're quite an operator," he said admiringly.

Acknowledging his compliment with a slight smile, she added, "I arranged for a place for you on the truck that's taking us tomorrow."

He tore the edge off an old program lying about, took out his pen, and wrote down an address. "I'll meet you in Kassel at this address, waiting for you, after ten o'clock tomorrow morning."

"Remember, I will be alone in Kassel. You have to meet me," she said and added, "But..."

"But, what?" he asked.

"I need some money for a taxi to get to this address," she said apologetically. He handed her a few American dollars.

When Franya returned to their barracks, Stasha jumped up to greet her. "Franya, I've been sitting at this window waiting for you all afternoon. Are you all right? It's been three hours since you left. What happened?"

"At first, he was very suspicious, angry. But our story worked and he's agreed to meet me in Kassel, at this address," she told him, handing him the slip of paper.

"I'll let Kemeris know so he can set up his team in Kassel," Stasha said.

"Let Kemeris know?" she repeated. "How can you get to Kemeris now?"

Stasha did not reply. He went out on the veranda and turned over a chair, leaning it against the railing. When he returned, she asked about the chair. He told her that by turning over the chair, he had just informed the CIC of their success with Antek. She was puzzled by this signal, asking what would follow.

"I have no idea," he replied. "That's what Kemeris told me to do. The rest is up to them. We did our part."

"We're in the pipeline. No more Germany! No more Antek!" she called out and, as she was about to embrace Stasha, there was a knock on the door. Stasha asked, "Who is it?"

"It's me, Moishe Gruenwald."

Stasha opened the door only slightly. "Moishe, hello. I'm sorry, but we're very busy."

Gruenwald put his foot in the door so Stasha could not close it, walked into the room, and asked bluntly, "What message do you have for Lieutenant Kemeris?"

Stasha was speechless. He looked at Franya, who grasped his arm for support. He stared at Gruenwald, who offered no explanation. "Kemeris didn't prepare me for this, didn't mention you," Stasha mumbled.

"The less we each know, the safer we all are," he replied.

Despite Gruenwald's assured demeanor, Stasha was dumbfounded.

"It all seems so improbable – chairing the Drama Circle, Jadzia's accidental meeting with Esther, and the principal asking my wife to volunteer to be a chaperone."

Gruenwald replied, "Nothing was accidental. It was prearranged so that I could be near the two of you without arousing anyone's suspicion."

"And the Drama Circle?" Franya asked.

"That too," he said. "Even the last-minute plan for the picnic in Kassel, before your ten-day stay in the camp expired. Now, what about Antek?"

Stasha handed him the piece of paper with the address in Kassel. "He'll be there tomorrow at ten."

Gruenwald looked at the piece of paper, dropped it on the table, and said, "There's no such address. That section of Kassel is totally destroyed. The entire area was leveled by Allied bombing. Antek suspects you and wants you out of the camp."

They were both devastated. Stasha slammed his fist on the table, blurting out a Polish curse, "*Psiakrev*." Franya grabbed her husband by the arm and began to weep. He held her as she sobbed like a wounded child while he tried to maintain his own countenance in front of Gruenwald.

"He smelled a CIC agent a mile away," Stasha said.

"I'll get back to you," Moishe assured them.

A pall of sadness descended upon them. As Gruenwald was leaving, Jadzia skipped into the room.

"Hi, baby. Mama has a headache. Run down to Esther's and ask her mother to take you both to the dining room for supper."

Later that night, as they were getting ready for bed, Gruenwald returned with instructions from Kemeris.

"Both Kemeris and I feel that Antek suspects you," he told Franya.

"What does that mean?" Stasha asked.

"He's playing your game. He probably wants to get Franya out of the camp."

"Do you think he'll be there?" Franya asked.

"He or his agents," Gruenwald replied. "That means you're in mortal danger."

"Then what do I do?" Franya asked.

"Nothing. We'll start over with our own agents. For your own safety, get yourselves out of the camp quickly. We'll have a car waiting for you outside the gate in fifteen minutes."

"Never!" Franya blurted out. "I know I enticed him. I know he's trapped.

If there's a chance of his being there, we must continue with our plan. I'll keep my appointment with him and you find a way of taking him."

Unaccustomed to being opposed, Gruenwald said firmly, "The CIC has procedures, methods of conducting clandestine operations..."

Franya held up her hand to stop him and just as firmly announced, "I will be in Kassel. I will keep the rendezvous. I know I have him caught; he's interested in me and I am certain he will be there."

The CIC agent began to argue, but Franya firmly repeated her determination to be in Kassel. He looked at Stasha, hoping to get him to change Franya's mind. Stasha shrugged.

Franya courteously asked him to leave, bluntly stating, "You just tell the CIC that if they're not in Kassel tomorrow, they'll miss capturing Karpov."

As he was leaving, Gruenwald looked at his watch. "I don't even know if I can reach Kemeris at this hour. And if I do get through to him, I can't guarantee that he'll agree with your plan."

*

On Sunday morning, a convoy of three two-and-a-half-ton trucks pulled out of the Eschwege DP camp, headed for Kassel. At the park near the circus, the trucks unloaded more than 150 wildly excited children and about twenty-five parents.

Franya had little to cheer about. Standing next to Reva Gruenwald, she whispered, "I only hope Kemeris and your husband know what to do."

The taxi she found was a broken-down, converted van that used a wood-burning engine. She had to haggle with the driver about the exorbitant fare he quoted. Once they settled on two dollars, she asked him to take her to the address on the piece of paper she showed him.

"There's no such address," he shouted. "The whole area is kaput. Only ruins."

"That is where I want to go."

"Lady, there is no such house, no such street any more. Even if I get you near there, you'll have to go the rest of the way on foot. About two hundred meters."

She climbed up into the passenger seat, ordering him to drive her. For ten minutes, they drove in silence through rubble-littered streets. Then the driver stopped the truck and pointed to a heavily bombed area.

"That's your address."

Lifting the front of her skirt, Franya walked carefully through the huge pile of ruins. The footing was treacherous, and she knew that each step carried her further into no-man's-land. With great care, she stepped from one mound of debris to the other, half hopping, half stumbling. About halfway, she slipped and fell, wrenching her ankle. She sat amidst the rubble massaging her foot.

"I'm sorry," she heard a voice.

It was Antek, standing there giggling. She looked around and saw him lying under a pile of rubble. She was relieved, but she resumed her acting, glaring and shouting at him, "How dare you! How dare you!"

"A person like me must be very cautious."

"A person like you!" she repeated. "You bastard! You're not a person. You're an animal. How could you put me through all this? Take me back to the circus, take me back this minute. I don't want to know you."

"Who are you? I need to be convinced," he replied.

"I have to convince you?" she said, feigning even greater fury. "Go to hell."

"You're very pretty when you're that angry." He smiled and reached for her hand but drew back.

"Avrum," she whimpered, "please take me back to the picnic. Take me back, please. I'm in no mood for games."

"Come, your anger has finally convinced me," he said, picking her up and carrying her about a hundred meters to a clearing in the ruins where a blue car was parked. A driver was sitting at the wheel. Antek helped her into the car, but when he got in, the driver turned around, pointed a gun at his head, and barked, "Out of the car, now."

Instantly, four men, one of whom Franya recognized as the driver of the taxi, surrounded Antek and hauled him away.

Out of nowhere, Gruenwald pulled up in a black sedan. "Franya, in, quick!" he ordered, accelerating as she slammed the door. They sped out of the city onto the autobahn. After driving about half an hour, without saying much, he pulled to a stop behind a parked military vehicle. Franya gasped when she saw Stasha and Jadzia in the army sedan.

In less than an hour, the three were ushered into the office of the commanding general of the Third Infantry Division where Lieutenant Kemeris greeted Stasha like a long-lost friend.

Turning to the imposing two-star general, Kemeris saluted and said, "General, the entire story can't be revealed yet, but these folks are Stasha and Franya Wojchiechowski. They've just rendered invaluable service to the United States of America. We request they be officially commended for their singular contribution."

The general read a formal resolution and presented Stasha with the US Army's Silver Star. Kemeris then escorted them out of the office and led them to a waiting car, ordering the corporal to drive to Frankfurt. As the lieutenant got into the passenger seat, Stasha said, "What was all that about? The last thing we need now is a medal."

"That's the start of the pipeline. Next, you will be driven to the US consular office in Frankfurt, where you will receive a visa, and get on your way to the United States."

Embracing their child, Stasha and Franya hugged each other and then broke into applause. Kemeris handed Stasha his business card. "If you ever need anything, contact me through my headquarters in Washington DC. And I've got something for you, little one," he said to Jadzia, handing her the white and blue Third Division patch.

After their surprise had subsided, Kemeris described the procedure that awaited them in Frankfurt. Stasha and Franya bombarded him with questions about how they would travel to the United States, where they would live, and how they would make a living. "My people will find you a job and a home," he replied.

When the car stopped in front of his office, he turned to Stasha, "Would you please come with me for a minute? I have papers for you to sign dismissing you from military employment. Franya, it'll only take a minute."

Once the two men were alone in his office, Kemeris dropped his jovial Texas facade and looked at Stasha gravely. "I want to say this to you in private because I don't want to frighten your wife. The Russians will never forget you or forgive your part in Antek's capture. They'll hunt you down and won't give up on you until they get you back to Russia. We strongly recommend you change your name. It will make it a bit harder for them to find you. We will eliminate your name from all our lists. It will not even appear on the plane's manifest. As far as we are concerned, and hopefully in the eyes of the Russians, the Wojchiechowski family will disappear. And the quicker we get you out of Germany the safer you will be."

As Stasha got into the car, Kemeris poked his head in and said to Franya, "Hey, you can't go to the US with a name like Wojchiechowski."

"We need a new name?" Franya asked.

"You don't need one, but you'll get along better in the States with a new name, something shorter, more American."

"It's a good idea," Stasha said to Franya. "We're starting a new life, and a new name would be fine."

"I thought of a name for you. 'Wycliff'. It's a nice-sounding English name. You could be Stamford Wycliff. How's that? You even retain enough letters to remember Stanislaw Wojchiechowski."

"And me?" Franya asked.

"Simple," Kemeris replied, "it's either Fran or Francine. Which do you prefer?"

Franya quickly replied, "Francine. It's closer to Franceska."

"How about me?" Jadzia asked. "Do I get a new play name too?"

"Actually," he said, "I have something in mind for you. My little sister's name is Jodi. That sounds like Jadzia."

They repeated their names, joking and laughing at the new experience. He wrote their new names on a slip of paper and gave it to Stasha. He also handed a sealed manila envelope to the corporal, ordering him to introduce them to the consul and give the sealed envelope to him.

"Good luck on your trip," Kemeris said.

When they arrived at the consular office in Frankfurt, the corporal introduced them to the consul general, who ushered them into his inner office, past a long line of civilians waiting to be interviewed. They sat down side by side at a long table in his office, where he tore open the manila envelope and read its contents. He then handed them forms to be filled out.

"This has to be in English, so I'll help you," the consul said. "Let's start by using the names Lieutenant Kemeris gave you."

When they reached a question dealing with the work Stasha had done during the German occupation of Poland, the consul checked the instructions from Kemeris's sealed file and wrote, "Slave laborer in Silesian mines."

He handed Stasha a "United States Identity Card in Lieu of a Passport" for the family. It bore their entry visas to the United States.

As they walked out of the consular office, they saw the corporal waiting to take them to the airport. He said, "Well, you're on your way now. Congratulations, you've just been granted a paper-clip visa."

On the way to the Frankfurt airport, Stasha and Franya laughed as they practiced their new names. Jadzia Wojchiechowski, now Jodi Wycliff, aged five, going on six, had never seen her parents so lighthearted. Although Stasha knew the reason for the name changes, he joined in the laughter.

*

The converted B-25 bomber landed in New York's Idlewild Airport on a dreary December day in 1945. Stamford and Francine Wycliff didn't notice the cold or damp. To them, the moment they set foot on American soil was the most beautiful day of their lives.

Chapter 10

Dr. Szymon Berson's fate took a turn for the better in March, 1945, when he was transferred to the Polish Fourth Division to head the Polish military hospital in Warsaw.

"It may not be the Czyste," Dr. Berson said to his former commanding officer, Major Dworin, "but I'll make it the best military hospital in Poland."

"You can try, but remember, you'll still have to work with the Russians and they give nothing away."

The military hospital was a small clinic, just a few wards set aside in the City Hospital of Warsaw. Berson's staff consisted of a maintenance man, a nurse who doubled as a secretary, and Dr. Pawel Dereszewski, an old physician he knew from before the war. The old doctor was a scion of a Polish noble family, but he had been reduced to poverty by the Communist regime. He was grateful when Berson arranged for him to sleep in one of the wards, and soon the hospital became Berson's home as well.

"I know that you deserve better," Dereszewski said one evening to Berson as they were eating dinner together in a darkened hospital lounge. "I remember your work at the Czyste Hospital. You should be the head of the entire hospital."

"Just to be back in Warsaw is satisfying," Berson replied. "There is so much going on, so many challenges. After all that Warsaw's been through, I'm glad to contribute in some way to Warsaw's recovery."

Very soon, however, he discovered that Major Dworin was correct. The Russians gave nothing away. They turned down his numerous requests for funds to improve the clinic. And even when he recommended patients – Polish military veterans who required special treatment – Warsaw Hospital would not admit them.

Old Dr. Dereszewski told him, "Szymon, you might as well get this straight. You're not a member of the Communist Party, so you're not going to get anything from it."

Dr. Berson's enthusiasm did not wane. He applied his energies to what he always called "the Reconstruction of Poland."

Lacking proper medical facilities, Berson created a new department of rehabilitative services in his clinic to care for Polish soldiers who had been wounded in battle. He turned to Haskel Kornblit for help. Within a matter of days, Haskel delivered various bits and pieces of athletic equipment, weights, pulleys, mats, and parallel bars, which Dr. Berson used to rehabilitate his handicapped patients. The doctor also hired nonmedical personnel – people he selected primarily for their ability to engage patients in physical therapy, fully utilizing Haskel's equipment. Before the year was up, Berson's Rehabilitation Center became the most sought-after clinic in Warsaw. Its patients' recovery records were exemplary, and the facility earned high praise from professionals and nonprofessionals alike.

Berson was not disillusioned when his Russian overlords consistently withheld much-needed funds for the clinic. They even questioned the Rehabilitation Center's expenses.

"You know the Communists only provide for the party's needs," Dr. Dereszewski said. "The rest of us are out of luck."

"But I understand why," Berson responded, intending to teach Pawel a lesson. "The city is in a crisis. In time, the Russians will straighten it out."

Berson was an optimist, but also a realist. He used his connection with Haskel to get more equipment to expand his Rehabilitation Center. Gradually, he opened additional offices around Warsaw as branches of the center. Berson did not ask Haskel how he acquired the equipment; nor did he ask why Haskel did not ask to be paid. To show his gratitude, however, Berson would invite Haskel from time to time to dine at a local restaurant, where they ate, drank, and talked until all hours of the morning. On one of these occasions, Haskel warned Berson about Poland's worsening economic conditions.

"You know, Doc, your Rehab Center is at the bottom of the ladder when it comes to the Russian's priorities here. Be careful that they don't close you down and leave you and your staff standing on the street. Poland is on the verge of economic collapse. The whole country is like an occupied country. Thousands, hundreds of thousands of Polish citizens will flee to the West to escape poverty and Communism."

"Then why are you staying?" Berson asked.

"To make money from the illegals," Haskel replied with cheerful candor.

"Illegals?"

"Jews and non-Jews are leaving Poland illegally for Germany. If they can get there, UNRRA will take care of them as war refugees. But everyone needs documents to be recognized as bona fide stateless persons. They have to prove where they were during the war. Some also have to produce proof of residency by showing police records. I supply any documents they need and arrange for their transportation to Germany. I am what you might call a *Spekulant*. I speculate in order to make a profit. The work is a gold mine because many of those who are fleeing can pay nicely."

"What about those who can't pay your price?"

"The Jews have an organization that helps them get out of Poland."

"I'm looking for survivors of the Ghetto," Berson said. "Can you take me to that organization?"

"Any time you can get away from your hospital duties."

"Take me now," Berson said. "Dr. Dereszewski will cover for me."

"At your service, my dear doctor," Haskel complied, bowing. "My car is at your disposal."

As he drove, Haskel explained, "I learned about this organization when Rachel, my former girlfriend, left me to go to Germany. I never heard from her again."

"She was a pretty woman," Berson said. "I met her in the Ghetto's bunkers. I know how you must feel. But now, with your looks and your money, you can still find a nice girl to love."

Haskel stopped the car on Twarda Street, in front of an old, partially bombed-out theater near the train station.

"Thanks for bringing me here, Haskel," Berson said, shaking his hand, ready to get out of the car.

Haskel held on to the doctor's hand, saying, "I know you'll be able to refer some people who need to get out of Poland."

"So that's why you got me the hospital supplies," Berson said, patting Haskel's shoulder.

"Szymon, is there anything wrong with that?" Haskel asked. "I do for you, you do for me."

*

When Haskel drove off, Berson walked into the large, warehouse-like room. He saw about forty people lined up in front of a long registration table. He joined the line and when his turn came, one of the three registrars asked for his name.

"Berson, Szymon Berson."

"Dr. Szymon Berson!" a man sitting on the edge of the table called out.

"Tevye!" Berson shouted gleefully.

They locked in an embrace.

"My name is no longer Tevye. Here they know me as Yosef," Tevye whispered. Then he turned to the women registrars, "Just keep going. I'll be back shortly."

As it turned out, he didn't get back to the room that night. For hours, the two men sat, talked, and drank from a vodka bottle Tevye produced from his coat. First, they sat in the back room of the theater and then they relaxed in the unused lounge at Berson's clinic, reminiscing about their work with the Partizans and their service in the Red Army.

Tevye enthusiastically described his fortuitous meeting with the Jews of the Palestine Brigade in Italy. "My work with the Bricha is my ticket to Palestine."

"Bricha?" Berson asked.

"Hundreds, thousands of Jews survived the Nazi hell by hiding in countries overrun by the Germans. And thousands more survived in Russia," Tevye replied. "They're all returning, all coming out of hiding. But they have no place to return to. We gather up these remnants and whisk them into Berlin."

"Two questions," Berson said. "Who's the 'we'? And why aren't the survivors returning to their former homes?"

"Your first question first. 'We' is the Bricha, made up of a bunch of young kids from Palestine and survivors like me," he replied. "It's super secret."

To describe the Bricha's operation in this area of Poland, Tevye drew a jagged line on a piece of paper. "This is the border between Poland and Germany." He then drew two circles – one the German side, which he marked "Berlin," and the other, a border city in Poland about ninety kilometers away, which he marked "Stettin."

"Our Bricha unit collects Jews from all over Poland, provides transportation within Poland to Stettin and, from there, transports people by rail or truck, or by ship on the Oder River to Berlin," Tevye explained. "Crossing the borders illegally is no simple matter. It requires bribing Polish, Russian, and German border guards. They all want watches, cigarettes, and the like."

"Why Berlin?"

"In Berlin, Jews become wards of the UNRRA, which runs large Displaced Persons camps. There, they can be processed, again clandestinely, for travel to Palestine."

Tevye proudly explained that the Bricha maintains the same setup in almost every country bordering with Germany.

"What about my second question?" Dr. Berson asked. "Why aren't the Jews returning to their former homes?"

"Szymon, you are fortunate," Tevye said. "You returned to your city and were given back your old job in your hospital. Others who returned were given a hostile reception."

Dr. Berson thought a while and, instead of telling of his plight with his return to Warsaw, he changed the subject.

"What about your plans?"

"Working for the Bricha is my ticket to Palestine," Tevye repeated. "The Zionist ideal of building a Jewish national homeland in Palestine gives meaning to my life. Had there been a Jewish state before the war, hundreds of thousands of us would have been saved from the Holocaust."

"I'm impressed with your emotional attachment to Palestine, but not with your logic," Dr. Berson said. "The war's over. A new Europe is in the making. Palestine is far off. Poland is here and now."

Tevye said he couldn't believe what he was hearing, and bluntly said he refused to accept Berson's defense of Poland's treatment of its Jews.

With enough vehemence to match Tevye's passion, Berson continued, "Poland was a war casualty, as you can see in the microcosm of my hospital. Meanwhile, don't lose hope. Changes are in the wind. In the future, Jews and Catholics will unite in building a Polish democracy that will be a model for the world."

"Szymon, you're dreaming." Reaching out to touch Berson's arm, Tevye said, "I feel as close to you as if you were my brother. If you remain here, you'll be lost to us and maybe even to medicine. I'm not talking Zionist philosophy to you. I'm talking about you. I'm talking to you as a brother, my brother. Get out of Poland while you still can."

Long past midnight, Berson called a halt to the debate. "OK, OK, Tevye, I'll think over what you've said. I understand you see tomorrow only in Palestine."

"I know what's really keeping you here," Tevye added as they walked back to the old theater, holding onto each other. "It's not Polish nationalism. It's your dream of getting back Czyste Hospital, your baby."

"Now, enough. No more debate for me," Dr. Berson emphatically replied. He clasped Tevye's hand to say good-bye and headed back to the hospital.

"Czyste protected you from all the Stashas of Poland," Tevye persisted, trailing after him. "You judge all of Poland based on your own safety in your cloistered hospital."

"You sound like Dr. Poliakov," Berson said, turning to look directly at Tevye again.

"Who's Poliakov?"

"Someone who criticized me as you are doing now. Regrettably, he also thought what he was doing was right," Berson said. "I'll tell you the whole sad story some other time. For now, good night!"

Dismissing Tevye's blind faith as a fabrication or false hope, Berson returned to his work with greater zeal for the next three weeks. He urged old Dr. Dereszewski "to see a new Warsaw in the making" and not to be disillusioned by the "transitory political or financial crisis."

But Szymon Berson was in for a life-altering shock.

Late one afternoon, he was called to an accident in a crowded section of Warsaw. When he arrived in the ambulance, he saw a young man lying in the courtyard, bleeding from every part of his body. The injured man was barely breathing. His feet were fractured and bleeding profusely. While he tended the victim, the doctor was surrounded by the huge crowd who were shouting obscenities, jeering him as he tried to help the stricken person.

Someone ranted at the victim, "Zyd, come by here again and you won't need an ambulance! You'll need a hearse!"

Another male voice shouted, "Hitler didn't kill them all!"

Amidst this pandemonium and while trying to stop the man's bleeding, Dr. Berson pieced together the details of the tragedy.

The young man, a Jewish survivor, had returned to Warsaw to his former home in the apartment complex where Berson had been summoned. He had shown his prewar deed to the man occupying the house and asked for the return of his apartment. The negotiations turned ugly when the resident physically pushed the man out of the apartment, fought with him on the veranda, and steadily beat him with an iron poker. Their fighting and shouting attracted the neighbors, who joined in cursing the Jew. When the man fell from the third-floor veranda down to the cement courtyard, the neighbors burst into applause.

Berson looked around at the crowd. "I need volunteers to help carry this man to the ambulance."

No one came forward. The driver and Dr. Dereszewski helped Dr. Berson carry the wounded man to the ambulance. As they trudged through the hostile crowd, one neighbor shook her fist in rage, "We've had enough of you Jews."

"And tell the other Zyds they'll get the same treatment if they ever come back here," another voice shouted.

At the hospital, Berson transferred the young victim to the emergency ward where, despite the feverish work of a group of doctors who desperately tried to save his life, he died on the table. Walking wearily out of the ward, Berson threw his surgical gown and rubber gloves on the floor in disgust. He refused any food Dr. Dereszewski offered him and remained secluded in his tiny bedroom.

In the middle of the night, he awakened Pawel. "That young man survived the war but was killed in liberated Warsaw. I can't sleep. I can't get his disfigured face out of my mind. I can't block out the virulent anti-Semitic shouts of the mob. I don't know what to do."

"You need to see the pattern," Pawel said gently. "They rejected you for Czyste Hospital. The university also rejected you. You can't get supplies from the Russians. And now, this warning that Jews will be killed if they try to take what is rightfully theirs."

"You're right, Pawel, all of that is anti-Semitism. It's brutal," he said.

He went back to bed, but could not sleep. It was still dark when he left the Rehabilitation Center and walked to the theater, where he hoped to find Tevye. The registration center – where people were sleeping on the floor – was lit by a single electric bulb hanging from the ceiling. Stepping over the sprawled bodies, Berson lay down on the bare floor, folded his arm under his head and immediately fell asleep.

Tevye awakened him a few hours later, offering a hot cup of coffee. "What brings you here?"

Berson yawned, stretched, and looked around the empty room. "Where's everybody?" he asked.

"On their way to Berlin," Tevye responded. "And you slept through it all."

"When's the next transport?" Berson asked.

"I thought you couldn't decide whether to go," Tevye said.

"I still haven't."

Tevye shrugged in exasperation. "You still can't decide. I give up on you."

"I can't decide whether I should report to the truck with or without my uniform."

"Why, thank you, Szymon, at last!" Tevye said, hugging him. "The next transport leaves tonight, at eight."

Berson returned to the hospital and worked as diligently as he had every day for the past year. When he finished his rounds, he sat with the old doctor and gave him an envelope containing money he had saved.

"Pawel, I decided to get out of Poland."

"You can be caught and punished severely as a deserter," the old doctor said.

"I know the danger," Berson nodded. "Nonetheless, I've decided to chance it. So, hold down the fort for me and don't report my absence. Give me a few days before the military comes around to inspect."

"I'll keep it running. The military won't suspect a thing," Pawel promised. He got up and rummaged through the cabinets, filling a small canvas pouch with a few bottles of aspirin, some mild sedatives, and a handful of medical supplies. "These may come in handy," Pawel said. "A doctor should never be without his stock-in-trade."

Later that evening, Berson walked out of the hospital in his uniform. He carried a small knapsack, in which he carried his civilian clothes, in case Tevye advised him to change.

*

Tevye embraced Dr. Berson at the entrance to the old theater. "Here at last, Szymon," he said. "And now you must give me your documents."

"My Polish passport, my medical certification, my military ID card," he enumerated, putting them reluctantly in Tevye's hand. "I admit they give me a sense of belonging, a sense that I am still somebody."

"When you come with us, you are a stateless person, requesting aid from UN agencies. You have no passport, you have no identity card, you're nobody – at least not on paper. But I'm returning your medical certification."

"What will happen to my documents?"

"They will probably be put to good use," Tevye replied, without elaborating. "From now on, you follow orders."

"Whose?"

"A twenty-one-year-old kid's," Tevye said with a chuckle. "He does business with police chiefs, Komisars, and border patrols."

They were interrupted when a young man stuck his head through the doorway and yelled, "The truck is here!"

Tevye sprang to his feet and ran down the hallway to speak to the group before he allowed them to board the truck.

"The first leg of your trip will be to Sochaczev, a railway station north of Warsaw. You will be met by one of us and get further instructions," Tevye called out, reminding Berson of the time Tevye was the Partizan leader issuing orders in the forest. "From there, you'll board a train for a long ride, about five hours, to Kutno."

"What about me?" Dr. Berson asked Tevye as they both boarded the truck.

"What about you?" Tevye asked.

"With or without the uniform?"

"We'll ask the Bricha man when he meets us at Sochaczev."

After about two hours, the truck pulled up to a siding at the far end of the Sochaczev train station, where the passengers were asked to quickly and quietly board a waiting boxcar. The transfer went smoothly until one of the passengers refused to leave her position in the corner of the truck, where she cowered, sobbing. When someone tried to carry her out, she became hysterical. Her screams brought a railway official scampering over to the boxcar to investigate.

"What's going on here?" he demanded to know, lifting his whistle to summon the guards.

"Nothing, friend, nothing," a young man stepped in front of the official and, taking him around the shoulders, led him away from the boxcar. The young man took a wad of bills out of his battered briefcase and handed it to the official, saying, "Thank you, thank you for helping us get the train underway. I think we're all set."

The official pocketed the wad, gave an offhand salute, and walked back toward the locomotive.

"That's him, the Bricha leader," Tevye told Berson. "He's in charge of this transport. He'll take you to the border."

Tevye returned to the truck, where he spotted the still-cringing passenger. Amid tears, the woman begged not to be put into the boxcar.

"I survived one concentration camp," she wept. "I won't go to another."

"Now, now," Tevye quietly explained, "this boxcar is not going to any concentration camp. It is going to Berlin, to safety. We Jews paid for this boxcar. *We* control its destination."

When she showed no signs of moving, Tevye became stern – the Partizan commander again. "I warn you, if you don't get onto the train by the time I count three, I'll leave you here with the Polacks and the Russians. Now! One..."

Before he finished his count, the frightened woman scurried into the boxcar.

"Well, that's as far as I go," Tevye told Berson. "Come, I'll introduce you to Avi."

Avi had a boyish, round face with rosy cheeks tinged with freckles. "Welcome, Dr. Berson. I see you're a colonel. Impressive."

"Do I wear it, though?" Berson asked. "Should I change into civilian clothes instead?"

"For us, it's safer to have you in uniform," Avi replied.

"Why?"

"If anything goes wrong," Avi quietly said, "we could always resort to some military persuasion."

"What could go wrong?" Berson asked, alarmed.

Avi replied in a stilted accent that Berson could barely understand, "Hoodlums on the train often start fights with Jews. The mere presence of such a high-ranking military official would make them think twice."

Tevye explained, "Trains have been a danger zone for Jews. We've had several incidents where roving bands of Polish thugs have thrown Jews out of speeding trains."

"But I hope that your uniform doesn't get you in trouble, Dr. Berson," Avi added.

"What kind of trouble?"

"Well, what if someone stops you to ask for your military orders?"

"I don't know what would happen. I hope no one asks," Berson replied.

"Then don't ask me. You must decide whether to wear it or not," Avi declared. "I don't like trouble with the military."

"For the time being, I'll keep it on. We'll see what happens."

"Fine," Avi concurred and, as they boarded the train, he asked, "Doctor, would you stay close to the woman who got upset? We want to make sure she doesn't attract the attention of railway officials as we make stops during the ride. It'll be a long journey."

Berson searched for her in the dim glow of the oil lamp and saw her sitting crouched in a corner, hiding her face in her kerchief.

"I'm Szymon Berson," he said, talking to her above the babble of voices as he squeezed into a space next to her. "I'm a doctor and I'll be taking care of you till we get to Berlin."

"Thank you. I'm sorry I caused such a ruckus," she replied haltingly. "My name is Sonya. Sonya Gruber. I'm still a bit shaky."

As the train started moving, Dr. Berson gave her two tablets of the sedative he had taken from the hospital. She took them with water from his canteen. "I apologize for getting hysterical," she stammered. "But when they ordered me into the boxcar, I was seized by uncontrollable fear. I could only think of being herded into a boxcar and taken to a concentration camp."

"It will take all of us a long time to overcome the dread and terror we experienced under the Nazis," Berson said. "Do you want to tell me about that boxcar?"

"No," she whispered, "I can't."

Berson gazed at her still-youthful face, wondering how old she was. He felt like a father, quieting a child after a bad dream. "Why don't you try to get some sleep," he suggested.

After a vain attempt to comply, she turned to him, "I don't want to think about my situation," she said. "Tell me about your work in the Polish army."

He briefly described his duties and then added, somewhat diffidently, "For now, I'm a deserter."

"You'll be in trouble if they catch you," she said.

"I was a Partizan," he replied. "I can handle myself."

"Partizan!" she exclaimed, perking up. "Tell me."

He told her how Leon Viner had forced him out of the Warsaw Ghetto and then described the year he spent in the woods, going from one hideaway to the next tending the sick and the wounded. He broke down when he described Ketzalleh's death. Sonya listened with rapt attention, not speaking until he mentioned the AK's refusal to cooperate with the Jewish underground.

"Do you think this war has brought an end to anti-Semitism?"

He shook his head. "Did you really believe that this war, the war against Hitler, would rid the world of anti-Semitism? The fact that we have to travel clandestinely through Poland should burst that bubble of hope."

Sonya buried her head back in her folded arms, remained silent for quite a while, and then murmured, "So, all my family and friends who were killed in Majdanek – they died for nothing." She began to sob softly.

"Help me understand," Berson said, reaching out to touch her arm. "Tell me about your experiences there."

"No, Doctor, I can't. It's been two years since my liberation, and I can't talk about it yet."

"The fact that you panicked before getting into this boxcar shows that Majdanek is still very much part of you," Berson said, as if offering a diagnosis. "It might help you if you talked about those experiences."

And so she began.

*

"Lublin was my home. I was born there, went to school, and worked there. I enjoyed both my professions – teaching Hebrew in the Jewish school and teaching English in the university. When the university was closed down in 1939, we all knew that war was imminent and that the Germans would make us the next target. But no one knew, no one could believe the horror they would bring to our lives. I think our camp, the one at Majdanek, was the first concentration camp built. It was just a few kilometers from Lublin. Even then, before the crematorium was built, the camp was already a death factory.

"I was hauled there together with about twelve other women – my close friends from the university and some students from the Jewish school. Every one of us was taken to what the Germans called the 'Arena', a former outdoor basketball court. There, they tattooed us. I nearly fainted when they were tattooing my arm. There are no words to describe my inner pain, my shame, my anguish, as they jabbed that number into my flesh. In Western movies, I had seen animals being tattooed. That's what I was reduced to – an animal. Several days later my friends were called out again to the Arena, where they were lined up against the wall and shot, one by one.

"I was spared from being killed in the Arena only because I was in excellent health. You see, I participated each year in the Maccabia Games we sponsored in Lublin. I was a runner and a high-jump competitor.

"So, that put me in a different category. I was what the Germans called an 'able-bodied Jew.'

"I was assigned to a labor battalion. In my group, thirty-eight of us were marched off each morning at sunrise to a construction site about four kilometers out of the camp. It was a two-hour march to the work site. We dug trenches for foundations for some buildings or factories. Digging those trenches was hard labor...some parts of the terrain were solid rock, requiring us to break through the hard surface. And, keep in mind, we were not allowed to stop nor were we given any food. At nightfall we were marched back to receive our only meal for the day. During the first year, I kept up with the regimen. I learned many tricks to stay alive, like saving a few crumbs from the evening meal to eat stealthily while working the next morning. Anyone slowing down would immediately feel the crack of a whip or the butt of a rifle on his back. I saw many of my fellow forced laborers either shot to death or savagely beaten. The Germans made the rest of us bury their bodies in the trenches.

"Even though I began as an able-bodied person, I soon felt weakened; my hands were blistered from holding the shovel and pickax. More than once, I was beaten, blows pounding on my body, because I paused to stop the flow of blood from my hands or to wipe sweat off my face. The last blow of one of the beatings was so severe, I fell on my face in the ditch I was digging. I think I passed out, although I do remember thinking how pleasing the cold mud was to my pained body. Some of my fellow workers tried to pick me up, despite the fact that they knew what punishment they would endure for stopping their work.

"I managed to get up without their help, though. Perhaps it was because my desire to live was even greater than my fear of dying. But I also knew that sooner or later my fate would be sealed by a shot in the head or a fatal kick – like the killings that I saw so often about me.

"I began to deal with death realistically. Despite my will to live, I realized that I had cheated death too often. Sometimes, in a mystical frame of mind, I would welcome my death, recalling stories about the hereafter from my childhood, stories that I had sometimes told the children in my Hebrew classes. I often imagined that when they would kill me, I would be united with my murdered friends or I would finally be with my loving grandparents. Those thoughts gave me some comfort.

"Then came the day when I thought death was certain. I simply could no longer join my labor battalion at daybreak. I could not move my body. Every bone ached; every limb was inflamed. My barracks partners were already lined up for the four-kilometer march and I was not in the line that morning. A German guard entered the barracks and began shouting obscenities at me like a wild man. He literally dragged me to the Arena to be shot. He ranted that this was to be a lesson to others in my labor battalion. At that time, the ovens had already been installed, but nonetheless, he marched me to the Arena so that 'no one would dare shirk the labor.' Weak as I was, I stood up with my back to the bullet-ridden wall, begging, pleading, shouting in German, in Polish, even in English, that I wanted to live.

"They didn't shoot.

"The German firing squad leader walked toward me. He stopped and asked if my English was good enough to translate English into German. When I said it was, he took me to the commandant of the camp, who gave me a pad and pencil and told me that Roosevelt was about to make a speech and he wanted me to translate it, as he was speaking.

"I survived Majdanek because I became the official translator of English, Russian, Polish, Latvian, Czech, and even Spanish. Languages I knew because I had majored in linguistics.

"Surviving Majdanek did not mean I was freed from the labor battalions. It only meant that when I was needed, I would report for translation duties. Otherwise, the beatings, the starvation diet, and the hard labor continued, and would have killed me.

"But the worst experience in my two years in that concentration camp was seeing the chimneys – chimneys that daily belched smoke, that gave off the odor of searing flesh throughout the camp. I could count the number of burned bodies by counting the number of absentees in our labor battalions on our morning marches.

"To this day, I cannot fall asleep without seeing those ghastly sights – the beatings, shootings, burning – replayed before my eyes."

*

By the time Sonya finished her story, the buzz and chatter in the boxcar had died down as people prepared for the long ride. Lulled by the staccato rhythm of the speeding wheels clicking against the rails, Sonya tried to sleep, but the swaying motion of the train kept jerking her head from side to side. Dr. Berson lowered his shoulder so she could lean on him. When he thought she was asleep, he covered her with his greatcoat.

"This is not such a bad ride in a boxcar," he softly whispered.

He knew she heard him because her lips curled up in a smile as she made herself more comfortable, leaning closer to him. She slept through the ride without waking. But, like the previous night, Dr. Berson was up all night, unable to sleep, not because he was troubled as he had been the night before. He simply enjoyed feeling her so near. Several hours later, Avi, the Bricha leader, opened the door slightly, allowing the morning sun to light up the car and wake up the group.

"We're coming into Kutno in about fifteen minutes, and I want you all to get up and pay close attention to my instructions," Avi called out.

He gave them a few minutes to stretch and then told them that although they would be traveling together the rest of the way, they were not to stand close to each other in the railroad station or give any appearance that they were an organized group. He announced that each family would be given money to purchase a rail ticket to Stettin and that each traveler must purchase a ticket separately and also enter the train alone.

Since Berson could not fully understand Avi's announcements, he asked Sonya if she could.

"He speaks more Hebrew than Yiddish, with a few Polish words thrown in," she said, giving Berson the gist of what Avi was saying.

"On the train, don't talk, not even Polish. Your Yiddish accent will attract the attention of those crazy Polacks," Avi continued in his stilted Yiddish. "When you get to Stettin, we'll assign places to stay. Some in hotels, some in rented rooms. I cannot tell you how long you will remain in Stettin before you are taken across the border, but you must remain at your assigned residence, ready to move out at a moment's notice.

"And remember, never, never say to anyone that you are hoping to go into Berlin," Avi announced. Then, staring at Sonya, he added, "Remember, don't draw attention to yourself. Always be in the background. And don't worry, the colonel and I will always be near you. You are always safe."

"Dr. Berson, you have very broad shoulders," Sonya whispered. "I think l would be safe with you always."

"Sonya, if you want another shoulder pillow from me, you must call me Szymon."

"I'll call you Szymon, even if I do not need your shoulder," Sonya replied with a smile.

Berson helped her out of the boxcar and they walked to the terminal together. "Stay here with the luggage," he said, pointing to a bench, "and I'll go buy our tickets."

She agreed, but held his arm as he was about to walk away and said softly, "What will happen if someone asks for your military papers or travel orders?"

"It has never happened before," he replied. "So why should it happen now?"

"Because there's always a first time."

He smiled broadly, ridiculing her fears. Before marching off to the ticket window, he asked her to drape his greatcoat over herself. Although she did not understand why, she followed his instructions. As he was walking over to the ticket window, she saw a Polish military police officer approach him with a salute and then point to a special window marked "Military Personnel." Sonya, who could not hear the conversation, was worried, wondering if the officer would ask to see Berson's travel orders. She noticed that Berson was whispering a few words to the policeman and then pointed to her.

"What was that all about?" Sonya asked when Berson returned with their tickets to Stettin.

"He told me I could get free rail tickets at the window marked 'Military Personnel'," Dr. Berson replied. "I pointed to you and told him I was traveling with my friend on a nonmilitary journey and asked him whether you were worth the price of a ticket."

As they boarded the train to Stettin, Sonya asked, "What did the policeman say to you?"

"He agreed you were worth the price of a ticket."

Concerned about possible harassment on the train, Berson tried to stay awake during the three-hour ride to Stettin, but he dozed off, his head resting on Sonya's shoulders. She woke him when the train pulled into the station in Stettin.

"I wasn't sleeping," he quipped. "I just like the feel of your shoulder."

"If you weren't sleeping, what was the snoring noise I heard?"

They both laughed until Sonya grasped his arm and said, "Szymon, I can't remember when the last time was that I laughed."

"So it's a good omen," he replied.

Before the passengers got off the train, Avi gave people slips of paper bearing the addresses of their lodgings. Sonya and three other women were assigned to a room in a pension and Berson was given a hotel room, which he was to share with Avi.

The young Bricha agent told him, "Tomorrow morning we'll begin moving people across the border into Germany. After that, we have a two-and-a-half-hour ride to Berlin in trucks. We must not arouse the interest of any local officials, because this group is totally without papers. If they suspect we are an organized body, they can stir up trouble or prohibit any later group from staying in Stettin.

"Will you help me alert everyone to be ready for the move, not to unpack luggage, and if possible, to sleep in their clothing?" Avi asked before he left, explaining he had several details to work out to ensure their successful departure from Poland.

After carrying out Avi's instructions, Berson spent the evening touring the quiet city with Sonya. When he returned to his room in the wee hours of the morning, Avi was still awake.

"Things aren't running smoothly," he said somberly.

"What's wrong?"

"The truck we sent through last night is still halted at the border and we don't know what the Russians will do with the people. Until that's resolved, we'll have to wait until the Bricha clears us to go."

They heard a knock on their door. Avi opened it, and a young man came in, speaking hurriedly to Avi in Hebrew, which Berson did not understand. The young man finished and left, without acknowledging Berson's presence.

"He's the local Bricha leader," Avi explained, "and he wants you to decide about the group's next move."

"Me?" Berson asked. "He didn't even nod to me."

"All he knows is that you're a doctor and he needs you. Here's the problem: Ordinarily, when a group arrives in Stettin, they are taken to the *punkt*, that's the processing center, and immediately placed on trucks to Berlin, before the authorities here get wind of their presence," Avi said. "But the Russians interdicted our last transport, so this time no refugees can move through the *punkt* until that's settled."

"So why do you need my advice?"

"Should we move the group to the *punkt* or let them stay in Stettin until we get clearance?" Avi asked.

"What's the difference?" Dr. Berson asked back.

"The *punkt* was a police barracks. The Germans bombed it out when they invaded Poland. It's been abandoned in disrepair ever since. No water, no electricity, no toilets."

"Terrible, not fit for people in this weather," Berson said. "What's the problem with staying here until you get clearance for us to move?"

"All sorts of complications," Avi explained. "When the locals find out that Jews are in Stettin, how long will it be before they start harassing us or before the city officials ask for documents? So, the question is: Leave them here until we can move them out to Berlin or bring them to the *punkt* now for safety's sake?"

"The conditions you describe at the *punkt* could lead to serious health hazards," Berson said. "We have no way of managing sick people. Let's stay here in Stettin as long as we can before moving there."

"Then you will be responsible for the group's safety here?" Avi asked.

"Me? I'm a passenger like the others. Of course I can't take responsibility for this group's safety in a Polish town! I only have a uniform, not an army! I recommend staying here only because I wouldn't choose to invite health problems that we can't handle."

"Well, if they can't be protected here, they must go to the *punkt* nevertheless," Avi said. "The Bricha can't protect them either. We are very few and we must operate underground."

Avi, Berson, and Sonya visited everyone in the group, to inform them that when they are ordered to move to the *punkt*, each will be given a specific time to ride the town's trolley to the last stop. From there, they will have to walk a half a kilometer.

Avi took Berson to the *punkt* the next morning, ahead of the group, in the hope that they could set up some hygiene facilities and ward off the possibility of illness among the refugees.

"I had it better with the Partizans in the forest," Berson told Avi as he looked at the garbage left from previous groups that was piled high around the bombed-out former police station. "The flies and rats here are a real menace."

Avi shrugged his shoulders and lifted his hands up in the air. "Doctor, speak to the Russians or to God. As soon as either one gives the word, we'll move."

Suddenly they heard shouting and yelling coming from the road in the valley below. They were amazed to see the entire group making its way up the incline to the gate of the *punkt*.

"You were instructed to make your way individually," Avi stormed as the group entered the gate.

Sonya came up to him. "This was not our decision, Avi. The police captain ordered every member of our group to show identity and travel papers. That's what caused the stampede. I'm afraid the police will come here and maybe arrest all of us."

"I'm going to Itzik," Avi said.

"Who's Itzik?" Berson asked.

"He's like your friend Tevye, a local Jewish Pole who's working with us. He's now the Bricha's negotiator with the locals."

"What do you mean?" Berson asked.

"Well, now the Stettin police will also have to be bought off," Avi said bluntly. "Why don't you come with me, in uniform, to city hall and we'll talk to Itzik."

When they found Itzik, a hulking, balding, middle-aged man, he was already drinking coffee with the Polish police captain. As they entered the captain's office, they heard Itzik offer him two packs of cigarettes per each member of the group to call off the inspection of identity documents. Before the captain replied, Dr. Berson whispered to Avi to ask for a brief postponement to allow them to discuss the matter privately.

Huddling in a city hall corridor, Berson said in a hushed tone, "You can kill two birds with one stone if you make your payment to him contingent on the Russians allowing our truck to cross the border."

"The police captain has as much authority with the Russian border patrol as I do," Itzik responded.

"So let's negotiate with the Russians."

"I can't do that," Itzik explained. "In the past, we've negotiated everything with the police captain."

"What will you accomplish if the captain allows you to remain here? All you get is a few days' reprieve with no guarantee that your trucks will be permitted to cross the border. If the Russians rule the border, that's where you want to go. Where's the Russian Komisariat for this town?"

"Upstairs," Itzik replied. "Right here in city hall."

"In Warsaw, the district Komisar controlled everything including the hospital's toilet paper," Berson said. "So this local Komisar undoubtedly controls the border guards as well as residents' rights."

"But the Komisar is no local police chief," Itzik warned. "He's much more demanding."

As expected, the Komisar was a large, cigar-smoking man, pontificating from behind a massive desk in an office heated beyond stuffiness. He greeted Itzik, "How can I help you, my friend?"

"We have a group that needs to cross the border, but the Russian border guards are holding up one of our trucks there."

"Now what could I do about that?" the Komisar asked. "Those guards have their own officials, their own payment schedules."

Itzik whispered to Berson, "That means higher bribes."

The Komisar continued, "We would have to get clearance from them."

"Tell me what you would need, Komisar," Itzik said, "but assure me that our group will be allowed passage across the border in the morning."

The Komisar named a huge amount of gold as well as the usual number of cigarettes and cans of coffee. Itzik agreed to the items mentioned but not the gold. Instead he offered several brand-name Swiss watches and again insisted on guarantees that the trucks will be allowed to leave Poland. The Komisar made a hasty phone call and then said, "Bring me the stuff this afternoon and your group will be cleared tomorrow morning."

Avi, Itzik, and Dr. Berson hurried back into the *punkt*, where Avi gathered everyone together and shouted, "Listen, everybody! We're leaving for Berlin tomorrow morning!"

Pandemonium broke loose. Amid the whooping and hollering, Dr. Berson embraced Sonya, twirling her around like a kid with a doll. There was no letup in the joyous clamor, the shouting, and the singing. Sonya and Szymon left the regaling group and found a hillock just outside the gate, where they sat sharing their thoughts about finally getting to Berlin.

"Berlin has become a symbol for all of us," Szymon said. "It represents our escape from tyranny and the jumping-off point for our future."

"Isn't it amazing," Sonya said. "Berlin – the place where evil sprung, is for us the first step toward our new future."

Before long, they had a heated discussion about where that future was to be. She stressed the merits of establishing a Jewish national homeland in Palestine and the need for an end to Jewish homelessness, while he emphasized his love for medicine and his need to grow in his field, something he could accomplish only in the United States.

"Let's stop debating," Sonya said. "We both need some sleep."

He leaned his back against the gate, motioning her to rest her head on his lap. He stroked her hair, caressed her face, and bent down to kiss her. She embraced him around his neck, whispering, "Thank you. I didn't think I'd ever feel a moment of happiness again."

They soon fell sound asleep.

They were awakened by the sharp grind of a truck's engine as it backed up to the gate. Daylight was creeping in, and in their dazed condition they were confused as to whether the diffused light was dawn or twilight. Itzik jumped off the truck, startling them both.

"Good morning," he called. "Let's get everyone on the truck!"

Avi stumbled out of the *punkt* just in time to hear Itzik bellow, "Everybody has to be on this truck in less than half an hour. We must get on the road!"

As the group quickly shook off their drowsiness and frantically gathered their belongings, Itzik told Avi and Berson, "I've arranged with Stefan – that's the police captain – to get us out of the city at exactly 6:40 A.M. At 8:40, Mischa will be at the border to get us through. By 9:40 he's gone and when he's gone, we're through, finished."

"Who's Mischa?" Berson asked.

"He's the guardian angel with whom I negotiated the border crossing."

"I thought that was arranged with the Russian at city hall."

"Later, I'll explain later," Itzik said. "We must leave in seventeen minutes."

Avi, Sonya, and Berson ran up and down the *punkt* waking up stragglers and shouting, "We're leaving now! Grab your baggage and get on the truck immediately!"

Avi and Itzik then stood beside the tailgate, helping people board the truck. The group shouted their good-byes to Avi and let out a loud hurrah as the truck lurched forward, leaving the *punkt*. When the truck neared the border, Itzik stopped the truck and spread the tarpaulin over it. Before he laced the tarp completely shut, he stuck his head into the truck and ordered everyone to be completely silent. The ride to the border lasted only a few minutes, but the stop at the checkpoint was interminable. Because the tarpaulin blocked any fresh air, they could barely breathe beneath it.

"What are you carrying?" they heard a guard asking in Russian.

"Fifteen cows," Itzik's voice boomed out. "All slaughtered."

They could hear the border guards' footsteps at the tailgate and saw the rustling of the canvas as though someone was trying to untie it. Sonya could see a guard's hand reaching inside the truck. She heard Itzik's voice asserting that the documents he was showing them were in order. The guards' steps retreated from the rear of the truck and then they heard another voice demanding fifteen watches.

"Seven," Itzik argued. "Mischa agreed to seven for this transport."

"Mischa is not here." The guard's voice sounded threatening.

"OK, ten," Itzik bargained and, to sweeten the pie, he added, "The best – Omegas."

Then there was a long pause. Finally the belching engine roared and the truck was on its way. The group burst into a spontaneous shout, "Goodbye, Poland!"

Their joy was short lived. They soon stopped at the border crossing into Germany, where again they heard voices negotiating with German border patrols and with another set of Russian guards. Itzik again haggled with them for a price, but this time it was a simple matter of arithmetic. The Russian officer counted forty-two persons – and demanded forty-two cartons of cigarettes.

*

Late on that May afternoon in 1946, Itzik called out, "Berlin!"

He helped each member of the group off the truck and then told them that he had to return to his post in Stettin. "Here's what will happen next," he explained. "After a mandatory delousing procedure in the French sector, you will be transferred by a UNRRA vehicle to a Displaced Persons camp in the American sector. Then he motioned toward a rangy young man with a winsome smile. "This is Yakov," he said. "He'll guide you through the American sector."

As they boarded the UNRRA bus, someone asked Yakov, "What's this 'sector' business?"

"When the Allies conquered Berlin, they divided the city into four occupation sectors: American, French, British, and Russian," Yakov replied. "The Americans set up DP camps in their sector for survivors."

"What's 'DP'?"

"Displaced Person," Yakov replied. "That's you. You were torn away from your home. You'll be in a DP camp only a few days. Then they'll take you further south, to the Munich area, so that soon you'll be away from the Russians and on your way to Palestine."

Acting as a tour guide, Yakov described what the bombed-out areas they were passing were like before the war. He became ecstatic telling them about the famous Tiergarten, the zoo, and the once-fashionable Kurfurstendamm Avenue as the bus lurched through the gutted street, now strewn with postwar debris. His excitement was mirrored by the passengers as they poked their heads through the open windows to get a better view of the utter devastation before them.

They gasped when Yakov pointed out the ruins of the chancery where Hitler had committed suicide and where his body was cremated by his loyal officers. They sat quietly as the bus made its way down the broad, unscathed tree-lined avenue, Unter den Eichen. At its western end, the bus entered a barbed-wire enclosure. As it passed through the police-patrolled gate, Yakov announced, "Welcome to Schlachtensee! Our safe haven."

Chapter 11

TIRED, HUNGRY, DISORIENTED, BUT HOPEFUL, the refugees got off the bus in the massive central courtyard of the sprawling Displaced Persons camp. Yakov shepherded them into the huge communal dining room for their first meal in the camp. Having been given only meager rations the previous night amid the filth of the *punkt*, they fell on the hot stew with gratitude. An hour and a half later, they assembled in the administration building's reception room to be welcomed by Harold Fisher, the camp's director.

Fisher, a stout man, with a perpetual smile and constantly chomping on a cigar, gave an immediate impression of being sincere and compassionate. He explained that they had now come under the protection of the United Nations, whose Relief and Rehabilitation Agency – UNRRA – administered the camp. Speaking with warmth and affability, but using an odd mixture of German and Yiddish, he explained that they would each receive daily rations of eighteen hundred calories, the minimum the international agency required.

"You have just eaten your first meal, and I hope you liked it. I did," he said with a smile, patting a waistline that gave evidence of considerably heartier meals. "It was cooked by camp residents. The dishes were washed and the room was swept clean by camp residents. No Germans and no Americans work here. Only you, the Jewish residents. The police guarding the installation are Jewish residents. In fact, it's the volunteers from among the five thousand Jewish refugees who live here who run the whole camp. The few of us on the UNRRA staff are professionals working on your behalf. We include two Americans and several Scandinavians who are social workers and administrators. However, even with the UNRRA's devoted service, this camp would be impossible to operate without your help, as volunteers."

"How long will we stay here?" someone from the rear asked.

"We'll discuss that when you are rested and settled. But right now, I encourage you to volunteer as carpenters, plumbers, kitchen staff, or office workers. Use your skills here. Your compensation will come to you in the form of increased food rations in exchange for your work."

He introduced his American and Norwegian staff members, and then added, "You are safe here. Of that I can assure you. But to continue to be safe, do not venture into the Russian sector of Berlin."

Mr. Fisher ended his briefing, speaking like a father to his children, "Now, let's get you settled. If you go to the waiting room just through that door, you can register and get your room assignments."

Dr. Berson stood with Sonya in the queue that formed in front of one of the registration desks, waiting for their names to be called. Eventually, a young UNRRA official, reading from a list that Yakov had given him, called out, "Berson, Szymon."

"Doctor Berson," Berson corrected him.

"You are a doctor? A medical doctor?" the registration official asked.

"Yes."

The registrar's face beamed, extending his hand to greet the doctor. He quickly picked up the phone and announced, "Harold, we have a doctor, a medical doctor, in the new group that's just arrived." Then, putting down the receiver, he said to Dr. Berson, "The director wants to see you right away. Please come with me."

"I shall be glad to meet the director," he said, "but I don't want to leave Miss Gruber until I know she is properly settled."

"Doctor, she will be right here in this room, well taken care of, when you finish your interview with the director."

Berson followed him to Fisher's office, occasionally looking back to check on Sonya.

"Dr. Berson! Welcome, welcome! We are very glad to have you. You are a gift sent to us from heaven," Mr. Fisher's voice boomed out in his very bad blend of Yiddish and German.

"Thank you," Berson replied. "You may speak to me in English, if that is easier for you, and tell me why I'm a gift from heaven."

"Do I detect a New York accent?" Fisher asked, laughing with some surprise, hands folded across his rotund paunch.

"Before the war, I did one year's internship in the Stone-Winthrop Hospital in New York City," Berson said. "I hope to contact my friends at the hospital and return there for a medical appointment and updated training."

"Wonderful, wonderful. You know, our UNRRA Resettlement Department can help process your emigration to the United States."

"That is good news," Berson responded. "Now, I am curious to know why I'm a gift from heaven."

Mr. Fisher explained that since the Schlachtensee camp had been established, about a year earlier, it had been what the refugees call a *durchgangs lager,* a transit camp. Refugees would come in from Poland and would be immediately transferred further south, to the Munich area, where permanent DP camps were well established. During that year, about twenty thousand Displaced Persons had passed through the Schlachtensee camp – none of whom ever stayed more than a day or two. Neither the US military nor the survivors themselves wanted DPs to remain in Berlin. It was too close to the Russians.

Fisher bluntly stated, "Doctor, I and my staff are well aware that most of the Jewish survivors want to be closer to Europe's southern ports for their emigration to Palestine."

"What about resettlement in other countries?" Berson asked.

"That's a major issue," Fisher replied. "The war has been over for fifteen months and still no country, no nation anywhere in the world, is willing to open its doors to the refugees."

"What does that mean?"

"It means that as of two weeks ago, this transit camp has become a permanent holding center for those desiring resettlement in Palestine or elsewhere."

"Why?" Berson asked, shocked.

"The cold war between the Russians and Americans is heating up. The Russians are pressuring the Americans to pull out of Berlin."

"How do strained relations between Russia and the United States affect a DP camp?"

"The US is standing up to the Russians by showing its determination to stay in Berlin," Fisher said. "Keeping the Displaced Persons in Berlin is proof positive to the Russians that the Americans intend to remain here a long time. And now we have a severe medical problem."

As Mr. Fisher was about to continue his explanation, a Norwegian official stepped into the office saying, "Excuse me, Harold, everyone in the new group has been assigned to their quarters and they're ready to go."

"Thanks, Sven. Please take them to their barracks."

"Excuse me," Berson said. "Is Sonya Gruber in that group?"

"Yes, yes," the official said. "I asked her to wait for you."

Fisher walked out to the reception area to get Sonya. "I'm sorry, my dear," he said, leading her to the office and offering her a seat next to Dr. Berson. "I should have asked you to come in with Dr. Berson."

"Mr. Fisher was just about to tell me why I am a gift from heaven," Berson explained dryly.

"Call me Harold," Fisher said, drying his bald pate with a clean handkerchief and then lighting a fresh cigar. He offered one to Berson, who courteously refused. "Well, let me explain our severe problem, then you can judge how God has worked miracles by bringing you here."

For Sonya's benefit, Fisher again explained the changed status of the DP camp, from a transit camp to a permanent holding center. "I'm afraid there will be no more transports out of Berlin in the foreseeable future."

Sonya stared at him, her face hardening. "Yesterday, Yakov told us that we would stay in this camp only a few days and then be on our way to Palestine."

"When it comes to this critical matter, Yakov doesn't run the show – nor does the UNRRA. The US Army does," Fisher replied. "Movement out of Berlin is now totally controlled by the Army. We are not permitted to send anyone down to the Zone unless we get clearance from the military. They have given us only three exceptions to the strict ban against the onward travel of Displaced Persons: family reunions, unaccompanied children, and a hospital train for the chronically ill."

"So, how can I get on my way to Palestine?" Sonya asked angrily.

"Like everyone else," Fisher replied candidly, "you'll have to remain in Berlin for a while, possibly a long while."

"What do you mean? That's not possible," Sonya insisted.

Dr. Berson, reached for Sonya's hand and, trying to calm her, he changed the subject. "Harold, tell me about your medical problem in this camp."

"Let me answer her question first," Fisher replied, recognizing Sonya's keen disappointment. "Miss Gruber, I know you are upset, but I have to give you the facts so you understand your situation realistically. Who's stopping you from going on to Palestine? Everybody. The British are still blockading ships headed for Palestine; the Americans are playing footsie with the British; and the Russians are erecting unnecessary but impenetrable obstacles to travel out of Berlin. And we, an agency of the United Nations, instead of solving the refugee problem, can only stand by on the sidelines as the superpowers go at each other's throats."

"So it isn't just the DP camp's rules – it's everything," Sonya sadly realized. "I'm sorry for my outburst, but as you understand, I expected, that is, we all expected that as soon as we made it to Berlin we would get out of Germany right away. The prospect of staying here indefinitely is shocking."

"I know, I know only too well," Fisher replied.

"Excuse me, Mr. Fisher," Sonya said speaking slowly, her voice choking, "you don't really know. You don't know what the word 'Germany' means to us. It fills me and others with terror, with fear, with pain."

Mr. Fisher walked over to her, held her hand, and softly whispered, "I hope that my predictions of a long and arduous stay in Berlin are wrong."

Sonya nodded and dabbed her eyes. Then, her face lighting up, said, "Szymon is a doctor. He could go on the next hospital transport and I could go as his nurse."

Mr. Fisher did not reply. He stood up, took a thermos from the shelf and poured them each a cup of lukewarm, black coffee. As he relit his cigar, they drank their coffee, saying nothing.

"From your silence, I gather that you're not so pleased with my suggestion," Sonya said. "Does it have anything to do with Dr. Berson's being your gift from heaven?"

"It has everything to do with that," Fisher responded. "You're very quick."

He unfolded a map of the camp's area and explained that in Berlin there are two Jewish DP camps, Schlachtensee and Tempelhof. Between the two camps the DP population is eight thousand souls. He pointed to an area on the camp's map marked "clinic" and explained that it had served adequately as a clinic because it had barely been used. Since becoming a permanent camp over the past two weeks, however, serious medical problems had arisen.

"We have only one UNRRA doctor, who's running himself ragged. As long as the camp was temporary, his small infirmary could do a creditable job. Now that this is a permanent holding camp, he can't possibly cope with our growing health problems. We now need an entire medical facility. And that requires a hospital and trained medical personnel. I've been bombarding my UNRRA headquarters for action and, so far, all I get is promises. And this little clinic is a joke."

He folded the map, put it back on a shelf behind his desk, and said, "Dr. Berson, we need a medical facility and a full-time medical leader who will stay with us as long as the Displaced Persons are forced to remain in the camp. Your fellow Jews need a doctor, not a Band-Aid."

Then he turned to Sonya and added, "That is why I did not respond to your suggestion about you two leaving Berlin on a hospital train."

When Dr. Berson did not reply, Fisher continued, "We have another, even more serious problem. We have about three thousand school-age children in the two camps, probably the largest concentration of children in Germany, for whom we must provide a school – something else we didn't have to do when this was just a transit camp. I can't neglect these responsibilities, these burdens. We must care for our sick and educate our children."

"Mr. Fisher, can we have a few moments to discuss this in private?" Dr. Berson asked.

"By all means, and pour yourselves another cup of coffee. It's still warm," he said. "I'll wait for you in the next room."

Szymon and Sonya whispered briefly together and then joined Fisher in the reception room.

"We have decided to help you carry this burden," Berson said.

"Since we're both forced to stay, I'll help as well," Sonya added.

"Do you have a medical specialty?" Fisher asked her.

"No, I'm a teacher, a graduate of the Teachers' Institute."

"Wonderful!" Fisher's voice boomed, his face lighting up with an infectious smile. "Then you'll help our principal, David Hershkovicz, who is setting up our school."

Fisher stuck his head out of his office door and called out, "Sven!"

The Norwegian official reappeared promptly. "This is Sven Carlson," Fisher told Szymon and Sonya. Then he turned to his aide, "Sven, would you set up living quarters for Miss Gruber and the doctor in the barracks across from the administration building."

As they were leaving, Fisher called after them, "Wait. We have a staff dinner tonight. Why don't the two of you come?"

They were assigned to a small room with two windows, two narrow cots, and a slender clothes closet at each end. A small table with two folding chairs stood in one corner.

"You have several hours to rest," Sven said as he turned to go. "At 6 P.M. a car will pick you up in front of the administration building to take you to Harold's home outside the camp for dinner."

*

Alone with Szymon at last, Sonya burst out, "I can't bear it that our freedom is halted yet again! How can they, the entire world, deny us our travel to Palestine? It isn't fair."

Szymon solemnly reminded her that they promised Mr. Fisher to help carry the burden, and complaining about it now was useless. Sonya bemoaned her frustration in having her dream shattered, the dream of getting out of Germany, of getting to Palestine.

Szymon sat down on the bed across from hers, clasped her hands, and, in a rare burst of emotion, quietly said, "Palestine may be the best place for us, but it's somewhere far away in the future. The fact is that we're here, stuck in Germany."

"It's still not fair," Sonya said, on the verge of tears.

"Sonya, Harold Fisher said that I'm God's gift to him. But right now, having found each other is God's gift to us. These past two days will loom as the most important days of our life. So let me help you and you help me through this wretched delay. At least we are together!"

He drew Sonya to him, holding her head as she came to rest on his shoulder. He kissed her forehead, stroked her hair, and whispered, "We've known each other only two days. To me these two days have been the gift of a lifetime."

She cupped his face in her hands, kissed him on his lips, and with a faint smile said, "Szymon, I love you dearly. These two days have given me a future. I had none until you came along."

He stood up and said briskly, "Right now the dinner party at Fisher's is in our immediate future and we'd better clean up."

Sonya rifled through her meager belongings for her threadbare robe so she could go to take a shower in one of the public washrooms. On her way out, she handed Szymon a fresh sheet from the stack of linens at the foot of her cot.

"Szymon," she said, "I do like my privacy. Would you find a way to hang this between our beds?"

After he hung the sheet across the room, he smiled and said to himself, "I like my privacy too. But what's wrong with being private together?"

At exactly six o'clock, Fisher's car pulled up at the barracks' entrance. The taciturn driver took them to Fisher's home, a few blocks away from the camp, where Fisher enthusiastically introduced them to the rest of his staff. Each of the six staff members echoed his excitement at having both a doctor and a teacher in their midst.

During dinner, Fisher sat next to Berson and quietly told him, "I looked through your records, and I see that you were in the Polish army. The Russians will undoubtedly be interested in returning you to stand trial for desertion."

Berson asked with alarm, "Can the Russians come into the camp?"

"Officially, no. But I can't guarantee that they won't try. I can't even guarantee that they haven't already slipped in one or two of their agents, posing as Displaced Persons to spy on the likes of you."

"You mean we're in danger?" Sonya asked.

"I seriously don't really know. Just be careful," Fisher said.

During his first three weeks at the camp, Berson worked closely with Dr. Joseph Rebak, the UNRRA physician, to organize a functioning hospital. With Fisher's permission, workmen were called in to break through several walls to extend the clinic. Even more important, Berson established close ties with the US Medical Corps and with the local German hospital. The Americans gave him supplies to equip the camp's expanded facility, and the Germans agreed to allow him to refer serious cases for treatment at their hospital.

Sonya, for her part, worked for the school, assisting the principal, David Hershkovicz, who was also a camp resident. Before the war, Hershkovicz had headed a large Jewish school in Pinsk and was now trying to establish schools for the two DP camps.

*

David Hershkovicz was in his forties when the Russians marched into Pinsk in the summer of 1939. The Russians occupied that part of Poland as provided by the Ribbentrop-Molotov prewar agreement. Hershkovicz, a teacher in the Tarbut School, soon found himself without a school because the newly established Communist regime closed it as it was based on Zionist and Hebrew culture. Despite the new Communist ordinance prohibiting Zionist instruction, Hershkovicz continued his leadership of the Zionist organization and also privately taught Hebrew and Bible studies. Appearing before the dreaded NKVD, he was found guilty of "fostering counter-revolutionary activities."

Fortunately, after his sentencing, Hershkovicz's wife prepared for what the regime called *chiska*, "cleansing" – ridding society of undesirable citizens, who were to be sent for "Resettlement" to Siberia, another term for slave labor. She packed clothing and food in a special suitcase, which David would carry onto the boxcar that was to carry them off to their exile.

Two days later, at midnight, David, his wife, and their two children were marched to the train station, where hundreds of other Jews were assembled to be exiled to Siberia as "bourgeoisie Zionists – enemies of the people." They were all "undesirables" – owners of private businesses, religious leaders, and Zionist activists, who could not be integrated into the new social order that Russia was to establish in Yanow. Many were weeping and crying, certain that they were being taken to their deaths in frigid Siberian labor camps.

Packed like sardines in the locked boxcars, they all faced untold tribulations during the twenty-nine-day passage without food, water, or ventilation. Soon hunger and thirst ravaged the group. Children and adults became ill, vomiting on the train. Hershkovicz collected bottles from other passengers, which he tied to long strings so that when the train would stop at a station the bottles could be lowered from the openings of the boxcar.

The locked-up passengers would beg for water from the passersby, offering money or clothing in exchange. Before reaching their unknown destination, several passengers died. Their corpses lay next to the living.

Their end destination was a tiny village where the group was let out to fend for themselves before the authorities could place them in labor camps. Somehow, David and his family, together with several others, were able to find an unoccupied hovel where at least they had roof to shelter them from the seasonal rains and storms. While in the village, he learned that, because of certain political considerations, Polish citizens residing in Russia were given a reprieve and would be given residence rights to live in the Soviet Union. David quickly returned to his family and negotiated with the trainmaster to allow the group to travel anywhere away from Siberia. When the next train arrived, they all boarded the cars, which, after weeks of travel, brought them to areas that David knew only from his geography classes: Kazakhstan, Uzbekistan, Kyrgyzstan – 130 kilometers from the Chinese border.

How some survived the next four years, suffering hunger and disease, and watching others die, was a miracle. But, for David, the suffering was bearable because the remnant of the original group was constantly heading southeast, closing in on Iran, getting nearer and nearer to Palestine.

When the war was over, none of the survivors of that group considered returning to Yanow. News of anti-Jewish rioting in Polish cities reached them as they crossed the border into Poland. Aimlessly, they wandered for months, until the Bricha found them and transported them to Berlin's Schlachtensee Displaced Persons camp.

*

Working with David Hershkovicz in the DP camp, Sonya helped register one thousand children. But while student registration was spectacularly successful, teacher enlistment went badly. So far, the faculty had only eleven teachers, hardly enough to begin, even for a few small classes.

"Why aren't teachers signing up?" Sonya asked David in frustration.

He explained that few teachers survived the Holocaust. Educated leaders, he said, were the first to be exterminated because they were not considered "able-bodied," fit for hard labor. Moreover, among the DPs in both camps, David explained, very few people were willing to be trained to teach. He asked her to consider teacher-training, which might help in their recruitment efforts.

"I've taken up this issue, teacher recruitment, with the chaplain," Hershkovicz said.

"What chaplain?"

"The Americans assigned a very energetic, young rabbi, Chaplain Michael Goldberg as liaison to the camp. He's helping us set up the schools. Actually, we have a meeting with him at the Chaplain's Center on Thursday night. You should come. The teachers we've enlisted so far will be there. A special bus will be picking all of us up from the central courtyard at eight. Bring Dr. Berson."

"I'll certainly be there," Sonya said. "As for Szymon, he is terribly busy, far too busy for a teachers' meeting, much less a discussion with some eager beaver American rabbi."

"Ordinarily, I wouldn't insist," Hershkovicz said, "but I strongly suggest that you urge Dr. Berson to join us. He'll experience something both of you will long remember."

During the next few days, Sonya forgot about the meeting with the rabbi, giving all her time to recruiting and training new teachers. Before the meeting with the chaplain, Sonya was able to double the number of teachers on the faculty. On Thursday evening, as she prepared for the meeting, Sonya asked Szymon to accompany her to the Chaplain's Center. His reaction was as she predicted. "We have so little time to be together," he said. "I can't see us wasting it in a rabbi's office."

*

Chaplain First Lieutenant Michael Goldberg was as American as apple pie. He was born in Hartford, Connecticut, where he was a reliable Little League pitcher and a pretty good student. As a boy, he delivered newspapers in the early mornings, before school started, pulling the heavy load in his faded red Flexible Flyer wagon. To augment his income, he collected discarded milk bottles and turned them in for the three-cent return deposit. His parents put his earnings to good use. They bought him a typewriter. During his high school and college years, he earned most of his income typing term papers for students and research reports for faculty members. He was a fun-loving, happy-go-lucky young man and his academics were good enough to merit scholarships that supported him until he graduated from college.

However, Michael had no idea what career to pursue until he put in a stint as a counselor at a children's summer camp. While training for his Red Cross Water Safety Instructor certificate to help counselors learn to be lifeguards, he became involved with several college students who had gotten in trouble with the police for joyriding while drinking beer. Somehow, they gravitated to him, looking to him for guidance. His success with them inspired him to consider the rabbinate as a career. As a rabbi, he figured, he could continue to help solve people's problems.

During his first year at rabbinical school, World War II broke out. As Hitler's tanks were gobbling up Europe and destroying Jewish communities, Michael found himself deeply affected by the reports of concentration camps. Immediately following his ordination, he volunteered to serve as a US Army chaplain and convinced his superiors to station him in Europe so that he could help the Jewish remnants, the survivors of the Holocaust.

Chaplain Goldberg, now in his mid-twenties and as wiry and intense as he had been as a teenager, was stationed in Berlin. He served both American and British Jewish military personnel. He was thrilled when the Army designated him as the liaison between the Jewish refugees and the United States Army. He visited the Displaced Persons camps as often as he was in his own Chaplain's Center. Additionally, when Yakov, Berlin's Bricha representative, approached him for covert help with their operations, the chaplain proved a worthy participant in their work.

*

Sonya had agreed to go to the teachers' meeting at the Chaplain's Center, only so that she could get to know the other teachers. When they arrived after a ten-minute bus ride from the camp, she saw Chaplain Goldberg standing at the door, welcoming the group. He greeted Sonya with a kiss and showed her to a seat on the sofa in the spacious living room. She noticed that he also greeted Mr. Fisher heartily and fondly.

"Harold," Sonya said, "I'm surprised that you're interested in an educational meeting."

He replied cryptically, "This is no ordinary meeting."

With that, Fisher left her and escorted the young chaplain around the room, introducing him to several of the newcomers. With more than twenty people packed into the room, it became unbearably hot and uncomfortable. Goldberg took off his military jacket and started the meeting by explaining that this was to be the second in a series of seminars aimed at giving the volunteers more teaching skills. They all laughed when he quipped that learning to be a teacher would help them get even with all those teachers they did not like while going to school as children.

"Misha, please describe how you were recruited to teach," he said to the seventeen-year-old, newly appointed math teacher.

"I met Chaplain Goldberg on our soccer field. In one of the plays, when I bumped into him and we both fell, he asked me how much was two plus two. I said, 'Four.' 'Fine,' he replied. 'You'll be our arithmetic teacher.' The chaplain played soccer on my team at the DP camp, so I couldn't say no to him," Misha said, laughing hysterically.

The assembled volunteers joined in the laughter because everyone knew that Misha was stating an experience shared by everyone who had dealt with the persuasive chaplain. When the laughter died down, the group listened intently as Misha shared a more serious concern.

"The problem is, I know how much two plus two is, but I have no idea how to handle classroom discipline problems," Misha confessed. "The kids have got me coming and going. That's what I'm here to learn."

As the newly elected president of the nascent Teachers Association, Hershkovicz introduced an elderly survivor who had been a school principal before the war. The old man lectured knowledgeably about maintaining class discipline, describing several methods teachers could use to enforce proper behavior. Sonya considered his presentation thought provoking, but not earthshaking. The question period, however, fascinated her because of the heated arguments between the teachers on how to implement the lecturer's pedagogic principles.

She added to the discussion, asking, "How can we run a school and maintain discipline in overcrowded classroom conditions? Without more teachers we won't be able to implement even one of the suggestions we have heard tonight."

"That's my surprise for the evening," Hershkovicz replied. "Our recruitment problems should be over soon, because now we can offer a meaningful incentive to all volunteer teachers."

He reached for a paper bag and emptied its contents: three packs of American cigarettes, one pound of coffee, and three chocolate bars. The group gasped at the sight of these lavish gifts. "People who volunteer to teach will receive these items every week."

Someone called out, "With that you can buy whatever you want anywhere in Berlin."

"Be careful!" Harold Fisher exhorted, quickly rising to his feet. "That's anywhere except in the Russian sector. Remember, stay away from the Russian sector. We cannot help you there."

Hershkovicz rose to thank Chaplain Goldberg for providing the precious gift items, and announced that Sonya would set up a teacher-training program for both camps.

In the midst of the heated and excited discussion, the chaplain scampered up the makeshift dais and, calling a halt to the speeches, proceeded to lead the group in singing Zionist and Yiddish songs. Soon, laughter and rejoicing filled the room. Even Harold Fisher got into the act, singing the one Yiddish song he remembered from his childhood. The rhythmic clapping and the spontaneous hora dancing rumbled like thunder across the room throughout the evening.

Swept up in the emotional charge that surged through her whole being as she joined in the singing and dancing, Sonya whispered to Harold, "I'm so sorry Szymon didn't come. He'd love being here."

Harold grinned, "I sent my car to get him."

As they were talking, Berson entered the crowded room, snaking his way through the dancing crowd to hug and kiss Sonya. He stepped in beside her in the whirling, dancing circle as onlookers clapped and sang.

Shouting above the din, Szymon asked Sonya, "Where's the rabbi?"

"Right there, flying through the air," she laughed, pointing to Michael Goldberg, just as Yakov, the Bricha leader, hoisted the chaplain onto his shoulders. They danced about the room like whirling dervishes, with everyone following and dancing in a hora-beat conga line.

"That's a rabbi?" Berson shouted. "Where's his beard, his *kapote*, his sideburns?"

Berson joined the revelry and merrymaking, which continued way past midnight. When there was a break in the dancing, Fisher introduced Dr. Berson to the chaplain and the three slipped away from the party and conferred for a long time in Goldberg's office, adjacent to the living room. They returned to the party when the teachers were mingling around a long table with trays of food. Dr. Berson and the chaplain also filled their plates and joined Sonya.

She smiled at them and asked, "Do you know what time it is?"

"Who cares," Szymon replied. "I'm only sorry I didn't come earlier."

"You also missed Hershkovicz's announcement about the special gift packages we can give as incentives to teachers."

"I know about the packages," he replied. "When Harold introduced me to the chaplain, that's all we talked about – the gift packages. I'm meeting the chaplain tomorrow."

"What for?"

"For some gift packages for me," Szymon replied.

"Are you going to teach?" Sonya asked.

"No," Szymon replied, hugging her. "You'll see."

When the group finally left the Chaplain's Center at two o'clock in the morning, the chaplain found Yakov waiting in his office.

"Michael," Yakov said, pulling a piece of paper out of his pocket, "here's what we'll need for the next transports."

Chaplain Goldberg scanned the list and let out a low whistle. "Two cartons of cigarettes for each person we take through their border! Twelve watches for each vehicle! The Russians are getting pretty expensive and I've got a legal problem with this requisition."

He explained that the military had been impounding his packages, containing the cigarettes, coffee, and chocolates he had been receiving from hundreds of friends from the United States. The CID, the Criminal Investigation Division, suspected him of dealing on the black market.

"They're giving me the choice of sending the packages back to the donors or facing a criminal investigation."

"Are you in trouble with your superiors?" Yakov interrupted. "Because if you are, we'd rather close up the Stettin operation."

"Nope. Things haven't reached that stage yet."

However, at 7:30 the next morning, an army captain arrived to see the chaplain.

"I'm Captain Sean Murphy from the APO, the Army Post Office. I've been ordered to investigate you on possible postal fraud charges."

Chaplain Goldberg smiled, extended his palms, and said, "You caught me. I confess. Here, put the handcuffs on me."

"No, seriously, Chaplain, we've never had a problem like this before," Captain Murphy said. "Do you realize that all those cartons addressed to you are taking up almost the entire space reserved for military parcel post?"

"So release my packages to me and you'll free up that space," Chaplain Goldberg said, still smiling.

"You don't understand, Chaplain. You're under suspicion for black marketeering. Usually this would be up to the CID. But the brass want to stop you without creating a public outcry in the DP camps, so they thought they'd charge you with mail fraud instead. Here is the charge," the captain said, reading from an official charge sheet, "'Using the APO for personal profit.' I'm supposed to investigate you and recommend action to be taken. Our men have been secretly following you around Berlin for about two weeks, but they can't quite keep up with you. You've been seen in the French sector, the British, even the Russian sector. You'll admit that raises suspicions."

"Okay, let's make a deal," Chaplain Goldberg said. "We'll do it together. Everywhere I go, you go. You'll see how I dispose of these black market goods."

"Don't make jokes, Chaplain," Captain Murphy said. "This is more serious than you think."

"Deal or not?" Chaplain Goldberg asked, disregarding the warning.

Hesitantly, the captain extended his hand. "When do we start?"

"Right now," Goldberg said, leading the captain to his jeep.

He let the captain sit in the passenger seat. Carrying a large duffle bag, Chaplain Goldberg jumped into the rear of the open jeep and told his driver, "Schlachtensee DP camp."

Much to Dr. Berson's surprise, Chaplain Goldberg showed up in his clinic at the DP camp's newly expanded hospital at about 8:30 A.M. The chaplain introduced Dr. Berson to Captain Murphy as the camp's doctor.

"I've just finished the rounds," he said to the captain, then, turning to the chaplain, Dr. Berson added, "We didn't leave you until 2 A.M. When did you sleep?"

"I got a bad case of insomnia. If you can cure me of that, doctor, you can name your price."

"Ever try praying?" Berson asked jokingly.

"Yup, it only woke me up," the chaplain quipped. "Why are you up so early? Maybe you pray too much?"

"Nope, it's my patients. They don't let me sleep," Berson said.

The doctor showed them around the hospital – a converted barracks in the middle of the huge, sprawling DP camp. He proudly pointed out many of the changes he had made, converting a ramshackle facility into a well-ordered clinic.

In one ward, Dr. Berson introduced them to a young woman who had given birth three weeks earlier. The doctor whispered that she was slowly dying because they could not stop her internal bleeding. The doctor explained that only one drug, cryoprecipitate, could save her, but it was unavailable either through UNRRA or other military sources.

"Can you get the cryo-whatsit anywhere?" Chaplain Goldberg asked.

Berson hesitated, glanced at Captain Murphy, and replied, "Chaplain, you know there's nothing you can't get in Berlin."

"How much?" the chaplain asked.

"Six cartons, maybe seven."

"Wow! Seven cartons to save her life," Chaplain Goldberg mockingly said and, turning to the captain, he asked, "Can we afford eight bucks to help this woman?"

When the captain nodded, Chaplain Goldberg opened his duffle bag and took out the necessary cartons of cigarettes, plus some tins of coffee and boxes of Hershey bars.

"Thank you, Chaplain. I can meet a lot of the hospital's needs with such valuable means of exchange."

"Now we're off to see the Russians," Chaplain Goldberg said to Captain Murphy as the jeep sped through the heart of the city. They arrived in Spandau, in the British sector. The chaplain led Murphy into the Kazimir restaurant, which was crowded with Russian, British, French, and American personnel. The two men sat at a table near the door and ordered coffee and slices of dark pumpernickel bread with butter. Soon they were joined by a young man wearing a leather coat and a black felt fedora.

"Avi, meet my friend, Captain Murphy," the chaplain said. "You called to tell me we're having trouble with our brothers. What's up?"

Avi uttered a few unintelligible phrases and walked away to wait at the door.

"What was that all about?" Murphy asked. "And, who's Avi?"

"First, Avi was speaking Hebrew. He travels often from Stettin to Berlin to transport the Jewish survivors. He told me that four families with a total of six children are stuck in Poland, waiting to be transported to the American sector in Berlin. The trucks were paid for in advance, but the border guards want an extra payment of two cartons per transported person – that makes twenty-eight cartons of cigarettes to get fourteen people out of Poland."

"Who are they? Why do they need to come here?" Murphy asked.

"Probably concentration camp survivors, or survivors of the Partizan groups in the forests, or from Siberia. They've all been through terrible trauma and want to start over as free people. They can start a new life only by going through the US zone."

"Why?"

"That's the only place we can process them for travel to Palestine."

"Is it legal?" Murphy asked, overwhelmed.

"Is it legal to disregard their plight?" the chaplain asked. "The war's over, but they're homeless refugees still in flight, still in life-threatening danger."

"You know, I've been in the Army a long time and I never realized what's really going on with the survivors."

Chaplain Goldberg lit a cigarette and slowly blew the smoke away. "Tell me, Captain," he said, "is the freedom of these people worth twenty-eight cartons of cigarettes?"

"Don't ask," Murphy said, getting up from the table. "I'll leave you two alone to take care of business."

The chaplain then walked over to the door and whispered to Avi, who quickly disappeared amid the crowd on the urban streets of Spandau, where he helped himself to the cartons of cigarettes from the chaplain's jeep.

As the captain and the chaplain were about to leave, a Russian officer approached Goldberg. Murphy watched their animated conversation. Within minutes, the Russian officer shook the chaplain's hand and hastened away.

"What was that all about?" Captain Murphy asked.

"He's a *polkovnik*, a colonel, and he's my broker."

"You're kidding, Chaplain," Murphy said. "Your broker?"

"Yes, Sir. I buy human cargo from him and he gets me a good price per head."

"You mean, the two cartons of cigarettes per head that your guy asked for?"

"Yes and no. He wanted three cartons and I had to haggle. This time I won. But he gave me bad news."

"What's the bad news?" the captain asked.

The chaplain did not reply. Instead, he looked at his watch. "We're running late and we have one more stop."

Sunset was near when Goldberg and Murphy got to the *kinderheim*, the Jewish orphanage in the French sector. More than one hundred children were gathered in the gym of a local school for a special birthday party. They sat at long tables filled with food, including the traditional birthday cakes.

When Chaplain Goldberg came in, the kindergarten director, Frau Anna-Carolina Hammerschlag, was speaking to the children. She interrupted her lesson, saying, "Today, we all want to thank the US Army for the new clothes you are wearing and the presents you've received," she said.

Then, turning to Goldberg, she announced to the children, "This is Chaplain Goldberg, who brought you these gifts from your American army friends."

The chaplain waved, said hello in German (thus using up almost his entire German vocabulary) and then, in English, exhorted, "Boys and girls, let's sing." Soon he had them singing English and Hebrew songs, complete with hand gestures and clapping.

On the drive back, the chaplain explained, "All those gifts – the clothes for the kids, the special treats, the birthday presents and cakes – I traded for them, using the contents of all the packages I've gotten from my friends and from various organizations back home. Anna-Carolina lets me know what the children need and I try to find it on the German market."

"Chaplain, do you realize, what I saw today is very much in the spirit of the Eisenhower Directive, giving Holocaust survivors priority in feeding, housing, and resettlement. And the American Post Office is directly abetting in the distribution of all the items I witnessed today…much to its merit."

It had been a tiring day for both of them. They sat silently through the long drive to Berlin Command HQ. When they reached his office, Captain Murphy said, "Now, come have dinner with me at Harnack House. You might have a chance to meet with some military brass who're always hanging around the posh hotel. In the meantime, I'll firm up a decision on your impounded packages."

As they sat down to dinner in the officers' mess at tables set with china and white tablecloths, Murphy said, "As you might have guessed, Chaplain, I'm impressed with what I saw today. I'm going to recommend clearing your packages."

The chaplain feigned a sigh of relief. "What, no handcuffs?"

Sipping his coffee slowly, Murphy explained, "When I originally got the order to look into this problem involving packages to the Chaplain's Center, I discussed the whole deal with my brother in Frankfurt; he's a major in G-2. I can't wait to tell him what I've seen today."

"Don't forget to tell him about my meeting with the Russian colonel," the chaplain said jokingly.

"About your meeting with the Russian, you said you had bad news. Can you tell me?"

"He warned me that the KGB is asking the US military to hand over one of our DPs, a man they claim is a deserter from the Polish army."

"Chaplain, you can trust me. Who's the deserter?"

"Tell your brother it's our doctor, Szymon Berson. You met him this morning in the Schlachtensee camp."

"I'll take it up with my brother," the captain said, lifting a glass of wine. "Now, let's toast your mission. You're doing a fine job."

The Chaplain's Center primarily served American Jewish military personnel, but its religious services also attracted Jewish worshipers from among the British troops in Berlin and even a few Jewish members of nearby Russian units. One Russian visitor, a soldier the chaplain knew only as Yoina, said he came to the center to study in the library. Once, while Yoina was there, Harold Fisher called the chaplain, quite agitated. "Chaplain, I'm on my way over. We have a big problem – one of our residents, Mottel Blosztein, has been arrested by the Russian police."

"Don't come. I have to be at the camp soon anyway. I'll come straight to your office."

The chaplain quickly left Yoina to join Fisher and Berson in the DP camp. Goldberg found them both quite upset.

"I came to you instead of having you come to me, because I worry that this Yoina, the Russian who uses my library, might be a security problem."

"You acted wisely," Fisher said. "We've lost another DP and my people tell me that the Russians have him."

"Who?" the chaplain asked.

"Blosztein is a Russian Jew who managed to escape from Russia and enter the camp as a Displaced Person. This morning, he was with friends on the U-Bahn when Russian soldiers grabbed him and carried him off the train."

Before the chaplain could say anything, Dr. Berson said, "There is only one way the Russians could know that Mottel was in the camp. They have spies here."

Fisher shrugged, "Doctor, we admit thousands of people. I have no way of recognizing a Russian spy. That's why I fear for you and Sonya."

"We're anxious too," Berson admitted. "We've asked Fisher to put us on the next hospital train out of Berlin."

Goldberg nodded, "To tell you the truth, Szymon, the Russians are already demanding to hand you over as a deserter from the Polish army. I don't want to frighten you. I can tell you the US won't oblige the Russians, since the cold war is getting hotter. But if you are ever on that hospital train, even as the accompanying doctor, the Russians can whisk you off when the train passes through the Russian zone."

Fisher concurred, "You're safest here. Don't leave the American sector. And don't let Sonya go out either. Just call me or the chaplain if you need something from the city."

A crisis occurred a few evenings later when Sonya and Szymon visited the chaplain. As they were about to leave the Chaplain's Center after a pleasant dinner, the chaplain noticed a black Mercedes pulling up in the driveway. Yoina was getting out of the car followed by two burly Russian soldiers. Immediately realizing the danger, the chaplain said, "Szymon, Sonya, go upstairs and wait in one of the bedrooms."

When Yoina stalked in, trailed by his Russian guards, the chaplain smiled, "Why Yoina, what brings you here tonight? The library won't be open until tomorrow morning."

"I am here on business," Yoina said in Polish. "I have a request from the Polish ambassador to deliver Szymon Berson to us to stand trial as a deserter."

Yoina began to repeat his orders in English, but the chaplain interrupted, "Yoina, you have been a guest in my home for more than a year. You know this building is a US Army installation. From your first day here, you made me suspicious about you, so suspicious that I have taken precautions in case you ever struck against us here."

"We take Berson and you need no precautions," the Russian grunted.

Chaplain Goldberg put his hand on the telephone. "Yoina, when I dial one digit, within two minutes, an MP vehicle will pull up to escort you back to the Russian sector. I remind you this Center is a US installation. Leave quietly now and avoid embarrassment for you and your group."

Yoina got up, glanced at the telephone, and immediately led his guards back to the car.

Driving back to the camp an hour or so later, Goldberg told Berson, "You have Captain Murphy to thank for this reprieve. The CIC warned me about Yoina and they decided that whenever he came to the Chaplain's Center, the Army would park a truck across the avenue."

"So our only safety is to be locked up in the immediate environs of the camp," Sonya said.

"You have no other choice," the chaplain replied.

* *

Every Thursday night, Szymon and Sonya attended the teachers' seminars at the Chaplain's Center and quite often stayed afterward. The chaplain visited them in the DP camp almost daily, and the relationship among the three steadily grew closer. On one such visit, Chaplain Goldberg pointed to the curtain separating their beds, and said, "Someday, I hope that sheet can come down."

"Chaplain!" Sonya chided the rabbi. "No morals!"

"When one is married, one does not need a separation."

Neither said a word, and the chaplain rapidly changed the subject.

Although they were deeply in love, Szymon and Sonya had not considered marriage. Their eighteen months under the dismal living conditions in the camp had taken its toll. They saw no end to life in the cramped barracks behind barbed-wire fencing. Despite their gratifying work in the hospital and in the school, their spirits were dampened. Over time, they became infected with the utter despair, the despondency that pervaded the entire camp.

Although the weekly teachers' sessions in the Chaplain's Center continued, gloom set in there as well. The packages from the chaplain were still much appreciated, but the participants had lost their initial excitement. To try to boost their spirits, Fisher invited the international UNRRA director, then on an inspection tour of Berlin's DP camps, to listen to their concerns.

"Sure there is a serious malaise in the camp," Sonya told the guest. "It's October, 1947. We were liberated in the spring of 1945. We came to Berlin a year and a half ago, but we are still living behind a fence, still lining up for food rations. We are still Displaced Persons. When we were liberated from the Nazis, we were certain we would be free. But we are not."

"I can commiserate," the UNRRA official said, "but I wish I could offer more encouragement. I can't do much, but I can increase the sports and educational facilities you have to work with, if that will boost morale and help you with the students."

Fisher introduced the chaplain to the visiting official as the camp's "bit of sunshine," and Goldberg proved he deserved the title by passing along to the group the latest news.

"There's a vote coming up next month in the General Assembly of the UN on the Partition Plan to create a Jewish state and an Arab state in Palestine," he told the assembled teachers. "I think it's going to pass. If so, the floodgates will open for the immigration of all Jewish Displaced Persons."

"We'll plan something big for all our schoolchildren," Sonya said.

After the meeting, Goldberg called Sonya and Szymon aside. "I didn't mean to put my foot in my mouth the other night when I joked about the curtain," he said apologetically, "but what are your marriage plans? I'd be glad to give you a grand ceremony here."

"Thanks anyway, Chaplain, for all your kindness," Sonya said, "but no. It would still be like getting married in jail. We want to wait until we can have a normal wedding."

*

A few days later, Sonya called and asked the chaplain if they could come to his office right away to discuss an urgent personal problem. Certain they had nevertheless decided to discuss marriage plans, Goldberg was utterly surprised when Tevye entered the Chaplain's Center with the couple.

"Well, hello, Tevye, I mean Yosef," the chaplain said, hugging him. "Are you still in Warsaw? I thought they'd given you your certificate to Palestine by now."

"They did and I'm on my way," he said, "but Sonya should be also. She got her certificate. She's supposed to leave at the end of September."

"So what's the problem?" Goldberg asked.

"I will not leave without Szymon," Sonya said with finality.

"If she doesn't use the certificate and emigrate to Palestine, she'll lose her priority status. She'll have to wait God knows how long for another opportunity. Help me, Chaplain," Tevye pleaded, "I'm trying to convince her to leave Szymon for a while. We'll do everything we can to get him to Palestine as fast as possible."

"Tevye, you want me to decide for Sonya?" Chaplain Goldberg asked. "You know her better than that!"

"Just talk some sense into her."

"Szymon, what do you have to say?" the chaplain asked.

"I'm in contact with the medical director of the Stone-Winthrop Hospital. He's trying to get me a non-quota visa to the US, as a medical expert," Berson said.

"Since Szymon can't come with me to Palestine," Sonya added, "I have to pass up the certificate. I don't want to leave without him."

"Tevye, you and I have little to say here. We can't interfere in such a personal matter," Goldberg said.

Tevye threw his hands in the air, shaking his head, and repeating over and over, "How can anyone give up a certificate – a chance to get out of here, to go to Palestine?"

"My dear Tevye," the chaplain said, "Szymon and Sonya know what they're doing. We can't interfere in their private lives."

So saying, he brought a bottle of wine out of his cabinet and poured each of them a glass.

"*Lechayim*, Tevye, a safe trip!" Goldberg raised his glass, and the evening became a farewell party as they toasted Tevye.

"Thank you, thank you all," he said. "I have to go this minute, to be on time for my transport."

He gave Sonya a parting look. "Ah, Sonya, someday we'll meet in Palestine!" he declared, shutting the door behind him.

With Tevye gone, the chaplain said, "I must confess to you that when you called asking to come by, I was certain that it was about your wedding plans."

"We've decided to do it here," Szymon said, surprising the chaplain.

"What changed your minds?"

"Love breaks the chains of servitude," Sonya quoted from a Hebrew poem.

"True, true," Goldberg replied. "Set the date and I'll be there."

"Sunday, November 23, 1947," Szymon replied.

*

Harold Fisher suggested that the wedding should be a festive affair, a morale booster for the entire camp. He decided, with their approval, to hold it in the central courtyard with thousands of residents present. Plans proceeded quickly. The chaplain and camp rabbi would officiate at the religious ceremony and all the DPs would then share a generous open buffet. The teachers and scores of Dr. Berson's former patients volunteered to help set up the tables and serve the guests. The UNRRA staff would attend, along with many military officers of the US Medical Corps.

One guest was invited at the very last minute because he arrived in Berlin a day before the wedding. He was the US representative Joseph Stanton from the sixteenth District of New York City. He was a fixture in Congress, where he had served almost fifteen terms and was now chairman of the powerful House Armed Services Committee. On his present mission to Berlin, he was part of a congressional committee touring Germany and Austria, investigating the living conditions of the American men and women in the Army of Occupation.

The day he arrived in Berlin, he went to stay at the posh Harnack House. At the time, Chaplain Goldberg was in the Harnack House meeting with Colonel McDuffy, commanding officer of Berlin Command. The colonel rose to greet the congressman and then introduced Goldberg as the Jewish military chaplain for Berlin Command.

"I represent lots of Jews in my district," Stanton said, pumping the chaplain's hand. "What do you have going on here that would be of interest to them?"

"The biggest Jewish wedding you've ever seen in your life," the chaplain responded.

"Count me in, Chaplain. I love that Jewish gefilte fish and chopped liver."

That was how Congressman Stanton, chairman of the House Armed Services Committee, came to attend the wedding of Sonya and Szymon Berson.

The congressman not only got his fill of gefilte fish, but he took a starring role in the ceremony, joining Fisher in leading the groom down the aisle. At the wedding feast, he sat next to the bride and groom, amid the large contingent of military brass who tagged along with him. He danced the hora with the bride and above all, beamed when Chaplain Goldberg introduced him as "the most famous statesman in Washington, next to President Roosevelt, of blessed memory."

Congressman Stanton relished the sustained applause that greeted him and the instant adoration he received from the camp's residents. He stayed with the partying mob, singing and dancing past midnight, when the wedding celebration finally ended. As they were walking to the car, Dr. Berson asked Representative Stanton, "Do you happen to know Dr. Samuel Neufeld?"

"Chief cardiologist at Stone-Winthrop? Do I know Doc Neufeld!" Mr. Stanton replied. "Sammy and I are bosom buddies. He visits me in Washington all the time. I set him up with the big politicos he needs to see for research funding."

"Mr. Stanton," Dr. Berson began, "before the war, I worked under Dr. Neufeld. I wrote to him more than a year ago, when I first came to this camp, about the possibility of coming to Stone-Winthrop Institute to continue my work there."

"What did he say?"

"He promised me a position in the hospital if I could get a visa to the United States."

"Simon – that's your name, isn't it?" Mr. Stanton said. "Here, write down your name on this pad and you can bet your bottom dollar that if Sammy wants you, you'll get your visa. I'll personally see to it!"

Berson wrote his name and handed the pad back.

"Sonya and Simon Berson," the congressman read the doctor's scribbled handwriting. "I like the sound of it, 'Sonya and Simon.' I won't forget you. You'll hear from me as soon as I get home."

*

Six days after the wedding, on November 29, 1947, thousands of camp residents listened avidly to Armed Forces Network radio, which was broadcast over the camp's public address system. Volunteers brought the hospital's ambulatory patients out to the central courtyard, some in wheelchairs, to listen to the program. It was broadcasting the United Nations vote on the partition of Palestine, which would create an Arab and a Jewish state and would end the British mandate of Palestine. To prepare for the historic event, Sonya had the schoolchildren produce huge placards, artistically printing the exact words of the resolution. Children were assigned to carry them through the crowd. They read:

> The British Mandate for Palestine shall terminate…INDEPENDENT ARAB AND JEWISH STATES SHALL COME INTO EXISTENCE…NO LATER THAN OCTOBER 1, 1948.

When the voting was underway, each time they heard a "yes" vote over the public address system, three thousand people cheered. Many counted the "yes" and "no" votes aloud. When the United Nations chairman announced, "The resolution on the Partition of Palestine passes by a majority vote of thirty-three to thirteen, ten abstentions," the entire camp erupted in wild cheering and hysterical shouting. The celebration in the camp lasted through the night, as people sensed the end of their long imprisonment.

*

Szymon and Sonya now had to face the practical choice between legal *aliyah* to Palestine or waiting for the US visa that Mr. Stanton had promised. Every evening when they came back to their small room, now without the divider, they argued heatedly over this issue.

"Please understand me," Szymon said. "I am not against Palestine. But my priority is medicine. When I go to Palestine, I want to arrive there as a medical expert, which I can become only after studying in the United States."

"But there is no guarantee that immigration to the United States will ever be a reality," Sonya said. "You haven't heard from Congressman Stanton, have you?"

"But, suppose that tomorrow we are informed that my visa is approved?"

"Szymon, I will make you a promise," Sonya said solemnly. "If, at any time, you receive a visa that would enable you to intern at Stone-Winthrop, I will come with you to the United States, but you have to make me a promise also."

"And I know what it is," he answered. "I promise you that when I complete my studies at Stone-Winthrop, I will come back to Palestine with you."

And so they waited.

For the first month after Stanton's visit, Berson checked the incoming mail at Fisher's office daily. Fisher's answer was always the same.

"Nothing, I'm sorry."

"Why fool yourself, Szymon?" Sonya said one day. "You can't get to the United States. Palestine is your only option."

The moment of truth came in the late summer of 1948 when the Bricha's unit director, Yakov, announced that both Sonya and Szymon were to receive certificates for legal immigration to Palestine.

Sonya reminded Szymon of her promise. "I will keep my promise. If your US visa comes through, we will leave Palestine and go to the US so you can study."

A few days later, Yakov brought them their tickets and told them to prepare to leave for the port of Bremen to board their ship. The following day, they went with thirty or so other DPs to Fisher's office to await the bus that would transfer them to Berlin's train station.

Much to their shock, Fisher stepped out of his office and addressed the entire group, sorrow written all over his face, his smile erased.

"The train to Bremen has been canceled. In fact, all trains have been canceled. The Russians set up a blockade around Berlin, prohibiting any vehicle, rail or motor, from leaving or coming into the city."

To avoid panic, Fisher called a public emergency meeting of all residents in the central courtyard. Within minutes, thousands showed up in the courtyard, wondering what the emergency was. Fisher stood on a platform, his voice booming over the public loudspeakers, announcing the Russian blockade of Berlin. He told them that as a result of the sudden blockade, all American military personnel were ordered to wear helmets and sidearms.

"But remember, all of us, military personnel and civilians, are under the protection of the US Army. We are all subject to the blockade the Russians have imposed on Berlin. But I assure you that except for a halt in travel to the Zone, this will have no effect on the safety of the residents of this camp. We are safe because the United States is undertaking a massive airlift to transport the lifesaving supplies into Berlin, to its military and to us."

Harold Fisher turned to Chaplain Goldberg, who introduced Colonel McDuffy, commanding officer of the US Army's Berlin Command, who further assured the huge assemblage that the military force of the United

States would protect them from any incursion by the Russians. Then the colonel added an expression they had never heard before. "In this standoff between us and the Russians, you are really the heroes in the present cold war. By keeping you, the survivors, the Displaced Persons, here in Berlin, we are showing the Russians our determination to stay in the city. Your suffering here is as important as the presence of our troops who are stationed here. You are our heroes."

As the group was disbanding, Chaplain Goldberg privately told the commander, "Thank you for your remarks, Sir. You not only gave them a sense of security, but you lifted their spirits by acknowledging them as allies of the United States."

Watching the colonel drive off in his sedan, the chaplain heard an announcement calling him to the administration office to take a phone call. "Chaplain," his secretary said with excitement, "a letter has just come from Representative Stanton in Washington."

"I'll be right there."

Goldberg jumped into his jeep and took Szymon, Sonya, and Fisher with him to the Chaplain's Center.

"This just came for you," the chaplain's secretary said, handing Dr. Berson an envelope bearing the insignia of the US Congress.

"I told you Stanton wouldn't forget you," Fisher said. "This letter might even help you get through the Russian blockade via the airlift."

Berson slit open the envelope and handed it to Sonya to read aloud.

Dear Simon,

I have taken up the matter of your immigration with the State Department and have been informed by the secretary of state that at this time there are no non-quota visas available for any Displaced Persons.

However, I have been personally assured by him that as soon as the US Displaced Persons Bill that is now pending in Congress becomes operative, you will receive priority consideration for your immigration to the United States.

I have also received official confirmation from my friend Sammy Neufeld of your appointment in the Stone-Winthrop Institute.

Rest assured that I will do everything to expedite your emigration to the good old USA.

My best wishes to Sonya.

Sincerely yours,
Joe

Berson crumpled the letter, threw it into the trash can, and angrily mumbled, "I have a good friend in Washington. He signed it 'Joe'."

*

America's response to Russia's blockade of Berlin, the massive airlift, was a blessing for Berlin's residents but psychologically disastrous for the Displaced Persons. The constant roaring of the US Air Force planes flying in and out of Berlin only reminded everyone that the blockade also blocked their resettlement. More than before, because of that constant reminder, they began to feel like prisoners, counting the days of their incarceration in the bleak DP camp. Despite the residents' high regard for them, neither Harold Fisher nor the chaplain could dispel the despair.

Three months later, Dr. Berson, busy in the hospital, was summoned to come urgently to the director's office. "Szymon, the camp is to be evacuated by the US Army," Fisher said, showing him an urgent telex from the military. "You have to prepare your patients for immediate transfer to hospitals in the American zone. We're all going to Frankfurt."

Dr. Berson worked feverishly to close the hospital. He had to contact hospitals in the zone to reserve beds, update patients' charts, and prepare sick patients for air transport.

The US Air Force carried out the evacuation of the Berlin DP camp without a hitch. Sonya and Szymon, assigned to the Zeilsheim camp near Frankfurt, were among the last to leave. When they went to Fisher's office to say their good-byes, Harold was not there. The chaplain told them that he was already at the airport, attending to the residents' needs.

As the chaplain drove them to Tempelhof Airport, he explained, "I called Stanton's office and alerted him of your reassignment to the Zeilsheim camp near Frankfurt. I want him to be able to find you when that visa clears."

At the airport, they got out of the jeep and Goldberg disappeared to find a parking spot. Fisher found Sonya and Szymon waiting patiently in line to board their flight amidst the hubbub of people pushing to get on planes.

"There you are," Fisher called out, embracing them. "I want to wish you a safe trip."

Then, pausing as though to catch his breath, he said, "In my work with the Displaced Persons, I've become involved in the lives of thousands of people. But I've never met a couple as lovely as you." His eyes moistened and, to hide his embarrassment, he abruptly turned and left them at the gate. "Sorry, must run," he mumbled over his shoulder, "I have loads of paperwork waiting back at the camp."

They boarded soon after he left and as they took their places in the plane's bucket seats, Sonya said sadly, "I'm sorry we didn't get to tell the chaplain good-bye." But as the crew was about to close the plane's doors, Chaplain Goldberg appeared in front of them and took a seat next to them.

"Hello," he smiled, "you're not rid of me yet!"

"Good," said Sonya. "I wanted one last chance to talk to you. I hope you realize what you have meant to us these past two years. Yes, we suffered a lot, but, as Harold said, you were always there, our bit of sunshine during those dark days."

Berson added, clasping the chaplain's hands, "I can't tell you how badly we felt when we couldn't say our proper good-byes to you and thank you for all you've done for us and for the camp."

"I'm just grateful to get you both out of Berlin," Goldberg said. "Frankfurt is only an hour away, but it makes a vast difference. Ever since you came to Berlin, I've only wanted to help you leave."

"Wherever we go, the US or Palestine, we'll never forget you," said Sonya.

"I have no idea where I will be when I return to the States," the chaplain said, giving his business card to Berson, "but if you get there, call the number on the back of the card. It's my parents' home. They'll know where you can find me."

"Here, let me have it," Sonya said. "I'll put it in my album where I keep all my memories of Berlin, from the worst to the best."

He told them he had also called Israel's office in Frankfurt, informing them that Dr. and Mrs. Berson would be at the Zeilsheim camp so that they could reissue their certificates to Palestine. When the plane landed and as they were about to disembark, Goldberg kissed them. He remained in his seat.

Szymon asked, "Well, what about you? Aren't you coming?"

"The plane is turning around. I'm going back to Berlin for now."

"You mean you only came along for the ride?" Dr. Berson asked.

"No, I came along only to be with you. Now you're on your way to a new life and I'm glad that I could be with you as you start on the first leg of your journey."

*

When Szymon and Sonya deplaned in Frankfurt, they were met by a representative of the Jewish Agency, asking them to follow him to the El Al desk. The stranger, who introduced himself as Benni Arad, informed them that their immigration to Palestine was approved at an emergency meeting of the Aliyah Commission. Mr. Arad also informed them that he had reserved seats for them on the next flight to Tel Aviv.

Sonya was ecstatic. At that moment, however, they heard their names being called. A voice on the public address system was summoning them to the information desk.

"Hello, hello! You must be the Bersons!" a short, bronzed-faced man shouted amid the din, welcoming them when they approached the information desk. He introduced himself as the director of the DP camp at Zeilsheim, near Frankfurt, explaining that Harold Fisher had phoned and alerted him of their arrival.

"I had set up fairly good quarters for you at the camp, but about an hour ago, I received different instructions from our HQ in Geneva. I'm to hand you over to the American consulate here in Frankfurt. Your immigration to the United States has been approved."

As he led them to his car, Sonya, walking unsteadily, whispered, "Are we doing the right thing, Szymon, going to America…when Palestine is open to us?"

Berson patted her arm. "Let's wait and see. Our departure for the US may still be months away."

Sitting in the anteroom at the US consular office, amid hundreds of other people who were waiting to be called, Sonya could not contain her anxiety.

"Szymon," she said resolutely, "we have lived among the *goyim* all our lives and what did it get us – a Hitler! It's time to be free of them."

He sighed. "I know, Sonya. I know your passion for Zionism and it makes a lot of sense – and I share it. The only long-term solution to Jewish homelessness is our homeland. But let me arrive there as a useful man, as an expert in my field. Going now to Palestine, when an opportunity to continue my studies in the United States is literally knocking on our door, is simply not an option."

Sonya did not reply. She wiped a tear from her cheek and squeezed his hand.

"My problem is not Zionism," he whispered. "My problem is medicine. I've been away from current practice for almost eight years. Do you know what these eight years mean? A whole new world of antibiotics, new surgical methods, new technologies – it has all passed me by. At last I have a chance to catch up at Stone-Winthrop. I can't deny myself that chance. Above all, remember my promise. We will go to Palestine after my course of studies."

"Fine," said Sonya. "It's America – but only temporarily."

After they filled out their immigration forms, the DP camp director ushered them into the consul general's office where the vice consul greeted them warmly and handed them a telex. "It's from the visa Section in Washington," he said. "I've been ordered to expedite your immigration to the States. I don't know how you know Congressman Stanton, but he's gone all out to get you stateside."

He led them into a special nook in the office, offered them some refreshments, and went to his desk. Moments later, he joined them and said, "Your visa will be ready this evening. You leave on the next transport, at midnight."

Chapter 12

THREE YEARS EARLIER, in December of 1945, Stasha, Franya, and their daughter, Jadzia, had arrived in the United States. They had presented their special INS visas that abruptly renamed them Stamford, Francine, and Jodi Wycliff.

A State Department messenger who met them at New York's Idlewild Airport drove them from the airport to Grand Central Station. He presented Stasha with an envelope containing three hundred dollars, train tickets to Miami, and a copy of Stamford's employment contract with a farmer named Joe Platek. Twenty-four hours later, their train pulled into the Flagler Street railroad station in Miami.

Platek greeted them in Polish and threw their luggage into the back of his big pickup truck. He drove them to Homestead, a rural suburb half an hour south of Miami. He pulled up in front of an apartment building and unlocked the door of a small, sparsely furnished, two-bedroom apartment overlooking fields of winter vegetables.

"Well, here you are," the lanky farmer said to the travel-weary family. "Mr. Wycliff, do you need to rest a day or two before you come into work?"

"No, no, I don't," Stasha answered, still speaking in Polish. "I rested long enough on the plane and on that long train ride."

"Fine. I'll pick you up in the morning," Platek said, leaving them to get settled.

Early the next morning, as they were driving to the farm, Platek asked, "Stamford, do you know anything about packaging vegetables?"

Stasha did not answer immediately – he was not yet responding automatically to his new name. But when the farmer repeated his question, Stasha replied, "No, in Poland we never bothered with packages. We took our produce directly to the market and the customers used newspapers or whatever they had for wrappings. But I'll do whatever you tell me."

"Here it's important to pack produce properly," Platek explained. "If it is not packaged properly, we face huge losses. Things get crushed or they rot during transit."

Within a month, Stasha proved himself a capable packer, carefully and diligently doing as Platek instructed. Over time, he devised several improvements using the farm's new packing material, Styrofoam. Before long, Stasha's innovations were implemented throughout the produce industry, though he was not aware of anything that happened outside of Homestead.

While Stasha only gradually got used to his new name, Jadzia and Franya adapted to theirs almost immediately. Two days after their arrival, for example, Francine registered Jadzia at the local kindergarten as "Jodi Wycliff." Within a week, when her parents gave her a baby doll with a gift card inscribed, "To our beloved Jadzia," Jodi remonstrated with her parents. "My name is Jodi," she protested, stamping her little foot. "Call me Jodi, only Jodi."

Stamford worked diligently for Platek and, to augment his income, he labored extra hours at neighboring farms. Francine, always a churchgoer, regularly attended services at the local Catholic church. One day after services, she struck up a friendship with Sally Winters, an attractive woman near her own age. Her husband was an officer stationed at the SAC Air Base in Homestead, where Sally volunteered as an English teacher, working with the Mexican migrant workers who came in droves to pick South Florida's crops.

When Sally and Francine met for lunch at a small coffee shop, Sal smiled as Francine labored over the menu.

"This hamburger, it is with ham?" she asked.

"No," Sal said, "it's ground beef."

"I do not understand. And this hot dog, there is no dog, yes?" Francine guessed.

"Correct. It's probably pork," Sal answered, adding, "You're working awfully hard at that menu. I'd be glad to give you private English lessons at my house. Ordinarily, I would tell you to come to my classes, but all those folks speak Spanish."

With a few weeks of private lessons, the two became fast friends. Francine became used to being called Fran and she finally learned to call Sally, Sal. At one of these lessons, Francine brought Jodi to Sal's home, a military bungalow on a shade-covered street in Homestead. As she introduced the child, Francine said to Jodi, "I told my teacher about you. Would you sing a few songs for her?"

After Jodi sang a couple of simple songs in English, Sal hugged her.

"Jodi, that was lovely. I'd like you to sing in the children's Christmas play at church."

Sal was describing the play to Jodi and Francine, when a tall man in uniform entered the living room.

"Hi, honey," Sal said, getting up and kissing her husband. "This is my newest student, Francine Wycliff, and her daughter, Jodi." Then, turning to Francine, she said, "This is my husband, Captain James Winters."

Captain Winters greeted them warmly as Sal continued, "You should hear Jodi sing. She's just wonderful. I'd love to have her sing at the Christmas party."

Squatting down on the floor to be near Jodi, Winters said, "That's what we need – a little singer like you. Will you please, please come?"

Giggling at his serious tone, Jodi said, "Sure, I'll come."

He turned to Francine, "We would like to have your whole family come to our annual Christmas party."

"We'd love it," she replied enthusiastically.

The party was held several weeks later in the air base's mess hall. The room was filled with military men, children, decorations and gifts. Jodi sang Christmas carols, delighting the gathered airmen and their families.

During the next few months, Stamford and Captain Winters also got to know one another while working together to remodel the captain's military quarters. They worked evenings and on weekend afternoons. Most Saturday nights, after the men put away their tools, the two couples would go out together to Miami Beach for what Sal called "R&R" parties.

At his wife's insistence, Stamford also took private English lessons from Sal, showing exceptional progress and gradually eliminating his Polish accent. Over the course of lessons and many R&R parties with the Winters, the two families cemented a friendship that lasted beyond the remodeling and even beyond the captain's tour of duty at the Homestead air base.

Captain Winters was reassigned to Boston almost two years after the Wycliffs came to Homestead. Francine and Sal arranged an outing to Miami Beach as a farewell party. The next day, Stamford drove the Winters to Miami airport in the captain's jeep, which he would return to the air base on his way home. As the Winters were about to board the plane, Stamford presented them with a well-packaged carton of fresh vegetables.

"You'll like these Florida tomatoes when you eat them in Boston's cold winter," Stamford said. "Let me know anytime you want me to send some more."

Before the week was over, Jim called Stamford with a hint of excitement in his voice. "Hey, Stamford, listen to this. I met a local produce distributor here, in Boston, and gave him a taste of one of your tomatoes. He'd buy as many tomatoes as you can send, if you can find a cheap enough way to ship them by air."

"That's great," Stamford said. "You market them at your end and I'll ship all I can."

The first few shipments of tomatoes from Joe Platek's farm were not profitable, but as Stamford gained experience, making contacts with independent pilots and private charters, profits rose. In the process, he stumbled on an idea that started him on the road to riches. Stamford began to present gift baskets of Florida fruit and vegetables to key Air Corps personnel at the airport as they were about to travel up north.

"Try these," he'd say, "and show them to some produce distributors in your area. I'll pay a good bonus for any contact you make with a buyer."

In his first year of operation, Stamford soon surpassed Platek's farm's ability to meet the demand for fruit and vegetables. He had to quit doing farm labor because the network of produce outlets he had created was spreading throughout the United States. Gradually over the next five years, he established joint ventures with his far-flung distributors. Bringing to business the same focused ruthlessness he had applied in Poland, he formed a company that bought huge tracts of farmland. And, using his contacts at the air base, he purchased several surplus C-24s.

Stamford Wycliff was soon an acclaimed businessman, well known and well connected. He moved his family from Homestead to a pleasant suburban apartment in Miami so Jodi could attend a better private school.

A year later, he drove Francine in their wood-sided station wagon to a two-story, stucco home on Biscayne Bay. Bougainvillea trailed up the cream-colored walls.

"What are we doing here?" Francine asked as they walked around to the swimming pool at the back.

"It's ours," he beamed with pride, "paid for in cash. Hire the best interior designer in town. We can afford it."

Within days, he had his name inscribed in gold leaf paint on the door of a black Cadillac.

*

But his greatest achievement, he would say, was becoming a citizen of the United States. The day the three of them were sworn in as citizens, Francine invited their friends and business associates to a gala party in their now beautifully furnished home. For entertainment, she arranged for a well-known pop group to sing and dance for her guests. At the party, without consulting Jodi, already thirteen, Francine called on her to sing for the guests, who applauded her enthusiastically.

The party was a huge success. Before it broke up, Stamford, somewhat drunk, offered a toast, "For us, this day is our Day of Liberation. Today we are finally free, free from guilt, no longer harassed victims of war. Today we are citizens of America, proudly wearing its colors as our badge of honor."

Later that evening, Jodi sat with Francine in the corner of the large dining room and asked, "Mom, what did Dad mean when he said that he's free from guilt?"

Stamford heard her question and looked at Francine who shrugged, motioning for him to reply. He reached out to Jodi, asking her to sit on his lap, but she edged back and emphatically repeated her question.

"After the war," he explained, "all survivors were burdened with a sense of guilt that they survived while others met their death at the hands of the Nazis."

"And, becoming a citizen rids you of that guilt?" Jodi asked.

"Becoming a citizen of the United States gives us a sense of security we did not have before," Stamford said. "We are now part of the land of the free."

"I don't understand the word 'guilt', Dad," Jodi responded, "but anything you say is OK with me."

When Francine and Stamford were alone in their bedroom, she looked up at her husband as she brushed her hair at her dressing table. "Stamford," she said softly, "it's time you really did feel free from guilt. You're not Stasha and I'm not Franya. Those days are over."

"Maybe I shouldn't have used the word 'guilt,'" Stamford said. "But, now that we're citizens, we do have a sense of security we didn't have before. No one can touch us."

"What do you mean?" she asked. "Who would harm us?"

"Do you remember Lieutenant Kemeris?"

"Of course."

"It was he who was responsible for changing our names immediately, for our safety. He said Stasha and Franya had to disappear to avoid being captured by the Russians."

"The Russians, why?" Francine asked, shocked.

"They could seek revenge on us, for exposing Antek, the Russian spy."

"But you travel everywhere," Francine said. "Are you safe? Are we really free from the Russians now, because we have new names?"

"We have the full protection of the United States," he assured her. "I am a citizen of the United States. You're right, I'm no longer Stasha. He is dead."

*

Within a few years, he was as far removed from Stasha, the Polish thug, as the earth is from the moon. He was now chairman of the board of the reputable Wycliff Corporation, listed on the New York Stock Exchange. His financial success catapulted Stamford and Francine Wycliff into Miami's highest social circles, where they became widely known and respected. Posh country clubs sought them as members and various charities heaped honors on Stamford for his contributions.

The Wycliffs moved once more, now buying a waterfront mansion, a gray Colonial with white shutters and bay windows, on four lushly landscaped acres in Coral Gables, the city's most established luxury suburb. Their stately waterfront home off Old Cutler Road soon became the hub of Miami's society as parties flowed between the burnished, oak-floored salon, the broad, white-pillared porch, and the keystone patio surrounding the pool, its fountain framed by pink hibiscus.

Each day, Jodi was chauffeured to the Russell Academy, an exclusive, private high school. At her mother's insistence, she joined the school's drama club. During her four years at Russell, she starred in several student productions. She began dating at fourteen and spent her high school years rehearsing student productions and then staying out with her friends until the early hours of the morning. When her parents questioned her behavior, she stormed at them that she was just behaving "like an average American teenager, not a Polish villager." Her parents were stung, but decided not to engage her in a debate.

In her senior year, when she turned eighteen, her parents presented her with a fire-engine red Jaguar. Despite her innate intelligence, she graduated from Russell with no better than a C average, yet she had become the homecoming queen. Because Jodi was selected to lead "The Star-Spangled Banner" at graduation, Francine bought her an original Dior, a formal, white lace gown.

At the reception following the graduation, Stamford and Francine caught up with Jodi to tell her how proud they were of her singing. She didn't seem to be listening – her eyes darted around the room looking for her friends. Before her parents even realized, Jodi had jumped into her car with several classmates, leaving them on the steps of the auditorium. Just before she roared off, she called to them, "Don't wait up for me. We're going to a graduation party."

Her parents did not wait up, but when Stamford awakened at 5 A.M., he peeked into Jodi's bedroom and then woke Francine to tell her that Jodi had not yet returned.

"Stop worrying," she said. "Be calm. We have to get accustomed to having a grown-up daughter."

Pacified, he went back to sleep. In the morning, after a quick breakfast, he headed to his office. By noon, when Jodi still hadn't come home, Francine called him. "Perhaps you were right and we should have worried last night. She's not back yet and I'm getting scared."

Stamford called Coral Gables' chief of police to report Jodi's absence. The chief calmly informed him that several groups of Russell graduates had slept on the beach. Nonetheless, the chief promised to send out a couple of officers to find Jodi.

He called back within a half an hour. "She's fine, Mr. Wycliff. My guys are driving her home. But if it is OK with you, I think I'd better run by your office and tell you the whole situation."

He sat down with Stamford and explained, "The police helicopter spotted the red Jaguar in an outdoor parking lot near the beach. That's where we found Jodi asleep. While examining the car to make sure that it was hers, we found this bag."

He emptied the bag onto the polished mahogany desk. "Three nearly empty packets of pure coke," the chief said. "And, Sir, I don't know how to say this, but the police also found several used condoms right where your daughter was sleeping."

Stamford took a moment to compose himself. Then he thanked the chief for his concern and for letting Jodi off with a warning. He knew that almost any other teenager in Miami found with that amount of cocaine would have spent the night at the juvenile detention center; and any other parent would have been waiting in line to make bail. Stamford hurried out of his office, rushing to get home.

"She's upstairs in her room," Francine told Stamford as he came into the house. "She won't talk. She won't answer any questions."

"Something is radically wrong with her," Stamford said, showing his wife the contents of the brown bag. "This is just the first thing to hit us in the face, but her behavior throughout the year proves something is off, even her lousy grades prove it."

They sat down, talking in hushed tones, trying to figure out how to approach Jodi about the items found in her car. To make matters worse, Francine told her husband that when the police brought Jodi home, she was wearing a boy's pair of pants, a plaid shirt, and no bra.

"I just don't know how to talk to her," Stamford said.

"You don't have to talk to me," Jodi called out angrily as she came down the stairs. "I'll do my own thing and I don't need anybody's advice."

"Sit down," Stamford ordered.

"I will not," she retorted. "I'm going out. But I want you to know, you can't control me and you can't control what my friends do or don't do! And, for your information, I did not have sex and I only wore those pants because my dress got wet because we all went into the ocean."

Jodi ran out of the house, slamming the door.

Stamford was about to call her back to confront her with the police findings, but he thought it best to let her cool off.

"She's having sex, sniffing coke, and lying," he told Francine. "She's doing all the stuff we read about in the newspapers. I just hope she grows out of it."

"I still think something is wrong," Francine said.

She was right. Something was wrong with Jodi. She was not like other girls from the prestigious high school she attended. All her classmates had already selected the college they would attend, but Jodi claimed that college did not interest her. For the first six months after her graduation, she did nothing but sleep late most mornings and stay out almost every night. She frequented bars and refused to explain her behavior to her glowering father and increasingly frantic mother.

Finally, to give in to Francine's pleading to do something productive and to appease her father's growing annoyance and disappointment, Jodi enrolled in the local Florida Drama and Arts Academy. When she had completed the acting courses, she took up with a local theater group. She landed parts in various plays that the group performed but, after being with the troupe for two years, neither Jodi nor her mother were happy with the troupe's accomplishments.

"They're a bunch of amateurs," Francine said to Jodi one evening as they were discussing her future. "You are a born actress. You've wasted two years with the Drama Academy. Dad has an interest in the Theater Guild of New York. He can get you started there."

Jodi hesitated, then replied, "I'll give it a try."

Back in her room, Jodi whispered into the phone, "It's New York! It's my chance to get away from the house. Wow. Can't talk in case they hear me. Bye."

Francine and Stamford set Jodi up in an elegant apartment in New York, where her father found work for her as an actress. She stayed with the theater company for a year and a half, attaining only mild success. She fell in love with the lead actor in one of their productions and moved in with him. Jodi chose to be married by a local magistrate rather than have an elaborate ceremony. Her parents learned of her marriage only through the headlines in Variety. They were neither consulted nor invited, despite the generous allowance Stamford's bankers added to her account each month. The marriage lasted less than a year. Jodi took up with the actor's crowd of jet-setters, roamed the world with them, and got a reputation as a social gadabout, beautiful, smart, wealthy, but aimless and a slut, sleeping with numerous men, married or single.

*

Suddenly, without giving her parents a hint that she was coming, Jodi returned to Miami, showing up one Sunday with a pile of Louis Vuitton luggage and a hangover. She remained strangely silent, often staying in her room or sitting alone on the porch and staring out at the bay. After their first couple of tries, neither Francine nor Stamford asked her for explanations about her failed stage career or her failed marriage. Nor did they pressure her about her future plans. Jodi cavalierly thanked her parents for their support, but she told them that she needed time to sort out her feelings. One evening, however, after a quiet family dinner, she joined them in the spacious Florida room and this time, she didn't abruptly dart away when the conversation turned to her future.

"Why don't you go to college?" Francine asked Jodi tentatively. "You're twenty-three years old. You can still make something of yourself."

"I can get you into any college you like," her father added.

Jodi sat in the corner of the sofa, saying nothing, immersed in thought.

"Dad is on the board of trustees of Gates College in New York," Francine said. "You could study there and still maintain contact with the stage."

When Jodi did not reply, her mother continued, "Jodi, acting can still be your career. You're a born actress."

Jodi got up from the sofa, walked over to the window, and for a long time stared out at the bay. When her father walked over and put an arm around her, she wriggled out of his embrace. Annoyed and frustrated, he walked out to the patio, leaving the two women alone.

"Now, Jodi, you've upset Daddy," Francine fussed. "I'm pleading with you to get a hold of yourself, go back to college, go back to acting."

"Mother! Stop badgering me about being an actress," Jodi shouted, stalking across the room, away from her mother.

For a rather long time, both remained silent.

Francine then walked over to Jodi and put her arm around her. "I only wanted to help," she said with a tremor in her voice.

Jodi embraced her mother. "I'm sorry, Mom. I didn't mean to yell at you. But you just keep pushing and pushing."

Stamford walked in, saw them together and patted Jodi on the back. "You need to tell us what is happening with you. We have waited too long," he said. "There is only the three of us, but we are a family. Unburden yourself."

Jodi sighed, sat down next to Francine on the overstuffed brocade couch, and began, "I have done a lot of thinking these past few days. I realized something important, something you and I never spoke about."

"Something I did? Something Dad did?"

"Yes, something you both did," she replied. "But I don't want to upset you and I'm sorry if I've disappointed you or let you down."

"Say it," Francine said. "The time for apologies is long over."

"Mom, I never wanted to be a singer or an actress."

Francine was surprised, but said nothing. Stamford, standing behind the armchair that faced the sofa, looked at Jodi intently.

"I recall that as a child I did it because I knew it always made you happy. But for me, it always reminds me of singing to soldiers, of staying in those camps, of the train rides. I never said this to anyone. You know what I mean?"

"No," Francine said. "Tell me."

Jodi spoke slowly, pausing between phrases, "When I am on the stage, I sometimes get the shivers. I see blurred images. Soldiers. Swastikas. Guns. I'm singing to them. I see words that frighten me, like 'Gestapo', 'spies', 'ghetto', 'major'. And all the time that's what you want me to do – sing, act, dance."

For the first time in twenty years, Jodi spoke her true mind to her parents. But once she had started, her words flowed like a cascading river.

"Then there's another thing," Jodi said, looking at her father. "Dad, do you know what it was like growing up and everybody relating to me not as Jodi, but as Stamford Wycliff's daughter?"

He was too stunned to reply.

"In school, to my teachers, my principal, even to my friends, I was not me. I was you. I was an outsider. With my lousy grades, I became president, valedictorian, everything, because I was Wycliff's daughter. I hated the school, the teachers, and the kids. I wasn't allowed to be one of them. Do you know why I sniffed coke? Because my friends said, 'They'll never hurt Wycliff's daughter.' Even in New York, I knew that I got my theater jobs only because I was Mr. Wycliff's daughter.

"Do you know why I traveled all over the world, with all kinds of people? To get away from you, and it didn't work. And now, Mom, you tell me, 'Dad can get you into this theater, into that college.' I can't take it anymore. I can't."

She began to cry and continued repeating, "I can't. I can't," as tears were gushing down her cheeks.

Francine reached out to her daughter, who was seated with her head bowed, her hands hiding her face, bawling like a baby. She put a handkerchief into Jodi's closed fist, stroked her hair, and bent down to kiss her. Jodi looked up and embraced her mother, tears still flowing freely. Stamford walked over to them and they clasped each other without saying a word.

*

Jodi applied to college, choosing the School of Journalism at Northwestern University. She knew her high school grades were poor, so she wrote a special essay entitled "As the Phoenix Flies" for the admissions committee. In her four-page essay, she described her experiences and her personality development, pointing out that as a child she was victimized by the war that raged about her. She described how while going through those stormy years, she did not feel the victim, yet those searing experiences had a profound effect on her character development, stunting her moral and intellectual growth. Finally, she wrote, at age twenty-three the feathers of the phoenix were growing back. Her essay concluded, "Please let me fly, let me soar to the heavens where I can one day reach the rays of the sun."

She was accepted. Several years later the dean told her that the admissions committee voted in her favor because the essay showed exceptional writing talent. He encouraged her to recognize her skills as a writer and be prepared to enter a profession that is highly competitive. His remarks made a profound impression on her. For the first time in her life, she was accepted as Jodi, not as Stamford Wycliff's daughter.

She stayed at the top of her class throughout her four years at Northwestern, graduating summa cum laude and winning the prestigious Sinclair Award in Communications. That netted her a job in New York City with Network International Corporation, NIC, a leading, global television consortium. At twenty-seven, she was certain that her new post would launch her career. But for almost two years she was only assigned to do research for news segments, tape voice-overs, or write brights – the short, light features that ended news reports.

Over dinner one night in her comfortable Manhattan condominium, she complained to her visiting parents, "I'm almost thirty years old and my career is frozen at being a gofer for the studio's hotshots." She was pleased that her father did not offer to get her a job with a company he owned. He did tell her that she possessed the potential of being a top-rated TV journalist.

Her break came during her stint as a weather reporter on a Saturday evening news show. That evening, she was wrapping up before the main newscast when the NIC anchorwoman suffered a stroke, just minutes before she was to go on the air. The frantic director whirled his hand, motioning to the producer to stretch the local segment and prepare several advertisements. As the studio dissolved into chaos and stretcher-bearing paramedics rushed in, Jodi approached the director. "I wrote the next segment," she said. "Want me to deliver it?"

The director hardly had a choice. Jodi took her seat behind the anchor desk, ran her fingers through her hair, and, instead of delivering her cute feature on the pandas at the National Zoo, she ad-libbed the breaking story of the anchorwoman's stroke, dramatically reporting the work of the emergency team attending to her. The astonished director motioned her to keep going. Without a script, Jodi related the anchorwoman's career accomplishments and closed the program by sincerely wishing her well from all her colleagues.

Despite Jodi's informal clothes and her unkempt hair, her descriptions were so vivid and her reactions to what had happened were so heartfelt and sensitive that NIC's phones began ringing off the hook. Jodi became an instant celebrity and earned a slot on the air. The company brass sent her to their local affiliate station for seasoning as a newscaster and within two years made her the coanchor of their national morning show.

A year later, she began doing live broadcasts from several world capitals, and through NIC, the name and face of Jodi Wycliff became known around the world. Soon her series *Jodi Wycliff Specials* earned its own prime time slot, featuring interviews with famous national and international personalities.

On the fifth anniversary of *Jodi Wycliff Specials*, NIC's chief news anchor interviewed her on the air. Toward the end of the show, he asked her to describe her happiest moment during the long run of the program. To his surprise and to the surprise of her crew, who thought they had finally figured out what she might do next, Jodi replied that her happiest moment came when she covered her father's recent election as the national president of the US Chamber of Commerce.

"That victory party was a crowning moment for me," she stated firmly.

"Why?" asked the anchorman. "Why that particular program, in comparison to coronations, Olympic gold medalists, and everything else you've covered?"

"My father is a self-made man," she said. "I'm proud to be the daughter of someone who climbed the rugged mountain of success using only his bare hands."

At her condo that night, Stamford mildly chastised her. "I appreciate the accolade, Jodi, but I think you diminished your stature and the fifth anniversary show by giving such a personal and childlike reply."

"I had the chance to say something that mattered to me," she protested, "instead of doing what my PR specialists were telling me."

"I'm sorry to say this, but you sounded like a first-grade schoolchild," he said. "After all, your fame stems from your ability to interview world-famous personalities. The list of dignitaries you've interviewed reads like a who's who of world leadership. You didn't have to talk about your dad."

Jodi hugged her father. "Dad, I love you and I'm proud of you. Not just because you're the president-elect of the Chamber of Commerce, but because you are a living miracle."

"Hardly," he said.

"You just don't see it that way," she persisted. "You came here penniless, a war victim, with both hands tied behind your back, and you pulled yourself up to sit with kings and princes."

"You should do a story on him," her mother said.

"One day I will," Jodi replied. "And do you know what the lead line will be? 'From Stasha to Stamford.'"

Untying his bow tie and removing his cummerbund as he mentally shook off any reminder of his life as Stasha, Stamford said, "A better title for your next show is, 'He Tamed the Market but not his Daughter.'"

"Well, I'm almost tamed," she said. "I may surprise you yet. Cal and I have decided to announce our engagement."

Francine sprang up like a ballerina and brought out cocktail glasses while Stamford opened a bottle of champagne. They toasted each other, rejoicing at Jodi's announcement.

During the past year, Caldwell Boynton, a brilliant attorney and the scion of one of the South's oldest families, had become Jodi's constant companion.

"When will you announce your engagement officially?" Francine asked.

"As soon as I return from my next assignment."

"Where are you headed now?" her mother asked.

"Ismailia," she replied. "The Egyptians and Israelis are meeting in Ismailia to try to work out a peace plan and I have a long day of flying ahead of me. I just hope I can get an interview with Egypt's president."

"Don't forget Sunday, January 14, the installation dinner of the US Chamber of Commerce in Miami Beach," Stamford said, reading from an embossed invitation and handing it to her. "That's where I will be officially installed as president."

"I wouldn't miss it for all the Arabs in Ismailia," she promised.

Chapter 13

It was an unseasonably warm, sunny day in April, 1948, when the first Displaced Persons transport tied up at pier 65 in New York.

"Dr. Berson! Dr. Berson!" Szymon and Sonya heard a voice calling out as they were walking down the ship's ramp.

They were among the first people off the vessel that had brought more than six hundred Displaced Persons to the United States. Dr. Sam Neufeld edged his way through the crowd to embrace Dr. Berson.

"Sam, I want you to meet my wife, Sonya," Szymon said.

He looked at Sonya as though she were a model, and jokingly said, "You are every bit as lovely as Joe Stanton described you. Just twirl around a minute so I can see you."

He held her hand as she made a graceful pirouette, laughing as he explained, "When Stanton returned, he told me all about the wedding at the DP camp," Dr. Neufeld said, kissing Sonya's cheek. "According to him, it was the event of the century."

"It took Stanton two years," Szymon said, "but he finally came through. He got me a priority visa and, by the way, he also gave me my new name, Simon."

"Then Simon it is," Dr. Neufeld said, stressing the name. "Simon, let's go to the baggage area to claim your luggage, so that we can get out of here."

"That's it," Simon said, lifting the one valise he was carrying.

"One bag? That's all you have?" Dr. Neufeld asked with surprise.

"Two dresses, one sweater, one extra suit, two shirts, three pairs of socks, and plenty of warm underwear," Sonya said.

"And one stethoscope," Simon added.

"What about money?" Dr. Neufeld asked when they were seated in the back of the limousine.

"What can I get for two cartons of cigarettes?" Dr. Berson laughed, and went on to explain Berlin's means of exchange to Dr. Neufeld.

*

During their first two years in the United States, while Simon trained and prepared to take the US medical boards, they lived in a small apartment provided by the Medical Institute. When he passed the boards and received his license to practice medicine, they held a small party in their apartment. The guests included Dr. Neufeld and Congressman Stanton, but Sonya was surprised when Stanton brought a young couple, Peter and Gloria Reinert, whom she had not invited, to the party.

"Peter is my protégé," Joe Stanton said, introducing them. "He'll be running for my seat in the Sixteenth District when I step down next fall."

Peter Reinert, a young, affable attorney, told them how he decided to go into politics the day he met Joe Stanton.

"When Uncle Joe offered me the opportunity to run as his successor with his endorsement," Peter said, "I grabbed it even though I knew that nobody could replace him."

The Bersons and Reinerts struck up an immediate friendship. Although Gloria Reinert was ten years younger than Sonya, she spent most of her time with her either window shopping on Sundays, at the Berson's home, or spending leisurely evenings built around spaghetti suppers and great conversation. Peter joined them whenever he could, but he was preparing for his run for Congress so was most of the time out on the road.

Two months later, when he stood for election, Sonya did the unthinkable. She took a leave of absence from her studies at Hunter College to campaign for Peter, addressing every Jewish group in the Sixteenth District, either in Yiddish or in her recently acquired Brooklynese English. And on election day, when Peter announced his victory at two o'clock in the morning, Sonya stood at his side with Gloria receiving the applause of the huge gathering. After the election, Sonya returned to her studies.

Two years later, she received her doctorate in education. The college's Continuing Education Department hired her and, in the space of a few years, she established herself as an expert in career planning. As director of the program, she set up an innovative program creating joint ventures with business and civic organizations to help students choose careers after experiencing on-the-job training in areas of interest to them.

Since many of her students ended up training at the Stone-Winthrop Institute, where Simon practiced medicine, Sonya became a well-known figure there. Without intending to become a "mother" to trainees, lab technicians, nurses, and interns, over the years she became the unofficial advisor to hundreds of her former students employed at the Institute. She often said that the abiding affection they showed her was the prime motivation for her work. She, therefore, put in long hours at the university and the Institute.

When Gloria called Sonya from Washington DC, inviting her to see the new home she and Peter were buying in Georgetown, Sonya dropped everything and flew there. She had planned to spend a day or so with them, but she ended up staying the entire week, helping Gloria decorate the new home.

Simon also grew in his profession, demonstrating his worth to Dr. Neufeld. In his fourth year at the Stone-Winthrop Institute, he was appointed research physician, working directly under Neufeld. He was soon recognized as Neufeld's protégé, often appearing with him at state and federal government committee hearings, where they represented the Institute either to contribute medical information or to seek government grants.

On one occasion, they were scheduled to appear before a House committee when Neufeld came down with the flu. Simon called Peter Reinert to delay Neufeld's testimony.

"Simon, we can't postpone his appearance. It's the committee's last meeting for this session," Peter Reinert said. "You'd better get here. As far as the committee members are concerned, no one questions your expertise."

When Berson relayed Peter's recommendation, Dr. Neufeld agreed and the nationally-televised committee hearing, where Simon fielded questions from its members, produced a new media star in the medical world. Three years later, Simon earned his sabbatical. He and Sonya took a six-month vacation in Israel, traveling the length and breadth of the country. Sonya was delighted with Simon's new-found love for the Holy Land. True to the promise he had made to her in Berlin, he looked about for a position that would enable them to settle there. First, he was interviewed by the Hebrew University's president and was offered a teaching position in the university's medical school. The salary was small, but they figured that Sonya could easily get a teaching position and, with that income and their savings from their work in New York, they reckoned they would have enough to make ends meet. With time, they would have enough to put a down payment on an apartment.

Before beginning his teaching, a five-day visit from Gloria and Peter became a highlight of their sabbatical stay in Israel. Although the trip was politically motivated since it was almost required for the congressional representative of New York's Sixteenth District to be seen with Israel's leadership, Sonya and Gloria were together from the moment the Reinerts landed at Ben-Gurion Airport.

One evening, while they were all dining at a seaside restaurant, Simon told them about his teaching position in Israel and calmly stated that he was going to resign from the Institute. Peter's fork dropped from his hand.

"Simon, don't," Peter argued vehemently. "Why take such a radical step? You've built up a wonderful reputation and a great career in the States."

"Who knows how much higher you can climb," Gloria added.

"It wasn't an easy decision," Sonya said, "and it took us a long time to make it. But we decided we need to be in Israel and that's it."

Peter and Gloria soon realized that debate was useless but, several days later, when Sonya and Simon took the Reinerts to Ben-Gurion Airport, Peter asked, "Simon, have you talked to Dr. Neufeld about your decision to stay here?"

"I sent him a long letter explaining my decision to accept the teaching position at Hebrew University," Simon replied.

"What was his opinion?"

"No opinion. He cabled back four words," Simon said, quoting the wire: "'Your resignation not acceptable.'"

Peter embraced him, and with a lump in his throat, wished him good luck, and quickly turned to leave.

"I don't know what I'm going to do without you," Gloria said, hugging Sonya. "One thing I always wanted in my life…a sister. God sent you to me. Now, you're leaving."

Simon wrote to Dr. Neufeld, explaining his enchantment with Israel and how happy Sonya was with their decision to remain there. Through a barrage of phone calls, Neufeld persistently questioned Simon's decision to leave, while stressing his contribution to the Institute and the brilliant future it offered them. Despite Dr. Neufeld's efforts to convince them, Simon submitted his written resignation to the Institute and Sonya submitted hers to Hunter College. To implement their decision, they went to the Aliyah Department to learn what furnishings they, as immigrants, could bring into Israel without paying the huge tax on such goods.

Three weeks later, Neufeld called Simon from New York to have one last try. "Simon, think about this," Neufeld begged. "The board of the Institute is offering you the position of chairman of the Research Department. The position has just become available and your name will be first on the list at the next meeting."

Once again, with this significant offer in hand, Sonya and Simon deliberated returning to America or making their future in Israel.

Quite by chance, they spied Tevye one evening at the opera house during an intermission. Berson, who was never really too enamored of opera, suggested an impromptu dinner at a local restaurant. Tevye was delighted and the women, Sonya and Tamar, Tevye's wife, went along reluctantly.

The evening turned out to be a wonderful reunion, as they caught up with each other on their past and their accomplishments. Tevye bragged about his steady rise in the Aliyah Department, attaining the position of "*rosh hamachlaka*" – head of department. He was enthusiastic about his position, singing praises of working for the government on something so dear to him. Tamar winked at Sonya as the two made for the powder room.

"His love for Israel is so great," Tamar said, "that he's willing to tolerate the government's red tape that has him all snarled up."

Sonya told her about her husband's offer to teach at the University, waxing poetic about their possible future in Israel.

"You sound like my husband," Tamar said, wishing her a hearty "mazal tov" on their decision to make *aliyah* and adding, "I hope you're not disillusioned."

Sonya decided to share their dilemma with Tevye.

His advice was simple. "Take the university job. You won't make much money, but you can easily create a private medical practice and before you know it, you will strike it rich."

To make his suggestion more attractive, Tevye promised to find the right place in Jerusalem for Berson to set up his practice. Tevye did not truly understand the problem facing Simon as he simply stated, "Taking Neufeld's job offer means you're giving up on Israel."

After much talking in circles, Sonya suggested a new tactic. "Why don't we go back and talk to the president at Hebrew University? Let's see what he thinks we should do."

"It would be unwise to turn down such a stunning offer," the president said, surprising both Sonya and Simon. "After several years as head of the Research Department at a world-famous institute, you would have excellent credentials for a top appointment in Israel, much better than I can do for you now."

Sonya and Simon returned to the States.

*

Over the next decade, Dr. Berson achieved national prominence guiding the Stone-Winthrop Research Department. Sonya went back to the college and, though they had little time for friends, they maintained their warm friendship with Peter and Gloria.

Simon gained stature both from his leadership of the Research Department and from his medical writings, which over the years set the benchmark for medical research in the United States. Dr. Neufeld took special pride in Simon's meteoric rise as a medical expert and often boasted that he had discovered him. When the time came for Neufeld to retire, medical circles acknowledged that Dr. Simon Berson would be named as his successor. At the crucial board meeting, Dr. Berson was indeed appointed to the exalted position of chairman of the Stone-Winthrop Institute.

Dr. Neufeld introduced Simon at his installation ceremony with the words, "I now present your new chairman, a man who came to this country barely eighteen years ago with only one valise, containing one suit and several shirts – and not one medical book. And today, he qualifies as one of the foremost physicians in the United States."

Responding to Dr. Neufeld's remarks, Dr. Berson first thanked Dr. Neufeld and then his staff, and closed his short acceptance speech by saying, "I may have had only one valise when Dr. Neufeld saw me off the boat, but I had something else that helped me reach this day." He turned to Sonya, seated next to him. "I had the support, the love, and the help of my Sonya. She sacrificed her dream to settle in Israel so that I could arrive at this moment."

The applause that greeted Simon's declaration grew thunderous when

Sonya, the mentor of many of the professionals present, rose to acknowledge Simon's grateful praise.

For the next fifteen years, Simon Berson worked such long hours that he required three private secretaries to keep up with his output. During that time, he made valuable contacts in Washington, obtaining substantial government grants for the Institute. His close friend, Congressman Peter Reinert, had become an important personality in the nation's capital, chairing the House Finance Committee, where Simon was a frequent witness on medical matters. His reputation was so widespread that when he would testify about the cutting edge of research before a congressional committee, the meetings became media events and he often ended up on the evening network newscasts.

After one newscast, the sparkling host of the *Jodi Wycliff Specials* interviewed him for one of her broadcasts, "Frontiers of Science," which received rave reviews. One critic said, "The good doctor made the show worthy of an Emmy nomination."

*

At the peak of Simon's career, everything turned to ashes. Sonya suffered a massive heart attack. Despite the efforts of the best doctors in the country attending to her, she remained in critical condition.

Simon spent every day in her hospital room, leaving her only when she was sedated or asleep. Throughout her illness, Sonya remained mentally alert and spiritually strong. She knew she was dying, yet she consistently consoled her husband, encouraging him to continue his work. Late one night, he held her hand, gazed at her pale face, and finally forced himself to unburden the guilt he had been carrying heavily since she became ill.

"I am deeply troubled that I never took you back to Israel," he confessed to her.

"I remember you said that at your installation. But after a while, I stopped asking," she said, "because you were doing so much good here. I cherished our visits to Israel, but I have only contentment and joy in my heart when I think about our lives together."

He rested his head on her chest as she wrapped her arms around him, both of them overwhelmed by love and grief and loss. When it became clear that Sonya was dying, Gloria Reinert came to New York. Peter followed her as soon as Congress recessed. They split their time between Sonya's hospital room and the Bersons' spacious Riverside Drive apartment.

"You're in New York, America's theater capital," Sonya reprimanded Gloria. "Take your husband to the theater. Enjoy your vacation."

"We came to New York to be with you, not to go out and watch costumed strangers on stage."

Sonya died six months after her heart attack. Simon was inconsolable. That day, Peter and Gloria took him home to his apartment, where he asked to be left alone in his den. He sat there by himself, brooding as he kept leafing through Sonya's old photo albums and address book, which read like a diary. He shuffled through folders of yellowing papers dating back to their days in the DP camp in Berlin. Peter, who was making the funeral arrangements, poked his head into the den to ask Simon which rabbi to call.

"Chaplain Goldberg, Michael Goldberg," Simon said, showing him a picture of Sonya and the chaplain in Berlin.

"That was more than thirty years ago," Peter said.

Dr. Berson took Goldberg's business card out of Sonya's scrapbook and handed it to Peter, saying, "Here, this has a number on it."

"That's probably twenty-five years old, Simon," Peter said. "But I will try to track him down."

Peter dialed the number on the card but the man who answered had no idea who Rabbi Goldberg was. Peter then called various funeral homes but could find no trace of a Rabbi Michael Goldberg. Gloria finally succeeded in tracing Michael Goldberg, the former chaplain of Berlin, after calling dozens of Michael Goldbergs listed in the phone books of all five boroughs of New York City. Peter notified him of Sonya's death, requesting him to officiate at the funeral. Without hesitation, he agreed, and immediately came to visit Dr. Berson, staying with him most of the day. After the funeral, Simon stayed home for the traditional seven days of mourning. Rabbi Goldberg was often at his side. The rabbi tried to get Simon to talk, to reminisce about their days in Berlin, to recall his first meeting with Sonya, or their wedding. Simon was uncooperative, remaining silent or just mumbling courtesies of how deeply he appreciated Goldberg's presence.

When the *shivah* week was over, Simon returned to his office, where he found a pile of work, invitations to speaking engagements, committee meeting schedules, and a vast stack of mail. He could not handle any of it.

He sat in the office, staring at the wall, brooding, and finally left early to continue brooding at home.

Back in Washington, Peter was distressed when Simon did not show up for an important Finance Committee hearing where he was scheduled to appear as a key witness on pending legislation affecting the Institute. That evening, Peter took the shuttle to New York and headed straight for the Bersons' apartment, where Gloria was still staying to try to help Simon. When he arrived, he found three Institute doctors with Dr. Berson. They were trying to convince him that his physical condition was perfect and that there was no reason why he could not continue to serve the Institute in his present capacity.

"For a sixty-nine-year-old, he's in perfect health. He simply refuses to face up to the fact that it's Sonya who died, not him," one of the doctors said to Peter.

"Simon, they tell me you're nuts," Peter said later, when he and Berson were alone, sipping herb tea that Gloria had brewed for them. "But they also tell me that you're healthy enough to continue your work and that I can reschedule you to testify before our committee."

"Peter, get off my back," Simon said quietly and with a little testiness. "I just want to quit. I don't want the Institute. I don't want your committees. I just want to be left alone."

"You're absolutely right," Peter said, giving Simon's shoulder a gentle tap. "They're all bugging you for no reason at all. You want to quit. I'll even help you quit."

Simon smiled. "You need a favor. You smart, little bastard. What do you want from me?"

Peter pulled up a chair next to Berson and said, "I have to go to Miami Beach to attend a dinner in honor of some rich guy who's being installed as president of the US Chamber of Commerce. Even the president has to go because this guy is a big, big contributor. The president asked me to be a member of the congressional delegation honoring this big shot. So I have to be there. Gloria won't come on these duty trips because I usually leave her alone in some hotel room when I have to go make nice to the big brass. Come with me; give her some company. It'll make her happy to hang out with you."

"Gloria, come here," Simon called out. "Is he telling me the truth or is he feeding me a line?"

"How would you like to stay alone all day in a hotel," she replied, "while the big shot congressman hangs out with some bigger big shots. I long ago decided that I don't care to be a prisoner even in a posh hotel. But if you come down to Miami Beach, we'll go strolling on the beach and visit all the tourist sites."

"Gloria, you're a delightful liar," Simon said, reaching for her hand. "Of course, I'll go with you."

The installation dinner was no ordinary affair. The presence of so many dignitaries gave the formal dinner the aura of a diplomatic event, complete with strict security and precise protocol. The incoming president of the US Chamber of Commerce, Stamford Wycliff, marched in, flanked by his wife and his famous daughter, Jodi Wycliff. They entered to the accompaniment of a twenty-seven-piece orchestra. The dignitaries, including a good cross section of America's top industrial giants and enough influential politicians to get almost anything done, rose and greeted Stamford and his family with waves of applause. After they took their places at the head table, the emcee, a leading Hollywood star, announced, "Ladies and Gentlemen, the President of the United States."

The audience remained standing and applauded as the president and his wife slowly walked in to the band's rendition of "Hail to the Chief." The audience sat down when the president took his seat. Then he stood up again and crossed over to the other side of the dais, where he embraced Stamford and held his hand high as though declaring him a champion. The audience rose to their feet again, clapping heartily for the president and Wycliff.

Amidst this raucous reaction, Peter Reinert noticed that Simon had left his place at their table and was edging over toward the dais. Gloria quickly slipped over to him to bring him back, but he remained standing near the stage, even after the master of ceremonies asked the audience to be seated. He returned to his seat only when ordered to sit down by one of the president's Secret Service men.

"Does he just want to see the president?" Gloria whispered to Peter.

"No, that's what I don't understand," Peter answered. "He's met the president a dozen times or more."

"What's wrong, Simon?" Peter asked Berson once he had returned to his seat but kept staring at the head table.

"I have to get up to the dais, Peter," Simon replied.

"You'll see the president later. We have you scheduled for a cocktail and photo op session in his suite," the congressman replied, gently touching Simon's sleeve to keep him in his seat.

"I'm not interested in the president. I must get a closer look at the honoree, what's his name," Berson said, reading from the program, "Stamford Wycliff."

"When the speeches are over," the congressman replied, wondering why Berson seemed so upset.

Berson continued twisting his head, squinting his eyes, removing his glasses and putting them on again, staring at the man seated in the center of the dais. He asked Peter persistent questions about the honoree, even whispering with uncharacteristic discourtesy during the emcee's brief speech extolling Wycliff as an American business pioneer. Berson could not sit still, even when the archbishop of Miami was giving his invocation.

As soon as the archbishop concluded the invocation and the waiters began to serve the first course, Congressman Reinert motioned to one of the security men. "Excuse me," he said, "I'm Congressman Reinert. I would like to go up to the head table with Dr. Berson."

"Certainly, Congressman," said the security man. "I'll escort you."

Simon, walking ahead of Peter, stopped in front of Stamford, who rose, extending his hand, ready to be introduced.

"Stasha Wojchiechowski," Berson breathed raspily.

Stamford Wycliff did not reply. He remained standing. His hand slowly dropped to his side, his face frozen.

"Stasha, Stasha…the Satan of Warsaw," Berson said, his voice trembling. "You Nazi pig."

Peter, completely surprised, grasped Berson by the shoulders and whispered urgently, "Simon! I'm taking you back to your seat."

Squirming out of the congressman's grasp, Berson leaned over to Stamford and said in a steely but low voice, "I'm Berson, Dr. Szymon Berson of the Czyste Hospital in Warsaw. Stasha, I'll get you, no matter who you think you are now."

Berson walked woodenly back to his table and apologized to the others there for having to leave. He quickly departed with Peter trying to catch up to him but being delayed by the numerous people who reached out to shake the congressman's hand.

"Simon, what the hell was that all about?" Peter asked when he caught up to him in the outer lobby.

"Your honoree is Stasha, the chief collaborator with the Nazis in Warsaw, the one who confiscated Jewish property, took over Jewish homes, and rounded up countless Jews and sent them to their deaths."

"Couldn't you confront him some other time, not surrounded by half of America's business establishment and with the president there, for heaven's sake? I can't understand your behavior."

"Only someone who saw death in the Warsaw Ghetto could understand my behavior. Right now, I don't even understand myself, how I didn't just scream at him and keep screaming."

"We'll deal with this later, Simon," Peter said. "Come back to the table. Remember, we're meeting with the president after dinner."

"No, I can't, Peter. You go back to Gloria," he said, still seething. "I have to get out of here. I can't stay in the same room with that son of a bitch."

Peter Reinert saw the shaken doctor to a taxi and returned to his table, where he found Jodi Wycliff sitting next to Gloria. He began to apologize for Dr. Berson's behavior.

"Peter," Jodi said, "I heard Dr. Berson call my father a Nazi pig. I know Simon Berson from interviews with him. I thought I knew him well. What would prompt him to do such a vulgar thing?"

Before he had a chance to reply, Gloria stepped in. "Peter, I told Jodi that Dr. Berson just lost his wife and that he also quit his chairmanship of the Institute. He's obviously still emotionally upset."

"That's true. He was shattered when she died," Peter said and added, "Jodi, forget the incident. Nobody could hear anything. Even me, standing right next to him. I could barely make out what he said."

When Jodi went back to the dais, Peter turned to Gloria, "Thank you for explaining Simon's crude behavior so tactfully."

"It wasn't tact, it was compassion for a daughter whose father is being honored in the presence of the president of the United States," Gloria replied. "I wouldn't let anything spoil such a beautiful evening for her or her family."

But the evening was spoiled. Stamford was visibly shaken. His face drooped. His smile was gone. Throughout the dinner, he ate nothing. Francine constantly assured him that no one had heard the man's ranting, certainly not the president on the other side of the dais. Jodi, too, made light of the episode, repeating what Gloria told her about Dr. Berson's shaky emotional condition. Stamford was not listening. He kept ordering the waiter to refill his glass.

After he was officially installed as the national president of the US Chamber of Commerce, Stamford staggered to the podium to respond. He fumbled with his glasses, dropped the pages of his prepared remarks, and inadvertently hit the microphone with his hand. He delivered his address poorly but he saved the day when he turned to the president and said jokingly, "Be careful not to drink from that pitcher, Sir, I think the waiter spiked the drinking water."

*

After the banquet, Stamford realized consciously what he had always suppressed: his money and success were a barricade he erected to block out the past. Sure, he enjoyed the status, the money, and the power. But he knew if he worked hard enough and long enough, he would never have to think about the old days.

It just wasn't safe to stop. Stopping might bring up the memory of Dr. Berson and make him see his angry face – or another face that may crop up in the crowd, in any crowd.

Despite the enormous amount of liquor Stamford Wycliff consumed at the installation dinner, he did not sleep at all that night. Neither did Francine. They sat up most of the night, but she could not get him to unburden himself. In the morning, she gently turned to him and said, "Talk to me, Stamford. I need to know what's eating you."

"I just have a stomachache, that's all," he said.

"Are you in pain?"

"My stomach hurts, that's all. Don't badger me," he snapped.

"The amount you drank last night would kill a horse," Francine said, handing him a couple of antacid tablets.

She made him a light breakfast and tried again. "Now, please, talk to me about what happened last night."

"Never mind that," he said. "I have already taken steps to counteract any eventual action against me."

"I'm surprised that you already took action to prepare a defense."

"In all these years, it's never left my mind," Stamford confessed. "I took it up with my lawyer."

"Your lawyer?" she asked. "You already discussed this with your lawyer?"

"Some time ago. Two or three years ago. With John Butnow. He's the former director of the Immigration and Naturalization Service. He's in private practice in Washington."

"You were worrying all these years and you never told me a thing."

"Didn't want to frighten you," Stamford said, walking over to the marble-top bar where he poured himself a tall glass of scotch.

"That's not going to do you much good." She took the glass out of his hand. "It'll only make your stomach worse."

"I know," he replied. "But I need it now. It helps me forget Stasha."

"That happened thirty years ago. It's gone and forgotten."

"Not as far as Berson is concerned," he replied, reaching for the phone.

When he got Butnow on the phone, he spoke tersely, relaying to him the events of the previous night. "John, Berson called me Stasha and kept repeating it. 'I'll get you' – that's precisely what he said."

For quite a long time, Stamford listened on the phone and finally hung up.

Francine looked at him with concern. "What did the lawyer say?"

"He said not to worry about a thing," Stamford replied. "He said these things are so complex, so muddy, that most of these cases are dropped before they're even brought to trial."

Simon Berson discovered the same reality when he phoned Peter Reinert from New York, asking, "Peter, what should I do? How do I proceed against Wycliff?"

"A case like this takes years to process," Peter responded. "Why don't you refer the entire matter to the Office of Special Investigations."

"Office of Special Investigations? What's that?"

"It's called the OSI. Congress authorized establishing it about five years ago. It's a section of the Department of Justice set up for the specific purpose of investigating and prosecuting Nazi collaborators who've gained admission to the United States by fraud or misrepresentation.

"You could lodge your complaint against Wycliff at the Federal Office Building in New York, or right here in Washington."

"Peter, I'll come to Washington right away. I want this to move quickly. Can your office get me an appointment with someone who has some clout at OSI?"

"Hang on."

The Congressman made a quick call, spoke briefly, and clicked back onto Berson's line. "Simon, you have an appointment with Sheldon Haar, the director of the OSI, tomorrow morning at ten thirty. Can you make it?"

"I will, but can you come with me?" Simon asked. "I'm not fond of Washington bureaucrats. I want to avoid the usual foot-dragging."

"Sorry, I have a full calendar," Peter replied, "but when you finish with Sheldon, call me. We'll have lunch."

Dr. Berson took an early shuttle to Washington and went directly to the OSI office.

Sheldon Haar, a short man with intense brown eyes and thinning, curly hair, met with Dr. Berson and took copious notes as Berson listed his charges against Stamford Wycliff.

"This man collaborated with the Germans," Dr. Berson concluded his report on Stasha. "He took part in killing Jews in Warsaw. He's more than a collaborator. He's a Nazi."

"I have the overall picture. Now, go back to the beginning," Haar said. "I need dates, places, people, as many exact details as you can give me."

Berson methodically reported the events he had personally experienced. He recalled incidents involving Stasha and his role in decimating the Warsaw Jewish community. Every now and then, Haar asked him to slow down so he could get everything in writing.

"From what you've told me," Mr. Haar said, "I'm satisfied that we have something to go on to build a case against Mr. Wycliff. However, I need you to repeat your story in the presence of two interviewers who will tape-record your testimony and will ask you questions to clarify your accusations. We'll use that deposition to research our records for evidence that substantiates your allegations, so you must be sure of your facts."

"My facts are solid," Berson said, "and I'm glad to submit to your interview. Just tell me when you want me back here."

Haar buzzed his secretary and told her, "Please set up a meeting for Dr. Berson with two of our interviewers, preferably people who know the Warsaw files."

"He's an important person now – president of the US Chamber of Commerce, masquerading under the name Stamford Wycliff," Dr. Berson said while they were waiting for the secretary to confirm the appointment.

"He's really Stasha, Stasha the Satan of Warsaw. He shouldn't be allowed to escape now."

"Dr. Berson," Haar said, "I assure you, if the evidence supports your claims, we are as anxious as you are to prosecute this case, to denaturalize him, and to deport him back to Poland."

"Denaturalize?" Dr. Berson asked.

"After Congressman Reinert called yesterday and told me what happened at the Chamber dinner, OSI started looking into the case of Stamford Wycliff. He became a citizen in 1952. Our first step would be to strip him of that citizenship. A citizen of the United States cannot be deported. We must now prove that when Wycliff entered the US, or when he became a citizen, he lied about his past, that the Immigration and Naturalization Service was not told about collaboration with the Nazis. Your testimony is invaluable but we have to substantiate it with evidence that can stand up in court."

"Mr. Haar, how can you or anyone find evidence when the Germans destroyed all the records after the war?"

"After your interview, I will assign several investigators to the case," Mr. Haar said. "From what you have told us, rest assured that we would be able to pick up his trail, either here or in Europe."

He reached over to answer the buzzer on the intercom, "Yes?"

"Can Dr. Berson be back here next Monday at nine for his interview?"

Haar looked at Berson, who nodded.

"That's fine. You can confirm it."

"I'm impressed by your quick action," Berson said. "I must confess that I thought I would have to fight against the political bureaucracy to pursue my case against Stasha."

"Dr. Berson, it's no longer your case," Haar said firmly. "It's our case – the US Government against Stamford Wycliff."

"How long would the deportation proceedings take?"

"Cases that involve denaturalization and deportation of an American citizen are very complex," Haar acknowledged. "They often take years to process."

"Years!" Berson repeated in dismay.

"My last case, which was a relatively easy one, took five and a half years. You know what they say about the wheels of justice."

Berson could not hide his annoyance at the delays ahead, but he replied grimly, "Just let me know what I can do to move it along. I can wait. I have nothing but time on my hands."

Over lunch, Simon told Peter, "I'm grateful to you for putting me in touch with Haar. He seems aggressive and eager to pursue this case."

"He is," Peter assured him, "but by their nature these cases take a long time to unfold, no matter how aggressively Haar investigates."

"Haar said the same thing about the time this takes. Are you both trying to discourage me from pressing this case?"

"Simon, I'm not trying to dissuade you but to forewarn you," Peter said. "First of all, from now on, you will have very little to do with processing this case beyond testifying against Wycliff. The OSI will take charge. And second, have you ever heard about the wheels of justice – how slowly they grind? Well, in these cases they often grind to a halt."

"Yeah, Haar mentioned those balky wheels too."

"Just leave the whole thing in the hands of the OSI, Simon. Try to carry on with your medical work."

Berson pushed away his plate, his Caesar salad only half eaten. "I wish I could, Peter, but ever since I saw Stasha, I can think of nothing else."

Peter drove Dr. Berson to the train station, and urged him to try to nap during the three-hour ride back to New York.

The following morning, at his office, Berson scanned his calendar and ordered his personal secretary to cancel all his appointments. She brought him a stack of neglected correspondence, which he also waved off. "Delegate it to other people on the staff," he ordered.

He sat in deep thought for an hour, even ignoring his private phone, which rang once or twice. Then he telephoned the deputy chairman of the Institute's board of governors and, after the shortest of pleasantries, told him, "I'm putting my resignation in writing, and I want you to know about it before it's circulated to the entire board."

He wrote a one-paragraph letter in longhand, stipulating that his resignation was effective immediately. He gave it to his secretary, instructing her to make copies and mail them to the board members.

"I only want someone to clean out my desk and pack up my personal belongings," Berson said, putting on his coat to leave.

"I'll do it, Doctor," she said. "Shall I send it to your home?"

"No," he replied, "just put the box away here until I let you know what to do with it."

Looking at her stricken face, he added kindly, "I'll tell the deputy chairman that they should keep you on as the next chairman's secretary. I'm grateful for all your help."

He walked out of the hospital and headed to his apartment, where he paid his housekeeper a month's wages in severance. After she left, he canceled the phone, his *New York Times* subscription, and the cable television service, and set the thermostat on low. He packed a suitcase, caught a cab to Grand Central Station and took the first train back to Washington, leaving New York and the Institute behind.

When he got to Washington, Berson called Gloria. He spent the night at the Reinerts' and, with Gloria's help, made an appointment with a real estate agent for the next morning. By noon, he had signed a one-year lease on a small, nicely furnished apartment on Connecticut Avenue.

Using the phone in the leasing office, he called Sheldon Haar. "Sheldon, I just wanted to let you know that I've moved to Washington. Now I can be instantly available for any meetings or hearings related to the Wycliff case."

"Well, after your interview on Monday, we will have to schedule a deposition for Wycliff, and I'm sure we'll have to set a time when his attorney can come too."

"And then?" Simon asked.

"Dr. Berson, I have cautioned you about the length of time a case like this can take," Haar repeated patiently. "We not only have a tough case, but we're going up against a very tough defense attorney. Wycliff has hired John Butnow, the former director of the INS. He knows how the Immigration Service works, and he completely understands all the legal loopholes that have a chance of working in the Immigration Court."

It took three weeks to set a date for the first deposition. When it was finally held, Butnow, Haar, and Wycliff met at the Justice Department. When Dr. Berson was informed about the results of the deposition, he was annoyed at the deference everyone showed Wycliff, as the lawyers apologized for scheduling the deposition in Washington, rather than in Miami. Simon was also annoyed that he had not been invited to be present at the proceedings.

*

"Mr. Wycliff, we want you to know that our only source of information about you is Dr. Simon Berson, and before we proceed with a full investigation of his charges…"

"I object," John Butnow interrupted. "These are not charges. No charges are pending against Mr. Wycliff. There are only allegations from one old man, not formal charges."

"Agreed," Haar said. "Mr. Wycliff, if these allegations prove to be incorrect, we would just as soon drop the entire case. Can you tell us briefly what you did as a policeman in Warsaw during the German occupation of that city?"

"Stamford, don't answer that," Butnow called out. "Mr. Haar, you're jumping the gun. He may have not been a policeman at all, and your reference to the German occupation implies that he was part of the German war machine. Let's just call him a 'civilian guard.'"

"Fine, I'll put it another way," Haar said. "I'm not trying to entrap anybody, just to get to the truth."

He turned to Wycliff, "Will you tell us what you did as a civilian guard in Warsaw between the years 1939 and 1945?"

"Hold it," Butnow called out again. "That's like asking, 'When did you stop beating your wife?' You haven't established that he was a guard all this time. As a matter of fact, Mr. Wycliff was a slave laborer in the German mines during those years."

Before agreeing to Butnow's objections, Haar asked the court reporter to go off the record. He pleaded with Butnow, "John, all these facts are going to come out in the interrogation, so stop nitpicking."

"This whole case is going to depend on whose nit is being picked," Butnow said, smiling broadly. "So, Shelly, you might as well get used to it right from the start."

After another fifteen minutes of this kind of quibbling, Butnow allowed Wycliff to give a brief description of his work as a guard. Stamford stressed that the Germans shipped him off to the mines in Silesia to work as a slave laborer. He was recalled from the mines through the intercession of a Polish civilian official who was then killed by the Germans.

Referring to his notes, Haar asked Wycliff, "Why did you return to Germany after the liberation of Warsaw?"

"Don't answer, Stamford," Butnow said. "Haar, you know the German military may have ordered his return. How would Mr. Wycliff have access to those records?" Again, a heated argument ensued between the two lawyers over legal issues of the case.

Eventually, Haar turned to Wycliff and asked, "Can you tell us how you received your immigration visa to the United States?"

"You don't have to answer that," Mr. Butnow flatly stated. "Sheldon, the circumstances of Mr. Wycliff's immigration are classified by the federal government."

At this point, Haar terminated the deposition. Clearly, the release of classified information was the immediate crux of the case, and only an interdepartmental panel could determine whether to proceed with the prosecution of the case.

"What's an interdepartmental panel?" Dr. Berson asked after the session, when Haar was filling Dr. Berson in on its outcome.

"Whenever an issue comes up that involves various governmental departments or agencies, they are called together to determine if that specific issue is of particular interest to any of them. That's how we avoid situations where the right hand doesn't know what the left hand is doing. In this case, the interdepartmental panel will consist of the OSI, the INS, the CIA, and the JD."

"Pity, you left out some letters of the alphabet," Berson responded angrily.

About a week later, the interdepartmental panel met in a special session. Haar chaired the meeting and called upon the INS to submit its records pertaining to Stamford Wycliff's immigration to the United States.

"The Immigration and Naturalization Service has taken note of the allegations brought against Mr. Stamford Wycliff," said the INS senior agent representing the service. "Let the record show that upon the recommendation of the Central Intelligence Agency, the service is constrained from releasing any information or entering into any inquiry in the matter of Stamford Wycliff, pursuant to Article VIII, Section 16 of the INS Code."

The CIA representative concurred that material relating to Wycliff's immigration was not open to any further investigation or inspection. After Haar huddled briefly with the INS representatives, he cancelled the hearing.

He dreaded telling Berson that the session had been indefinitely canceled. And he was right. Berson was infuriated. "What do you mean the session is canceled?" the doctor stormed.

"Article VIII, Section 16 pertains to issues of national security," Haar replied. "The entire file on the entry of Stamford Wycliff into the United States is considered secret. We have to get the file declassified before we can proceed."

Sheldon Haar called his friend Frank Gabelli, chief security agent of the CIA, and invited him to lunch.

"Frank," Haar said while they were eating, "what's so important about Wycliff's special paper-clip visa that the CIA can't clear it?"

"Shelly," Frank replied, "they won't even clear it for me."

"Thousands, hundreds of thousands of collaborators were admitted to the US with paper-clip visas," Shelly said. "What's so special about this case?"

"The CIA claims that it had to have a legal opinion from the Justice Department as to whether the case may be reopened. When that opinion was requested, the department responded that the file could be made available only in an executive session of the State Department, but not in open court."

When Peter called Simon to explain the legal maneuvering taking place regarding the Stasha case, the doctor replied, "Washington's red tape is not only stuck, but even worse, it's all tied up in knots."

Six months later, Berson still saw no progress. If it hadn't been for Haar's constant restraint and reassurance, he would have acted on his threat to "go public," to give the media his information about Wycliff.

"I told you when we started that this would take time," Haar reminded Berson, "and then you said, 'I have nothing but time on my hands.'"

"I'm just not satisfied with absolute inaction," Berson explained furiously. "Should I bring in a private lawyer to get this case moving? I think you are well intended, Mr. Haar, but you're still a member of the Washington scene, and this foot-dragging is part of the game you people play. I have money to pay for a good lawyer."

For the first time since they met, Sheldon Haar let Berson see that he was angry. He got up, paced the floor, and faced Dr. Berson, "Doctor, you are overreaching. First of all, no lawyer can intervene in CIA matters; and second, all the money in the world couldn't move this case any faster."

"Sheldon, I'm sorry if I overstepped my bounds here," Berson responded, "but Wycliff has every advantage going for him in this, and the case is just bogged down."

"Look, Simon, I assure you, before the year is out, Stamford Wycliff will face denaturalization charges in federal court. Even John Butnow can't stall forever."

Chapter 14

In early December, the *United States v. Stamford Wycliff* case opened before Judge Edwin Bailey in Miami's federal court, almost a year to the day when Dr. Berson first encountered Stasha at the installation dinner in Miami Beach. The young attorney representing the OSI read the opening statement. Listening from the front row, Dr. Berson thought the declaration was clear and cogent, forthrightly accusing the defendant Wycliff of entering the United States under false attestations.

"In his visa application," the attorney stated, "Mr. Wycliff was asked whether he was a member of any organization that sought to overthrow the government of the United States," the lawyer said, "and Mr. Wycliff responded in the negative. Yet, we have an eyewitness to prove that the defendant served as police chief in Warsaw and participated in the Nazi atrocities by helping to build the Warsaw Ghetto, confiscate Jewish property, and herd Jews onto the death trains, thus collaborating with the German military occupation of Poland. Based on this evidence, we hold that the defendant lied in his application for admission to the United States and therefore must be stripped of his citizenship."

Butnow calmly set forth his defense of Wycliff, stating that the defendant was one of the millions of Polish citizens who were forced to work for the German occupation forces. Butnow quoted legal precedents from similar federal court cases in which participation in such forced labor had never been grounds either for having admission to the US blocked or for having citizens denaturalized. He challenged the plaintiff to prove, by reliable evidence, that Mr. Wycliff had ever belonged voluntarily to any organization that worked to overthrow the government of the United States.

Much to Berson's frustration, the entire proceedings veered away from Wycliff's crimes almost immediately and became bogged down in arguments about precedent and legal definitions. The judge ordered the OSI to submit documentation describing the kind of organization for which Mr. Wycliff worked. By mutual consent, the lawyers agreed to a three-week postponement so that both sides could present the judge with the documentation he required.

The defense, under John Butnow, clearly won the first round.

*

In the Wycliff household, however, the trial was already taking its toll, particularly on Stamford. He paced up and down, constantly replenishing his glass of scotch while watching the evening news on the major television networks where his trial was the lead story. Each network featured leading citizens who praised him and commentators who questioned Dr. Berson's credibility. They all agreed that Berson was reporting incidents that supposedly took place more than thirty years earlier.

A law school dean who was interviewed by one network assured listeners, "In view of the then-raging war, it is highly doubtful whether the government can prove its case without relying heavily on pure hearsay. In that case, Dr. Berson's testimony would probably be inadmissible in a court of law."

The head of a national chain of supermarkets appeared on one newscast declaring, "The very idea of accusing an upstanding citizen like my good friend Stamford Wycliff of having anything to do with the Warsaw Ghetto is patently absurd."

One anchorman even closed his segment about the trial by adding, "Dr. Berson is undoubtedly an outstanding medical man, but being a Holocaust survivor may have totally blinded him to the American standard that a man is innocent until proven guilty."

Francine watched the array of dignitaries and experts with comforting satisfaction. "Look, Stamford," she said, "didn't Jodi do a good job of lining up just the right people to be quoted?"

The phone rang throughout the evening as friends called to express their support and sympathy. Many callers vilified Berson as the "Jewish doctor." Others called Berson a "vengeful Jew." After the first few calls, Stamford quit picking up the phone.

"You talk to these people, Francine," he said, walking away from the television set. "My stomach is upset."

"I'll get you an antacid," she said, "but you won't feel better until you put down the scotch. You know your stomach acts up when you're tense and drinking only aggravates it."

When his wife left the room to get his tablets, Stamford threw his half-filled highball glass against the fireplace, smashing it against the bronze andirons. Francine ran back and saw her husband standing by the fireplace, his head leaning against his fists over the mantelpiece.

"Damn that son of a bitch," he growled, turning to his wife. "I remember Szymon Berson. I remember him like it was yesterday. And I know that he remembers me. Now he's smeared my name all over the world. I met him in Karl Greifler's office when I was very sick. He's the one who told me that I had a coal tar infection and prescribed special medication and treatments for me. I remember him arguing with the Nazi commanders to try to save patients they wanted to transfer.

"Berson had the guts to stand up to the Germans and he won't give up until he gets what he wants."

"Now, honey," Francine said, trying to calm him, "Mr. Butnow pointed out in court that no one has ever been found guilty of working for the Germans under the kind of conditions you faced."

"That doctor has courage," Stamford said, disregarding his wife's assurances. "I tell you, Berson will push the OSI until he gets his way."

"You have the best defense money can buy, no matter how hard that nasty man pushes," she countered. "Listen to what the *Miami Herald* says about Butnow: 'In the eleven years that he has been in private practice he has not lost a single immigration case.'"

Stamford shook his head, "Just leave me alone, Fran, and just answer the phone."

She patted his shoulder and went into the den to answer the call. Over the course of the evening, he heard the phone ring several times, and Francine, each time she answered, thanked the callers for their good wishes. He was eventually able to block out the jarring, ringing sound and to sink into his own thoughts, still sipping the scotch. When Francine walked in with the phone in her hand, he was irritated until she handed it to him.

"It's Jodi. She wants to talk to you."

"Did you hear the newscasts, Daddy?" she asked. "They really did a good job presenting your side and didn't you love that law school dean! And he's even Jewish!"

"Thanks for all you did, Jodi, I mean, for the people you got," he replied weakly, "but I really don't feel like talking."

"But we have a lot of talking to do," Jodi insisted. "I'm in Washington with Cal. We're coming to Miami tomorrow. Don't make any appointments. We are going to talk."

He hung up the phone without even saying good-bye.

When she arrived from Miami International Airport late the following morning, she found Stamford just as depressed as he had sounded on the phone. She spread out the major morning papers, reading paragraphs aloud to show him the favorable treatment he had received.

"The *New York Times* headlined the story 'A Case of Mistaken Identity'," she read. "Here, the *Washington Post* goes one better: 'Unproven Accusations of a Misguided Survivor'."

Her father scanned through the papers, but said little.

"I know it's all due to your hard work, Jodi," her mother said. "Dad and I are grateful. But he's taking it very hard."

"Who wouldn't?" Jodi said. "It's dreadful being dragged through the courts by this bastard of a Jew. But this will be over soon, Dad. I'll keep up the PR pressure so it doesn't do you any long-term harm. If things go the way I plan, everyone will see you as the victim of unbridled attacks from an undisciplined person in collusion with government bureaucracy. And Mr. Butnow agrees with this sort of publicity."

As she saw her father finally begin to relax a bit, she asked him point-blank, "These charges are false, aren't they, Daddy? This is all just a pack of lies, isn't it?"

He looked at her and quietly replied, "Whatever I did, I did with a gun pointed to my head. If I hadn't obeyed, I would be dead."

"You can't imagine what it was like, Jodi," Francine added. "Under the German occupation everyone in Warsaw worked for the Germans: the bakers who brought fresh bread each morning; the plumbers who fixed their bathrooms; the machinists who drove their cars; the farmers who delivered their vegetables.

"And your father was made a guard just like twelve thousand other

Polish workers," Francine concluded. "The people of a whole city became slaves to the German occupiers. Even you, Jodi, even you danced and sang for them when they ordered you to."

"Is that true, Daddy?" Jodi asked.

"As a little four-year-old, you entertained German troops," he replied. "They said, 'dance,' and we got you to dance."

"That's not what I asked," she said. "You did guard duty for them at the point of a gun. That's it, right?"

"Absolutely," he answered.

"That's all I wanted to know," Jodi said, cuddling up to her father and kissing him on the cheek. "I'm sorry, but I needed the reassurance."

"Those were strange and difficult times, Jodi," he said.

"Daddy, I love you, and now I know what you went through during the war. What Berson and the OSI are doing to you is so unfair and I have to stop them. Can you get Butnow on the phone? I would really like to hear his update. How does he think this is going?"

When he contacted the attorney, Stamford put him on speakerphone so Francine and Jodi could listen. Butnow was clear, "I have to warn you all that this case could be dragged through the courts for several years because the government intends to present hundreds of survivors as witnesses, just to create an atmosphere of revenge. However, I can also assure you that if it comes to a full-blown trial, the OSI cannot get a guilty verdict."

"But this means that my father's name will be dragged through the mud, nationally, for several years then?" Jodi cried out.

"There's no way to stop it," Butnow said. "They are calling hundreds of people to testify."

"I'm going to Sheldon Haar," she said. "I'm going to have him drop the charges."

"That would be great, if it works," Butnow said. "But I don't think it could possibly work."

"I have several questions first," Jodi said. "One, how did my father enter the United States?"

"Legally. His papers are in perfect order."

"Two, why was he brought to the US?"

"After the end of the war, thousands of people were left homeless. They were cared for in DP camps, where they were fed and housed, and some were allowed to enter the United States."

"Three, why weren't they returned to their former homes?" Jodi asked.

Butnow replied, "It's no secret that many of the refugees were fleeing from the Russians and returning home would have meant that they would end up in Russian slave camps. The State Department was authorized to issue so-called 'paper-clip' visas to thousands of war refugees who had either helped the United States military or who were known to possess certain scientific or weapon skills needed by the United States."

"Finally, why did my father qualify for one of these visas?"

"Your father qualified under the former provision," Butnow said. "As a matter of fact, both your father and mother qualified. They were both heroes."

"Why, then, couldn't my father's contribution be disclosed in the judge's chambers so we could get the case closed?"

"What I told you is off the record," Butnow said. "It's all classified and the CIA won't budge on that."

"I'm going to see Sheldon Haar," she said defiantly. "He's got to drop the charges against my father."

"Give it a try," Butnow agreed. "Sheldon's job is to apprehend war criminals and he's very persistent about it, but he's fair. When you talk to him, don't argue the law. He's one of the most brilliant lawyers in the business. You'll have to find some other grounds to persuade him. Should I soften the ground by giving him a call before you phone him? I have his private number."

"No, absolutely not. If you call him, he'll know we're seeking some way out of this legal quagmire," Jodi answered. "But do give me that phone number, if you would, and thanks for filling me in."

Jodi called Mr. Haar, and briefly told him the problem her father would have if the case dragged on for years. He agreed but apologetically explained that the justice system was such that there seems to be no way to shortcut the process. He sounded sympathetic. Having interviewed hundreds of people, Jodi thought she was a pretty good judge of character, even based on first impressions. She found Haar focused and fair-minded, as Butnow had reported.

"Can we meet?" she asked. "Maybe we can find some way out of this cumbersome process."

"I'll welcome you anytime you can come by," Haar said.

"I can only come to Washington right after Christmas, because I will be in Miami with my parents for Christmas."

"I'll make it easier for you," he said. "I'm coming down to visit my mother in Miami Beach, so I can meet you down there."

Because her father was so depressed, Jodi stayed around the house instead of joining her fiancé, Cal, at the Brickell Avenue condo. All week long, Stamford was in a dour mood, and she could do little to cheer him up, even though she and Cal tried to get him excited about their wedding plans. When they took him and Francine out to dinner at some of their favorite places, he remained depressed and dejected.

During that week, Jodi went Christmas shopping with her mother and when they got home, she suggested having a big Christmas party for all their friends to cheer him up. At first, neither Francine nor Stamford was interested in a party, but Jodi would not let them wiggle out of it.

"I want you to regain your self-respect," she lectured her father. "This trial will produce nothing to incriminate you, or diverge the public's perception of you, but it has already damaged your self-esteem. So I'm rounding up all your friends, just for you to see how many people are standing by you."

The party turned out to be exactly that – a show of support. A crowd of more than one hundred guests gathered in the Wycliff's sprawling home overlooking Biscayne Bay. When the orchestra leader announced that Francine and Stamford would dance a Chopin waltz, all the guests applauded as though they were at a wedding.

"People really love my parents, don't they?" Jodi said to Cal as they joined the other couples dancing on the poolside patio.

The Wycliff Christmas party turned out to be the social event of the holiday season, attended by the governor and Archbishop McMurray, as well as the community's ranking political and business leaders. Butnow, acting as emcee, introduced the governor, who called Stamford "our state's favorite son." Archbishop McMurray joined the tribute, saying, "Stamford is the most honorable and most charitable person in this diocese. He is Poland's gift to the United States."

During the course of the evening, Jodi informed the archbishop that she had arranged to meet Sheldon Haar over the holidays in the hope of getting him to drop the charges.

"Very good, Jodi," the archbishop said. "You might want to consider contacting some Jewish leaders to help you since this has already become a 'Jewish problem.' If you decide to go that route, I can direct you to some people who might help."

Jodi made a mental note of the archbishop's offer. "Thank you," she said, "I'll contact you if that seems to be needed."

Before the night was over, Stamford thanked everyone for coming, calling their show of friendship "the nicest Christmas present a man like me could receive."

Despite his public pronouncement, he privately whispered to Francine, "I wonder how these same people would react if the court were to find me guilty."

Francine was aghast at his bitterness. She pushed him onto the dance floor, scolding, "Now, don't be such a pessimist."

At around midnight, as the party was beginning to wind down, Cal whispered to Jodi, "Sweetheart, you have a phone call – Sheldon Haar."

"What a time to call!" Jodi said as she was picking up the receiver. "Hello, Sheldon, if you hurry to Coral Gables, you can still make the party. I'll try to keep the governor and the archbishop around until you get here."

"That's the best offer I've had all day," he said, "but I'm afraid I can't make it. I've been called back to Washington. We'll have to change our appointment. I'll be in the office tomorrow. Call me."

"Shame," Jodi said, "I was serious about my invitation to the party. You would have seen an outpouring of love for my father that you wouldn't believe."

"How long will the party last?" he asked.

"It's beginning to break up," Jodi said. "What do you have in mind?"

"I know what this trial means to you," Haar replied. "My plane leaves at eight o'clock tomorrow morning, so I can meet you anytime between now and then."

"I have a better suggestion," Jodi said. "Fly with us. My fiancé's company plane is also flying north tomorrow morning. Join us, and we can have a couple of hours to talk with no interruptions."

He hesitated a while and then agreed, giving her the address where he was staying.

"Fine, Cal and I will pick you up in the morning."

*

"Caldwell Boynton, your name sounds familiar," Haar said when they picked him up.

"General Electronics," Cal said. "You represented us in LA on that famous class action suit."

"Yes, of course," Haar said. "Are you still with them?"

"Mr. Haar, he's not with them," Jodi answered. "He owns them."

"No, I don't own them; I'm in charge of acquisitions," Cal replied and, jokingly nudging Jodi, he added, "One day I'll acquire Wycliff Corporation too."

"That'll be the day," Jodi laughed.

"My name is Sheldon, my friends call me Shelly."

"Thanks," Jodi replied. "I like that better."

"Shelly, if you ever consider quitting government work, give me a call. You can get a much better job with us," Cal offered.

"I might just do that right after this trial," Mr. Haar said, "because I've got a hot potato on my hands. And I know that's what you want to talk about."

They boarded the plane and made themselves comfortable over the small bar, where Jodi repeated her concerns about the case dragging on for years.

"Jodi, you're right. Your dad's trial could stretch over three years or more. It has already attracted national attention – even international attention. I'm under tremendous pressure – from both sides. I'm hearing from political bigwigs, business magnates, and religious groups. I make it a point not to get involved with any of them," he said. "But, from the very start, I knew the emotional stress that you must be going through. So when you called, I decided to meet with you. Incidentally, how did you get my private number?"

"From John Butnow," she replied.

"I hope he didn't put you up to this," Haar said, "because if he did, I'd have to look out for potential legal traps."

"No, not at all," Jodi said. "As a matter of fact, when I came up with the idea, he volunteered to call you, but I didn't permit him to for that very reason."

They took their seats in the cabin area and relaxed as the steward served a light breakfast.

"Shelly, my father is innocent," Jodi said when the attendant was clearing the dishes, "but everyone I talk to, including you and Mr. Butnow, expect a long, drawn-out process that might not resolve anything in the end. I would do anything, either on my television series, or by making any contribution to any charity you want to name, anything, to get these charges dropped."

"In some ways, I'd be willing to help you, but my office is in a bind," Haar responded. "From the moment that Dr. Berson brought the allegations to us, the OSI was legally bound to investigate the facts and if they turn out to be valid, to prosecute the case."

"So charges can be dropped only after your investigation?"

"That's right."

"And, in the meantime, you're putting my father through the wringer for no good reason?"

"In the meantime," Sheldon repeated, "our investigators are in Europe digging up old war records and our agents are inviting survivors to testify."

"Those damn survivors of yours are so uptight," Jodi retorted. "They get all wound up at the mention of the word 'Holocaust.' They'll testify to anything."

"Jodi, I assure you, our interviewers are trained to screen out hysteria and racial hatred. But it's true that the process is very touchy and requires careful handling. Those witnesses are anxiety ridden and petrified. Remember, they've been traumatized."

"You Jews are really out for blood, aren't you?" Jodi said angrily.

Cal reached out to take Jodi's hand to stop her from sounding like an anti-Semite, but she waved him off. "I know you Jews are out to bring my father down!"

Haar smiled and took out his wallet. He handed her a small photograph. "This is the only picture I carry," he said. "It's my daughter's first communion at St. Luke's."

"I'm terribly sorry," Jodi said, embarrassed at her outburst. "You see what this case is doing to me. It's turning me into a bigot. And after years of working with and interviewing people of every kind...But I simply can't stand by watching my Dad suffer so much. It's tearing me apart. It's hurting my entire family."

"I understand your feelings, Jodi," Haar said, "and I know what anxiety these frustrations can cause, but the OSI doesn't work on vendettas. We are only after the facts. So far, all we have is Dr. Berson's testimony and we can't go to court on that alone."

"So what's going to happen?" Jodi asked.

"I will try to speed up the case so that it can be resolved as quickly as possible. But I have to warn you that Dr. Berson is a well-known and highly respected person and, as you say, he's out for blood. He truly believes he is bringing a mass murderer to justice."

"Shelly," Jodi asked, "do you think I could gain anything by talking to Dr. Berson?"

"Yes. You could learn how well Berson knew your father in Warsaw and how determined he is now to get your father to the gallows."

"Can you set up an appointment for me to meet him?" she asked.

Haar wrote down Berson's number in his notebook, ripped out the page, and handed it to her. "Here, Jodi, call him yourself. He may be on a rampage, but he's also a gentleman."

When Haar went to the washroom, Jodi asked Cal, "Well, what do you think?"

"He's probably the smartest lawyer in Washington," Cal replied, "and I don't know why the hell he stays in this meat-grinder of a government job when he could name his own price at any law firm."

"By the way, did you offer him a spot at General Electronics just to soften him up?" she asked. "It sounded like you were trying to buy him off."

"Well, I learned a long time ago, there's no harm in sweetening the pie when you want to make a deal," Cal said.

"Haar is no dummy," Jodi said. "He can probably see right through you, and that's not going to do us much good."

"That's true," Cal said. "I'll apologize to him."

"Is he that good a lawyer though?" Jodi asked. "Would he be qualified to be a corporate attorney for you?"

"Sure, he's the tops. That's what worries me about your dad's trial," Cal stated. "Haar is shrewd but so is Butnow. They will spar in the ring for as long as it takes. Between them it's now a matter of personal pride."

They stopped talking when they saw Haar returning to his seat.

"What will you be doing in Washington?" Haar asked Jodi as he sat down.

"I'm not going to stay in Washington," she replied with a kittenish smile. "Cal's going out west and I'm going back to Miami. We just came along for the ride."

"You and Cal are taking this long plane ride just to talk to me?" Haar asked.

"What's another landing and takeoff?" she said.

"Well, that's one for the *Guinness Book of Records*," he said. "Now I've seen everything."

"I would fly to China and back if it would help my Dad."

"Incredible," Haar replied. "I now know you are dedicated to your father, but this beats anything I've ever seen."

"Dedication!" Cal turned to Haar, "Shelly, did you see Jodi's feature 'From Stasha to Stamford' in the *New York Times*?"

"I saw it. I thought, at the time, her words were a supreme tribute to him."

"Thanks for the compliment," Jodi said, sitting quietly as the men talked.

Haar turned to her and said, "Jodi, I hope you don't mind my asking you one thing that bothered me about that article. You didn't mention your Dad's war years in Warsaw, just his life before the war in that small farming village and his rags to riches success here in the States."

"He has never talked to me about those years," she replied. "In fact, I understand that most survivors don't like to talk about their lives under the Nazis. Perhaps he wanted to forget those years."

Haar nodded as though agreeing with her but said nothing.

"That's what I figure, about those years," Jodi continued. "But this trial, this whole ordeal, is making my father despondent and irritable. The looming trial and the daily media reports have taken their toll. His ego is shattered. I've done what I can, getting him favorable PR and holding that party to lift his spirits, but nothing has really helped."

"Jodi, you understand my position. What can I possibly do to help?"

"I need your advice," Jodi said.

"On what?"

"How to get the charges dropped," she said.

"Jodi, I explained to you that even if Berson dropped the charges, OSI would have to continue its investigation."

"Even if Berson confesses that he dreamed them up?"

"You raise an interesting legal point," Haar said. "If Berson came into my office and stated that none of what he said was true or that he was completely mistaken, we probably would consider closing the file."

"Shelly, I would do anything for Dr. Berson if he would do that."

"Do you really think that he would even listen to anything you have to offer?" Haar asked, waving off the attendant who came to offer drinks.

"Listen, Shelly, I know what Berson's late wife meant to him. I'm ready to finance any project in her memory, either in Israel or in America, that he could think of. He can name his price."

"You've really done your homework. How did you know about Sonya?"

"You should watch my TV shows," she replied. "I'm known for my research. I interviewed Sonya Berson with the doctor about seven years ago. She was more interesting, more exciting, than any of her husband's medical experts. She made the show."

Sheldon sipped his coffee, thought a while, then said, "Jodi, you're brilliant. If Sonya's memory is involved, Simon might listen to your scheme."

"I would do anything to help restore my father's sanity," she said.

"If Simon contacts me to withdraw his allegations," Haar said, "I'll intercede with Judge Bailey to drop the suit."

"That's all I wanted to know," Jodi said. "Now I know why I came to Washington. To get through to Dr. Berson. Thanks, Shelly."

Jodi moved to a couch, covered herself with a soft blanket bearing the General Electronics logo and slept soundly. Cal smiled at Sheldon, "Let's go sit at the bar in back so we don't wake Jodi up. She's become a different person since this case came up, more fretful, more serious. Her sole interest is her father's plight," Cal said. "I wish I could do something to help."

"None of us can do anything for her," Haar whispered. "I think someone ought to tell her that this is totally out of her control. And that sooner or later it will control her."

"By the way, Shelly, I hope you didn't misunderstand my offer to work for us at General Electronics," Cal said. "I did not mean it in any way as an attempt to influence your case against Stamford."

"Cal, if you hadn't offered, I would have been surprised," Shelly replied, only partly in jest. "I know my worth on the open market, but I have a job to do at OSI."

Jodi slept soundly until the pilot announced their landing in Washington. Cal looked at his watch and said to Haar, "I'm being picked up by the company's limo. We can take you into town."

"Thanks anyway, Cal, my secretary is coming for me."

As they disembarked, Haar shook hands with both of them. "Jodi, good luck with Berson," he said in parting. "And thanks for the ride."

Jodi had Cal's driver drop her at NIC's Washington studio and dialed Berson's number from an empty conference room. The phone rang several times before he answered.

"Dr. Berson, I'm Jodi Wycliff. Please, before you hang up, would you meet with me? I'll come any time that is convenient for you."

"I am not surprised that you called me," he said, pausing to cough several times.

Jodi recognized that his cough was affected, but responded quickly, "You don't sound well, perhaps I can come to you so you don't have to go out."

"No, no," he said, "I'm still a little feverish. I could be infectious."

"I'm not afraid of catching a cold," she said. "All I want is to speak to you for just a few minutes."

Again she heard him cough several times and again it sounded to her like a bad actor trying to pretend to be sick.

"Dr. Berson," she said, "I made a special trip from Miami only to see you. Please let me talk to you, even if we must talk on the phone."

"I can't," he replied.

"Can I see you tomorrow or the day after?" she asked. "I'll wait for you to get better."

"Miss Wycliff," Dr. Berson said, "I do not wish to sound disrespectful, but I do not want to meet with you or listen to anything you want to tell me."

"Dr. Berson, seven years ago, I interviewed you and Sonya," Jodi said calmly. "At the time, you thanked me for whatever benefit that interview brought you or the Institute. Now, I ask you, I beg you, please talk to me."

"Miss Wycliff," he said, "when I did your show, things were on an entirely different basis. I've been expecting your call ever since I saw you at the installation dinner sitting next to your father. I am determined to press on with my charges against Stasha and I will not be swayed by you."

"Are you that vindictive, Dr. Berson?" Jodi asked plaintively rather than angrily. "You can't even hear me out for a few minutes?"

"Not vindictive, Miss Wycliff. I don't want to hurt you any more by telling you even worse things about your father."

"You already hurt me," she said, "and you're hurting me more by refusing to meet me."

"You are innocent. You do not deserve to be in pain. I understand that," Berson said, "but your father must pay for his crimes."

Having no concept of what Berson had witnessed, Jodi was incensed at his bland indictment, but she continued to plead, "Hear me out. My father is willing to make amends."

Berson interrupted her, "Miss Wycliff, please, you must understand there can be no amends for the deaths of hundreds, thousands, of innocent men, women, and children."

"Dr. Berson, even if my father were guilty, which he is not, this whole legal rigmarole is so unnecessary. He is ready to make a sizeable contribution to any charity honoring your wife's memory, in Israel or in the United States."

Dr. Berson did not reply. She could hear his heavy breathing.

"You designate the price, the commemoration, anything, and my dad will pay any amount."

"Miss Wycliff. That is an obscene offer," Berson said grimly. "Money cannot cover the blood of innocent victims."

"Dr. Berson, the offer comes from me and my father. And if it is a mistake, it is my mistake. But I am heartbroken. You are destroying a fine, decent person."

"You are his daughter and you must love him very much," Dr. Berson said, with no remaining trace of a cold. "But I hate him as much as you love him, because I know what he has done and you do not. I will do anything to unmask him."

"You're not a vindictive man, you're a hurt man, as hurt as I am," Jodi said. "Let's talk this over, please."

Dr. Berson did not reply, but she could again hear him breathing heavily. Then she heard the click of the phone. He had hung up.

Jodi sat at the empty conference table for a long time. She dialed his number again, but there was no reply. She dialed three more times, four, and still no reply. She picked up the phone and hurled it to the ground. Ten minutes later, impelled by fury, Jodi called a taxi and went to the Justice Department. When she arrived at the OSI office, still seething with anger, she asked the gray-haired receptionist if she could speak with Mr. Haar, "for just a few minutes."

The receptionist soon reappeared with Sheldon, who was surprised to see her again so soon. "Jodi, I'm sorry, but I'm in conference," he said. "If you don't mind waiting, I'll see you in just a few moments."

Jodi sat in the corner of the reception area, paging through old magazines. She turned down the receptionist's offer of a cup of coffee and, every so often, glanced at her watch. Twenty minutes had elapsed when Haar opened his office door.

Looking up, she saw the attorney-general of the United States coming out with Shelly. "Why, Jodi Wycliff, how are you?" he exclaimed.

"Mr. Attorney-General, how good to see you again," she responded, standing up for his kiss on her cheek. "What brings you here?"

"Shelly will tell you," he said, "but it's not for publication."

"Wow, you must really rate around here," Jodi said, walking into Haar's office. "The big boss himself came down to your office!"

"And the bigger boss probably sent him," Haar replied. "That's why I had to cut short my vacation in Florida."

He told her that the attorney-general came to express his concern over her father's case and broadly hinted that the president was following its progress.

"In Washington's lingo that means, 'get rid of it.'" Haar explained.

"And one lousy Jewish doctor can rule the roost over the attorney-general and the president," Jodi blurted out. "I called Berson, Shelly. The old bastard wouldn't even see me. His Almighty Lordship wouldn't grant me an audience."

"This is not your day, Jodi," Haar said, handing her a telex that had come in from Germany over the holidays.

She read the telex: "Wycliff file found in German documentation center. Soon as we get it authenticated we're coming home with it. Wycliff is a dead duck. Steve."

Jodi sat down and, letting the telex drop to the floor, she buried her face in her hands and began to sob.

"Poor Dad, he doesn't deserve this," she whimpered. After a few minutes, she dried her tears and asked, "What kind of evidence could be in that file? Will Butnow know about this?"

Sheldon ignored the first question but answered the second, "Yes, when we get through evaluating the material my investigators bring back from Germany, we'll pass it along to your father's counsel."

Jodi thanked him and got up to leave, but when she reached the door, she turned back and asked, "Shelly, can you set up an appointment where I can run into Dr. Berson?"

"What do you mean?"

"Set up some bogus meeting where he and I would have to sign some papers, or some such scenario where our paths would cross," Jodi said.

"Sit down again for a minute, Jodi. When you said you were going to call Simon, I tried to warn you: he can't be bought off and he can't be dissuaded. Even your idea of playing the Sonya card didn't work. If he were to come into this room right now and see you here, he would storm right out."

"Can you talk to him?" she asked.

Haar thought a while, then replied, "I don't think anyone can."

"But my only hope is to get him to drop the charges, and I'm not giving up," Jodi said. "I'm going to get to him. May I use your phone?"

"Are you calling him again?" Haar asked.

"No, I have one more card to play," she said as she dialed Cal's private number at General Electronics.

"Hi, Cal," she said. "What time will your plane be ready to go back to Miami?"

"As soon as I wind up some work here, say in about two hours," Cal answered. "I was planning to stay overnight in Miami and then fly to the coast. But you sound terrible. Did something happen?"

"Oh, Cal, nothing is going right – not Berson, not the OSI investigation, nothing is working out," she cried.

"Listen, Jodi, I'll shift my California trip a few days so I can stay with you, you sound so upset."

"Thanks, Cal, I am upset. I'm too upset. We have to keep trying. Could you have your secretary call the archbishop and make an appointment for us any time tomorrow or even this evening?"

Cal was waiting for her on the tarmac. She fell into his arms, telling him about her exasperating phone call with Dr. Berson as they walked up the gangway into the jet.

"We'll approach it another way," he reassured her. "We have a meeting with the archbishop tomorrow morning at ten. Now, tell me what else is going on. You are beside yourself."

Tense and unhappy, she told him about her bitter conversation with Berson and about Haar's inability to schedule a meeting with Dr. Berson – but she found herself unwilling or unable to tell him about the telex at first. When she complained about Berson for the fourth time, Cal asked, "Did you really expect anything better from Dr. Berson? He's a vindictive old man."

"It's no longer just Dr. Berson," Jodi said, finally telling him about the disturbing telex from Germany.

On the way to Coral Gables from the airport, Cal tried again to console her. "You know the case is in good hands," he said. "Butnow is a great attorney, an expert."

"I know that," she said wearily.

"Listen, hon, instead of running around trying to save your father, maybe you should back off and let the lawyers solve Stamford's problems."

"I can't believe you are lecturing me!" she cried out. "Don't you realize that his problems are my problems?"

She had to wait quite some time before she was able to calm down after her outburst at Cal. Finally, when they entered her parents' home, she called out, "Hi, everybody, are we here in time for supper?" acting as though she had good news.

During supper, she recalled her conversation with Sheldon Haar on the plane that morning and ended by telling them that tomorrow she would meet with Archbishop McMurray to get him involved in helping out in the case.

"He already filed a deposition as a character witness," Stamford reminded her.

"He promised to do more," Jodi replied. "The archbishop offered to get some Jewish leaders, maybe even a prominent rabbi, to intercede with Dr. Berson. Won't you come with us to see him in the morning?"

Stamford hesitated, but Francine urged him to go with Jodi. "It'll do you good to get personally involved in solving our problem."

Stamford reluctantly agreed.

In the morning, they went to the rectory, where Jodi related her bitter experience with Dr. Berson. Father McMurray nodded with understanding, "There now, Jodi. I'm glad to help you in any way."

"The OSI would consider dropping the case if Berson were to withdraw the charges," she whimpered.

"I know Berson," Stamford interjected. "He'll never drop the charges."

Disregarding her father's pessimism, Jodi reminded the archbishop, "At our Christmas party, you suggested that it might be worthwhile to enlist help from some Jewish leaders. Is that still an option?"

"Absolutely. I'll call the president of the Rabbinical Council," Father McMurray enthusiastically replied. "We can ask the rabbi to meet you in his office or I can ask him to come to your home."

"Which do you think is better?" she asked.

"To the Jews, Stamford is the Satan of Warsaw," the archbishop regretfully explained. "But if the rabbi meets you, Stamford, in a friendly setting, man to man, in your home, he might help you get to Dr. Berson. The current head of the Rabbinical Council is Samuel Cohen. He's a very compassionate person."

"Invite him to our home," Jodi said after giving it some thought.

"Hello, Samuel," Father McMurray said into the phone, "I have a favor to ask you."

He paused to listen and then said, "Don't be so hasty, Rabbi. This is one favor you may not be able to grant. It's about Stamford Wycliff. His daughter, Jodi…that's right, the famous newscaster, would like you to meet with her father at his home in Coral Gables."

Jodi could not hear the rabbi's response, which seemed rather long, but she was relieved when Father McMurray said, "I understand and I even agree. So tomorrow at three at their house, Gables by the Bay, last house next to the water. Thank you so much, Rabbi."

"Thank you, Father, but what did you agree to?" Jodi asked.

"The rabbi knows about you, Jodi, and about all the publicity you've created for Stamford. He stipulated that there is to be no press release or public statement about his meeting with your father."

Jodi and Stamford barely made it home before the storm struck. Local newscasters had been tracking the angry red swirl of a hurricane on their maps for most of the week. At last, it veered off to the west, posing no threat to the mainland, but torrential rain and blistering winds pounded Miami's coastline from the edges of the storm. Palm trees and power lines were felled, cluttering the city's streets. The high tide of the bay flooded the Wycliff's manicured lawn, dumped seaweed and saltwater in the swimming pool, and swept over the patio, scattering the potted impatiens.

By that evening, the winds had died down, but the rain continued unabated. Jodi sat by the window, looking out at the flooded garden in the dark gray light of a sunset with no sun.

"Dad," she said, "I think the roses around the pool are gone, but the hibiscus by the fountain is a native plant, maybe it'll bounce back. This storm is such a mess for the whole town. Do you think I should call Rabbi Cohen in the morning and reschedule our appointment?"

"I prefer not to meet with him anyway, so this rain is exactly what I wanted," Stamford replied. "He will probably cancel anyway. Just as well, I just can't face him. I know what his reaction to me will be."

"Remember, Father McMurray says he is a compassionate person."

"But he's Jewish, isn't he? And I'm their Satan."

At exactly three o'clock that blustery afternoon, Rabbi Samuel Cohen, a compact man with a neatly trimmed beard, stood at their door, closing his umbrella and taking off his water-drenched raincoat. Jodi welcomed him and called her father to come down to meet him.

Before Stamford came into the salon, Jodi told the rabbi, "There is more evidence being gathered in Germany. The OSI case is getting stronger. It doesn't look good at all. Our only chance for a reprieve is if Dr. Berson rescinds his accusations to the OSI."

Rabbi Cohen did not respond because he heard Mr. Wycliff coming down the stairs. Jodi introduced her parents. Francine thanked the rabbi for keeping the appointment despite the weather.

Stamford did not wait to be introduced and said bluntly, "Rabbi, I recognize how deeply the Jewish community feels about the Holocaust. I don't really expect you to be able to help me."

The rabbi listened attentively but said nothing as Stamford continued,

"I am the product of the raging anti-Semitism that existed in Poland before the war, and I don't expect to be forgiven for what I have done."

Both Jodi and Francine tried to break in, to mute Stamford's bluntness, but he continued, "Yes, I was an anti-Semite and, as a result of the war, I did a lot of bad things, Jodi. I even helped the Nazis attain their demonic goals in Poland. And I'm sorry for what I did."

Jodi was stunned when she heard this abrupt confession, which contradicted her father's declarations of innocence, but she was able to hide her feelings in front of the rabbi. Stamford noticed his daughter's surprise. He walked over to her seat, took her hand, and said, looking into her eyes, "I also did some good, something I can't talk about."

"Dad, tell the rabbi about how you helped the Americans when you were in the DP camps," Jodi urged.

"There is no point in talking about anything I did right. I can't talk about it," Stamford said. "For the rabbi, the bad will outweigh it."

"I am impressed with your candor and sincerity," Rabbi Cohen said. "On the scale of justice, there is good and evil. The good can counterbalance the bad. Please, do tell me about any good you also accomplished."

Stamford merely shook his head, maintaining a stony silence.

"The good and bad that my father did in Germany is a matter of record, Rabbi," Jodi said. "What we need now is to have Dr. Berson drop his charges."

"I am surprised at your request, Miss Wycliff," Rabbi Cohen said calmly. "You know the Jewish community is aligned with Dr. Berson."

"I'm sorry, Miss Wycliff, but your father's name, Stasha, is an anathema to the Jewish community because the name symbolizes Jewish suffering under the Nazis. As a result of the pretrial publicity, Stasha is not merely some obscure figure from Warsaw."

"The man is right," Stamford proclaimed. "He's a realist. Nothing can be done."

"No," the rabbi replied, turning to Jodi. "Despite all that I have said, I see the anguish, the suffering that you and your father and mother have been put through. If I can do anything to ease or eliminate your pain, just ask."

"Only one thing," Jodi replied, thanking him for his offer, "I would like to talk to Dr. Berson, just to beg him to see me. Can you help?"

"That should be easy," Rabbi Cohen said as she handed him a slip of paper with Berson's number.

When Berson answered, Rabbi Cohen introduced himself. He pleaded with Berson to talk to Jodi, quoting some biblical phrase in Hebrew that Jodi did not understand. There was a long pause and a short click.

The rabbi hung up and ruefully said, "He refused to speak to you, Miss Wycliff, and he scorned me for interceding on behalf of 'Stasha'. I regret I could not accomplish this small favor, but I do have a congregant, a well-known doctor, who might be able to intercede with Dr. Berson."

"Thanks, Rabbi, but if you can't get through to Dr. Berson, nobody can," Jodi said. "By the way, what were the Hebrew words you spoke to him?"

Rabbi Cohen hesitated a bit, looked away from Stamford and replied, "I told him he must listen to you because of the biblical principle which states that children cannot be held accountable for the misdeeds of their parents."

"Rabbi, you hit the nail on the head," Stamford said. "Tell it to Jodi. She must not suffer on my account."

"I wish it were that easy for a daughter to look aside when her father is so tormented," Rabbi Cohen said. "If you think of anything else I could do, don't hesitate."

When Rabbi Cohen left, Stamford said, "I'm impressed with him. He came here despite the storm. He tried to contact Dr. Berson. He understood your suffering. He's everything that the archbishop said about him. I like him. He was honest, warm, and understanding."

"But useless," Jodi added.

*

The judge agreed to hear arguments in chambers before allowing the OSI's new evidence to be heard in court. Haar handed the judge a copy of two documents that his investigators discovered in Germany. One was a scroll commending Stasha Wojchiechowski for the help he gave the Gestapo and the other was a Gestapo certificate, promoting him to the rank of major.

"This document clearly indicates that Mr. Wycliff belonged to the Gestapo, an organization calling for the destruction of the United States," Sheldon Haar stated.

John Butnow argued that first of all, the certificate was a copy and might not be the exact official record of the German Wehrmacht, and second, the scroll did not indicate the kind of help Stasha rendered to the Germans.

"He may have provided them with fresh vegetables from his farm or he may have provided them with any other amenities that in no way contributed either to German military success or political oppression," Butnow argued.

"What about the elevation in rank?" the judge asked. "It seems quite incriminating to be a major in the Gestapo."

"Your Honor, let me explain the real issue facing us," John said. "US intelligence has a complete roster of all the Gestapo officers who had served in Warsaw, which we can produce in evidence. Yet nowhere is there a Stasha Wojchiechowski listed as an officer. My assumption is that Stasha was never officially promoted to be an officer of the Gestapo. The only explanation for this document is that this may have been done as a joke, a spoof, solely for the entertainment of the German troops. It's like the mayor of Miami being named an honorary quarterback of the Dolphins."

"That's sheer nonsense," Mr. Haar replied.

"Is it?" John Butnow asked. "Have you any other example of a Polish citizen serving in the Gestapo as an officer – a major, no less?"

"Your Honor," Haar argued, "this certificate of promotion indicates that he held the simulated rank of a major. In every army a civilian may serve with this rank."

"Not in the German army, and not a Pole in the German army," John Butnow claimed, reminding the judge of the *herrenvolk* theory, the master race theory, which held that the Poles, like the Jews, were an inferior race.

"And," Butnow continued, "this document cannot be valid because it does not bear the official endorsement of the German High Command that normally authenticated every officer's promotion."

"Until the government proves the validity of this certificate," the judge ruled, "I will not admit it as evidence."

Haar immediately asked for a continuance, explaining, "We have tried to avoid bringing in other survivors to testify about the harsh treatment of Warsaw's Jews by the Nazis, abetted by Stasha. We tried to keep this trial from becoming a public spectacle, grist for the media mill. However, we will now search for other Warsaw Ghetto survivors."

Butnow immediately moved for a dismissal since the OSI's case "was based on a useless piece of paper from Germany."

Haar asked for a three-month continuance, arguing that the OSI would require that amount of time to authenticate the documents and to continue interviewing witnesses. Despite John Butnow's vehement objections to any postponement, the judge ruled in favor of Haar's request but warned, "Mr. Haar, that will be your last opportunity to present witnesses and character testimonies. Meanwhile, any disclosure of the contents of these documents will be considered contempt of court. In other words, I am issuing a gag order and I will enforce it strictly."

When the two attorneys left the judge's chambers, a battery of reporters waiting outside the courtroom asked for the status of the case. Haar only stated, "This is a difficult case and the government needs more time to prepare its evidence."

But John Butnow, with his usual broad smile reserved for the press, avowed, "What Mr. Haar means is that the government failed to prove its case against Mr. Wycliff, who is innocent of all charges as we will demonstrate in open court."

Jodi was on cloud nine when Butnow called to report that the prejudicial documents would not be accepted as evidence. She asked him about the arguments in chambers and the reason for the postponement.

"The judge has issued a strict gag order. We are not allowed to disclose anything about these documents. He gave Haar more time to authenticate them, but I am confident that we will get Stamford cleared of all charges at the next session of the court."

Stamford, however, was not as happy as was everyone else. At dinner that night in a fine restaurant in Washington, he spoke little and ate less. "I don't feel like eating and I'm not in the mood to celebrate," he said curtly, sitting at the dinner table as though he were not involved in what was going on, as though someone else was being tried.

Dr. Simon Berson was also saddened by this turn of events. He was annoyed with the silence that greeted him when he asked Haar to explain the reason for the continuance. He became even more upset when the attorney mentioned the judge's gag order.

"This is unacceptable, Sheldon," Berson argued. "I'm going to go to the press myself and tell my side of the story."

"Simon, that might be considered a violation of the gag order and may result in the whole matter being thrown out of court. How many times do I have to remind you, this is not your suit against Mr. Wycliff? It's the government's case. We are not ready to proceed and your going to the press will not move this case any faster. In fact, it could do irreparable damage."

"Then tell me why you need three months," Berson demanded.

"No, I can't and I won't," Haar replied calmly. "I can say nothing to you or to anyone else. But if you want to help, find some other survivors to testify against Stasha Wojchiechowski – if they knew him in Warsaw."

At his own expense, Berson placed advertisements in the newspapers, the Yiddish press, the Anglo-Jewish press, and the newspapers in Israel. He rejoiced when, almost immediately, several letters came in response to his query. Most of the letters were from people who knew Stasha before the war, and they characterized him as a young hoodlum who harassed and beat up Jews in Warsaw. Several Jewish organizations wrote to offer their assistance in his quest. Dozens of letters came from survivors who were eager to testify against Stasha. More than thirty persons were prepared to come to court, each telling a tale of horror. But their testimonies actually gave Haar's staff little to go on because none of them could claim that they actually saw Stasha kill or even strike any Jews.

"Shelly, since our witnesses can't testify that Stasha personally murdered anyone, does all the testimony we've gathered this month amount to nothing?" Berson asked unhappily.

"Not at all," Mr. Haar replied. "Their testimony creates an atmosphere of credibility. They will make it clear to the court that Wycliff was capable of collaborating with the Nazis. However, since there isn't much to go on, you personally must testify to Stasha's collaboration in acts of terror."

Mr. Haar set up an appointment with OSI lawyers to prepare Dr. Berson to present his testimony at the next court session. Berson was deeply concerned about his forthcoming appearance in court, avidly anxious to present the true facts, which he was certain would prove Stasha's guilt.

"Dr. Berson will be a highly qualified witness," the OSI agents assured Haar. "We've hammered every point over and over. He's fully prepared to take the stand."

It was late in the afternoon when Dr. Berson finally stood as witness to testify in open court against Wycliff. At the very outset, however, when the judge announced that the case involved the United States versus Stamford Wycliff, Dr. Berson shouted, "He's not Wycliff. He's Stasha, Stasha Wojchiechowski, the Satan of Warsaw!"

The judge banged his gavel, ordering him to be quiet or leave the courtroom. The OSI lawyers were amazed at Berson's intemperate outburst. They did not anticipate his behavior. But Butnow reveled at the doctor's uncontrolled rage. He saw an opening that might let him totally discredit the witness.

"Does the name 'Wycliff' upset you?" Mr. Butnow calmly asked, assuming a paternalistic attitude to the witness.

"It certainly does," Dr. Berson stated angrily. "He's parading under false colors."

"Do you believe that it would only be fair if Mr. Wycliff would resort to his name rather than, as you say, 'parade under false colors'?"

"If you want honesty in this court, then you should never refer to this demon as Stamford. He is Stasha."

"You may be correct, Dr. Berson. However, let me ask you, does your temper indicate that you might need the help of a psychiatrist?" Mr. Butnow asked.

Haar jumped to his feet, "Objection!"

"Sustained," said the judge. "Strike that from the record. Watch it, Mr. Butnow."

Despite the judge's prompt action, Butnow's allusion to Dr. Berson's mental state made quite an impression on members of the jury, some of whom laughed out loud.

After establishing the doctor's sterling credentials, Haar asked Berson to describe Stasha's actions. The doctor calmly related numerous incidents in which the Polish militia, under Stasha's command, shot students, bashed in the heads of Jews while herding them into the Ghetto, confiscated Jewish property, refused food and medicine to hospital patients, starved the Jews in the Ghetto, and sent Jews who escaped the Ghetto to their deaths in concentration camps.

But Berson again flared up when his attorney, Mr. Sheldon Haar mentioned Stamford Wycliff as the defendant.

"That is a phony name, a cover up," he hissed and sputtered, almost like a madman.

Butnow was able to put Berson's erratic behavior into the record and next called on several prominent government and business officials and Archbishop McMurray. In a quiet, orderly manner, they heaped kudos on Stamford Wycliff as a great humanitarian, an outstanding citizen. Butnow's star character witness was former lieutenant John Kemeris, now seventy-two years old.

Haar had shown little interest in the defense's presentation of previous witnesses because, in the end, they would have little effect on the legal outcome of the trial. However, when Kemeris took the stand and stated that he had been an officer in the CIC stationed in Germany and that he had personally worked with Mr. Wycliff, Haar looked up from his papers to listen.

"Mr. Wycliff rendered a great service to the United States," he said, his Texan accent unchanged by the years that had passed, "though I am not permitted to testify as to the specific nature of the service because it is still classified."

"Can you testify as to the result of the service Mr. Wycliff rendered?" Butnow asked.

Kemeris took a sheet of paper out of his pocket and said, "Before you enter this into evidence, Mr. Butnow, you should know that the intelligence service has authorized the release of this statement but will not elaborate upon it. It says, 'Mr. Stamford Wycliff, formerly known as Stasha Wojchiechowski, rendered valuable service to the US Occupation Forces in Germany. For his contribution to the security of the United States, he was awarded the Army's Silver Star and was recommended for priority immigration into the United States.'"

The spectators in the courtroom burst into applause and the reporters hurried out to file Kemeris's disclosures. The judge, unable to control the commotion, immediately ordered a recess in the proceedings. The judge called both lawyers to the bench, reminding Haar in hushed tones that he had less than a month to come up with evidence authenticating the document that promoted Wycliff to the rank of major in the Gestapo.

"If you cannot substantiate the validity of that document, upon which this entire case rests, I will rule in favor of dismissal of this case without prejudice."

When Butnow left the judge's presence, Jodi hugged him, gleefully congratulating him for destroying Berson's character and thanking him for the array of character witnesses he had presented. Walking out of the courtroom, she saw Dr. Berson standing in the foyer.

"Dr. Berson, you said you didn't want to hurt me, so just listen to me," she said, speaking rapidly as he tried again to avoid her. "I now appeal to you on my behalf, not on behalf of my father. I only want to talk to you so that I can go on with my life."

Berson did not reply. He sidestepped her and quickly walked back into the courtroom, joining Haar who was sitting at the lawyer's table, stuffing papers into his attaché case.

"Our key evidence is on hold. We now have twenty-six days to come up with substantiating evidence. We're in trouble. And your behavior on the stand today didn't help."

"I'm sorry I lost my temper," Berson said. "It's my fault that this didn't go well."

"No, it's not you. It's Butnow. He took advantage of your genuine pain. You and I both need a drink. Come, I'll buy. I'm leaving for Berlin tomorrow."

"Berlin?" Dr. Berson asked.

He could not disclose that the OSI had to authenticate Stasha's Gestapo promotion. Instead, he explained, "I might be able to find other incriminating evidence."

They entered a local bar, where they watched the television broadcast of the Wycliff hearing. As expected, the report headlined the Kemeris statement, hailing Wycliff as a hero, a champion of American security. One reporter editorialized, "The case against Mr. Wycliff should never have begun."

Berson and Haar found a table in a corner of the bar and downed two stiff drinks in rapid succession.

"You did the best you could, Mr. Haar," Berson stated, "and I undermined you by being so outraged. I'm sorry I was such a poor witness."

"Simon, your testimony and those of the character witnesses have little to do with the outcome of the case. What we find in Berlin will determine its outcome. But meanwhile let's drink to Stasha," Haar said, lifting his third double scotch. "May he live long! In Poland!"

"Shelly, that's the first time you called him Stasha," Berson said. "So you really do believe me."

"Simon, I believe, I believe. And that's the first time you called me Shelly," Haar said, trying a bit of humor to fight off his depression. "I don't want to hear any more about the case. Why don't we plan what to do with the money that Jodi offered you as a bribe, I mean, a contribution, to any charity you would name?"

After the fourth drink, both were smiling, slapping each other on the shoulder, still playing the game of allocating Jodi's money to farcical causes. Each came up with all sorts of suggestions, amusing themselves by conjuring up imaginary organizations.

"No, wait," Shelly whooped, "I have it – the National Association of Zoological Institutes."

"What's so funny about that?" Simon asked.

"Its initials spell NAZI!" Shelly said, laughing at his own joke.

He hailed a taxi, instead of driving his car, knowing they were both far too tipsy to drive. By the time they reached Haar's apartment in Chevy Chase, Berson was asleep in the back of the cab. With the driver's help, Haar put the old doctor on the sofa and fell onto his bed with his clothes on. When Simon awakened the next morning, he saw Sheldon sitting at the table sipping a cup of coffee. Holding his head, Simon reached out to accept a steaming mug from Sheldon and joined him at the table.

"Good morning, Simon, let me ask you a question while you drink your coffee. I was thinking about the case, and the one thing that I can't figure out is why none of the survivors ever saw much of Stasha."

"Because he was not just an ordinary guard patrolling the streets," Dr. Berson said. "When I first met him he was working in what the Germans called the Treuhandstelle, the Trusteeship Office, which was headed by a colonel, Colonel Karl Greifler, who was the most important officer in the German Military Government in Warsaw."

"So if Stasha was working in that department, he just didn't go around killing people," Haar said. "He was probably with some high official in a position in the top echelons."

"Well, sure, but what does that mean to us?" Berson asked.

"It means that my men in Berlin were searching in all the wrong places."

Chapter 15

Vice-consul Randolph McGowan, the US military attaché in Berlin, had worked with Sheldon Haar on earlier OSI cases. When Shelly got to Berlin in pursuit of information about Stasha, Randy assured him that the consulate would fully cooperate with him in his search.

"According to Dr. Berson," Haar told him, "Stasha worked in the Treuhandstelle."

"That's the Trusteeship Office, which was even more important to the Germans than their celebrated military units," explained McGowan, whose combination of bald head and neatly trimmed salt-and-pepper beard made him look as European as his local colleagues. "The purpose of the Polish invasion and, for that matter, of all of Hitler's invasions, was to transfer every bit of enemy property to the state."

"We're looking for anything with the name Greifler, Colonel Karl Greifler, commanding officer of the Trusteeship Office. Of course, we need his name linked to Wojchiechowski," Haar explained.

McGowan assured, "We have all the files from that department. After the war, we used the data to authenticate ownership of Polish properties and return them to Polish citizens."

McGowan drove Haar to downtown Berlin and dropped him off at the documents warehouse, where the archivist pulled out the Trusteeship Office's records, stored in fourteen huge cartons. They were neither indexed nor cataloged, requiring Haar and his team to search through every file in each carton.

With the assistance of two German-speaking associates from the consulate, Haar searched through hundreds of documents. Working for two days late into the night, they found Colonel Greifler's name mentioned several hundred times – but not a single reference to Stasha Wojchiechowski.

The next evening, as McGowan and Haar were commiserating over a cold beer, Randy suggested, "Shelly, come with me tonight to this cocktail party at the Siemans' extravagant spread in honor of V-E Day. There's a good possibility that the Russian military attaché, General Mieczyslav Kolcharski, will be there and he'll be able to advise you on tracking down your quarry."

"Who is Kolcharski?"

"He's the Russian expert on Polish collaborators," Randy said. "He's the man you want to know."

When they arrived at the Sieman's sprawling estate, McGowan asked for Kolcharski, but the parking attendant said the general's car had just pulled out. McGowan reached for the parker's phone and called the general in his car.

"Hello, Mitch, this is Randy McGowan. It's not an emergency but I hope you can come back. I think you might like to meet my guest, Sheldon Haar, chief of the OSI."

"Sheldon Haar!" the general replied. "Hold him. I'm turning around."

"I'm glad to meet you, General Kolknarski," Haar said, struggling with the Russian name.

"Another American," the general laughed. "Not Kolknarski, Kolcharski, 'ch' like in *Ach du lieber.*"

Haar tried to pronounce the German 'ch' but gave up, "Sorry, can't do it."

"Then call me Mitch," the general said, leading them to the bar.

"Call me Shelly," Haar said. "All my friends do."

"OSI, Office of Special Investigations? Tell me, Shelly, how does it feel to lose the Stasha Wojchiechowski, alias Stamford Wycliff, case?" Kolcharski asked, slapping Haar's shoulder.

Almost spilling his drink, Haar replied, "The battle isn't over until it's over."

Carrying their drinks, the three men took a table under a trellis in the far corner of the garden.

"Mitch, can you tell me what the Russians know about Stasha that we don't know...yet?" Haar asked.

"We know we'd like to get our hands on him," the general said, "but you'll never get him deported. During the war he was a pain in the ass to the Committee of Polish Liberation, you know, the legitimate Polish government following the war."

"Legitimate," Randy McGowan responded, "from the Russian point of view."

"Now, Randy, let's not get into that again," the general said. "Wojchiechowski was a thorn in our side working for the Germans. Now he's your thorn! I drink to your success."

Kolcharski was charming. He laughed easily, affably teasing Randy about the "Communist bogeyman" scare and joking that the US embassy was still protecting collaborators as "anti-Communists."

"You say that Wycliff, or Stasha, collaborated with the Germans," Haar said, as they accepted a second round of frosty beer from a waitress. "How is it that we can find no record of his collaboration anywhere we look?"

"You're probably looking in the wrong places," the general said.

"Give me a clue, then. We've raked through the Trusteeship Office records."

"You don't understand the Germans yet," Mitch said. "They would never admit that a Pole helped them in such a sensitive department. Look at their Resettlement files. You will find him listed for special resettlement in Germany; that happened just as our Red Army marched into Warsaw."

"A Resettlement record of Stasha in Germany would not help the OSI's case," Haar said. "I have to prove he was a Nazi collaborator."

The general suddenly became serious. "I can give you pertinent records incriminating Stasha, but I need something in return."

"What do you need?" McGowan asked.

"I want the US government to deport Nicholas Klatchko."

"Who's Klatchko?" Haar wondered.

"He was a UN employee in New York," McGowan explained to Haar. "He was convicted as a Russian spy and he's now doing fifteen years in a federal prison."

"General, that's not my department," Haar said. "But when I get back, maybe we can do business."

"For Klatchko, we would open our file on Stasha. Go back to America and send me Klatchko. Now, I have to leave. Shelly, good luck in the trial."

"Wait, General, we'll walk you out," Haar said.

As the three men stood in the dark by the outer gates waiting for their cars, the general said, "Shelly, I should tell you one other thing. Trust your Dr. Berson. He knows what he's talking about."

"You know Berson?" Haar asked.

"I was a nineteen-year-old military tank driver when he saved me from a burning tank," Kolcharski said. "He won't remember me. But I will never forget that he saved my life."

As he drove off, he called out, "Don't forget. Give my regards to Dr. Berson."

Haar and his team spent the next day completing their search through the Trusteeship files and then, following up on the general's tip, they combed the Polish Resettlement files.

They also tried to trace "Zahn," the Nazi officer who signed Stasha's commission as a major. The files held no record of the promotion, or anything to implicate Wycliff, except a memo from Colonel Zahn with instructions "not to proceed against Stasha despite the Rynek involvement."

Rynek was a new name to the investigators. It was not mentioned in any of the cases they had searched.

Over coffee with McGowan the next morning, Shelly told him about the Rynek name in the memo.

"Now, I'm overflowing with questions," Haar said. "Maybe I should go back to Washington and appeal the judge's throwing out that commissioning certificate. I think he was wrong to declare it inadmissible. What do you think?"

"Well, I think taking anything before the Supreme Court is a pretty cumbersome, vastly time-consuming job," Randy said. "First, tell me what have you discovered thus far?"

"Does the name Rynek mean anything to you?"

"If you've hit a name that's not in any of our records, ask Kolcharski about it," Randy advised. "He's the only one who knows anything about the contents of the Gestapo records. They've never been released. When we get back to the office, I'll call him."

*

"Mitch, Randy here. Mr. Haar is about to leave and wanted to say good-bye. Do you have time to see us?"

"Can you bring him out to my house?" the general asked. "I'd be happy to talk to him again before he goes."

The general greeted them at the front door of a large Gothic house on a shady street. Although the house was very formal, the general himself was warm and affable.

"Come in, come in," he said. "Shelly, I am pleased you came to say good-bye."

"Well, as you might have guessed, I have ended my investigations here with a couple of questions," Haar admitted.

"I assumed as much," the general said. "Take a cup of tea and sit down. What else is on your mind?"

"We found an order from Colonel Zahn telling the Germans not to take action against Stasha 'despite the Rynek involvement'. Do you have any clue what that is about?"

The general thought a moment. "Zahn was the last Gestapo chief in Warsaw. But those Gestapo files are in Moscow and they might be there because they might also contain the evidence, explaining why we want Stasha."

"General, can I see the files?" Haar asked.

"Sorry, Shelly," the general said. "Even if I could get clearance to show them to you, it would take six weeks, maybe longer, to get those files to Berlin or Washington."

"What if we deliver Klatchko to Moscow?" Haar asked, taking Kolcharski by surprise. "Would Moscow send me the file on Colonel Zahn now?"

"Can you get Klatchko here today?" General Kolcharski smiled.

"I will do my best to deliver Klatchko, if you get me the Zahn file," Haar said. "The OSI works in close cooperation with the CIA, and Frank Gabelli, its security director, is a friend of mine."

"I know Gabelli. He's a friend to nobody. That's not his job to be a friend," the general said. "I want to help, but your assurances are too flimsy to get anyone in Moscow to move an inch. Can you give me more than that?"

"May I use your phone?" Haar asked.

"Careful, Shelly," McGowan whispered. "Very big leagues here."

Haar gave him a small smile and dialed a number in Washington.

"Hello, Frank, Shelly here. I'm with General Kolcharski. He has a file that is critical to the Wycliff case. He'll give it to me for Klatchko. Can we do it?"

"Shelly, that's an interesting thought," Gabelli said. "Let me talk to the general."

He handed the phone to Kolcharski, who abruptly hung it up, waited a few minutes, and redialed.

"Hello, Gabelli, it's Kolcharski," the general said laughing. "Sorry for the delay. I still don't trust you Americans, so I dialed you myself."

They were on the phone for almost half an hour, using phrases and code words that neither Haar nor McGowan understood.

When he hung up, the general said, "Now, Shelly, go back to Washington. In about a week our plane will bring the Rynek file. You just make sure that Klatchko is on the plane's return flight."

"I will follow up with Gabelli," Haar promised. "Thank you, General Kon…Kolkarski, er, Mitch," again fumbling the pronunciation of the general's last name.

"Konkarski – again – Konarski," the general jokingly rebuked Haar, but he suddenly stopped short and said, "Wait. I remember something. Konarski? Dr. Vladek Konarski. He was part of that whole business in Warsaw. So that you don't return to Washington empty-handed, go look in the Polish civilian files under Konarski, Dr. Vladek Konarski, and you'll find something you may be able to use on Stasha, until you get the Rynek file.

"And when you get to Washington, don't forget to give my regards to Dr. Berson."

The archivist handed McGowan a file marked "Konarski" and the vice-consul thumbed through it quickly. "Holy smokes, Shelly!" McGowan called out. "This is a treasure trove on Stasha."

Randy pulled out an official document and translated: "Stasha Wojchiechowski is herewith commissioned Commandant of Warsaw's Police Department, signed by Colonel Karl Greifler."

The file included a memo on Colonel Greifler's evaluation of Stasha's work, noting that he was "of great help in implementing the German war policy."

"That's it, Randy," Haar said. "Now, can you get me back to the States as fast as possible?"

"How long will it take you to get ready?" Randy McGowan asked. "We've had the vice-president here on a quiet diplomatic visit and Air Force Two is taking off soon to return stateside."

"That's great. Vice-President Bigwell and I know each other well. I'm ready to leave now," Haar replied. "Here's the key to my hotel room. Just ship my suitcase back to the States. And do me a favor, call my office and give them the ETA of this flight so my secretary can pick me up."

Randy called the embassy's transportation desk to reserve space on Air Force Two for Sheldon Haar who had the requisite security clearance. Randy escorted him to the helipad on the embassy's roof where a chopper was waiting. The helicopter landed in Tempelhof's airport right next to Air Force Two, just as the plane's access stairs were about to be pulled back. Haar climbed the steps three at a time.

When the plane reached cruising altitude, Vice-President Stewart Bigwell sent a secretary back to ask Haar to join him in the plush forward compartment.

"Shelly, I'm glad we'll have a chance to talk," the vice-president said as Haar settled into the comfortable chair across from him. "You know that the president cannot officially intervene in your work over at OSI, but don't you think you've gone too far traveling to Berlin just to chase this Wycliff case?"

"Sir, I am constrained by the judge who will be hearing the case not to discuss that one aspect of the case with anyone because…"

"Come on, Shelly," the vice-president interrupted, "we know all about the faked certificate making him a major in the Gestapo. That's been thrown out of court. Isn't it time we just forget all about it?"

"Mr. Vice-President, may I ask how you know about this? There's a gag order." Haar asked.

"Sure. The judge told us. But don't worry, nobody else knows."

"If I could prove that Wycliff was commandant of Warsaw's police department and implemented German war policy, confiscating property, killing people, would it change your mind?"

"Hell, no," he said. "I wouldn't care if he was Hitler's right-hand man. Wycliff is too important to us to be harassed. Anyway, it's more than thirty years ago. The war's over. The Nazis are over. It's time to forget all that."

Haar leaned over to the vice-president so even Bigwell's hovering staff members couldn't hear him. "Let's cut the bull. I already know how this is going. The attorney-general told me of the 'president's interest in the case.' I know Judge Bailey is beholden to the president for recommending him to the Supreme Court and I also know that the president is beholden to Stamford Wycliff for support from the business and agricultural communities and for enormous campaign contributions. But now that I have hard evidence that this guy was a Nazi war criminal, will the president still pressure Judge Bailey to protect Wycliff?"

The vice-president did not reply. He straightened out his pillow, leaned back, and shut his eyes. When they landed at the Andrews Air Force Base, Haar stuck his head through the doorway of the front compartment. "Thanks for the ride," he called to the vice-president.

Giving him a wave, the vice-president said, "Good-bye, Shelly – and just ask yourself, isn't it time to let bygones be bygones?"

Haar did not reply. He was pleased to see his secretary waiting for him because that gave him a polite excuse to refuse the vice-president's invitation to ride with him in the White House limousine.

*

"Hi, Shelly, welcome back," his secretary said, as he got into the car. "You want an update from the front? Stamford Wycliff has been hospitalized and the press is all over it. Butnow is being quoted that OSI harassment brought on his illness."

"Has Butnow asked for a postponement?"

"Nope," she said. "With Wycliff sick, I think he's sure he can get the case dismissed."

The first call Haar received when he got back to his office was from John Butnow. "Shelly, you've heard about Stamford?"

"Yes. Is he doing OK?"

"I'm not sure, but he'll be better if you can tell me you didn't find any new evidence."

"You'd better come see for yourself, John," Haar replied. "You won't believe your eyes. We have a complete file on Wycliff. He was commandant of the Polish police under the Germans. Berson's story is true."

John Butnow rushed to Haar's office and scanned the file from Berlin. As he scanned the pages, Shelly asked, "So, John where do we go from here?"

"Shelly, I'm going to avoid a court fight," Butnow said. "I'll ask the judge to reject this evidence and dismiss the case."

"What are you talking about?" Haar replied. "This is an indictment, clear proof of collaboration with the German occupation."

"I will question its authenticity and, more important, you will have to prove that any action Wycliff took under German occupation, served the German Wehrmacht."

"John, I don't think you have a leg to stand on. But you're his attorney. You do what's best for your client and I'll do what's best for my agency."

Judge Bailey listened to both sides as they argued in chambers. He reviewed the file and turned to Butnow. "John, this information is prima facie evidence establishing Wycliff as a collaborator with the Nazis' occupation forces. The burden of proof is on you now."

"Judge, I want to move for dismissal!" Butnow protested.

"Sorry, John. According to this file, Stasha was, in effect, the extension of the military arm in Warsaw. Read the document, he was 'of great help in implementing the German war policy'. This is very serious, John."

Sheldon Haar watched John Butnow struggling to win his argument, expecting a favorable ruling from Judge Bailey. He tried not to enjoy himself.

"Your Honor, we are creating an historical anachronism," Butnow said. "We're putting a telephone in Ophelia's bedroom. We're injecting American standards of peacetime justice into an alien wartime situation. I'll tell you what, would you allow an American brigadier general to come here, to your chambers, to explain the duties of military police in battle conditions?"

"How is that relevant?" Haar protested.

"We'll know when we hear him," Judge Bailey responded.

Before the week was over, Brigadier General Victor Weiskof appeared before Judge Bailey. He briefly testified, "Civilian police implement the civilian laws of the country under occupation, not the military laws of the occupiers. We don't establish new traffic laws, or new tort laws, or new corporate laws. The civilian police of a conquered people are appointed only to avoid social breakdowns."

After the general's statement, Judge Bailey ruled that the general was not to be cross-examined and addressed both attorneys, "I want you both to sum up your arguments. I'll render a decision tomorrow morning."

From the judge's remarks and his reaction to the general's statement, Haar realized he could not expect a favorable decision. As soon as he left the judge's chambers, Mr. Haar called Gabelli at the CIA.

"Frank, that Rynek file from Moscow is vital now. The OSI can't make its case without it. What's the status with the Klatchko exchange?"

"We have Klatchko ready. He's actually been in our security section's jail cell at the airport since yesterday but I can't get through to Kolcharski and neither can Randy," Gabelli said. "I hope, for your sake, the old bastard isn't backing out."

The following morning the judge, summarizing General Weiskof's testimony, ruled in favor of John Butnow, who immediately moved for a dismissal of all charges.

"Judge, would you grant us a continuance?" Haar asked. "OSI is receiving new information from the Russians' wartime files on the Gestapo."

"The OSI simply hasn't made its case, Judge," Butnow objected. "It hasn't come up with a single piece of admissible evidence that compels denaturalizing Stamford Wycliff."

The judge turned to Mr. Haar, "When is this alleged incriminating evidence arriving?"

"When I was in Germany, the Russians assured me that it would be in Washington within a week," Haar said. "That was ten days ago."

"Mr. Haar, I will give you twenty-four hours," Judge Bailey said summarily. "If you don't have that evidence in my hands by then, I'll grant the defense motion to dismiss."

Berson, who had waited outside the judge's chambers all day, paled when he saw Haar emerge obviously dejected.

"Another failure?" Berson asked sympathetically. "Come on, I'll buy you a cup of coffee."

"We have exactly twenty-four hours to win our case, or your buddy Stasha will be cleared of all charges," Haar said, explaining the deal he had made with General Kolcharski.

"Kolcharski? General Kolcharski?" Berson asked. "Who is he? Sounds familiar, but I don't know why."

"He knows who you are and sends you regards. But unless we hear from him soon, how he knows you won't matter anyway," Haar said. "I have to go back to Gabelli now and try to break this loose."

*

"Kolcharski was not lying to you," Frank Gabelli assured Sheldon Haar who stormed into his office. "What's more amazing is that he was more interested in the deal than you were because getting Klatchko back to the Kremlin is a number one priority with the Politburo."

"So who can you call in the Politburo?" Shelly asked.

Gabelli snapped his fingers and pointed to Shelly. "Right!" he whispered.

He called Moscow and spoke briefly on the phone to his counterpart in the Politburo. When he got off the phone, Gabelli said, "You won't believe this. The plane actually left Moscow last week. The file is on board. But, the plane is heading east, making several stops along the way. Washington is its final stop."

Sheldon Haar said, "Can you call your friend back? Just tell him that if the file isn't here by eight o'clock tomorrow morning, Klatchko doesn't go to Moscow."

At exactly eight o'clock in the evening, the huge Aeroflot jet rumbled to a stop at Washington National Airport. A Russian officer deplaned carrying a carton. He headed to the black sedan where Klatchko sat in the backseat between Haar and Gabelli. Sheldon ripped open the sealed carton, examined its contents, and nodded to Gabelli. Gabelli stood up, letting Klatchko out of the car. The Russian officer escorted Klatchko to the plane; they climbed the steps as Gabelli's car sped away from the airport.

Sitting in his office, Haar and several of his assistants spread the contents of the carton out on a conference table and pored over the documents. Gabelli looked on as they quickly examined one folder after another.

"You'd better find something, Shelly," he said. "I have to know what we got when we gave away Klatchko."

"That's it. Pay dirt," Sheldon called, holding up a file marked Rynek. He showed Frank a sheaf of papers listing Stasha's accomplishments in assisting German intelligence. The file held something else just as important: the original, yellowing, officially stamped certificate commissioning Stasha Wojchiechowski as a major in the Gestapo.

Haar picked up a phone and called Butnow. "John," he said quietly, "this isn't over yet. Come on over to my office."

Wycliff's attorney sat in stony silence as the translator read page after page describing Stasha's services to the German Wehrmacht in full detail. The documents explained everything. The only mystery was a handwritten note on the last page: "Let him have his fringe benefit. Take no action. Zahn."

John Butnow put down the folder, fingering the original certificate and shaking his head.

"Shelly, he's in the hospital and this will kill him."

"John, call the judge," Shelly said. "Dismissal is out of the question now."

Back in his office, Butnow called the judge, and then he telephoned Jodi.

"I thought I would come down to Miami in a day or two to visit Stamford," he told her.

"They've listed his condition as critical, John," she said. "You may not want to wait. I've taken some vacation time from the network to stay here. He's terribly ill."

Butnow buzzed his secretary. "Please set me up on the next available flight to Miami, and find me a hotel room near the hospital," he told her. Then he drove to the airport.

*

"So good of you to come," Francine said, getting up from her chair beside Stamford's bed to greet Butnow. Stamford nodded weakly.

"Stamford had surgery three days ago," Francine said, "and the doctor assured us the operation went well. We're waiting for the pathology report."

"I hope he'll be on the mend soon," Butnow said, trying to hide his shock at Wycliff's ashen complexion and skeletal appearance.

"I've been in the hospital almost two weeks and I'm not getting any better," Stamford said hoarsely to his attorney. "I think they're holding something back from me."

"Well, you're going to feel a lot better next week when I get your case dismissed," Butnow said.

Stamford showed no reaction. Jodi smiled at the lawyer and stroked her father's hand. "Dad, the dismissal will end your legal problems, and the surgery will take care of your medical problems. And remember, we have a wedding to plan. Cal will be here as soon as he can leave LA."

"Look, Dad, your nurse is here. I'll be back in a few minutes. I'm just going to step outside with Mr. Butnow."

"What's the matter with you?" Francine chided her husband after the nurse gave him his medicine and left. "John came all the way from Washington just to give us good news and you didn't even thank him."

"I have other things on my mind," he said. "Now, Francine, tell me the truth about my condition."

"I swear to you, the doctor said your operation was a success and that he is only waiting for the pathology report."

"Promise me that as soon as the report arrives, you will tell me the results, whatever they are," he ordered.

In the adjacent room, Jodi brought coffee to John Butnow, and offered him something from the baskets of treats that were among the flowers and gifts their friends had sent.

After gathering herself, she asked him, "What are the chances that you will get a dismissal?"

"Excellent," he said.

"Did Sheldon bring anything back from Germany?"

Butnow told her a partial truth, "Yes. But I have several experts studying the file who will testify that it's a fraud, just like all the other stuff he brought from Germany."

The waiting room door opened and a nurse stepped in. "Miss Wycliff," she said, "Dr. Greenberg would like to speak to you and your mother."

When Dr. Greenberg and Francine joined Jodi in the hallway, she introduced John Butnow to the doctor.

"I have been following the newspaper accounts of the case," the doctor said to Butnow, leading them to his office. "I think you'd better stay to hear the report."

"Unfortunately, what I have to tell you is not good," Dr. Greenberg said, holding Wycliff's chart. "Pathology shows that Stamford has cancer of the pancreas."

Francine let out a stifled cry. Jodi put her arm around her mother's shoulders.

"How bad is it?" she asked.

"The technical term is adenocarcinoma of the pancreas. It's in its late stages and it's incurable," the doctor said. "I'm truly sorry."

"I have to tell him," Francine said, drying her tears.

"No, Mom. Please don't," Jodi said, tears dripping down her face.

"Jodi, I know your dad," she said.

"Whatever you decide," the doctor said, "do it quickly. I'm going to have to sedate him soon, because he's going to be in severe pain, which I'm afraid will be with him until the end."

"When will that be?" Jodi asked, adding hesitantly, "The end?"

"Not long. A week, maybe two," the doctor said. "Perhaps you want to talk it over. I'll be here if you need me, and I'll talk to him about the prognosis if you want me to."

"That won't be necessary, at least not until I've spoken to him," Francine said. "I have decided to tell him. I promised him. He's always been in charge and he'll want to be in charge now too."

"Doctor," Butnow asked, "could you give me a letter with your evaluation of his condition? That will assure getting the case dropped."

The attorney turned to Francine. "Do you want me to be with you when you tell Stamford what is happening?" he asked.

"No, John, but thank you. Jodi, I'd like you to come in with me, but if you're not up to it, I'll do it alone."

Jodi whispered, "I'll come, Mom."

She clutched Francine's hand as they walked into Stamford's room. Francine motioned the nurse to leave.

"How bad is it?" Stamford asked, trying to smile at them.

When they did not reply immediately, he said, "I suspected long ago that I have a serious illness. I'm right, aren't I?"

"You are," Francine said softly, sitting down beside him. "You have pancreatic cancer." She slipped into his arms, both of them in tears.

"Oh Daddy, Daddy," Jodi cried bitterly as she sat on the other side of the bed, holding him and her mother. "Daddy, I love you so much," she sobbed.

Stamford lay motionless, his eyes moist. "Now, sit me up and talk to me," he said to them. As they helped prop him up on the pillows he said, "Tell me how long this is going to take."

At first, neither woman could answer, then Francine said quietly, "Not long. When the pain gets too bad, Dr. Greenberg will sedate you to keep you comfortable."

"It's that bad," he said, reasserting himself. "Well let's not waste any of my precious time bawling. Ask McMurray to come as soon as he can and let John come back in. Jodi, if I'm going to see Cal before you marry him, he'd better find a way to leave Los Angeles."

When Butnow came in, Stamford shook his hand. "John, do you have an update for me, papers I need to sign, anything?"

"No, Stamford, you don't have to do a thing."

"John, thank you for your good efforts in trying to clear my name."

"My pleasure," said Butnow, taking Stamford's extended hand. "I'm leaving for Washington immediately. Don't worry about the case. Your name is cleared."

The rest of the afternoon, Stamford, Francine, and Jodi reminisced, running through happy memories, and then recalling serious moments in their lives. Several times, Stamford said, "Jodi, always remember that your mother was a heroine. She suffered through the German occupation of Poland and coped with deprivation in Germany until we came to America. And she made me into a gentleman."

When the two women burst into tears, Stamford took Francine's hand and jokingly said, "Maybe if you can give me more of those antacid tablets, it'll go away."

Instead of laughing at his attempt to humor them, Jodi fell on the bed, sobbing loudly, "Daddy, oh, Daddy. I love you. I love you."

The severe pains came that night as he was being prepared for sleep. He cried out, unable to catch his breath, his face contorted. The attending nurse quickly gave him a shot of morphine. When the pain subsided, Francine and Jodi came back in to sit with him.

"Jodi," he said in his weakened voice, "you have nothing to be ashamed of. I will make you proud of me."

Thinking that he was still concerned about the outcome of the trial, Jodi said, "I am already proud of you, Daddy. I always have been. Put all that out of your mind. John has assured us that your name will be completely cleared in court."

The following morning, Archbishop McMurray arrived at the hospital very early. He was alone with Stamford. Jodi and Francine were still asleep in the room adjoining his, part of the suite the hospital reserved for generous donors.

Stamford was awake and struggled to sit up to greet the priest.

"It's time," Stamford said.

"I know," said Father McMurray, donning his stole and preparing to administer last rites.

When he finished, Stamford asked, "Am I forgiven?"

"For what?"

"For being Stasha the Satan?"

"Stamford, Jesus forgives all who have faith in Him. His love will embrace you in eternal life."

Stamford rose his head from the pillow and reached for the priest's hand. “Are you sure? Father, are you sure? You don’t know what I really did.”

“I do know that the last rites are a guarantee of eternal life,” the archbishop said. “The Bible tells us, ‘He that believeth in Me shall not die.’”

The archbishop folded his stole and took a seat close to the bed. He looked up and asked, “Stamford, Rabbi Cohen told me you said you also did some good during the war, but that you refused to talk about it. Can you tell me now?”

Stamford lay back on his pillow and thought for a long while. Then he quietly related the details of Jodi’s adoption, recalling the night her parents brought her to his house before they were put on the death train.

“For almost two years, they were our friends. Francine became ‘Mama Franya’ to Jodi. When I discovered that her parents were Jewish, I sent them to their deaths,” he confessed, struggling to speak. “They gave us their baby – we took Jodi.”

Father McMurray was stunned. He walked around the room, then sat down on one of the chairs near the bed and put his hand to his chest to catch his breath.

“Will you tell Jodi that you adopted her, that you saved her?” the archbishop asked. “Do you need my help? Perhaps you want to discuss it with Francine first? Be assured, though, you saved the child’s life…you gained a devoted daughter.”

When Jodi and Francine came in, they found the archbishop and Stamford engrossed in conversation, so they waited at the door.

“Come in, come in,” Father McMurray said, trying to sound much heartier than he felt. “I’ve been here since early this morning and now we’re just chatting.”

“Thank you so much for being here, Father,” Francine said, “but, Stamford, you haven’t touched your breakfast tray. You have to eat to keep up your strength.”

He tried to answer, but his voice sounded raspy and he was obviously having difficulty breathing.

“I’ll leave you to be together,” the archbishop said. “I have to get back.”

Stamford struggled to regain his voice. “Father, thank you for your prayers.”

“Dad,” Jodi said, “I know that you’re worried about the case. John says it's coming up tomorrow. He's certain it will be thrown out of court. Please eat something so that we'll be able to celebrate your victory."

He had difficulty sitting up and was unable to coordinate his fingers, so Francine spoon-fed him some cereal. He only took a few bites before he muttered, "No more now, that damned pain is coming back."

Francine and Jodi stepped aside as the nurse injected another shot of morphine into his skinny, discolored arm.

When the pain subsided, Stamford told Jodi, "Go on to Washington and make sure that the hearing turns out OK, but come back soon. And, Jodi, don't try again to appeal to Dr. Berson."

"How did you know I approached Dr. Berson?"

"You're trying too hard to save me," he said softly, not responding to her question. "Not with Berson. He suffered too."

"Tell me, Dad."

Stamford lay back and closed his eyes. "Not now. I barely slept last night. I need to rest."

Throughout the day, Stamford spoke little. He slept most of the time. When he woke up in the late afternoon, he showed his first signs of disorientation, calling out "Franya" and rambling on in Polish. At one time, it seemed to Jodi that he did not recognize her at all.

"It's a reaction to the sedation," the nurse explained.

He soon regained his mental clarity and when they told him he called for Franya, Stamford was even able to smile at his own mistake. The two women stayed in the adjoining bedroom through the night, asking the nurse to call them if anything drastic happened.

The nurse smiled at them as they came into the room the next morning. "Mr. Wycliff slept through the night," she reported. "He's feeling a little better."

"Daddy," Jodi said, "the hearing is today. Do you really want me to go to Washington? I can be back this afternoon."

"Go! Bring me a full report," he said weakly, but turning to his wife, he added, "Francine, you stay with me."

"I ordered our pilot to have the plane ready at eight," Jodi said, "and the trial is set for eleven, so I should be back by three this afternoon at the latest."

Just as Jodi was leaving, the archbishop came in. Francine greeted him, then went out to accompany Jodi to her car.

"Have you talked it over with Francine?" the archbishop asked. "I mean about Jodi."

"No, I can't." Stamford lay back on his pillow. He winced in pain, sighed, and breathed heavily.

"I spoke with Rabbi Cohen about your adopting Jodi and told him how you saved her," Father McMurray said. "Do you want to know what he said?"

Stamford nodded and anxiously replied, "Of course. What did he say?"

The priest repeated the rabbi's words, "He who saves one life, it is as though he saved the entire world."

Stamford sat up and asked the archbishop to repeat the rabbi's statement.

"The Rabbi said it's a quote from the Jewish law books, 'He who saves one life, it is as though he saved the entire world,'" the archbishop repeated.

"Do you believe it, Father?"

Father McMurray repeated the phrase again and said, "Absolutely, Stamford, absolutely. You saved Jodi and you saved the entire world, yourself included."

Stamford grasped the priest's hand and kissed it. Then he smiled as he lay back on the pillow, raising his bony fingers as though trying to applaud or, maybe, pray.

*

Jodi arrived at the federal court and found the lawyers already discussing the case in the judge's chambers. She was allowed entry just as John Butnow produced the letter from Dr. Greenberg.

"This letter certifies that Stamford Wycliff has adenocarcinoma of the pancreas," Butnow said, "and that his condition is terminal. The doctor says he probably won't last a month.

"Now, I plead for dismissal without prejudice," Butnow stated.

The judge looked at Sheldon Haar, "Do you have any objection?"

"No, Sir, under the circumstances, the OSI does not object," Haar said.

"Dismissal granted without prejudice," the judge said. "This closes the case of *OSI v. Stamford Wycliff.*"

As the lawyers gathered their papers, Jodi asked Butnow, "What does it really mean, without prejudice?"

He told her, "Officially there will be no record that this case ever came to court. Your father is completely cleared."

"John, you told us that you were going to prove that all the documents from Germany were forgeries. What about that?" she asked.

"Jodi, sit down with me," he said. "I must tell you that one of the files, about a Jewish family named Rynek, is authentic, no doubt about it. Based on the facts in this file, your father could be indicted. That's why I begged the court to dismiss the case."

"But what will happen to the file?" she asked. "It may still be around to besmirch my father's memory."

"Sheldon Haar promised that no one will ever see the Rynek file. Not the press, not Berson. The judge's ruling is final. Your dad's name is officially cleared. I'll call Stamford from the office and tell him so."

"No, John, let me give him the good news. I want to see his face brighten up when I tell him. I'm going back to Miami immediately."

*

When Jodi rushed to Stamford's hospital room, she found a group of doctors huddled over his bed, working frantically over him. She headed for his bedside, but a young attendant stopped her.

"Miss Wycliff, this is not the time to interfere with the doctors."

"But I can't see my father past them," she said, distressed. "What is going on?"

Francine came to the doorway and gently took Jodi aside. "It doesn't look good, honey," she said. "Father McMurray was with Dad for most of the morning. He was in good spirits. Ate a full breakfast, even asked for a shower. But, suddenly, he took a turn for the worse."

From a distance, Jodi watched the doctors. When they finally left the room, she walked over to Stamford's side. His sallow, sunken face shocked and saddened her.

"Daddy, Daddy," Jodi cried out, stroking his shoulder. "You won. You won. The judge dismissed all the charges. You're free, Daddy. You're free. There's no shame. You are Stamford Wycliff, president of the US Chamber. Do you hear me? Daddy, wake up."

His eyes remained in a fixed stare. He was still breathing, but he was unresponsive to Jodi's words.

"Stamford, look, Jodi's here," Francine said to him in a pleading tone. "Your Jodi is back. Talk to her. Look at her."

He did not respond as he struggled to breathe. Every heave of his chest seemed liked an unbearable strain.

Jodi sat next to her mother, crying bitterly while massaging his hands. "Oh, Mom, why did you let me leave? I shouldn't have left him."

At that moment, Dr. Greenberg came in, said a few comforting words to Francine, and added some medication to Stamford's intravenous line. He remained at the patient's bedside a few minutes, told them, "I think the pain will ease now," and left the room.

"Jadzia," Stamford suddenly whispered, turning his head to look at Jodi.

"Yes, Daddy, it's me, Jadzia," she said, smiling through her tears. "It's me, Daddy. I'm back. You won. You're free. The case has been thrown out of court. No more shame! You can face the whole world."

"Listen…Alone. You listen. Just us. Alone."

Francine glanced at the nurse, who slipped out.

"Must tell you…the good…I did…" He spoke slowly, struggling with every word. He reached for Francine's hand. "Jodi, we…Mom and me…saved your life…adopted you…Jewish couple going to die…by Nazis…parents gave you to Mom. Saved your life…You gave me life…Franya…tell her."

"Oh, Daddy, no! No, Daddy," Jodi let out a shrill cry, bringing the nurse back into the room – but Francine motioned her to leave.

"Franya," Stamford said, barely breathing, "tell her. Tell her to be happy. For me…I saved her life…now she's saved me."

He took a long, jagged breath and gasped. His face fell slack, no longer contorted. His chest no longer heaved up and down. The gasping stopped.

Jodi stared at him and cradled his face, embracing him, crying, "Daddy, talk to me, talk to me."

The nurse brought Dr. Greenberg into the room. He listened to Stamford's heart and put down his stethoscope. Then he slowly closed Stamford's eyes.

"Francine, Jodi, I'm sorry," he said.

Jodi and Francine clasped one another, crying bitterly as the doctor led them into their room. "Stay here a while," he said. "I'll order a mild sedative for both of you."

Jodi cried hysterically, walking around the room, trying to find a place for herself. She was sobbing, unable to stop the flow of tears.

"Jodi, Jodi, Dad was very sick and in terrible pain," Francine said, hugging her, weeping. "He's at peace now."

"Mom," Jodi asked as Stamford's body was being wheeled out on a gurney, "what was that all about, what was Dad saying?"

"About what?"

"About what!" she challenged her mother. "About my being adopted."

"Not now."

"Now! I want to know now."

"Your father and I took you into our hearts from the moment you came into our life," Francine said, breathing hard, drying her tears. "We adopted you."

She fell into her mother's arms crying hysterically, "Mommy, Mommy. Tell me you are my mother. Tell me now."

Chapter 16

Hundreds crowded into St. Mary's Cathedral to pay tribute to Stamford Wycliff. Government officials and business leaders came to his funeral from all parts of the United States. They lined up to offer their condolences to Francine and Jodi, who were sitting in the reception room just off the main sanctuary. Amidst flowing tears, Francine acknowledged everyone's expressions of sorrow. But Jodi was unwilling or unable to acknowledge anyone's greetings. Cal, who arrived in Miami the evening Stamford died, shielded her, apologizing for her inability to respond to words of consolation.

The coffin, draped with the American flag, was wheeled into the church. Jodi, Cal, and Francine took their seats in the front row with the governor and the mayor. The governor, the new chairman of the US Chamber of Commerce and Cal eulogized Stamford after the archbishop said mass. They each extolled him as a giant in industry, a recognized civic leader, and a great philanthropist. Throughout the service, Jodi sat in stony silence, impassive, not listening or even hearing the speakers. Her nearly catatonic stupor didn't even lift when Cal read portions of her *Times* article, "From Stasha to Stamford."

At the cemetery, she stood with her eyes lowered, barely looking at the casket. She did not shed a tear during the proceedings. When Cal supported Francine, who fainted as the casket was lowered into the grave, Jodi did not extend her hand to help her mother. The service closed with a twenty-one-gun salute by a local military unit.

Driving back from the cemetery in the limousine, Cal tried to comfort her, repeating the many tributes extolling Stamford. Francine said she was grateful for the honors showered upon her husband, but Jodi did not, could not, say a word.

"Jodi, I know what's bothering you," Francine said when they were finally alone in their home after all the visitors left. "But I want you to know that he loved you more than any father could love his own daughter."

"I know," she said, bursting into tears for the first time since her hysterical weeping at the hospital the moment her father died. Cal held her until she stopped crying and helped dab her eyes.

Quietly looking at Francine, Jodi took a deep breath and asked, "Mom, who am I?"

"Jodi, here, have a drink, rest a little, and let your mother rest," Cal urged. "We can talk as much as we want later."

Jodi sternly waved him off and turned to her mother, "I want to know everything, Mom. I want to know how you adopted me."

Francine took a sip of the scotch and began describing the night Tomasz and Irena Rynek, Jodi's birth parents, brought her to their home.

"Did you know them before that night?" Jodi asked. "Mom, please, please start at the beginning. How did you know them? What were they like? Why did they give me up? What happened to them?"

Cal refreshed her drink and asked, "Francine, do you want me to leave, so you and Jodi can talk?"

"No, Cal, you're going to be family, you should know," she said, reaching for his hand. She walked around the room, smoothed her hair, and then sat on an upright chair facing Jodi.

"All right, as best as I can remember," Francine said, "right after I married Dad, I became pregnant. I miscarried and almost died. I needed extensive surgery. I was devastated after the operation because the doctor said I could never bear children.

"Without a baby, I felt as though I had no reason to live. I lived like a hermit, but once, when I went to church, a young couple sat down next to me and when they got up to go to the altar for communion, the mother asked me to watch their sleeping baby. That was you," Francine told Jodi, pausing often to recall details.

"Their names were Tomasz and Irena Rynek and, after that, I often arranged to be in church at a service where I was sure they would be there. I came to the service only so that I could be near you. Of course, we got to know one another and we would meet in the park or at the market. Eventually, we all became friends including Dad and Tomasz. I would visit their home; they would come to dinner with us. When we were together, I always played with you. I can never forget that beautiful, smiling baby. Jadzia, that was your name.

"Often, when the Ryneks had to be away from Warsaw, they would leave you with us. Those were the most precious moments of my life, particularly as the German occupation of Poland became more and more bleak. I became your second mother. You even called me 'Mama Franya'. Without you, I could not have gotten over my despair about going through life without a child of my own."

"Then what?" Jodi asked.

Francine spoke hesitatingly. "Then they came in the middle of the night. I remember Irena was carrying you in her arms. Your father handed you to me, telling me that I loved little Jadzia and little Jadzia loved me. Then they left quickly."

"That's all?" Jodi asked. "They didn't say anything. They didn't say why they were giving me up?"

"Jodi, please."

"No, Mom, I have to know."

Cal reached out to Jodi, "Sweetheart, your mother is exhausted. It's been a hard day. Can't we do this later?"

"No, Cal, we can't," Jodi said brusquely. "Please, don't interrupt. Mom, please tell me what happened that night."

"I can't recall. I was still half asleep. It was in the middle of the night," Francine said. "I…"

"Mom," Jodi said, kicking off her high heels and settling into the couch facing her mother, "I must know. Why did they come to you in the middle of the night? What did they say when they abandoned me, when they gave me away?"

"They didn't abandon you. They came from jail," her mother confessed, taking a deep breath and closing her eyes. "They were in chains. That's what woke me up, the clanging of the shackles. They handed us their baby, asked us to take care of you and walked back with their jailer."

Jodi persisted. "What did they say? What did Daddy do? Mother, tell me, I must know everything."

"Can we talk about that tomorrow?" she asked, holding her hand to her chest.

"No, Mom. It can't wait."

Francine leaned back in her chair, folded her hands on her lap, and rested a few moments before talking. Then she spoke rapidly in a staccato tone.

"They had escaped from the Jewish Ghetto. They had changed their names to Rynek and lived as Catholics on the Aryan side. But they didn't tell us.

"A year later, the Germans discovered that the Ryneks were living with false identity cards. They imprisoned them and shipped them off to Auschwitz or Treblinka. That's when they brought their baby to me. They said they knew what was going to happen to them."

"What did happen to them?" Jodi asked.

"Stop it, Jodi. Stop it!" Francine begged, staring at her daughter, tears welling up in her eyes. "You sound like a prosecutor." Looking about the room, she wiped beads of sweat from her face and forehead and with a quivering voice said, "And now I feel like the Ghetto is closing in on me."

"I'm sorry, Mommy. I really am. I don't blame you."

"Blame me?" Francine retorted, stomping out to the patio to compose herself, turning her back on Jodi.

When she walked back in a few minutes later, she practically shouted, "You don't blame me! Is that what you said! Do you know what the Germans would have done to us if they'd learned that we'd adopted a Jewish child? Do you know what they would have done to Dad if they'd discovered that he faked his report saying that you died in the prison?"

"I'm sorry, Mommy," Jodi said, embracing her mother and weeping on her shoulder. "I'm sorry. I love you. I loved Daddy. I'm sorry I hurt you. I didn't mean to. But I have to understand where I came from."

For quite a long time, Jodi and Francine sat on the sofa, holding each other. Then Francine got up. She lifted one hand to straighten her hair, but held tightly onto Jodi with the other.

"I have to go to bed, Jodi. Are you staying here are or are you going home with Cal?"

"I'll stay here as long as you'll need me," Jodi said.

When Francine's sleeping pill took effect, Jodi gently closed her door and went back downstairs, where Cal was waiting in the den.

"Why did you have to put her through the wringer?" Cal said severely. "Why did you torture her by questioning her about the gruesome past?"

Jodi quietly replied, "Cal, you can't know what torture is, unless you go through what I'm now going through."

"Jodi, it seems so uncalled for. You know I care about your questions, but couldn't they wait a day or so?" Cal asked.

He walked over to the bar and added, "Here, you've had a hard day too. Can I make you a drink? It'll make you forget your grief."

"No, Cal, thanks. You go on back to the condo. You must be wiped out too."

"You don't need me to stay?" he asked.

"No, I'll be OK," she said. "I need to be alone."

"All right, then," he said. "I'll call you in the morning."

Jodi saw him to the door and gave him a peck on the cheek as he walked out to his car. Returning to the den, she was deeply hurt that Cal did not realize, had no inkling of what she was going through. How she wished he really understood.

Alone in the den, she finally sat at her father's old rolltop desk to write down everything her mother had told her about the Ryneks. At times she became so upset, her hand quivered while writing. Soon it shook so badly that she had to stop. She switched on the television but as quickly turned it off, unable to concentrate even on the newscasts, unwilling to be reminded of her work.

She walked out on the veranda overlooking the bay and, staring out into the pitch black night, she sighed, "Irena Rynek...Tomasz Rynek! Where are you? What did you do to me?"

It was 2 A.M. when she walked back into the house and headed for her old bedroom. She selected a bottle of mellow Shiraz and a crystal goblet from the bar. Still in the black Donna Karan suit she had worn to the funeral, she sat on her bed, drinking one glass of wine after another until she had emptied the bottle. She knew she was getting drunk; she desperately hoped it would put her to sleep.

Hours later, still unable to sleep, she searched the medicine cabinet and took two Xanax capsules.

In the morning, Cal came by to check on her. He was planning to take her to Bermuda in a few days to help her forget the trauma of her father's death.

"Hi, Minerva, where's Jodi?" he asked the Wycliff's housekeeper.

"She is still sleeping, Mr. Cal."

When he stealthily walked into her room, he found her sprawled on the unmade bed, still dressed in her silk shirt and suit skirt.

"I haven't slept at all, Cal. I just need to sleep," she said when he suggested their taking a trip to Bermuda.

"No. Just sleep," she repeated, pushing him away as she closed her eyes and lay back, beyond exhaustion. He picked up her crumpled blazer from the floor, draped it over the back of the dressing table chair, covered her with a large cashmere shawl he saw folded neatly at the foot of her bed, and closed the door quietly behind him.

Cal went to his Miami office, and at mid-afternoon, he called Jodi to tell her she needed to get away from the death scene. Francine answered the phone.

"Francine, it's Cal. How are you holding up?"

"I'm numb, Cal. I hardly know what to feel or think, and I'm worried about Jodi."

"I wanted to find out how she is, if she wants me to take her anywhere."

"Jodi left," Francine told him. "She said she was going to the cemetery. I wanted to go with her, but she insisted on going alone."

Cal found Jodi crouching over the freshly covered grave, her hands smoothing the soil, her eyes filled with tears and her face streaked with wet sand.

He put his arm around her, "Jodi, sweetheart, let me take you home."

She did not respond to his pleading. She agreed to leave only when a cemetery attendant came by in a buggy and said, "Sorry, Miss, you have to go. It's time to lock the gates."

Cal followed her home in his car. She parked her car and walked over to stand beside his car window. "Cal," she said, "please go on back to the condo. Thank you for trying to take care of me, but I just want to be alone."

*

Over the next few days, Jodi did not fare any better. She either locked herself in her room or left the house telling no one where she was going. She often stayed away all night, returning the following morning and continuing her self-imposed isolation.

After about ten days of this, Francine's phone rang just after 3 A.M. "Senora," said a strange man's voice. "My name is Geraldo. Your daughter is here, in my pizza place. Very drunk. Sleeping. You'd better come for her."

"Give me the address," Francine commanded, instantly wide awake. "Someone will be there right away."

Francine called Cal, who immediately threw on a pair of jeans and drove out to the small restaurant on the outskirts of Hallandale. He found Jodi curled up on a bench beside one of the tables, passed out and reeking of alcohol. He recognized Geraldo from his mug shot in a recent story in the *Miami Herald*. The man was a drug dealer, just released from prison.

He confronted Geraldo. "What did you give her? Is she drugged? Did you sell her something?"

"I don't do drugs no more. Don't use 'em, don't sell 'em. I'm not going back to the slammer; I'm done with all that. I'm doing you a favor here, *comprende*?"

"Thanks, pal," Cal said. "Don't get excited. Just tell me what happened."

"She came in. She had a pizza, some Chianti, and she went to the bathroom, over and over. Probably sniffing coke. Then she passed out. Maybe it's an overdose, so I called the number on her key chain and got her mama. What else could I do?"

"You did fine," Cal said. "Thanks for calling."

On the way home, Cal called 911 from his car phone and described Jodi's condition. The operator said, "Don't take her home. Where are you now?"

"I-95," he said, "near the I-195 Miami Beach turnoff."

"You're not far from Mount Sinai. Take her right to the emergency room, immediately. I'll call and tell them you're coming."

Early in the morning, Dr. David Wolf arrived to check on Jodi. Francine followed moments later. She found Cal sitting next to Jodi's bed and was shocked at the sight of Jodi, asleep or unconscious, twitching and jerking under restraints with an intravenous drip in her arm. Her face was pale and drawn.

"She's apparently been on quite a drug binge," Dr. Wolf explained. "She came pretty close to the line. We have to keep her hospitalized until she's detoxed."

"Will she be OK?" Francine asked in a worried voice.

"She needs intravenous fluids and nutrition," he said, "and it might take a few days, but I think she'll be all right. I'm more worried about her emotional state."

Cal and Francine took turns staying by Jodi's bed. They never left her alone. Three days later, when her condition had stabilized, Dr. Wolf met with them in the waiting room.

"I'm about to discharge Jodi. You can take her home. Physically, she's clean. But like I said, I'm worried about her psychologically."

"So are we, Dave," Francine said. "I was with her all day today and she remembers nothing except that Stamford died. That's all. Nothing about the funeral, our conversations, the burial, taking drugs, drinking. Nothing."

The doctor assured them that in a few days she would come around.

As the doctor predicted, Jodi's memory returned. Within days, she could recall every detail of the funeral and the burial, about her adoption, even about her drugged vigil in Geraldo's restaurant.

A month or so later, Jodi went back to work in New York. She was grateful to slip into her old routine at the Network International and to begin planning her next series of *Jodi Wycliff Specials*. She commuted to Miami most weekends to be with her mother, spending time in both cities with Cal. She repeatedly told him how deeply grateful she was for his quick rescue at Geraldo's.

While enjoying their Christmas vacation in the Bahamas, Jodi and Cal began to make plans for their wedding, which they had scheduled for the following April. Francine was overjoyed at their having set a date at last and promised she would make them "a real wedding, with all the trimmings."

On Super Bowl Sunday, Jodi dropped the invitations in the mail, then she and Cal had brunch at a sidewalk café in Coconut Grove. Back at his condo, Cal settled in to watch the football game while she took the Sunday papers out on the balcony. Suddenly, Cal heard her shriek. He came running to the terrace to find her bending over the railing, holding her head and sobbing. He led her back to the sofa, shut off the TV, and handed her his frosty beer. She sipped it slowly and then held the cold can to her forehead. Gradually, her color returned.

"Jodi, what's wrong? Do we need to go to the hospital?" he asked with alarm.

"No, no, I'll be better in a minute, but I felt so dizzy and strange, so suddenly. Don't worry. I'm already feeling steadier. Go back to your game."

"No. Tell me how it happened," he said.

"It's nothing, honest," she said. "It's probably something I ate."

"Tell me exactly how it happened," he insisted.

She hesitated, then replied, "I was reading the paper. All of a sudden, everything went black. Not black, but like before a storm when the skies get dark and gray. I felt as if I was going into a spin. I couldn't move. That's when I called out."

"But you did move," he said. "You were bending over the railing, holding your head."

"Was I?" she asked.

"I'm going to call my golf partner, you know, Alan Kitcher. He's a lousy putter but he's a great psychiatrist."

"Cal, that's ridiculous. I had a fainting spell. Maybe I ate some bad tuna at lunch."

"You had a fainting spell. You're not sick. There may be some other cause. It can't hurt to call Alan."

He hit a number on his speed dial. "Alan, Cal here. We might need your help." He described Jodi's experience and asked if she needed professional psychiatric help.

"Put her on the phone," Dr. Kitcher replied.

Cal handed Jodi the receiver, which she took reluctantly, glaring at him angrily.

"Hello, Jodi," Dr. Kitcher said. "I need you to come in. After all, I never had a celebrity client before. If you need enticement, how about sharing a taco or two with me during my lunch hour tomorrow?"

Jodi smiled and put her palm over the mouthpiece, saying to Cal, “He’s some character.”

Then she said to the psychiatrist, “I’ll have to delay my return to New York, but I’ll do it if you make sure there is hot salsa on my taco.”

“You’ve got it. Tomorrow at noon.”

On Monday morning, Jodi and Cal woke up early, but lolled about in bed reading the papers. He took her into his arms and teased, “I like sleeping with older women.”

“You bum,” she laughed, “you’re only two and a half years younger than me.”

“Three,” he said, reaching to slip off her sheer negligee but clumsily tearing the thin ribbon of a shoulder strap. He said he was sorry.

“Never mind,” she said, “it’s coming off anyway.”

As they cuddled later, she nestled against his shoulder and asked, “Will it be this good after we’re married?”

“I’ll be more tender,” he said. “I won’t rip off your nightgowns.”

“You’d better,” she said, “or you’ll sleep alone.”

While driving to the doctor, she wondered why Cal insisted she had to see the psychiatrist. After all, she reasoned, she was creative, happy, content, and completely at ease. If not reconciled to her father’s death, she had come to peaceful terms with it. And that is exactly what she told Dr. Kitcher once she was sitting down on a comfortable leather chair in his office.

“Fine, fine, you feel great,” he said. “But since I can’t take my fee unless you talk, please say something, anything. About Cal, about yourself, or even about how Cal libels my putting. I promise not to listen.”

She instantly liked him. He was about fifty years old, with graying hair and expressive hands. His voice was soft and he seemed to have a great sense of humor. As she thought about what she might say, he offered her an iced tea and the promised spicy taco.

“I’ll be honest with you. I didn’t want the tacos and I didn’t want to come here,” she said. “I’m here because Cal insisted.”

“That’s fine with me,” the doctor said, biting into his taco. “You watch me eat and I’ll do you a favor. You can tell Cal we had a good talk. That’ll satisfy him.”

She laughed and asked him how long he had known Cal. This led them into chatting about unimportant things like what was good and bad about living in Miami, why she had never participated in sports, and her plans for her wedding to Cal.

"You'll be at our wedding, of course, but now you'll be my guest as well as Cal's."

"That's good," he replied. "After all, these five years as Cal's golf partner would justify it."

"You know, that's how long I've known him too," Jodi said, sitting comfortably in her chair.

"You've known each other for five years? What's taken you both so long to get married?" Dr. Kitcher asked. "Unless you can't afford a wedding…"

They both laughed.

Jodi sat up, leaned over his desk and, looking squarely at him, asked, "Alan, can a person involuntarily try to commit suicide?"

"Why bring that up?" Dr. Kitcher asked.

She described her experience the day before while sitting on the veranda.

"A decision to commit suicide may be made under duress, but the actual act is done when a person is in full control of his faculties. Why do you ask?"

"Cal found me bent over the terrace railing, practically unconscious. Could it be possible that I had planned to jump to my death? What really worries me is that I might have unconsciously been contemplating suicide. That's terrifying."

"Back up, Jodi. First tell me about the depression, the fainting spell."

"It's been happening quite often. Since father, on his death bed, told me that they adopted me from a Jewish couple who were on their way to the concentration camps. I was shattered by his death – even more so by the news of my adoption."

"You learned about that abruptly, amidst bitter grief," Dr. Kitcher replied, "and that may have provoked this reaction. How did you react to the death of your father?"

"I went on a binge. I did things I haven't done since I was a teenager – alcohol, cocaine. Heaven only knows what would have happened to my career if anyone had found out. Cal had to rescue me after I passed out in a drugged stupor in some hood's pizza parlor."

Under his subtle questioning, she told him in detail how she reacted to being told she was adopted, how she clandestinely bought drugs, taking them to "ward off feelings of distress that plagued her."

She agreed when he suggested that resorting to getting drunk or getting a high was a form of escape.

"I doubt that suicide is your problem," Dr. Kitcher said reassuringly. "The real question is, why do you feel the need to escape? You're back to your normal routines, so why escape? That is what you have to solve."

"Is it because of the anguish I felt when my dad died?"

"Death of a loved one can cause emotional stress. True. It's called separation anxiety. Also, in your case, learning that Stamford was not your father and that Francine is not your mother could certainly be a contributing factor. But why is there a need to escape?"

"Am I sick?" shc asked.

"No. I can understand your feelings. They're quite common."

"What's behind my blacking out so suddenly?"

"Jodi, there could be any number of reasons, physical and emotional. So, to start with, I suggest a good physical examination."

"Physically, I'm in great shape. What about the emotional aspect?"

"Well, tell me about your emotions."

She spoke at some length about her concern for her mother, who had always relied on her father, about her forthcoming marriage, and about her work at the network. She could talk about those topics easily but none of them were the source of the problem.

As the session drew to a close, she asked, "Is it OK for me to want to know more about my natural parents?"

"It is quite natural for adoptive children to seek out their past," he said. "Follow your instincts about pursuing your desire to search for your natural parents."

"OK," she said, "but I think I have to start with my mother, who might have more information for me."

"Remember that your mother may be suffering as much as you," he said. "Consider the fact that until your father's death she never told you about your adoption."

*

An hour later, Jodi took Francine out to lunch at a café beside the picturesque sailboat basin in the Grove. They sat in the balmy shade waiting for the sandwiches they had ordered. As they watched the sailboats tug at their moorings, Jodi finally said, "Mom, I know it's painful to talk about my adoption, but I have a lot of questions to ask you."

"Why, Jodi, why?" Francine asked. "Why can't you let the past be past?"

Remembering Dr. Kitcher's warning about her mother's sensitivity, Jodi fibbed, "I'm thinking of writing something about myself, like, 'From Jadzia to Jodi.' I want to start from the moment I was brought to you."

"Don't do that!" her mother interrupted.

"Why, Mom?" she asked. "There's nothing to hide. You and Daddy risked your lives to save mine."

"Jodi, let the past be past," she repeated. "I beg you, don't bring all this up again."

Jodi shook her head in disbelief. "Why not, Mom? I feel such a deep need to know more about all this."

"Try to put it aside," her mother said. "Those years were years of terror and only those who experienced them could possibly understand why I can't bear to talk about it. Now please, please just stop!"

"You must understand that even knowing as little as I do about the circumstances of my adoption, I love you more than ever. If it hurts you, I promise never to bring up the subject again. Now, tell me, how's the chicken Caesar club?"

As she paid for lunch, Jodi gave her mother Dr. Kitcher's name and address, asking her to send the doctor a wedding invitation.

"Sure, Jodi, but who is he?" she asked.

"Well, he's a friend of Cal's, and he's my therapist," Jodi admitted.

"You poor dear," Francine said. "You must be suffering a lot from what I've told you."

"No, I swear to you, I'm not suffering. Not at all," she said, adding, "I'm only following Cal's advice to get some counseling."

After she took Francine home, Jodi called Cal to thank him for recommending Dr. Kitcher.

"I really like your golfing buddy," she said. "We had a great conversation. He suggested that I should search for my birth parents. I tried to get some information from Mom at lunch, but it was impossible for her to even begin to talk about the war years."

"Why annoy her?" Cal asked. "Or rather, why annoy yourself? I'm not a psychologist, but the less you think about those years, the better off you'll be. Your mother's right. Let the past be past."

"Cal, I have to know about those years," Jodi said. "I want to know everything."

"OK, my love," Cal said, "but do me a favor."

"Anything," she replied.

"Fix the strap on your nightgown," he said. "I want to tear it again. That'll take away all your depression."

"I'd never object to a little recreational negligee destruction," she said, trying to pick up on his mood, "but this business about my past is serious to me. Don't you understand what I'm going through?"

"I know that you're driving yourself crazy," he said.

"One day you'll understand all the pain I feel about this whole revelation from my father," Jodi said.

"You're causing yourself more pain by wanting to search for your dead parents," Cal said.

"Let's stop this quibbling," Jodi said. "I know what I have to do. Don't worry about it for now. I'm running up to New York to work, and I'll be back in Miami for the weekend."

"Sounds good," he said. "As long as you're in New York, would you run by the Wycliff Corporation headquarters? There are papers there that need your signature. You're still listed as board chairman pro tem."

"Sure, Cal," she said. "What are your plans?"

"I'm heading for the West Coast office for a few days, but you know how to get me anytime you want me," he said. "We'll talk on the phone again tonight. See you soon, sweetheart."

Relieved to be back at her desk at the NIC office in New York, Jodi plunged into a mountain of work, arranging for the special series on the Middle East to be shot the following week, setting up coverage for the president's visit to a Veterans' Gala at the Lincoln Center, and tackling a thorny set of complicated production problems.

Jodi was in her office before seven each morning and rarely left before midnight. Her staff, relieved to have her back, ramped back up to her energy level as she dealt with myriad details. She also spent time at Wycliff Corporation headquarters, meeting with department heads, even plodding though the company's proposed budget.

To her staff's amazement, when Thursday night came, she was ready for her weekly taping, looking as dazzling as she had always been. Little did they know how eager she was to head back to Miami to unwind for the weekend.

But on Friday morning, NIC's CEO, Winston White, came into her office. "Jodi," he said, "we're meeting with the union's officers for final negotiations Saturday morning. We need you at the sessions because you know most of the participants, who will be making final contractual decisions so we can avoid a strike."

"No problem," Jodi replied. "Cal won't be back in Miami until Monday, so I can wait a day to head south. Just tell me where you want me and when."

"We'll have the labor meeting in conference room C on the fifteenth floor. We're going to start early tomorrow morning with breakfast at eight, but you're going to want to read this tonight," he said, handing her a bulky file about the tricky labor negotiations.

"I'm not sure 'want' is the right word," she grinned, "but I'll be ready in the morning."

The labor negotiations turned into a twelve-hour session that broke up Saturday evening. It was a crowning success for Jodi. Labor and management agreed to the conditions she suggested as compromises in their three-year contract.

She went from the meeting to La Guardia Airport and caught a late flight to Miami.

She fell into bed at Cal's Miami condo, exhausted, just before dawn. Late Sunday morning she spent a couple of hours at the health club, and left the spa feeling refreshed after a steam bath and a massage. She stopped at the coffee shop and had a quick omelet while she listened to a couple of elderly women arguing about vitamins, diets, and problems with their grown children. She laughed to herself, thinking they would be good subjects for a sitcom.

But when she returned to the condo, the symptoms hit her again, out of the blue – the excruciating headache, the chills, the sudden perspiration. She recognized the recurrence of her depression and called Dr. Kitcher's number, asking his service to have the doctor call her right back.

When the phone rang, she picked it up on the first ring. "Hello, Alan, it's coming back. The depression, the sweating, the headache."

"What did you do in New York?" he asked.

The question caught her off guard and annoyed her. "What in the world does my job at Network International have to do with my sudden symptoms that I can't account for?"

"Just tell me, Jodi. Tell me what you did in New York," he said patiently. "I'm looking for a reason."

She sighed and reeled off her week's activities, concluding with the successful negotiation that ended the strike.

"So you solved everybody's problems except your own," he said.

"Alan, how do I solve my problems when I don't think I have any problems?"

"If you have no problems, why did you call me?"

She sat silently, the receiver pressed against her ear.

"Jodi," he said steadily, "come to my office, now."

*

The medical complex was always quiet on Sunday afternoons. The parking lots were as empty as the waiting rooms. Walking along the long, darkened corridor, she saw the light shining under Alan's office door. She walked in and sat down, once again, in the leather armchair facing his desk.

"Alan, my only problem is that I suddenly black out and feel the chills coming on, the headaches, the sweating. Why? How can you solve that?"

"The same way you solved the strike," he said. "The same way you solved the problem of how to cover the president's trip. You know how to confront problems at work. You handle coordination, financing, who knows what. Now you have another problem. Something is causing this sudden depression."

"Why do you insist on calling it depression? Do I have a psychological problem?"

"OK, so you don't have any problems," he said, smiling at her. "Let's look at everything you did before the depression started today."

"Depression? That's exactly what I mean. I'm not depressed," she insisted. "I had the most pleasant morning I've enjoyed in a long time."

"Tell me exactly what you did," he repeated.

"I came in late from New York, so I slept very late, but I rested well. I went down to the health center, had a good work out, massage, and steam bath. I had a very good brunch in the coffee shop, went up to the condo and, wham, this hit me."

"Did you meet anyone?"

"No."

"Did you see anyone?"

"No," she said. Then she laughed and corrected herself, "Yes, in the cafeteria I saw some old ladies, like Jewish yentas, arguing about their diets. I thought it would make a good sitcom."

"Jewish yentas," Dr. Kitcher repeated her phrase. "Do you like Jews?"

"What the hell kind of a question is that? Are you accusing me of something?"

"No, I'm just asking, do you like Jews? Have you ever cursed, made fun of, argued with a Jew?"

She began to squirm, "Why do you ask?"

"Who were your parents?"

"Jews who escaped from the Ghetto and were shipped off by the Nazis to some crematorium," she replied, taking out a tissue to dry the sudden perspiration around her neck.

"Jodi, you don't have a problem. You have a dilemma," he said slowly. "On the one hand, you want to know who your natural parents are. That's normal, very normal. Almost every adopted child has that nearly compulsive need to know. On the other hand, you now know that your parents were Jewish and you're afraid to discover them because that would make you, what?"

"Jewish," Jodi replied in a whisper.

They sat silently for a long time.

"I have spoken disparagingly about Jews," she said slowly. "I've referred to Dr. Berson pejoratively, and once I accused Mr. Haar of being Jewish in a very insulting manner. He felt compelled to show me his daughter's first communion picture. I think of Jews, sometimes, as vengeful, like Berson, or as loud, or cheap."

"There's your dilemma," the doctor said. "You want to find your parents but that would make you a 'vengeful, loud, and cheap' Jew."

"That's what I'm escaping from?" she asked. "Is that what you were accusing me of in our first session?"

"Jodi," he replied. "Let's get this straight. I'm not accusing. And I don't know the answers. That's where your self-analysis comes in. You have to think through your own feelings, and that is going to be hard."

"Thank you, Alan," she said getting up, gathering her pocketbook and keys. "You were kind to see me on a Sunday. Let me think about what you've said."

"Jodi, when you think about your natural parents, remember, you're really discovering yourself," he added, writing down a number and handing it to her. "If it gets rocky, just call. It's my home number."

She went home and got into a steaming hot shower. Standing, thinking, the water streaming over her, she realized that the only information she had about her birth parents, so far, was the little bit her dad had told her and the scant stories her mother had filled in. Analyzing the situation like a journalist, she began to see that she could follow up with other sources. First there was Sheldon Haar, who discovered the Rynek file. Then there was Dr. Berson. As odious as he seemed to be, the salient fact was that he was in Warsaw with her father when her adoption took place.

Stepping out of the shower, she wrapped herself in a terry-cloth robe and called Sheldon Haar. Unable to get his unlisted home phone number, she dialed his private office number even though it was late Sunday afternoon. She was delighted when he answered the phone.

"Mr. Haar, it's Sunday," Jodi said teasingly. "What are you doing in the office?"

"The government doesn't pay me enough," he joked, "so I'm making it up with overtime."

"I need to see you," she said. "Can you fit me in tomorrow?"

"Sure. Come in around three."

Jodi reserved a flight to DC, made a cup of hot chocolate, and settled down in front of the television, channel flipping to find something deliberately mindless and soothing. She was watching an old *General Hospital* episode when the phone rang.

"Hey, how are you?"

"Cal," she smiled, "I'm OK now. I met with your friend Alan Kitcher again."

"Why?" he asked. "What happened?"

"That damn depression got me again this morning, but I think this time Alan helped me."

"How?" Cal asked.

"He made me think. Now that I know I'm adopted, I have to learn more about my natural parents so that I can know more about myself."

"Jodi," Cal said, "this time, I think Alan is wrong. To me, it's obvious that you bring on your own depression, just by thinking about this whole adoption thing."

"I thought so too," she said. "But I now realize that I get depressed when I force myself not to think about it."

"I just don't want you to hurt yourself," Cal said. "Let me tear your gown again and you'll forget your heartaches."

Jodi laughed, "Thanks for worrying about me. I miss you; when will you be back?"

"Well, I'm in Japan now. I'll be in LA day after tomorrow, so I can meet you in Miami next weekend."

"That sounds great," she said. "I'm going to meet with Shelly Haar in DC tomorrow to begin my search for my parents."

"Jodi, can't you wait for me to get home? You're on the wrong track. Stop this search before you get hurt. I'm afraid you'll be hurting yourself."

"No, Cal, I won't be hurting myself. I have to do this. I just have to."

On her way to Washington, she planned her campaign to search for her birth parents, to uncover their tracks, to find out who they were, and to learn what had actually happened to them. Even as she thought about the search, she knew the chances that either of them had survived were slim.

That is also what she told Haar later that day, thanking him for seeing her.

"Jodi, listen to me," he said, pointing to the jar on his desk. "There are a hundred jelly beans in there. Each is numbered. Pick a number from one to a hundred, write it down on this pad, and then see if you can come up with that number jelly bean from the jar."

She wrote down a number and took out a bean. It was not the number she wrote on her pad. The look on her face told him that she missed the point.

"Here, the odds against you were a hundred to one. With the Warsaw Ghetto, your chances of finding that young couple, or even finding out anything about their fate, are a half a million to one."

"My parents weren't numbered candies," she retorted. "They were human beings, speaking to people, lining up with them in soup kitchens, traveling with them, and, yes, having babies with them. Someone out there knows who they were, or are. And I intend to find out."

"How?" he asked.

"We'll start with you," Jodi replied. "I want to see the Rynek File."

"No, Jodi," Haar called out so loudly that his secretary rushed in. He shook his head and she quickly returned to her desk. "You can't have the Rynek file. There's nothing about your natural father in it, nothing."

"Then why won't you let me see it? There are names of people who can lead me to people."

"No," he said adamantly.

"Why? What's so secret about a thirty-year-old document?" she asked.

"It's a devastating indictment of Stamford Wycliff," he said. "And it'll devastate you. You will be hurt for the rest of your life."

"You sound like my mother or Cal," she said. "They didn't want to me to get hurt either."

"Jodi, listen to me. They're right. You are in real danger of getting yourself torn up by this quest," Haar pleaded. "Let go of the past. Forget this."

"Shelly, now you listen to me. you're in no position to tell me that. Your whole career is unearthing the past! Our past is what makes us," she flung the words at him. "I'm a big girl now. I can handle anything that's thrown at me. The only thing I can't do is run away from what's lurking out there."

"Jodi, you're like a kid playing with matches."

"Mr. Attorney," she said, "you may know the law, but you don't know a damn thing about human feelings. Do you know what it feels like losing your identity? It's like being a faceless person. Like being out on the ocean in a boat with no oars. I'm lost and I've got to find myself. Don't you understand?"

Sheldon did not reply. He sat at his desk and dropped his head in his hands. Then he looked up at her slowly, shaking his head. "Jodi, you have already accomplished so much. And your father established a fine record in this country. Leave it be."

"I'm not impressed, Shelly. Do I have to have my attorney subpoena the Rynek File, or are you going to give it to me?"

"You can have the goddamn file," he said, reaching into his drawer. He buzzed his secretary. "Here, copy this for Ms. Wycliff please."

When he handed the documents to Jodi, he warned her again, "If you think this will save you, you're wrong. It'll sink you and your boat."

"Thank you, Shelly," Jodi said, tucking her copy of the file under her arm. "You've been very kind."

When she got into a taxi, she began leafing through the Rynek File but she put it away, deciding not to read it until she could study its contents that night, alone, in her New York apartment.

By the time Jodi got home, it was after eight o'clock. She poured herself a glass of wine and began reading the Rynek File. Before she finished the first page, her hand began to tremble, letting the glass slip and spill on the ivory carpet. She sat and stared at the wall, fearing that another attack was coming on. She realized that Haar's warning was correct. The Rynek File was a devastating indictment of her father.

She recalled her analogy about being out in a boat without oars, and now she wondered if she was about to sink in her own boat – just as Shelly had said.

She began to sweat and, fearing another bout with suicidal depression, she put down the file and dialed Alan Kitcher's home number.

"Hi, Jodi!"

"Just one question," she said. "What is my problem? My inability to discover my birth father or my fear of finding out the true past of Stamford Wycliff?"

"Why do you ask?" he questioned.

"I got a file from Washington today that I hope will have information about my birth family's fate. I just started reading the first page detailing the commendations heaped on Stamford by the Nazis. I went all cold, Alan. I got a sort of sinking feeling in my stomach."

"Jodi, I don't know what information you've gotten your hands on," he said, "but basically, nothing that you discover can hurt you as long as you deal with it realistically."

"What do you mean?" she asked.

"Well, let's make believe that the worst thing in your life actually happens: You come into the office and the boss says, 'Miss Wycliff, you're fired!' What would you do?"

"Lots of things," she said. "I'd fight back or maybe I'd get a job with another network, or maybe I'd just settle down with Cal and have a baby."

"But you wouldn't go into a tailspin, would you?" he asked.

"No, of course not," she replied.

"Because you could deal with that problem realistically," he said.

"I get it. Thanks, Alan. Go take care of your sick patients."

"Hey, Jodi, if all my patients could recover like you, I'd have to close my office," he said. "Good luck in your search. Call back if you need me."

As she read the Rynek File, Jodi stopped every so often to write down names and episodes that she would have to investigate later. Around midnight, she typed her notes on her typewriter. She saved the document under the title, "Follow-Up List." It read:

Col. Rudolf Zahn – Author of file, Gestapo commander: Why did he name it the "Rynek File."

Sgt. Heinrich Glaubmann – Zahn's successor, last to see Stasha in Poland.

Col. Karl Greifler – Stasha's boss in Trusteeship: May have known of 'young couple'.

Father Grzybowski – St. Michael's Church, Warsaw: Was Jadwiga baptized? Did he know the Jewish parents?

Haskel Kornblit – Forger in Ghetto: Did he know the Jewish couple for whom he forged Rynek IDs?

Mendel Rozen – Chief of Jewish Police in Ghetto: Also in charge of ration cards. Would he remember names? What about special rations for babies?

Dr. Szymon Berson – Czyste Hospital Director: Ask about his relationship with Stasha as regards the Jewish baby.

She printed the list out, folded it up, and put it into her handbag. Half an hour later, after she had a fresh glass of wine and got ready for bed, she took it out again. Returning to her desk, she wrote in two additional names:

Archbishop McMurray – What did Dad tell him before he died?

Mom – get her to talk about 'young couple.' Handle with kid gloves.

Although it was past 1 A.M., she remembered she had promised to call Cal. To her surprise, when he answered the phone, he immediately admitted, "I called Alan Kitcher about you."

"You did what?" she asked.

"I told him to stop misleading you," he said, speaking rapidly before she could interrupt, "and I told him outright that his advice to you was wrong."

"I don't know whether to yell at you or laugh at you," Jodi said calmly. "But I want to know whether Alan told you about our conversation."

"Hell, no!" Cal replied. "I don't want to know about your conversations. I know more than Alan. I know what you need and I'm the only one who can give it to you."

"You can talk from now till hell freezes over," Jodi said laughing at him. "You're not only three years younger than me, but you're an absolute child to talk like that. I know what I need better than you do!"

"Jodi, this obsession about your birth parents is over the top," Cal scolded. "Why can't you leave the past alone? I think you're going way overboard and you could get hurt."

She listened to his harangue, paused quite a long time, and then quietly said, "Cal, good night."

She hung up the phone, cutting him off while he was still talking. She had never done that to him before and, for an instant, she thought about calling him back to apologize. Then she realized that she had to stop him from trying to block her quest, if only to make him realize how deeply she felt about it.

Despite her inner tension, she slept well.

Jodi knew that Francine was an early riser, so she called her mother the following morning, bright and early. "Mom, I'm planning to take a few days off from work and I want you to come to New York just to relax."

"I'm delighted you called and want my company," Francine said, "but I'm reluctant to accept your invitation."

"Mother, we can take in a couple of shows, go to the best restaurants and if you feel up to it, we can go shopping," she said. "Come on, you deserve a real vacation."

Francine confessed, "It seems awfully soon for me to go traveling."

"It will do you good to get over your mourning," Jodi said, hoping her mother would not react as she did when Cal used practically the same words and offered to take her to Bermuda.

Jodi coaxed and cajoled her mother until Francine agreed. "OK, OK, honey, I'll come up tomorrow, just as long as we don't go visiting anybody."

When they hung up, Jodi took out the "Follow-Up List" from her handbag and put a check next to her mother's name.

*

Jodi arranged a very pleasant vacation for her mother, exactly as she had promised, taking her to shows, going on shopping sprees, and dining in New York's most elegant restaurants. The highlight of the vacation was a Broadway matinee followed by a backstage visit with the stars. As they watched the cast take off their makeup and costumes, Jodi put on one of the wigs, went out onto the stage, and danced and sang one of the numbers in the musical to the empty theater. The cast gathered around her, applauding her performance. But Jodi had planned the seemingly impromptu recital to elicit a specific response from her mother, and Francine's reaction was exactly what Jodi wanted.

When they were alone in the darkened theater, Francine reminisced about the time when Jodi was a child actress, recalling how she had helped her dress for the occasion. She even bragged about her part, bowing to the audience in her tight-fitting dress after Jodi's singing.

"I think you had a bit of ham in you." Jodi said.

Francine laughed heartily. "I had a lot of ham in me in those days," she said. "But right now, let's get back and rest before dinner."

"The theater did play an important role in our getting a priority visa to the United States," Francine told Jodi when they were resting comfortably in their elegant hotel room.

"You never told me about that," Jodi responded.

"I had to play a role of an abused wife to trap a Russian spy who was hiding in our DP camp," Francine recalled. "His name was Antek Karpov and after we turned him in, the CIA helped us get to the States. As a matter of fact, it was the CIA agent, John Kemeris, a Texan, who changed our names and named you 'Jodi'. It was his sister's name."

"What was your Polish name?" Jodi asked.

"You'll never be able to pronounce it," Francine said, and began to laugh as she exaggeratedly pronounced, "Franceska and Stanislaw Wojchiechowski."

"That's a mouthful, Wojchiechowski," Jodi said. "Tell me how you captured the Russian spy."

Francine related how she had arranged for Jodi to perform before a large audience in the Community Hall of the DP camp. In their hotel room, she imitated Jadzia's rendition of a Hebrew song and reenacted how she tantalized Antek by her exaggerated bowing to expose her bosom. Jodi laughed hysterically as Francine lifted her dress, exposing her thighs and boasting that she enticed the spy in a small storage room. Francine proudly recalled how she lured Karpov to follow her to Kassel, where he was snared by the CIA.

Amidst their volleys of laughter, Jodi said, "I bet a lot of what happened back then you'd rather just forget. Like doing a semi-striptease to entice some spy."

Francine nodded quietly and whispered, "I'd like to forget everything with the Nazis. I often asked Stasha not to get involved with those Germans. I remember his reaction once. He picked you up in his arms and declared, 'If not for them, we wouldn't have Jadzia.'"

Jodi caressed her mother's hand, saying, "See, Mom, now you can talk about the past, even calling Dad 'Stasha,' and me 'Jadzia,' and not become paranoid about it."

Francine thought a while and then said, "You can't imagine how much better it is. Right now, it's almost like a curtain has been lifted from my eyes."

Listening to her mother, Jodi realized that she was listening to a description of her own feelings. She had been experiencing that sense of looking behind a curtain ever since learning about her adoption. She needed the curtain to be totally removed.

"I'd love to hear more about my childhood," Jodi said.

Francine freely reminisced about the farm in Grochov, about life with the American army and, finally, even a little about the young couple who brought Jadzia to her.

"I wish you had pictures of me from back then," Jodi said, curling up to her mother.

"I may still have some baby pictures."

"You do?" Jodi jumped up excitedly. "You never showed them to me."

"I gave them to your father and he hid them somewhere. I'll try to find them."

Jodi was ecstatic. "I'll be in Miami next weekend. Maybe I can see them then."

"Will you stay with me?" Francine asked.

"Absolutely. Cal will be in town, but he'll understand," Jodi said, kissing and hugging her mother. "As a matter of fact, I'll travel with you back to Miami tomorrow, so you don't have to fly back alone."

Her mother embraced Jodi, softly whispering, "Oh, how much I love you. How much happiness you've brought me, me and Dad."

She helped her mother get up from the sofa and said, "We should start getting dressed for dinner."

"I've had three wonderful days with you, Jodi," her mother replied. "Do you mind if we don't go out tonight? I feel a bit tired and I want you all to myself, without people staring at us in some restaurant."

Jodi prepared a light snack, which they ate at leisure on the terrace overlooking East River. Later, while her mother prepared for bed, Jodi put on a comfortable jogging suit and snuggled on the sofa to catch up on her reading. She was thrilled when her mother came up to her, hugged her, kissed her, and said, "I pray for your birth parents every night and bless them for giving me my daughter."

"I'm thinking of going to Europe to start searching for them," Jodi replied.

She was startled when her mother sat down next to her and said, "I wish I could go with you. I realize now how important it is for you to trace them. They saved your life, at a tremendous sacrifice. I hope and pray you'll find them…alive."

They sat for quite a while, holding each other. When Francine went to bed, Jodi took out her "Follow-Up List" and wrote under the "Mom" listing:

"My pictures!!! Possibly with Irena and Tomasz!!!"

She added the name John Kemeris to the list. Then she went into the bedroom and, seeing her mother asleep, she kissed her and put out the lights.

*

The next morning, Jodi got a surprise call from her lawyer, John Butnow. "I want to invite you and your mother to a special birthday party. My father is sixty-five years old and decided to retire, so we're celebrating his entry into his golden years."

The birthday party in Los Angeles was an exhilarating experience for Francine. Flying on the Wycliff private plane, Francine and Jodi traveled at a leisurely pace, making several stops and arriving refreshed at their suite in a Beverly Hills hotel.

Francine dressed in her most alluring attire for the special party and looked much younger than her sixty-two years.

At the party, she was seated next to Jason, John Butnow's father. When he was ready to blow out the sixty-five candles on the birthday cake, John called on Francine to help. While Jason blew his lungs out, Francine sprayed the candles with water, causing hilarious laughter. Jason and Francine danced throughout the night and were the last to leave when the party was over.

Jason and Francine saw each other almost every day during the two weeks she spent in Los Angeles. When winter came around, he took her on a skiing vacation in Aspen. Early the next spring, they were married in a simple ceremony in Los Angeles. John, Jodi, and Cal were the only guests.

Francine worried that maybe she should have waited a little longer after Stamford's death to get married again. But Jason represented such a carefree, new life. There was no history hanging over him, no farm life, no Nazis, no constant quest to climb higher and higher, no barriers. He was much less of a boss and much more of a companion. And she was very ready to have a good time.

*

When she returned to Miami after Jason's birthday party, Jodi began to search for the baby pictures her mother had mentioned. She ransacked her father's private office in Wycliff Towers, looking through every file cabinet, inspecting every drawer in every desk, but she found nothing. She carefully went through every closet in the house, every piece of luggage, even the medicine cabinets. Again, she found nothing.

Minerva, the housekeeper who had been with Francine ever since the Wycliffs built the mansion in Coral Gables, said she had never come across any pictures. "Jodi," she suggested, "you should look up in the summer place, in Vermont. There's a big safe in the den there where your father kept important documents."

A week later, intent on her quest, Jodi flew up to Northfield and went to the house set amid the rolling hills. The safe had not been used for years. No one had its combination. She authorized a local company to blast it open, but, once again, she found nothing.

"Jodi, this search is maddening and ridiculous," Cal said. "Your father had offices everywhere – in California, New York, Texas. Are you going to search every one of them?"

"Yes," she replied, taking his taunt seriously.

She personally visited each of Stamford's offices, but she found no photographs. The company's lawyers kept calling her, asking for appointments, because they had documents that required her signature. Refusing to abandon her search, she gave Cal her power of attorney to deal with the company's needs.

The power of attorney document was her liberation. Even Cal could not get her to make decisions affecting the future of the huge estate, because she had her mind set on only one thing: finding her baby pictures.

"Jodi, I think you're off your rocker," Cal shouted on the phone from the Wycliff Corporation's Miami office, after he tracked her down at her mother's home. "Stop all this fuss over searching for some silly baby pictures and focus on business. You're the titular head of the Wycliff Corporation and there are pressing matters that need your attention."

Calmly and dispassionately she said, "Cal, you make all the decisions. You sign all the papers. I trust you totally on business matters. As for me, I have decided that I have to uncover my past and the one key, the only key to that past, is the baby pictures. Please try to support me on this."

"I'm trying, Jodi," he answered, "but I think you are wrong to chase down all these skeletons. Leave them in their closets."

"Do you know what it would do for me to find a picture of me and my mother, my real mother?"

"I told you when we started this conversation that you're off your rocker," he said. "And I tell you now that your behavior about all this is really infantile. You have an unnatural craving to see yourself as a baby. You may be a big shot at Network International Corporation, but you have a lot of growing up to do."

"Your friend, Dr. Kitcher doesn't think so," Jodi said.

"He's just playing up to your ego, and you're vulnerable enough, or dumb enough, to fall for it. Since we're talking openly, I'll tell it to you straight. Your television persona has become your day in and day out personality. From the first day we met, I had hoped to break you from it, but now you have really sunk down deep to rock bottom. Jodi, you're beyond salvation."

"I didn't expect you to understand," she said firmly. "I'm telling you this for the last time. Then I'm going to hang up because this is getting us nowhere. In fact, these conversations are pulling us apart, further and further apart. Listen now and listen carefully. I need to know my past.

You're making a fetish out of denying me the right to search for that past. You just want to control me. Now good-bye."

As she hung up, she heard his voice, shouting, "I have to tell you…"

The phone rang, but when Minerva told her it was Cal, Jodi decided she wasn't ready to talk to him yet. In less than an hour, a messenger from Wycliff came to the house with a note: "Found an envelope with pictures in the bank vault, Cal."

She rushed to the bank, entered the bank president's office, and found Cal waiting for her, alone. He held an envelope in his hand but did not hand it to her immediately.

"Why didn't you answer my phone call?" he asked.

"I was too upset, Cal," she answered. "I couldn't go through another fight with you. Maybe we both just need time to think over our relationship."

"I don't need time," Cal replied firmly. "We have no relationship. We never had a relationship and we'll never have a relationship. You are today what you were twenty years ago – a spoiled brat."

She understood Cal. He did not mean to be shallow. He was just a busy man. The emotional storm of relationships never interested him at all. He expended his energies on business. She knew he loved her as much as he could love anybody, because she was successful, strong, smart, and sexy. She herself had always been as detached as he was, just as career-oriented, and not given to female flights of insistence. He was willing to bail her out now and then – like rescuing her from that pizza joint – but clearly, to him things were getting out of hand with her obsession over her Jewish birth parents. She realized that for him it was time to forget about romance and take care of business.

Although she understood him, she bristled when he handed her the envelope, saying, "Here. Go share these with your shrink. You're crazy and you need lots of therapy. I can't do anything else for you."

She left without saying good-bye.

Jodi peeked at the four pictures in the envelope while waiting for the elevator, then quickly put them back into her handbag. When she arrived at her mother's house, she sent Minerva to Cal's Brickell Avenue apartment, asking her to pack her belongings. She then called her secretary in New York and told her to cancel the wedding.

"The list is in my top desk drawer," she said, surprised at how calm she felt. "Just send everyone a letter. I'll call Archbishop McMurray myself."

Then Jodi called Cal to inform him that she was canceling their wedding. He was out, so she left a message with his secretary asking him to call her back.

Only then did she close herself in her room and open the envelope he had given her at the bank. The dog-eared pictures were brown-tinted, pasted individually on cardboard panels. She took out each one separately, handling them with extreme care.

The first picture, entirely out of focus, showed a group of men in German military uniforms. In the background she could make out the letters: BRISTOL HOTEL, and she could see a banner with a huge swastika hanging over the door. Studying the faces of the German soldiers with a magnifying glass, she assumed that the one dressed in a different uniform was Stasha. The second and third pictures showed a couple. In one shot they were sitting on a tractor and in the other they were posing with a priest in front of a church. Both photos had been taken from quite a distance, so the faces of the people were unrecognizable. But the picture taken with the priest, she was certain, was not of her natural parents.

"What would a Jewish couple be doing with a priest?" she thought, smiling to herself, contented that recognizing the Jewishness of her birth parents had no adverse affect on her.

The fourth picture, taken at closer range, excited her beyond imagination. It was a picture of two young women. One was Francine, she was sure; the other, a young beautiful woman holding a baby. She instinctively knew it was her mother. The tarnished, unclear picture had been taken in front of a brownstone-type home. She studied the faces of the women for a long time, but the baby's face was no more than an indistinct smudge. Jodi remained in the room most of the morning, studying every detail of the photos, especially the face of the young woman holding the baby.

Before putting away that picture, she touched the face of the young mother and softly said, "Mama."

In the late afternoon, Father McMurray called.

"Father, thank you for returning my call," she said. "I've decided to call off my wedding, and I wanted to tell you personally."

"Jodi, what are you saying?"

"Father, trust me, I know what I'm doing," she said.

"But why?" he asked. "Is it your business involvement?"

"I'd rather not talk about it, Father," she said. "It's very personal, but I know that it's the right thing to do."

"If there's anything I can do to help you, please let me know," he said.

"Yes, there is a way you can help me, but it doesn't have anything to do with Cal," she said. "It's about my father. I want to establish a memorial in the church in his honor. Whatever amount you think is proper, just let me know."

The archbishop thanked her, assuring her that he would establish an appropriate tribute. Then he asked, "And what are your plans, Jodi?"

"I'm thinking of going to Europe," she said.

"For a vacation?" he asked.

"No, to retrace my parents' past," she replied.

The archbishop encouraged her to make it a vacation, as a step toward overcoming her grief over her father's death. She thanked him and he wished her well on her travels.

The minute she hung up the phone, she called Cal. "You walked out on me," he said. "That just proves you are in no mental shape to make any decisions."

When Jodi said nothing, Cal continued his blistering tirade. "Jodi, you're not in front of a TV camera. Stop acting," he ranted.

"I'm not acting," she finally answered. "I only called to tell you I am canceling the wedding."

"I figured you'd do that," he said. "You've always been an independent bitch."

"It has nothing to do with being independent or a bitch," she said. "I simply realized that I'm no good to you or to anyone as long as I have this problem hanging over my head. You are right about one thing: this has become an obsession. It is my first priority, my only concern.

"Until this is settled, I wouldn't be any good as a wife," she said. "That's why I'm calling off the wedding. And, by the way, I thought you'd prefer it if I got my things out of the apartment, so Minerva is packing me up. That means you are free, Cal, and not committed to me."

*

She returned to New York a few days later and called NIC's Winston White to tell him she was bringing in her resignation. Once she arrived at NIC,

White soon stormed into her office, demanding to know what had gotten into her. She briefly related the circumstances of her adoption, telling him she had decided to try to trace her natural parents.

"Go ahead, Jodi, take a month off, even two months," he said wiping his bald head with a handkerchief. "I'm relieved. I thought you had gotten a job with another network."

"No, Winston," she replied. "I'm leaving. I'm going to Europe to find my birth parents. It's good-bye."

"You're wrong, Jodi," he said. "You'll end up discovering that your parents, your real parents, perished along with six million other Jews. The quicker you make peace with the idea that you were orphaned at age three, when the Wycliffs adopted you, the saner you will be."

"How do you know?" she asked.

"Unlike you," he said, "I have lived with survivors all my life. Few of them know the exact time, place, and date of their loved ones' deaths. They, all of them, accept the fact that they were robbed of their families and that the nightmare is over."

"They've had time to make the adjustment," she said. "I've only just become a survivor."

"How do you plan to proceed?" he asked.

She took out her "Follow-Up List" and explained, "Every one of these people had some contact with my birth parents. I'm going to contact every name on this list until I find out about them."

"So you intend to recall the Holocaust," he replied. "What do you think, it's like the instant replay we run in football games?"

"Winston," she pleaded, "don't make it any harder for me. I have decided to quit and nothing you or anyone can say will change my mind."

"Jodi, I wish you luck, of course. But, you know, there's no guarantee that this job will be waiting for you when you come back."

"Yes, I know. I'm not asking for any special consideration."

"Jodi, I only said that to get you to change your mind. There'll be a position for you any time you come back. I just hope it'll be soon."

"If you want to do me a real favor, help me get these old photographs reprocessed."

She reached into her handbag and handed him the envelope with the four pictures.

"I'll send them down to Tony Arbella in the photographic processing lab. He'll computerize these images and give them back to you in fine shape."

He began to explain the chemical nature of silver nitrate, which diminishes with time, and which can be calculated and computerized during the restoration process, but she put her hand up. "Never mind, Mr. White, I have no brains for chemistry. Just tell Tony not to destroy the originals in the process."

"I'll get them back to you later today," he said, walking away.

"Jodi Wycliff," he said, poking his head back through the doorway, "you're not very smart for quitting. If you'd let me fire you, you could collect unemployment insurance while traipsing around Europe."

She threw a pencil at him, calling out, "Get out, you petty thief billionaire."

She completed her preparations to leave for Europe, but now that she was ready to begin searching for her parents, she needed to talk to the only person who could help her now – number five on her "Follow-Up List" – Dr. Simon Berson. She dialed Sheldon Haar's office. When his secretary put her through, she brought Shelly up to date on what had transpired since her last visit.

"Now I have to ask you one more favor," Jodi said. "I want you to get Dr. Berson to see me."

"I can't," he replied.

"Why not?"

"He left Washington months ago and no one seems to know where he's living," Haar said. "Try calling Congressman Reinert. They were very close, even when Berson returned to New York."

She immediately called Reinert's secretary, who told her that the congressman was in The Hague attending a conference of the International Monetary Fund. She gave Jodi the phone number at his hotel. Jodi calculated the time difference between Europe and America and instructed her secretary to put the call through in two hours. While she was waiting, she took out the Rynek File and began reading it yet again.

Her secretary buzzed her. "I'm placing your call to The Hague now."

No one answered when the hotel operator rang Reinert's room, so Jodi called the news desk to find out who was covering the IMF conference for the network. She called the correspondent who was assigned to cover the conference and arranged a telephone hookup with Congressman Reinert. Within minutes Peter Reinert was on the phone.

"I have no idea where Simon is," the congressman told her. "Gloria and I lost contact with him. The one person who might be able to tell you is Rabbi Michael Goldberg. He helped Simon set up an apartment in New York when he left Washington."

He gave her the name of the funeral parlor that had handled Sonya's funeral, suggesting she call there to find Rabbi Goldberg's phone number.

"Miss Wycliff," Rabbi Goldberg said when she got through to him, "the last time I spoke to Dr. Berson, he sounded weak. I asked him if it was because the court had dismissed the Wycliff case. He said he was going to check into the hospital. He refused to tell me which one, but he called me about two weeks ago to tell me that he had undergone a successful operation."

"Why did he call you?"

"To ask me to set up a prearrangement with the funeral home."

"Is he that sick?" Jodi asked.

"I asked him," Rabbi Goldberg said, "but he didn't reply. He said he was alone in the world and was making arrangements for his funeral. He asked me to officiate when the time came."

"And you really don't know what hospital he was in?" Jodi asked.

"You won't believe this," the rabbi said, "and I'm embarrassed to tell you. Dr. Berson didn't want to tell me which hospital because he did not want me to visit. All he said was, 'When I die, the authorities will call you.'"

As she hung up the phone, Tony Arbella of the photo processing lab walked into her office. He apologized for his lab's inability to show any progress and returned the original four pictures.

"Can't you do anything with them?" she asked.

"Not much," Tony replied. "I don't need these any more. The data is in my computer, but I'm not getting a clear enough image. So I decided to return the originals because Mr. White told me to guard them with my life."

"Do you think you can do something with the images?" she asked.

"Our problem is that we're getting the grain in the paper mixed in with the picture. That's botching up the separation process."

"I don't know what you're talking about."

He explained that it was like getting two voices recorded simultaneously on an audiotape, although it would be relatively easy to separate voices but far more complicated to separate multiple images on a video recording.

"But we're not giving up," Tony said, heading for the door. "We're going to work on it all night."

"Here's my private number at home. If you succeed, call me at any time."

When Tony left her office, she began cleaning out her desk, packing up personal files and mementos she had accumulated over the years. She had numerous trinkets that guests had given her, plaques from various organizations for whom she had done TV specials, and pictures of her interviews with eminent world leaders. As her secretary passed each item to her, Jodi told her either to pack it or to throw it away.

Jodi added, "I'll come back and pick up the artwork, but if there is something you want to keep, I'd be happy to give it to you."

Her secretary thanked her and selected a Lladró porcelain sculpture of a delicate swan.

A recent publicity shot of her interviewing the surgeon-general of the United States, Dr. Kemp, was among the many autographed pictures Jodi was about to throw away. Kemp had succeeded Berson at the Institute. If Berson was in a hospital, Jodi reasoned, it had to be Stone-Winthrop. She asked her secretary to get Dr. Kemp on the phone. When he answered, Jodi reminded him about the "Pathfinders of Medicine" show she had done with him and asked him about Dr. Berson's condition.

"Miss Wycliff, I can't give you any information about Dr. Berson. The hospital and its personnel are not permitted to disclose any information about Dr. Berson's medical condition."

"You are telling me, in effect, that he is in the hospital as a patient, are you not?" Jodi asked.

"I'm not telling you," he said. "You've assumed that."

"Is that assumption correct?" she asked.

"Please, Miss Wycliff, don't ask me to breach a trust."

Jodi needed no further corroboration. She decided against calling Berson directly, remembering his last rebuff. Instead, she put a call to Reinert's hotel in The Hague, expecting to leave a message for the congressman that Berson was in the Stone-Winthrop hospital. However, Gloria Reinert answered the phone and introduced herself.

"I remember meeting you at the installation dinner in Miami Beach," Jodi said. "You were the pretty woman with the red hair."

"I'm a brunette now," Gloria giggled. "Tell me, what can Peter do for you?"

Jodi gave Gloria the Institute's phone number and asked her to have Peter call Dr. Berson to try to set up an appointment for Jodi to visit him.

Later that afternoon, Congressman Reinert called Jodi back. "I had the devil's own time getting through to Simon," he said. "I only got to talk to him after I threatened to storm the hospital the minute I get back to the States.

"And, when I finally delivered your message, he refused to see you. He simply does not want to relive his frustration over the Wycliff case."

Jodi was infuriated. When Reinert lamely apologized for his inability to help her, she suddenly came to life. "Mr. Congressman, I will show you the power of the press."

Jodi selected another Lladró figurine, a small ballet dancer, from her cabinet and hastened to the Institute. She sought out Elena Stole, the head of the Nursing Department, who had helped her during the shooting of the hospital segment of her "Pathfinders" show.

They spoke about their work and Jodi intimated that she might be doing a follow-up program. The head nurse assured Jodi that she would cooperate and invited her to stay for a cup of coffee in the staff lounge. Jodi then surprised Elena, giving her the lovely Lladró dancer as a token of thanks for her help in the production. The head nurse fingered the sculpture and thanked her profusely.

"It's really not much, Elena," Jodi said. "I should have given you something at the time, to thank you for your cooperation."

As she was about to leave, Jodi casually asked if Dr. Berson tolerated nurses in his room. The head nurse replied that she had even lectured Dr. Berson about his abrupt, even abusive, treatment of the nurses who attend him.

"He's really eccentric," Elena said. "Do you know that in all the years that I've been at this hospital, I never before heard of a doctor registering under a false name."

"Some day that would make a good story," Jodi said casually. "What name did the old man register under this time?"

The head nurse laughed, glanced about the room, and replied, "Jefferson. Would you believe it, Thomas Jefferson! But you can't blame him. Literally hundreds of his patients and students would flock to his bedside if they knew he was in the hospital. When one or two managed to sneak in, he raised the roof, so we now have a twenty-four-hour guard at his room."

That convinced Jodi not to try to visit Dr. Berson. She left the hospital, preparing some other strategy. Jodi stopped by the public library, took out several books on the Holocaust, and returned to her office. She asked her secretary to set up an appointment with Sheldon Haar in Washington. Then, for several hours, she studied the Rynek File and compared its contents with material in the Holocaust volumes. She was so engrossed in research that she was startled by the buzz on the intercom.

"Hi, Jodi," her secretary said. "Mr. Haar can see you at noon tomorrow."

"Please confirm that with him," Jodi said.

"Will do," her secretary answered. "Will you be coming back to the office after your meeting with Mr. Haar?"

"It all depends on what Tony Arbella tells me," she replied.

At about five o'clock, Tony walked into Jodi's office and showed her some reproductions that were no better than the originals. "Let me take the originals again," he asked. "My guys want to start over. I'll get them back to you tomorrow. My shop will work on this all night, to try to break down the chemical components. If it works, I'll give you a call."

When Tony left, Jodi finished rereading the sordid Rynek File yet again. She carefully underlined insertions that related to the Rynek family. The part that hurt her most was the comment: "Commandant Wojchiechowski apprehended Irena and Tomasz Rynek, whom he trapped living illegally on the Aryan side. The following day, he reported that the two adults were sent on the train, but that baby Rynek died in transit. No evidence to support that claim." In the margin, in clear handwriting, were the words, "Take no action," followed by Colonel Zahn's signature.

Early the following morning, her private phone rang.

"Come on over," Tony called out before she could even say hello. "We've got some great pictures to show you."

She dressed hurriedly, packed an overnight bag for her trip to Washington, gulped down a tall glass of orange juice, and took a cab to the network. When she walked into Tony's lab, she saw each of her four pictures enlarged and mounted on an easel. The pictures were sharp, and the faces were clear and in living color.

She recognized Francine and Stamford as they were in their youth. But when she looked at the picture of the young woman holding the baby, she stifled a cry.

"My God!" Tony remarked, "That woman looks like you!"

Jodi felt her pulse quicken, and her face flushed.

"The original pictures you gave us were pasted onto panel cardboard," Tony explained. "When we separated the actual pictures from the cardboard, we solved our problem."

He began to explain that the fuzziness was caused by the interaction of the ingredients in the cardboard with the images on the pictures, but Jodi was not listening. She walked over to the picture of the two women, remaining there for quite a long time. Then she turned around, embraced Tony, and thanked him for his work. He placed the pictures in a portfolio and handed it to her.

"These came just in time," she said. "I'm taking them to Washington."

From the photo lab, Jodi went into her nearly-bare office. She sat down, opened the portfolio, and stared intently at the photo of the two women and the baby. She reached for the phone and called Francine in Los Angeles. After she apologized for waking her mother up at such an early hour on the West Coast, she excitedly described the pictures and promised to send her copies. Her mother asked whether Jodi could spend the weekend with them.

"I'm not coming out to LA for a while, Mom," Jodi said. "I'm going on to Europe to start my search."

"You know I hope it goes well, Jodi," Francine said. "Do stay in close touch with me." She repeated what she had once told her daughter, "I pray for your parents every night and bless them for giving me my daughter."

Jodi stroked the picture, touching the faces of the women and began to weep softly. Suddenly remembering that she had to rush to catch her flight to Washington, she pulled herself together and hurried out of the building, clutching her portfolio and handbag in one hand and her suitcase in the other. As she tried to flag down a cab, a limousine pulled up. Mr. White opened the door for her and instructed his chauffeur to drive them to the airport.

"Jodi, you are not without resources in Europe," he said. "I instructed our offices in Berlin and Warsaw and, for that matter, anywhere this odyssey takes you, to give you full cooperation. Contacts, travel, hotels, anything you need. Don't hesitate to use your status with the company while you're trying to track down your parents."

"Thank you so much," Jodi said, gratefully. "You've already done me a tremendous favor getting Tony to process those pictures."

"If you approve," he said, "we'll flash them to our people around the world, asking if anyone knows about the woman with the baby. We can even distribute clips to other networks."

Deeply touched by his generosity, Jodi gave him a peck on the cheek. When they reached the airport, Winston said, "Oh, by the way, I hope you'll help us produce your search as a miniseries. We can call it *Mama, Where Are You?* It'll make a great show."

Jodi looked at him, not knowing whether to curse or laugh. She stepped out of the limousine, then she turned to him and said, "Winston, you're incorrigible."

He threw her a kiss and drove away.

*

"Question," Haar said, when she showed him the pictures in his office. "I agree that there is a remarkable resemblance between you and the woman holding the baby. But why did you come here?"

"I have to get in to see Dr. Berson," Jodi said. "He's the only one who has seen these people in Poland. He might be able to tell me something about my parents."

He reminded her that he had not seen Dr. Berson since the case against her father had been dismissed. "That was nine months ago. Since then, he's vanished."

"I know where he is," she said. "I even know the name he's used to register at the hospital, but I don't dare go to his room. I'm afraid he'll reject me again." She filled Shelly in on her conversations with Congressman Reinert, Rabbi Goldberg, and Dr. Kemp.

"You don't belong in television, you should be a detective," he said. "How did you get his alias?"

"That's a professional secret," she said, smiling impishly, "but it cost me a Lladró sculpture."

"And you came in all the way from New York just to ask me to accompany you to Dr. Berson's room, back in New York?" he asked. "You couldn't just call?"

"A picture is worth a thousand words," Jodi grinned. "I knew if you saw this picture, you couldn't turn me down."

"Jodi, no one can turn you down. Not even Berson."

"He did," she said, repeating what Reinert had told her. "I'm not taking another chance on losing him."

Haar called in his secretary who reported that he was booked up all week, right through Friday afternoon.

"Visiting hours at the hospital are till 8 P.M. Why can't you fly up with me this evening?" Jodi pleaded. "All you have to do is visit with Berson for fifteen minutes, just to get him to agree to see me. Then you can leave me with him."

"Why can't I call him on the phone and do the same?" he asked.

"One, he turned down Mr. Reinert, who is probably his closest friend. Two, he hates visitors. Three, a picture is worth a thousand words."

"Jodi, I realize that if I fail you on this one, I'll never forgive myself," he said. "Meet me down in the lobby at four-thirty, we'll make the five o'clock shuttle."

On her way out, Jodi handed his secretary an envelope containing a personal check from her account made out to Haar for $10,000 and his round-trip air ticket with an appropriate thank-you note.

When they had taken their seats on the shuttle, Shelly Haar returned the envelope. Jodi opened it and found his scribbled handwriting on the back of the check, "To Jodi. This is not a professional service – Shelly."

"I'll find some way to pay you back," she said.

"Don't send me a Lladró."

"Come on, Shelly, I'm not trying to buy you off."

"Let's drop the subject," he said. "Let's talk about Dr. Berson. What do you suggest? Do we go in together? Do you wait outside while I plead with him to see you?"

"Shelly, you're the high-powered attorney. You're supposed to give advice."

As they walked out of the terminal to the taxi stand, Jodi said, "You can't fail me. You have to get me in to see Dr. Berson."

In the taxi, he told her he had decided to go in first, alone, to see Dr. Berson, but that he would take the pictures with him.

"He may not want visitors, but he will be willing to talk about Stasha," Shelly said.

"Do you mean that he's still furious about the dismissal of the case?" she asked.

"No," he replied, "he's teed off that it was dismissed without prejudice."

"So if he's still vengeful," Jodi sighed, "he won't see me."

"That's not his motivation," Haar explained. "Berson thinks it was far more important to expose the acts of the Nazis than to punish your father. His primary interest was to bring to light the horrible events of the Nazi terror, not necessarily to punish Stanislaw Wojchiechowski or to expose Stamford Wycliff."

"You mean, if my dad had confessed to everything, Dr. Berson would have let it go at that?"

"Maybe if he had confessed publicly," Haar replied. "But that would have presented a problem to us. Simon Berson wasn't the litigant; the OSI was."

*

When they arrived at the hospital, Jodi asked the clerk at the reception desk for Thomas Jefferson's room number.

"I'm sorry, no visitors are permitted," the clerk said. "What is the nature of your visit?"

"This is Mr. Haar," Jodi said. "He's from the government on urgent business."

Seeing that they were unlikely to make progress with the receptionist, Haar asked to see the hospital's security director. They waited several minutes in the lobby and when the security officer presented himself, Haar explained who he was and why they had come. The officer told the surprised receptionist to admit them.

When they got to room 987, Haar took with him Jodi's pictures, instructing her, "Don't sit in the waiting room. Wait here, outside his room."

Through the partially open door, she saw the men greeting each other, but she could not hear what they were saying. After a few minutes, she stepped closer to the door and heard Sheldon say, "So Stasha adopted the Jewish girl and that is Jodi Wycliff."

Dr. Berson's voice suddenly boomed through the door of his hospital room. "Jodi, Miss Jodi Wycliff, you come in here!"

Chapter 17

"STASHA ADOPTED YOU! Stasha the Satan of Warsaw adopted a Jewish girl!"

Dr. Berson looked at Jodi and cupped his face with both hands in wonderment. He stared at Sheldon, then at Jodi, and whispered, "Why didn't you tell me?"

She said, "It's a long story. But, first, how do you feel?"

Berson sat up in his bed with intravenous tubes trailing from both arms. "I'm mending," he explained. "I've had the second in a series of surgeries and the prognosis seems encouraging. But enough about that. Why didn't you tell me about your adoption?"

"Peter Reinert asked you to see me, but you refused, just like the time I called you begging you to let me talk to you."

"You're right to be angry," he said. "But while the trial was in progress, I didn't want to see you because I knew that you loved your father and I didn't want to destroy that love."

"No one could," Jodi replied defiantly. "Even after I read the Rynek File, I still loved my father. Love him very dearly."

"What's the Rynek File?" he asked.

"It's some evidence we turned up in Berlin on our second trip," Haar replied.

"Then you dropped the case because of his illness?" Berson asked. "If there was anything incriminating in that report, it should have been made public."

"Simon, it was and still is an OSI decision," Haar stated bluntly.

Berson turned to Jodi, "Do you know why I really didn't want to meet with you? I was afraid that after meeting you, I might have followed Shelly's advice and recanted my story."

"You should have," Jodi said. "My father was also a victim of the raging terror. He too might be considered a survivor."

Berson retorted, "Stasha was not a survivor. He was a collaborator."

Jodi was incensed. Her face reddened as she angrily said, "How can you say that?"

"OK, stop this arguing," Shelly said, displaying the first picture. "You have more important things to do other than start the war all over again. You have to identify these people."

Berson adjusted his glasses and looked at the first picture, the one showing the group of German soldiers. He became quite excited as he pointed to the people in the photo and called out their names one by one.

"Colonel Greifler, Dr. Wolrauch, and this is Stasha," he said. "And this is the Bristol Hotel, which was the German military headquarters where Stasha had his office."

Jodi took away that picture and showed him the one of the two women.

"Here are my two mothers."

"She was hemorrhaging and we had to perform an emergency hysterectomy," Dr. Berson announced, pointing to Franya. "During the German occupation, this young woman was brought to the Czyste Hospital, bleeding profusely, but I was afraid to operate. We had no instruments, no sterile setting. And I had no experience in this kind of surgery. I looked around for a surgeon, but neither the Poles nor the Germans were even approachable that day. I'll never forget that case. Ultimately, I had no choice but to operate, to save her life."

"You saved my mother," Jodi said, reaching for Berson's hand, carefully avoiding the IV tubes. "This woman raised me. She convinced Stasha to take a chance, even at risk of their lives, to adopt me when I was brought to them by two condemned Jewish prisoners."

Berson looked up from the pictures and stared at Jodi, as though seeing her for the first time. He reached out, held onto her hand, and said, "I want to hear the whole story."

"You two have a lot to talk about," Haar said, "and I've got to get back to Washington."

Jodi hugged Shelly. "Thank you for all you've done, and for getting Dr. Berson to meet with me."

"Shelly," Dr. Berson called out to him as he reached the door, "thanks for bringing her to me."

A few moments later, an announcement was made over the public address system that visiting hours were over, asking all visitors to leave the hospital. As Jodi prepared to leave, Berson told her to stay. He again looked at the picture of Francine and said, "Yes, that's the woman. I saved that woman. But I guess, to you, I'll remain a culprit because I brought your father's past to light."

"Let's understand one another," Jodi said. "When you accused my father, I despised you. Because from that moment on, he became a broken human being. I saw an energetic, dynamic, creative person crushed like a rotten apple. Even if the government had lost its case, my father would have remained a beaten man. I still don't understand why he told me about my adoption. Perhaps that too was part of the pattern of self-destruction that you put in motion."

"What would you have done if you were me?" Berson asked, not intending to challenge her.

"I'm not accusing you," she said. "I want you to understand my feelings."

She described, in detail, her father's death, the shock she felt when she learned about her adoption, her subsequent struggle with drug addiction, and her need for therapy to overcome depression.

"Out of this torment came the realization that I had two sets of loving parents," she explained, "the ones who gave me up when they went to their deaths and the ones who took me in at the risk of their lives. No matter what you think about Stasha Wojchiechowski, or what I read about him, I can never forget the gift he gave me. My life."

"Which is exactly why I couldn't speak with you when you came running for my help," Berson said softly.

"But I need you now as much as I needed you then," Jodi said. "I must find my birth parents. You were with Stasha in Warsaw when he and Franya adopted me. You are the only person alive who can direct me in my search."

Just as he began to explain that he was not in Warsaw at that time and had never met her birth parents, they heard a soft knock on the door.

Dr. Kemp, the director of the Institute, came in. When Berson began the introductions, Dr. Kemp asked Jodi, "How did you get in here?"

"Never underestimate the power of the press," she said, smiling.

Kemp started to apologize to Berson. "Really, Simon, I'll find out who disclosed your room number and I will personally discipline them for breaching your confidence."

"Never mind," Berson said. "Whoever told her deserves a medal. Anyway, she came with Sheldon Haar of the OSI, who knows everything about me, right down to the fake name in the hospital registry."

Once again, Jodi prepared to leave, but Berson stopped her. "Stay around, Jodi. They're going to bring me up to date and then we can keep talking."

Kemp handed Berson the report about his surgery.

"I'll live," he said, after scanning the report and handing it back. "And now you'll excuse me. I have a very important guest."

When Dr. Kemp left, Jodi said, "If I were to ask you about your condition would you tell me the truth?"

"I always tell the truth," he protested.

"You're a delightful liar," she said. "You saved someone's neck by telling Dr. Kemp that Sheldon Haar already knew your 'fake' name and where you were hospitalized."

"That's not a lie," he said. "It's just a case of keeping them guessing."

"Well, don't keep me guessing," she said. "Dr. Simon Berson, how do you feel?"

"I should be good for about five years. At seventy-one, five years is a lifetime."

They then spoke at length about their experiences.

Berson told her much about Sonya's past and about his struggle to come to the States. Jodi told him how she had been spoiled as a child by her parents and their wealth, how she learned about her adoption, and how she needed to discover herself by finding her natural parents.

When the nurse came in again, it was close to midnight. This time, despite Berson's objections, she insisted on giving him his sleeping tablet and preparing his bed.

"Do me a favor," he said to Jodi after taking his medication. "I want you to leave these pictures with me and come back in the morning."

"Dr. Berson, I was hoping you'd say that," she said, writing her phone number on the portfolio.

"Call me Simon," he said.

"I can't," she replied.

"We have a lot of work to do and one day you will call me Simon."

Elena Stole, the head nurse, accompanied Jodi down to the hospital's exit. She said, "Miss Wycliff, I hope you didn't tell them that I told you about Dr. Berson."

"Of course not," Jodi replied. "But maybe I should have. Dr. Berson wants to give a medal to the person who got me in there."

Jodi returned to her New York apartment, wrote up the highlights of her day's accomplishments, and immediately got into bed, eager to get some sleep. She tossed and turned, unable to get the day's events out of her mind. She got up and began to reach for the pictures, only to recall that she had left the whole portfolio with Berson. Unable to fall asleep, she scanned through the accumulated newspapers and magazines, trying to push everything out of her mind. She could not. She realized that Berson was the only one who could help her search for her parents, but she was deeply concerned about his health. She reached over to her night table and picked up Aristotle's *Metaphysics* – ordinarily a well-proven path to falling asleep.

Her eyes simply would not shut, so she finally went to her medicine cabinet, took out two Nembutal capsules, and swallowed them in one gulp. At 3 A.M., she finally fell asleep.

The phone rang, jarring her out of a deep slumber. She fumbled for the phone and, at the same time, tried to focus on the digital clock. The amber numbers, 4:06, looked fuzzy as she clumsily put the phone to her ear. When she got her bearings, she recognized Dr. Berson's voice.

"Jodi, Jodi," he kept yelling, until she finally replied in a quivering tone. "Come quick," he barked, "I found it. I found it!"

Jodi sprang out of bed, sprinkled some cold water on her face, dressed quickly, gulped down a cold and stale cup of coffee she had brewed the night before, and called for her car. The parking attendant, noticing that she staggered into the driver's seat, warned her about drunk driving, and offered to chauffeur her. She sped up the ramp, almost knocking down the guardrail as she turned sharply onto the main street.

At the hospital she tried the front entrance. It was shut but a sign on the glass door directed her to the rear of the building, where she entered through the Emergency Room. The nurse in charge, noticing her unstable gait, offered to help her sober up. When Jodi asked how to get to room 987 to see Dr. Jefferson, the nurse called a security man who told her that visitors were not permitted at that hour. Jodi explained she had received a call from Dr. Berson. At the mention of the name, the security man called his superior and, after a brief conversation, he escorted Jodi to a bank of elevators.

"What took you so long?" Dr. Berson asked.

"Getting in to see you is worse than getting into the White House," Jodi said, slurring her words and sliding on the floor from the chair as she tried to sit down.

"Hey, what's with you?" he asked.

"I couldn't sleep. Took a couple of Nembutals."

As he lectured her about the dangers of strong narcotics, he instructed the nurse to give her an injection of Norcan. Within minutes after the injection, she regained her composure.

"Now, let's get to work," he said, taking out the photograph of the two women and the baby. He showed her the reverse side of the original print and pointed to a barely legible inscription.

"This is what I found!" he said triumphantly.

Jodi could not make out the smudged script and what she could read made no sense to her.

"It's Polish, your mother tongue," Berson laughed at her. "'*Dla…na pamiec dobrych chwyl, Irena.*' It says, 'To,' then the name is erased, 'In remembrance of our good times, Irena.'"

Jodi took the picture and held it to her chest as tears filled her eyes.

"In remembrance of good times," Jodi said, repeating the phrase. "They liked each other."

She said it again several times, then her countenance changed. She looked up from the photograph. "It doesn't tell us anything except that the woman holding the baby is my natural mother, Irena. But to whom did she write it?"

"That's why I called you," Dr. Berson said. Again, he showed her the reverse side of the original print. "You told me that this print had a cardboard backing. Whoever removed the cardboard erased the original inscription. We must get that cardboard because, like a decal, some of the writing may still be there."

Jodi picked up the telephone, dialed the NIC switchboard and asked for Tony Arbella at the photo lab.

"Miss Wycliff," came the response, "it's 4:50 A.M. No one is in the lab that early."

"Of course," she said, chagrined. "I'll call later."

"That's the only clue we have to go on," Jodi said to Berson. "If the cardboard isn't found, we're back to square one."

Dr. Berson, sensing her dejection, raised his hand and motioned her to come closer. He brought out a magnifying glass and called her attention to the background of the picture of the two women.

"What do you see right here, on the side of the shrub, right next to Irena's nose?" Berson asked.

Jodi squinted through the glass and read haltingly, "Ulita Notym 35."

"It's a name of a street. Notym Street. Does it still exist? Is anyone living there? Would anyone know who had lived there?"

Dr. Berson smiled benignly, again as though he had made a great discovery. "And that's not all."

They went through each picture and found bits of clues: a recognizable face, a military identification number, a Polish postman, a church with a priest standing at the door.

"And, the name on the church is St. Michael's," Berson pointed out, showing her the faint letters on the side of the building.

"So?" was all Jodi could say.

"So, if the priest or some of the congregants are still around, they may know something about the baby and the woman holding her," Berson explained, handing her another photo. "Even this tractor may be a clue. The faces are smudged and you only surmise them to be Franya and Stasha. Could they be…"

"My real father and mother?" Jodi whispered.

Berson said, "Maybe, and maybe I even met them. After all, I recognized several people in the other pictures."

Talking freely, he recalled his wartime experiences with Colonel Greifler, Stasha, and the Partizans, as well as his liberation by the Red Army and his struggles in postwar Poland.

"Jodi, in all these years, I never spoke about those times to anybody."

"When all this is over," Jodi said, "I want to do a series on your life. It'll be the best dramatization of the Holocaust ever done."

Before the first streaks of daylight could be seen from the draped windows, Dr. Berson barked his order into the intercom, calling for two breakfasts.

"It's 6 A.M., the commissary is closed," came the response.

"I haven't eaten in two days," he said, shutting off the intercom. "And now I'm hungry...that's a good sign."

Jodi reached for the phone and, while dialing, told Dr. Berson, "I'm calling the canteen at NIC, that's where I worked. It's open all night."

She ordered two sumptuous breakfasts to be delivered to the Emergency Room. Berson asked the night nurse to send the food up as soon as it arrived. In less than twenty minutes, they were eating heartily, laughing and chatting. As she left, she gave him a peck on the cheek. "I'll be back soon."

"See that you are," he said, "I never had a better time in a hospital room!"

*

It was still too early in the morning to go to the photo lab to retrieve the cardboard from the original pictures, so Jodi returned to her apartment and quickly wrote down the meat of her discussions with Dr. Berson. She showered and lay down to rest. When she awoke after what seemed just a short nap, it was already past noon, but she was completely rested. She called Tony to ask about the cardboard backing of the pictures, explaining that it contained vital information that should not be lost. He promised to search for it and to let her know if anything was found. Jodi sat quietly at her desk, sipping her coffee and reviewing everything that had transpired in the past two days. She methodically itemized every bit of information she had culled from the Rynek File, from Dr. Berson, and from the photographs. She then determined that going to Poland should be her first priority, but she also realized she could not even get started without Dr. Berson.

Her first stop was the hospital, where she burst into Berson's room without knocking. She was startled to see three people hovering over his bed – Dr. Kemp, whom she recognized, another doctor who was examining

Dr. Berson, and an assisting nurse. Jodi hurriedly apologized and backed off, preparing to leave.

"No, no, Jodi, come in," Dr. Berson called out weakly. "You've met Dr. Kemp. Now meet Dr. Burke."

"Simon, we're not taking you off intravenous. You're not out of the woods yet," Dr. Burke said, nodding to Jodi but not really seeing her.

He ordered Berson to rest and shooed everyone out of the room. Walking toward the elevator with Jodi, Dr. Burke explained that the patient had been up all night and had taken a turn for the worse. His blood pressure was dangerously low and his heartbeat was irregular.

"I'm afraid I'm to blame," Jodi said, standing in the elevator with Dr. Burke. "He called me in the middle of the night to come and I stayed with him till morning."

Dr. Burke looked up from his chart and said, "You're Jodi Whatchamacallit, from the TV."

"Wycliff," Jodi responded.

"I don't care if you're the Queen of Sheba," Dr. Burke said. "You can't storm into a sick man's room just to get your face on TV. You have no right to endanger a man's life."

Jodi bowed her head, apologizing and mumbling that she hoped that she did not cause serious harm to Dr. Berson.

"Before you visit him again, ask me," Dr. Burke bristled. "No more storming into his room."

"I didn't storm into the room," she said quite angrily. "And I didn't go there to get my face on TV. He called me and asked me to come, and I did."

Dr. Burke, towering over her in the small elevator, paid no attention to her. He kept turning pages in the chart, wrote a few notes, and then asked, "Why did he call you? We need to record it on his chart."

When she did not reply, he asked again, "Why did he call you?"

"You wouldn't be interested," she answered coldly.

"Anything that has to do with Dr. Berson's health interests me."

When the elevator reached the lobby, she strutted out, heading straight for the exit. He caught up to her and asked, "What did Simon call you about?"

"It's not about his health, so you wouldn't be interested," she replied, continuing her brisk pace down the crowded hall.

When they passed the doctors' lounge, he steered her into the empty room and demanded again, "Tell me why Dr. Berson called you in the middle of the night."

"Why don't you ask Dr. Berson," she said.

He did not reply at first, but walked over to the large urn and drew two cups of coffee.

"You must understand," he said, finally, motioning to her to sit down with him at one of the round, white tables, "Dr. Berson has done some things that have caused concern here at the Institute. He's retired and, officially, has no duties. But he does the weirdest things, like interrupting a class of interns and lecturing to them about lab techniques. And now he invites you in the middle of the night. Weird. We simply have to watch over him," Burke said, again referring to the medical chart.

"I don't find him weird," Jodi said, her voice betraying her anger.

"You don't have to put up with his antics."

"He is a brilliant, caring, dedicated man," Jodi said, emphasizing each word. "He's not weird and his actions are not antics."

"What do you want from him?" Burke said.

"Just tell me, what's his condition?"

"Are you related to him?" Burke asked, looking again at his chart and pointing out there was no reference to any family members. "You came in at 4:36 A.M. You had breakfast with him at 6:20 A.M. and left him at 6:35 A.M."

"Dr. Burke, put that damn chart away," Jodi said sternly. "Look at me. I'm a human being. I have feelings. I'm not just some face on TV or something you jot into a patient's chart. And Dr. Berson is human too. He's not just a body to stick needles and tubes into. If you would care for his feelings as much as you care for his body, then just ask, he'll tell you why he called me. Now good-bye."

Jodi immediately put her confrontation with Dr. Burke out of her mind as she left the hospital and then called Tony on her car phone.

"I'm sorry, Jodi," he said. "We're swamped here. With this workload, I'll have to get someone to stay after hours to look for your cardboard backing in the garbage bins."

"I'll come myself," she answered. "It's really important."

Tony met her in the lobby of the network headquarters and walked with her to the lab, talking as they hurried down the corridors.

"We had to separate the cardboard backings from your photos," he explained. "Then they had to be soaked with a chemical solution. I can't hold out much hope that you'll find any writing left on the cardboard."

He took her to the garbage disposal area off the garage and asked a maintenance man to pull out the trash bags from the photo lab. After Tony left, Jodi and the workman emptied all of the lab's plastic garbage bags and sorted through the debris. It took a long time, but she finally spotted several small, wrinkled, brown pieces of paper at the bottom of the pile. Her heart skipped a beat when she saw some Polish words on one of the pieces. She recognized only the imprint, "FOTOGRAFIA." She found several other pieces, but they had no markings. As the maintenance man was about to place the papers back into one of the bags, she noticed a brown piece, like a spitball, tucked into the crease of the bag. Carefully, she unrolled it and saw a faint trace of blue writing on the curled edge. She put it into her purse with the other pieces she had found, tipped the maintenance man, and headed for the hospital.

Her problem now was getting into the hospital. In view of her confrontation with Dr. Burke, she knew it would be quite difficult to gain access to Berson's room. Nonetheless, given that she had retrieved the scraps of cardboard, she could not postpone seeing him. The head nurse who had originally told her about "Dr. Jefferson" blocked her entrance to Berson's room.

"Dr. Burke put me in charge of Dr. Berson with strict instructions to let no one in, especially you," Elena officiously told Jodi. Then, just as the nurse turned to go into Berson's room, she whispered, "Don't leave, we have to take him out for his walk soon."

Jodi waited in the ninth floor visitors' lounge, keeping a close watch on the door to Berson's room. From the public phone booth, she called Sheldon Haar in Washington.

"I have decided to go to Poland to follow up on some of the leads Dr. Berson discovered in the pictures," Jodi said. "The military people whom he recognized might help me in my search. If those people are still around, I would get some information about my parents."

"Jodi, most of what you want is still tightly sealed," he said. "Neither the Russians nor the Americans will release any of the stuff you want."

"Shelly, I'm not giving up," she said in a calm, subdued voice. "Can you see me tomorrow in Washington?"

"Absolutely. Come for lunch."

As she hung up the receiver, she stepped out of the booth and heard Dr. Berson's raucous voice arguing with several nurses who were coaxing him to get out of his wheelchair.

"I don't want to walk. I want my phone back. Get Dr. Burke right away."

Then Elena explained that Dr. Burke had taken away his telephone and had ordered him to walk. She ordered the nurses to help Dr. Berson get out of his wheelchair. He waved them off.

"Damn it," he said, resisting their efforts to stand him up. "I want my telephone back."

In the melee, Jodi managed to get close to Berson, slipping past the security guard. Berson's face lit up when he saw her. "Come, let's go for a walk," she said.

He leaned on her shoulders as she held onto the IV pole, pulling it along as they started down the corridor.

"It's my fault," Jodi said.

"What's your fault?"

"Your phone being taken away," she replied. "Dr. Burke bawled the hell out of me for our midnight tête-à-tête. And that breakfast of kippered herring was not the best for your blood pressure. That's my fault too."

As they walked the entire length of the long hallway, Jodi told him that she had talked to Haar about her plans to go to Poland to search for her parents. He nodded repeatedly, "That's the only place where you might still find traces of them."

Jodi brought him back to his room. When he was comfortably seated in his easy chair, she handed him her collection of cardboard fragments. He confirmed that it was signed by someone, repeating the phrase he had earlier discovered on the photograph.

"I can barely make out the full name," he said. "It looks like 'Irena.'"

"I knew that name both from the Rynek File and from Francine's recollection," she said dejectedly. "We need to know what her name was before the forged documents named her Irena."

He too looked dejected and called for a nurse to help him get back in bed.

"How do you feel?" Jodi asked when the nurse left.

"I was doing so well up until our all-night session," Dr. Berson said. "Jeff's right about the restrictions."

"Who's Jeff?" Jodi asked.

"That's Dr. Burke."

"He's rough," Jodi said. "And rude."

Simon laughed, "Everyone accuses him of that, but Jeff is one of the leading oncologists in the country. He's been offered the position of head of the Institute's Oncology Department. He's also had a dozen tantalizing offers from private cancer clinics, and he has yet to make a decision about which one to accept."

"That's no excuse for being a jerk," Jodi said.

Again Berson laughed, "I've lectured him about his brusque manner several times, but to no avail. Anyway, you don't like him, so forget about him. I have something more important to tell you."

He asked her to close the door and sit down next to the bed. "I want to tell you something about myself, something I've never spoken to anyone about. After my second surgery, I lost interest in everything," he explained. "I waited to die, to be united with my wife, who's been gone for almost two years."

Jodi started to lecture him about the value of life. He politely asked her to hear him out.

"No one can accuse me of being a religious man, but ever since Sonya died, I could find consolation only in the thought that although she died, she was not entirely gone, that her grave was not all that was left of her. As a matter of fact, I hated visiting the cemetery. Never went there, not even on her *yahrzeit*."

"On her what?" Jodi asked.

"*Yahrzeit*, anniversary of death," Simon replied. "We Jews commemorate the day by visiting the grave, lighting a candle, and saying a special prayer."

"I understand," Jodi replied.

"I wish you could have met Sonya."

"Have you forgotten my interview with her? She was wonderful, electric."

"Then you know, she was a *goldene neshome*," he said.

"Golden what?"

"A golden soul, a way to describe a person's character," he said. "She was exactly that, a golden soul. So if there's a soul, which is not corporeal, then it's not in the casket and not in the grave. It's somewhere, but certainly not in the cemetery. Maybe she's with God. So I figure maybe we'll be united once again. That's what I lived for, death. My death."

Berson paused and looked away from Jodi so she would not see the tears in his eyes. "I'm sorry," he said, "I'm getting carried away."

Jodi urged him to continue.

"Then, only three days ago, you came to me with these pictures," he said, reaching for the photographs. "For thirty-odd years, I rarely thought about my life in Poland under the Nazis and, when I did, it was always with pain, with hate, with revenge. That's why I pursued Stasha, stalking him, like hunting down a killer."

Jodi winced, "I'm beginning to understand you. I might even be willing to forgive you."

"No. I don't want to be forgiven. What I want now is to help you find her," he said, pointing to the woman in the picture.

"But your health…" she protested.

"Remember, with proper care, chemo, or radiation, or both, I've got several years to live. I no longer want to wait for death. And whatever time I have, I want it to be creative, meaningful. To me, finding your father and mother would be exactly that."

"Exactly what?" Jodi asked.

"I want to go to Poland with you," he announced, leaning back and shutting his eyes.

She said quietly, almost in a whisper, that she had originally come to him to ask him to go with her to Poland, but that she was afraid to suggest it and even more afraid to ask Dr. Burke's opinion.

"Well, I'm not afraid," he said.

He rang for the nurse, and when she came he ordered her to call Dr. Burke.

"Jeff has many faults, but his worst one is his slavish loyalty to me," he said when the nurse left. "His concern for me brings out the worst in him. When he noticed my deterioration, that probably sent him into a tailspin. So he let out his fears on you."

"If he's so brilliant, why is he so childish?" Jodi asked, just as Dr. Burke entered the room.

"Why are you here?" Burke asked immediately, upbraiding Jodi for visiting Simon. "Didn't I order you to get my permission before visiting him again?" Without giving her a chance to respond, he turned to Dr. Berson, "Simon, what did you call me for?"

"I want to go to Poland with Jodi," Simon said.

"Simon, it'll kill you," Jeff Burke said. Then, turning to Jodi, he added, "Is that what you came for? To endanger my patient?"

"It's my idea, not hers," Berson spoke up.

Dr. Burke pulled up a chair, placed himself next to Jodi, and said, "Miss Wycliff, Dr. Berson is a very ill man. He has prostate cancer, but it's his heart that worries us even more. We're keeping him alive with paper clips and rubber bands. A trip to Poland will kill him."

"That's why I want you to come along, Jeff," Dr. Berson said, adding with a chuckle, "and bring your paper clips and rubber bands."

Jeff was stunned. His eyes darted from Jodi to Berson. "Are you crazy? Do you think you'd survive such a trip? Do you think I would sign this chart, discharging you from the hospital in your condition? No way!" he shouted, dissolving into furious sputtering.

"Easy, son," Berson said, raising his hands. "I haven't heard you shout like that since med school. But you're good at it. I always knew you'd make a fine drill sergeant."

Burke sat still for an extended moment, drew a deep breath, gave his mentor a long look, and asked, "What do you want with Poland?"

Berson explained Jodi's personal crusade to find her parents. He showed him the pictures. "She's at an impasse. I'm the only one who even knows where to begin searching. It's important for me to go."

"Why? This is her affair. Why is it important to you?" Burke asked.

"It would give me something to live for."

Dr. Burke threw his hands up in the air, shaking his head in disbelief. He paced the floor for several moments, then turned to Jodi. "Miss Wycliff, I appreciate your need to go to Poland, but for him Poland is suicide. Please talk him out of it."

"Only you can stop me from going, not her," Berson interrupted. "If you refuse to come along, I'll be forced to remain here as your ward and patiently wait for you to bury me."

Jodi began to say something, but Berson stopped her. He glared at Jeff and asked, "Is that what you want? For me to do nothing but wait for death? Read your chart."

"You're scaring me," Jodi said. "Dr. Burke, what is his condition, really?"

"My condition is critical," Dr. Berson said to Jodi. "The cancer will ultimately kill me. But people have lived with cancer, some even as long as five years."

Dr. Burke hung the chart on the bed's railing and then, after a long silence, turned to Dr. Berson and said with sincerity and compassion, "I'll cancel my calendar and go with you, just for a few days, as soon as you're ready to leave the hospital."

"And when will that be?" Simon asked.

"Well, before your relapse, we were planning to take you off the IV tomorrow. Now we'll have to wait and see."

Burke called Jodi the following morning as she was preparing to leave for her appointment with Sheldon Haar in Washington.

"Here's the deal," he said. "Just to be cautious, Simon won't be ready to undertake the ordeal of travel for another week or ten days."

Jodi suspected he was purposely delaying their travel to Poland, but she didn't want to aggravate him. "Can I make arrangements for our trip for a week from Friday?" she asked, trying to keep any challenging tone out of her voice.

"You can make whatever arrangements you want," he replied caustically, "but whether Simon will be there, is impossible to tell yet."

She heard him hang up. She looked at the phone in disgust and banged down the receiver. She was still fuming when she called the operational officer at Wycliff Corporation to order the company's plane for the trip overseas. The transportation coordinator told her he had to switch the call to Mr. Boynton's office. That surprised her.

"Jodi," Cal said. "Nice of you to finally check in. You've been replaced, you know. You're no longer a member of the board." Speaking rapidly and coldly, he explained, "At the last meeting, the board agreed that since you began searching for your birth parents, your behavior has been abnormal, erratic. This renders you unfit to be on the board."

"That's outrageous, Cal," she began. "What are you doing there? You have your own business to run."

"For now, I've been named acting chairman of the board."

"Be that as it may," Jodi said, "I'm still the majority stockholder of Wycliff, and only I will decide when I step down."

She immediately put a call through to Malcolm Donner, the company's attorney. His secretary meekly told her that he was in a conference and could not be disturbed. Looking at her watch, Jodi realized she would be late for her meeting with Sheldon Haar if she pursued this any further. As she sped off to the airport to catch the shuttle to Washington, Cal's words, "Since you began searching for your birth parents, your behavior has been abnormal, erratic," raced through her mind. Even on the plane to Washington she could hear his voice and imagine him smiling vindictively when he said, "This renders you unfit to be on the board."

*

Sheldon noticed her anger the moment he saw her sitting in his waiting room. She was twisting her handkerchief and nervously tapping her foot.

"Come on in, Jodi. You look furious," he said. "What has you so upset?"

She repeated what Cal had told her.

"Well, this is not my line of work," he said, dialing the phone, "but if something can be done, my friend Merv Houston, the biggest corporate lawyer in DC, can do it."

When Houston got on the phone, Haar repeated what Jodi had told him. Relaying information from her, he gave Houston the names and phone numbers of Cal Boynton and Malcolm Donner at Wycliff.

"Now that's that off my mind, I'll tell you why I wanted to see you."

"I know," Haar said. "Yesterday, you asked me all those questions on the phone."

"No, not just that, Shelly, I would like you to come with me to Germany, just for three or four days."

Haar was dumbstruck. But before he had a chance to reply, Jodi quickly told him that Dr. Berson had volunteered to go with her to Poland. "When we talked about it, he suggested a stopover in Berlin to get as much information as possible on Stasha, either from military records or State Department files. You could help me so much with that."

"Jodi you're talking about things that happened thirty-five years ago," Sheldon countered. "None of that stuff is around in the US military establishment. And I can't take three or four days out of the office for a wild-goose chase."

"Mr. Haar," she replied quietly but with rancor in her voice, "when you were prosecuting my father, you flew to Europe for weeks at a time. Now, when it's a matter far more important than prosecuting a broken man, you're too busy to bother."

Haar shuffled a few papers, swiveled in his chair, and said, "Be fair, Jodi, I've done almost everything you've asked me to do. Let me put a call through to Berlin. I think I can get you the backup you need. Then we'll both decide if I'm really needed there."

He asked his secretary to call Vice-Consul McGowan in Berlin. "It's about 4 P.M. there. He should be in his office. If not, try his home."

Within minutes, she connected Haar with Berlin.

"Hey, Shelly, I thought the Wojchiechowski case was closed," McGowan said.

"Randy, I have his daughter, Jodi Wycliff on the extension," Haar said. "Do you know her?"

"Hello, Jodi," Randy called out. "I was assigned to you when you did the story on the Berlin Wall. Remember?"

"Do I remember?" Jodi said excitedly. "You were with State and almost got me arrested by the Russians because you had me cross the Wall without clearance."

"Yeah, and that was the best part of your story," he teased.

Haar described Jodi's desire to trace her natural parents and asked Randy what he could do for her in Berlin. Randy waxed poetic, anticipating her arrival and promising her access to CIA field documents.

"You might also want to interview some Russian and German personnel who may have information on Stasha's wartime activities," he added.

"Do you need my help to get Jodi set up in Berlin?" Haar asked.

"You're always welcome, but Jodi and I can handle this. We'll be fine," he said. "Jodi, what flight are you taking?"

"I'll let you know, Randy," Jodi replied.

After they hung up, she turned to Haar. "Thank you, Shelly. Thanks for making the contact with McGowan. You're right, I can take it from there."

"So what flight are you taking?" Haar also asked.

"That all depends on what your lawyer friend tells you."

"We'll hear from him soon enough. Meanwhile, I have something for you. Right after you called me yesterday, I went through my files and found something that will interest you."

He told her he had traced John Kemeris, the CIC agent who had processed Stasha and Franya's immigration to the United States.

"My mother mentioned him," Jodi said. "Lanky Texas type. He gave me my name. I really want to talk to him. He may have some leads we can follow up."

"I'll call him and set up an appointment."

As she was about to leave, the light on his private phone blinked. He picked it up, listened, and motioned her to remain.

"Say that again, Merv," Haar said, "I'm putting you on the speaker so that Miss Wycliff can hear you."

"The company plane will be at Kennedy Airport next Friday morning," the voice said. "It'll go anywhere you tell it to go."

"Merv, how'd you do it?" Haar asked.

"Simple," the voice said, "I informed Donner that if the plane was not available to Miss Wycliff, she would immediately sue the board of directors not only for her reinstatement but for malfeasance and malpractice. And, pending the outcome of that suit, I would ask the court to put the company's assets in escrow. In effect, that would prohibit the company from doing any business with Miss Wycliff's stock. I gave the lawyer fifteen minutes to respond, but he didn't take quite that long."

"Merv, we're going to be good friends," Jodi said, thanking him. "When I get back, let's talk at length about Wycliff and what's going on there."

"You've got it," he said. "Have a great trip. Now they know you're going to fight back."

*

John Kemeris was old, probably in his eighties by now. He wore thick-lensed glasses that almost obscured his owlish red face. Looking at Jodi, scrutinizing her, he took off his glasses and put them on again.

"So you're Jodi Wycliff. The television woman. I think I can still recognize you," he said with a chuckle, excited about meeting a TV personality. "I figured all along that you were that little girl I named. Why don't ya come back next week after my cataract operation. Then I can see if you're still cute."

He sat back in his easy chair and, at Jodi's request, gave her the whole story. He recalled how the cold war had pitted the Americans and Russians against one another. He related how US intelligence used Stasha and his wife to ferret out a Russian spy who was masquerading as a refugee in the Displaced Persons camp.

"We promised them the US of A, and they took all kinds of crazy chances," he said.

"Did my mother ever tell you how she'd adopted a little girl?" Jodi asked when he paused to wipe sweat from his glasses.

"Adopted! They adopted you?" Kemeris called out. "No, nobody ever said a word about you being adopted. You were their baby."

"Would any record in the CIC files list the name of the little girl they adopted?" Haar asked.

"Nope," Kemeris said, shaking his head. "Miss Wycliff, CIC had a full record about Stasha Wojchiechowski, but I don't remember a darn thing about him adopting a girl. He and his wife had their daughter with them when he left for the States, but they never said a whisper about having adopted her, that is, you."

He looked at Jodi and proudly related how he had given her his sister's name. "I warned your daddy that a little singin', dancin' cutie-pie like you could mess up a mission like nothing else, but he insisted that they'd do just fine with you along."

Jodi listened to his stories and thanked him warmly, but she was disheartened that he could add no details about her natural parents.

There was little else to say. They chatted as they drank the lemonade he offered and then said their good-byes.

Driving back to Washington, she expressed her disappointment at having learned nothing from Mr. Kemeris. Haar stopped the car on the shoulder of the road and faced her squarely.

"You'd better get used to disappointment," he said. "In your attempt to find your parents, you're going to come to a lot of dead ends. This is the first one. There'll be lots more. Don't get disheartened and don't give up."

When she returned to her hotel, she found several messages from Francine.

"Hi, Mom," Jodi said, apologizing for not calling earlier.

"Jodi, you don't have to apologize. I know you're busy. I just called to tell you that Jason and I are leaving for a trip to the Far East."

"I'm leaving too," Jodi said. "I'm going to Poland in a couple of days with Dr. Berson and his assistant to search for my birth parents."

"I wish you well, honey," Francine said with excitement. "If you discover anything, anything at all, call me. I'll send you our itinerary so you'll know how to reach me."

As soon as she hung up the phone, it rang again.

"Where were you?" Dr. Berson bellowed. "It's been three days and I haven't seen or heard from you."

"I was in Washington. I met with Sheldon Haar who made contact with someone in Berlin for me. He also introduced me to a John Kemeris who was formerly with the CIC in Berlin. He's the one who expedited my parents' immigration to the US. But, more important, when did you get your phone back?"

"Jeff had the phone reinstalled and he's finally taken out the IVs," Berson said triumphantly. "We've begun preparing for the trip to Poland. And you know what? Jeff's hyped up, preparing himself to go. I think he's looking forward to the European excursion and can't wait for Friday. He's totally changed his attitude."

"I'll believe it when I see it," Jodi said. "Let me ask you a question. I've been reading that there are various organizations that maintain lists of survivors. Do you think there's any chance my birth parents might be on one of those lists?"

"What name would you look for on those lists?" Berson asked.

"All we know is 'Rynek'," she said.

"Then our first problem is to discover who they were before they became Irena and Tomasz Rynek."

"I'm glad you said *our* problem."

"It is our problem, yours and mine," Berson responded. "This has become my mission as well as yours."

Chapter 18

THE FOLLOWING FRIDAY, WHEN THEY boarded the Wycliff jet at JFK Airport, Dr. Berson behaved as though finding the Ryneks' true identity was, indeed, his problem. In fact, he behaved as though the entire excursion was under his command. First he checked with the pilot about their arrival time so he could prepare a work schedule for their first day in Berlin. Then he looked over Jodi's "Follow-Up List" to determine whether they had left anything behind that they were going to need in Poland. Finally, he checked over Burke's medical kit – amidst the younger doctor's protests – to make sure he had enough medication in case they had to stay longer in Europe. When he finished his inspection, he looked about the plane and, reaching for Jodi's hand, said, "I know why you insisted on flying the company's plane. It's like an ambulance plane."

After the plane took off, Burke sat next to Berson and, for the first two hours of the trip, hovered over him, often taking his pulse and checking his blood pressure. When the steward brought out the dinner trays, Jeff cleared which items his patient could eat.

Berson finally got exasperated. "Stop fussing over me, Jeff. Leave me alone. Go sit with Jodi. But be nice to her."

"I already apologized to her when we met at the airport. In fact, she told me she was glad I'd changed my tune. She figured that would make the trip less stressful."

Jeff slid across the aisle to sit next to Jodi, moving her travel bag from beneath her feet so that she could sit more comfortably.

"Did Simon order you to be next to me?" she asked teasingly.

"I wish he had done that a long time ago, so our first few meetings wouldn't have been so full of disasters," Jeff replied, peeking over her shoulder as she studied the latest version of her "Follow-Up List."

"Perhaps there are still some people in Poland who were with your mother when she gave birth to you in the hospital," Jeff suggested. "And maybe, during the year your mother spent with Francine in Warsaw, she talked about your birth. Perhaps Irena might have mentioned where it took place or who her doctor was, or where she lived after leaving the hospital."

"Where did you learn so much about my mother?"

"I've had a few long talks with Simon about your mission," Jeff said, adding, "not only about his medical chart."

Jodi thanked him and added his suggestions to her list. Next to the "Mom" insert, she wrote, "Call Francine from Berlin to ask if Irena ever discussed my birth."

She watched as Jeff made notes on Berson's medical chart and asked, "How's his condition? Are we sure he's strong enough for the trip? If something happened to him, Heaven forbid, I could never forgive myself," she whispered so that Berson would not hear.

"I can't guarantee anything. I'm glad you got this plane. It's damn good for any emergency. I'll be with him twenty-four hours a day."

They talked through much of the night, sharing experiences from their teenage years and discussing their professional successes. They were surprised how similar their lives had been. He admitted that he too had been a "wild kid," resorting to drugs after a difficult time at home.

"I straightened out after a good friend died from an overdose," he said. "And now, all I do is work, work, work. I'm afraid I'm going to be like Simon. Nothing exists for me beyond my work in the hospital."

When they arrived at Berlin's Tempelhof Airport on Saturday morning, Jodi released the company plane. Vice-Consul Randy McGowan greeted them on the tarmac and shepherded them through customs and immigration. As he drove them to the Excelsior Hotel, he explained, "I haven't made any appointments for you until tomorrow, so you have a day to get over your jet lag. Your first appointment is with a US employee in the CIA who's been authorized to let you read rough field reports about Stasha."

"What's a rough field report?" Berson asked.

McGowan explained, "CIC intelligence reports were routinely subjected to corroboration procedures, requiring two reliable sources of information before accepting any item as fact. Reports that were not confirmed through authentic sources were considered rough field reports and were filed away. These reports normally contain detailed information on people and places that might be useful to you. But, remember, they haven't been fully corroborated."

"What else is on for tomorrow, Randy?" Jodi asked.

"Your second appointment is with Heinrich Glaubmann, a master sergeant I discovered, who served under Gestapo head, Colonel Zahn, during the German occupation of Warsaw," McGowan said. "I also have to contact a particular general because Sheldon Haar asked me to make sure that Dr. Berson meets with General Kolcharski."

"Who's he?" Jodi and Dr. Berson asked in unison.

"Someone you saved from a burning tank when he was a young lieutenant," McGowan replied.

"I'm not here to reminisce about the war, so I'm not wasting my time with him."

"According to Shelly, if you're going to Poland," McGowan said, "Kolcharski can be a very big help."

After the porters took their luggage up to their rooms, they sat in the bar, where they had cocktails and snacks while their rooms were being readied. Jodi thanked McGowan for the arrangements and for the schedule he had prepared for them. Since the rest of the day was free, he offered to show them around Berlin.

"Dr. Berson, would you like to visit Schlachtensee, the DP camp you lived in?" McGowan asked.

"I have no interest in touring Berlin or visiting the camp," he said curtly. "However," he turned to Jeff, "why don't you and Jodi take Randy up on his offer?"

"Simon, let's get this straight from the start. I'm not leaving you for a single minute as long as you're here in Berlin," Jeff stated firmly.

Berson countered, "Jeff, if you are going to treat me like this, you'd better make plans to return to New York."

Jodi immediately came to Jeff's defense, "Dr. Berson, remember that you originally begged Jeff to come to Warsaw."

Berson murmured an apology.

"You guys kiss and make up," Jodi joked. "I'm going to run up to my room and call Mom in Hong Kong. I want to find out if Irena ever talked to her about the circumstances of my birth."

*

"Hi, Mom. How's Hong Kong?"

"Fine, interesting. How are you?"

"I'm in Berlin, safe and sound, ready to start my search."

"I hope it goes well, Jodi," Francine said. "I just wish I could help."

"You can, Mom. You spent a good deal of time with Irena Rynek in Warsaw, right? Did she ever mention where she gave birth to me or which doctor or midwife helped her?"

Silence.

"Mom, Mom, are you there?"

"I'm thinking," Francine said. After a protracted silence, she slowly added, "I remember telling Irena about my emergency surgery in the Czyste Hospital. I'm not sure, but I think she said that she also gave birth there."

"Mother, this is vital. Think. Can you be sure? Did she say I was born in the Czyste?"

"Wait. If I'm not wrong, I think she once visited me while I was hospitalized there, "Francine said. "This was later, after we had already become friends. I was hospitalized for a minor infection, and Irena visited me, and I definately remember that she told me that she had given birth to you there! I hope that helps."

Jodi practically howled with glee. "Thanks, Mom, you've been a great help. I'll follow that up when we get to Poland. You and Jason have a wonderful trip and stay in touch with me."

She called Jeff's room and excitedly gave him the gist of her conversation with her mother. "Jeff, Francine remembers that Irena told her that she gave birth to me at Czyste Hospital. Do you think there's a chance that Dr. Berson might remember Irena?"

Jeff did not wish to let her down so he quietly said, "For now, since we have no name for the woman and no firm date for the birth, let's wait until we get to Warsaw. Simon's memory will be jogged when we visit the hospital there."

*

The next morning, they arrived at McGowan's office early. He led them to the archives that contained hundreds of CIC reports as well as some German documents dealing with wartime conditions in Warsaw. Hans Braunschweig, a German archivist of the consulate, aided them in their search. Under his guidance, they found dozens of references to Stasha, mostly describing him as a hooligan working for the Sviatova Association before the war and listing his many arrests. Stasha's name also appeared several times in military records; his elevation to the rank of major, his appointment as police commandant of Warsaw – records that Jodi recognized because Haar had used them in his court hearing and were disputed by her attorney.

"Is there any file that specifically deals with the destruction of Warsaw's Jewish community?" Jodi asked Hans, hoping that Stasha's name would not be found therein.

He pointed to a stack of cartons that dealt with the Ghetto, which, he said, would take them weeks to plow through.

"But there is one file that you will find shocking," Hans said, opening one carton and extracting a slim folder marked "US Correspondence Exchange."

He explained that the file he was handing her contained copies of communications sent by various European consulates to their Washington offices. Jodi was attracted to a single sheet, titled, "Extermination of Jews," which was a copy of a telex sent by a vice-consul in Geneva to his superiors in Washington. Its opening sentence startled her:

I have in my possession unimpeachable evidence that the Nazis have a master plan to exterminate all the Jews of Europe.

When Dr. Berson and Jeff approached her desk, they noticed she was turning white as she read the rest of the telex.

"Dr. Berson, you gotta read this," she said.

The telex described, in minute details, "Concentration camps with ovens for cremating Jews killed in showers where prussic acid was used in the killing."

"So what else is new?" Dr. Berson asked. "We know about the six million Jewish dead and how they died."

"That's not what startled me," Jodi said, pointing to the date on the telegram. "It's August 1, 1942, when we, in the States, claimed to know nothing about Hitler's plans for the massive extermination of the Jews."

Berson took the telex from her hand, returned it to Herr Braunschweig, and said, "That's for the historians. Our job is to find Jodi's mother."

But, after working the entire day, they found no reference to Stasha's adopting a Jewish baby girl.

"Another dead end," Jodi muttered to Jeff, recalling Haar's warning.

*

When they returned to their hotel, it was too late to meet Heinrich Glaubmann, so Jodi called Randy to reschedule their session with the German sergeant for the following morning. That evening, during dinner at the hotel, Berson abruptly announced that he was tired and was going to bed. Jeff stood up to help Simon to his room.

"Sit down, Jeff," Berson again scolded. Then, imitating Jeff's earlier comment, he said, "Let's get this straight from the start. I'm not an invalid yet. I can get myself to my room and I can take my damn pills myself. I don't need you for that."

Chastened, Jeff backed down, letting Berson make his own way to his room. When they saw him take the elevator, Jeff said, "I have to be a psychologist to know how to tend to him."

Jodi smiled and said, "Wait till we get old. We'll behave exactly like the doctor you so admire. He's tough, but deep inside he's a pussycat."

When they finished their meal, Jodi and Jeff sat down in comfortable armchairs in the lobby and listened to a program of classical music piped through the hotel's public address system. It was almost midnight when they looked in on Dr. Berson and found him awake, reading some of the files he had taken from McGowan.

"Simon, you have a long week ahead. You've got to get your sleep," Jeff said, placing the bottle of sleeping tablets at his bedside. "Take two of these. It'll help you get the rest you need."

"Never mind me. Don't need 'em. Never felt better in my life," Berson replied. "Are you being nice to Jodi?"

In the morning, Jeff had a scare when he went into Berson's room to take him to breakfast. Simon was not asleep but he seemed disoriented. And when Jeff took his blood pressure, he noticed it had plunged to a dangerous level. Jeff counted the number of sleeping tablets in the medicine bottle and discovered quite a number of tablets missing.

"Simon, how many of these did you take?"

"Might have taken it more than once. Haven't slept yet," Berson muttered.

Jeff gave him a shot to offset the adverse effects of the tablets, and stayed until Berson fell asleep.

When Jeff came down alone for breakfast, Jodi immediately asked if Berson was OK. "He took too many sleeping pills," Jeff told her, "but he's not in any serious condition. He just needs to sleep it off."

During their breakfast, a waiter came to their table, telling them that a Mr. Glaubmann was waiting in the lobby. They quickly finished their coffee and went to meet the man who had known Stasha in Warsaw.

Heinrich Glaubmann was old, unshaven, and toothless, with deeply sunken cheeks. For this occasion he had undoubtedly put on a clean shirt, a slightly rumpled jacket, and an old, thin tie. He rigidly bowed to them, repeating over and over how honored he was to meet them and offering to be of service.

"Can you tell us about you and Stasha in Warsaw?" Jodi asked.

Glaubmann seemed unable to focus. He bragged about his military service in Warsaw and other military assignments, immediately pleading innocence to atrocities committed by his superiors. He rambled on, complaining about his government pension, which, he said, barely covered his daily living expenses. He said his throat was dry and asked them to buy him a glass of beer.

Realizing that giving the old man a beer would further disorient him, Jodi whispered to Jeff, "Don't order a beer yet."

She turned to Glaubmann, "I promise we'll get you a beer after you've answered our questions."

"I learned to speak English," he said, paying no attention to her request. His raspy voice made his speech difficult to follow, especially with his thick German accent and the whistling sound in his toothless mouth. "Und, if you can give me a few dollars, I would have very much appreciate it."

"Mr. Glaubmann, you are not here for a social visit. The money we might give you depends entirely on the information you can give us about Stasha Wojchiechowski," Jodi said sternly.

Glaubmann cackled, scratched his stubbled chin, and smiled. "I remember that Stasha," he said and, once again, rambled on, relating meaningless stories. He then took out a cigarette, and after fumbling several times to strike a match, he succeeded in lighting it. Puffing smoke into their eyes, he asked again if he could have a glass of beer.

Although they both urged him several times to recall incidents involving Stasha, the old sergeant wavered, repeating irrelevant stories he had already told.

Jeff asked in a commanding tone, "Glaubmann, you worked for Colonel Zahn, what do you know about the Rynek File?"

"Yes, Sir, the Rynek File," Glaubmann said in his garbled speech. "I was Colonel Zahn's adjutant, und I replaced him. *Ja*, the colonel was recalled to Berlin. Und I carried the Rynek File back to Germany und I knew all about the little girl Stasha stole from the Jews."

"Tell me all you know about Stasha and about that little girl. What do you mean, 'stole from the Jews'?" Jodi asked intently.

"Well, that little girl was his downfall and she was, like the Americans say, our ace in the hole," Heinrich grinned, showing his blackened gums. "Stasha was the chief guard over Jews to make them get on the Ostbahn, the train. About a year after he got that job, maybe later, no maybe more, Stasha reported that a baby girl died in the jail. I told the colonel he was faking. But the colonel said that Stasha was too valuable to be punished for that."

As Glaubmann spoke, Jodi scribbled in her notebook, trying to keep up with Glaubmann's mangled speech.

She angrily interrupted, "Mr. Glaubmann, you want cash and a drink. Tell me as much as you know about Stasha and the little girl, then I will give you all the beer you want."

"*Ja, ja*, I remember. I took Stasha and his wife and the baby girl to the train station in Warsaw. That was for resettlement to Germany. I teased him about this daughter. I even used her name. I joked that she was his fringe benefit of the war. That's what I said, 'fringe benefit'. He didn't think I was funny. Scared the hell out of him because he thought he would be punished for keeping the Jewish girl baby."

"You said that the little girl was Stasha's downfall," Jodi said, referring to her notes. "How did that little girl bring about Stasha's downfall?"

Heinrich thought a while. "You want dates, little details. It was a very complicated time. I can't give you that. It was a long time ago."

The old sergeant took out a sandwich from a paper bag and munched it, drinking it down with several cups of coffee that Jeff had ordered for him. Jodi watched the old man gobble his food. Then she picked up her notebook and addressed him again.

"Try now, please, to tell us how that little girl brought about Stasha's downfall."

"Forget everything I told you," Heinrich said, straightening his tie and attempting to look presentable. "Here's how it happened. First, Stasha and the Ryneks are good friends. Church, visits, dances. We, the Gestapo, knew everything. This goes on for about two years. You know what? He would bring their little girl to our parties to dance and sing for us. One day Stasha discovers they're not Ryneks, not Christians, but they are Jews with false identity documents. He comes to Colonel Zahn to ask special treatment for some other Jew from the Ghetto who worked with Rynek. I was there."

"Who was the other man? What does he have to do with the Ryneks? Why did he need special treatment from Colonel Zahn?" Jodi asked, inundating him with questions.

After sucking his lower lip, Heinrich said, "I can tell you some of that, not all. First, Stasha jailed the Ryneks for using false identity papers. Then he arrested the other man, the man from the Ghetto who made the document for them. Now do you understand?"

"No," Jodi replied, speaking slowly and looking squarely at the old man. "We're not interested in who else was arrested by Stasha. What we want to know is, what was Rynek's real name?"

"I don't know the Ryneks' names, but I know the forger's name," Heinrich Glaubmann replied slowly. "That is *gutt*, no? He was a Jew who made for many, many people fake papers. His name was Haskel. Haskel Kornblit. Find him and you'll find the Ryneks' real names. If Haskel made the false documents for the Rynek people, he knew also their real names. No?" He sat back, triumphant, tipping his now empty coffee cup sideways, just in case the dregs would yield another drop.

"Where is Haskel now?" Jodi asked.

"About ten years ago, maybe longer, he was right here in Berlin. Going back and forth from Poland to Berlin. I have not seen him since. But, like I say, find Haskel Kornblit and you'll find Rynek's real name. As for me, I want only *gutt* relations with the Americans. I never did nobody harm."

As he began to ramble again, Jodi stood up. "Thank you, Mr. Glaubmann," she said, handing him a $50 bill. "Here, that's your fringe benefit of the war."

The old man looked at her in surprise. "Thank you," he said, for a moment looking far more alert than he had been. Then he bowed slightly, tipped his cap clumsily several times, and finally shuffled away, still muttering.

Jodi and Jeff left the hotel, walked along the Kurfurstendamm, and stopped at an outdoor café. They sat at a table and began reconstructing the information they had gleaned from Glaubmann. Jodi shuffled through her notes and commented, "I think his remark about the forger was our first real breakthrough."

"So do I."

"What he said about the forger is correct. Maybe we should leave for Warsaw right away to pick up Haskel's trail. Can Dr. Berson travel? Do we have to meet with that Russian general?"

"Let's go find out how things stand," Jeff said, getting up.

According to the huge clock on one of the billboards, it was already past noon. They rushed back to the hotel and hurried up to Dr. Berson's room, where they found him lying in bed. Apprehensive, Jodi asked Jeff, "Is he all right? He looks comatose."

Berson opened his eyes, smiled at them, and immediately asked about their conversation with Glaubmann.

When Jodi reported what Glaubmann had told them, Berson said, "I knew Haskel well. I even did business with him in the Ghetto. I agree with Glaubmann. If Haskel prepared the Rynek's papers, then find him and you'll find your parents' real names."

Jeff heard the phone ringing in his room next door and bolted to catch it.

"Hi, I have good news," Randy McGowan told him. "General Mieczyslav Kolcharski will be coming to your hotel to meet Dr. Berson. So I arranged for dinner this evening at seven thirty."

Jeff came back into Simon's room to tell him and Jodi about McGowan's dinner arrangement. "Do you feel up to that, Simon?" he asked.

"Sheldon Haar asked me to meet this general, so I will have to be at the dinner," Berson begrudgingly replied as Jeff checked his pulse and listened to his heart.

"Well, you don't get a medical excuse," he said. "Everything's normal."

*

Randy McGowan introduced General Kolcharski to Jodi, Jeff, and Dr. Berson in the hotel's dining room.

"My doctor! My God!" the general called out, embracing Dr. Berson in a bear hug, practically picking him up. "I owe you my life. I owe you everything!"

Jodi and Jeff stood aside, watching the general sweep off his hat as he gave Dr. Berson an exaggerated bow. The general then called the hotel manager, and stated in a commanding voice, "Dr. Berson is my guest throughout his stay in Europe. Remember he is my guest. Dr. Berson, you can have my car, my house, anything!"

"If I had known you were going to turn out to be crazy, I would have let you roast in that tank," Berson grinned, shaking the general's outstretched hand.

When the laughter died down, McGowan again introduced the general to Jodi and Jeff.

"Welcome to Berlin. You must understand that I have waited all these years for this moment," the general said. "I have been so eager to express my thanks to Dr. Berson."

After aperitifs, they ate dinner as General Kolcharski related how he had been dragged out of a burning tank and how Dr. Berson had saved his life. "In fact," he announced, "I still have the official military account of that tank battle. It describes the good doctor's heroism in detail. I keep that on my desk and reading it is how I always start my day."

"This party is getting too serious," Berson said, raising his glass to the general. "To Mitch. You'll never go to hell. If that fire didn't kill you, there's no fire in hell that can even touch you."

"Since I don't believe in your God, or any other, I'll never go to hell," the general responded, raising his glass in return.

Throughout the meal, Kolcharski repeated his gratitude, and just as often, Dr. Berson kept making light of the entire episode.

When they finished eating, Kolcharski rose to propose his last toast. He reached into his pocket and brought out a velvet bag that contained a gold star for bravery. "This is a World War II medal, the highest military award," he explained. "It was presented to me by Stalin." He handed it to Dr. Berson with a flourish, and embraced him with tears in his eyes, repeating over and over, "Thank you for giving me my life."

For the first time since meeting Kolcharski, Berson was touched by the presentation. He said he could not accept the medal, knowing what it meant to a military man and what it meant to his family. On the verge of tears, General Kolcharski pleaded with Dr. Berson to accept it, saying, "How else can I express my sincere gratitude to one who gave me my life?"

Berson took the medal and the velvet bag, promising to keep it as a treasure as long as he lived.

General Kolcharski then turned to Jodi and, struggling a bit to revert to his standard persona as an intimidating military commander instead of a deeply grateful old acquaintance, he said, "I have one moment of business to conduct with all of you. Randy told me why you've come to Berlin. He also informed me that you are leaving for Warsaw tomorrow to continue your search. I want you to know that I have already issued orders to all the military units under my command to grant full assistance to you in your search."

He handed Jodi a copy of the order, saying, "Now, use it freely as needed." Taking it, she spontaneously bounced out of her seat to give him a hug and kiss him on both cheeks.

"From the bottom of my heart, I wish you success," he said, "all of you."

The following morning, McGowan met them at the hotel to drive them to the airport for their flight to Warsaw. As Jodi was about to get into his car, the concierge rushed out to tell her she had an urgent phone call. She went back and picked up the phone at the reception desk.

"Jodi, I'm glad I caught you in time," Winston White, president of Network International, said on the phone. "You've got to do me a favor. Pat Collins in Cairo just cabled that Sadat is flying to Tel Aviv next Saturday night and will speak to the Knesset in Jerusalem on Sunday. Can you get there for a one-on-one follow up with Sadat?"

"I'm on my way to Warsaw, Mr. White, and I don't know how long I'll be there, so don't rely on me to interview Sadat."

"We're not giving up on you," White replied. "He'll be in Tel Aviv until Monday. That gives you eight days. I will rely on you, indeed I will," he stated, hanging up and leaving Jodi saying, "Don't count on me" to the telephone's empty buzz.

During the hour-and-a-half flight, Berson regaled them with stories of his life in Warsaw. He spoke glowingly of the prewar years when he built up the Czyste Hospital, making it one of Poland's major health centers.

"It is different today," he warned Jodi. "You have to be careful dealing with the authorities in Warsaw since the USSR is still in complete control."

"I had no trouble with the Russians when I interviewed Brezhnev."

"You were a network correspondent then. Now you're just an ordinary tourist. And, remember, Mitch Kolcharski is not typical of the Russian rulers of Warsaw."

When the plane landed at Warsaw Airport, Chuck Knowles, the NIC bureau chief in Warsaw, pulled up in a station wagon, parked at the ramp, and facilitated their inspection at Polish customs and through immigration. As they drove to the Grand Hotel, Knowles told Jodi that his office was open to helping her during her stay in the city. He handed her the keys to the rented car.

"Mr. White and the Network are paying for the car and picking up all your expenses while you're in Warsaw," Knowles said. "And we can arrange your transportation to Jerusalem when you're ready."

"If he wants to throw away his money, it's OK with me," Jodi said as Knowles walked them to the hotel's bar. "But you can tell him I'm not committing to the Jerusalem assignment."

The local bureau chief argued with Jodi, but she merely put up her hand, telling him there was no use in arguing the point. When Knowles left, Berson excused himself to make a few telephone calls and soon returned.

"I just called the Jewish Committee, asking about Haskel Kornblit, who had had connections with the committee, and I'm already frustrated," Berson reported, "because the person I spoke to denied even knowing that name and hung up on me."

"That frustrated you?" Jodi asked.

"When the war ended," Berson explained, trying to control his anger by pouring himself a glass of water, "the committee was just a Russian tool, but now it's a recognized charitable organization, helping what's left of the Jewish community in Poland – five thousand poverty-stricken people."

"So what?" Jeff asked.

"I called back and simply asked how one would trace a survivor. I didn't mention Haskel's name. That's when they invited me to look through their records in their library."

Jodi agreed that the committee was covering up knowing the Kornblit person. "Should we go now?" Jodi asked.

Berson did not answer. He suddenly put his hands to his chest. His face contorted and he began breathing heavily. When he raised his glass of water to his mouth, it dropped from his hand. Jeff quickly forced a nitroglycerin tablet into his mouth and quickly lay Berson on a lounge chair. He unloosened his shirt around his collar, applied a cold compress to his perspiring forehead, and took his pulse. Jodi was aghast, watching Simon struggling to breathe.

After resting several minutes, Dr. Berson whispered weakly, "Remember, we have to get to the Jewish Committee to find Haskel."

"That can wait," Jodi insisted. "You listen to Jeff now."

"You have a history of angina, you know that. But this time, you had a more severe reaction. Your pulse is rapid and irregular," Jeff said, reaching for the phone at the bar. "I'm taking you to the hospital."

"Put down that damn phone," Berson said, trying to get up from the sofa. "I'm not going to the hospital."

"You're going and we're going with you," Jodi said, forcing him to lie back while they waited for the ambulance. When it arrived, Jeff introduced himself to the driver, filled out the necessary forms he was handed and asked permission for Jodi and himself to ride along with the patient. In the emergency ward, Jeff again introduced himself and requested an immediate cardiogram for Dr. Berson. When the registrar heard the patient's name, she called the head of the hospital, informing him of Dr. Berson's presence in her department.

"I'm Dr. Sobieski," he told Jeff while Berson was having his EKG. "I studied under Dr. Berson at the Stone-Winthrop Institute."

"I was his student also," Jeff said, "and at present I am the oncologist at the Institute."

"Myetek," Dr. Berson called out, hearing Sobieski's voice. "Get this contraption off me."

"What a phenomenal memory, Dr. Berson," Dr. Sobieski said as he handed the EKG printout to Jeff. "I was his student at the Institute eleven years ago and he remembers my name."

Jodi stood aside as the three doctors analyzed the EKG printouts.

"Simon, I'm going to ask Dr. Sobieski to keep you here for a day or two," Jeff said.

"Don't be ridiculous!" Berson protested. "That's totally unnecessary. Do you think you're some kind of nanny?"

Jodi tried to quiet him but the more she tried, the more he scowled. Despite his derisive remarks, Jeff asked Dr. Sobieski to arrange a private room for Dr. Berson.

"We have only dormitories," Dr. Sobieski said. "No private rooms."

"No way," Jodi called out. "No dormitories. We'll take you back to the hotel and I'll hire round-the-clock nurses."

"Jodi, he needs to be here. He needs blood tests, hospital facilities," Jeff protested.

Jodi refused to listen. "The hotel is ten minutes away. You take his blood as many times as you want. I'll run it to the lab at any hour, day or night."

"Dr. Burke, she's right," Dr. Sobieski said. "We can arrange it so that his hotel room will be an extension of the hospital."

"Dr. Sobieski, can you arrange for the nurses too?" Jodi asked.

"I'll come," the older nurse at the registration desk volunteered. "I'm Katya Barskaya. I remember Dr. Berson from my student nursing days at the Czyste Hospital."

Jeff and Jodi spent most of the afternoon with Simon in his hotel room. When he was fast asleep, they left Katya to care for him and went to Jeff's room, leaving the adjoining door open. They realized they had not eaten all day so they ordered a simple dinner to be sent to the room. During the meal, Jeff admitted he never watched TV and asked her how she became such a success. Jodi told him how she slaved at being a gofer after her graduation from college and how she got her first break in television. She described how she took over after the anchorwoman succumbed just before the opening of the live telecast. When he told her what drew him to oncology, Jodi related how her father had died from cancer. Jeff expressed his sorrow, then said, "I think cancer is a curable disease. In the next decade we'll erase this plague just as Salk did with polio."

"That reminds me, you're facing a big decision now, aren't you?" Jodi asked. "Have you decided what you want to do? Will you accept the Institute's offer to head their Oncology Department or go into private practice?"

"Yep, I decided to turn down all the other offers and stake my future with the Institute."

"Have you told Dr. Berson?"

"Yes. I told him my decision when he recruited me to come on this trip," Jeff said. "I wanted to make him happy."

"And I think you must take him home, right away, back to the States," she said, looking at the open door to Berson's room. "This episode should be a warning to us. You were right, Jeff, this trip to Europe could kill him."

Katya put her head in the doorway. "He's awake," she declared, "and he wants you to take him to the dining room. He keeps saying he's hungry. It's a sure sign he's better."

"Better, maybe, but no dining room," Jeff commanded. "Jodi, can you order something light for Simon and Katya?"

That evening, as Katya turned down the bed for Dr. Berson, he called Jeff and quietly said, "Thanks, Jeff. I'm a lousy patient. But I know I've got a good doctor."

While Berson slept under Jeff's watchful eye, Jodi found a moment to talk to Katya privately. "Let me ask you a question," Jodi said. "Do you remember, during the war years, a surgery Dr. Berson performed on a patient who was pregnant and hemorrhaging?"

"No, I don't," Katya said, "but I have friends who were with the doctor in those days. Let me ask them."

"Could you do that tonight?" Jodi asked. "Dr. Burke and I will watch Dr. Berson while you are away."

"What was all that about?" Jeff asked, coming in from Berson's room.

"I was just following up on the suggestion you made when we were flying to Germany. At the time, you said that we might trace a nurse who might remember my birth mother if she had been a patient in the Czyste hospital."

She reminded him of the phone call she had made to her mother in Hong Kong who recalled that when she was a patient in the Czyste hospital, Irene visited her and mentioned that she gave birth in the Czyste.

"If that's true," Jodi said with a tinge of excitement, "isn't it possible that a nurse who helped Dr. Berson on that hemorrhaging patient might remember the other woman who gave birth at the Czyste Hospital at that time?"

The following day, Katya returned with Ursula Kaminska, who had been a nurse at the Czyste Hospital and later married one of the doctors. Katya acted as her interpreter, because the woman spoke no English.

"She was in the Czyste Hospital when the bleeding woman was brought in," Katya said, translating the woman's terse statements. "There was no ether. He, Dr. Berson, asked her to hold the woman during the operation. After the operation, she was assigned to help the woman – Franya was her name – to overcome her postoperative depression. Poor thing couldn't have children after that surgery and she was so sad. She and Ursula actually became friends."

"Do you recall another couple who gave birth to a girl at the hospital at around the time you were tending to Franya?" Jodi asked Ursula. Katya translated the question.

"*Tak*," Ursula replied with a nod.

Jodi was ecstatic.

"What was the young couple's name?"

"I don't know. I just remember they had a girl. That is all."

When the nurse translated Ursula's statement, Jodi begged her to try to recall the young couple's names.

"*Ja nie wiem*," Ursula Kaminska replied.

"I don't know," Katya translated.

Jodi did not give up. Through Katya, she begged Ursula to remember, to think, to think hard, maybe she heard it somewhere.

"*Ja nie wiem!*" Ursula repeated. Katya didn't need to translate as Ursula picked up her handbag and slammed the door, storming out of the room in annoyance.

"Another dead end," Jodi sighed.

"It's not a dead end," Jeff said, squeezing Jodi's hand sympathetically. "When Simon gets better, we'll take him to what's left of the Czyste Hospital. Perhaps it will jog his memory and he'll recall the woman who gave birth to you."

"When Simon gets better," Jodi repeated. "Since we got here, he's had several episodes, which could have killed him. I'm so worried, I can't sleep. The thought of his dying here frightens the hell out of me. I want you to take him back home."

"He's not going to like it," Jeff said, "but you're right."

When Jodi awakened at 8:30 in the morning, she tiptoed into Dr. Berson's room.

"Hi, Katya. Where is Dr. Berson?" she asked the nurse, who was tidying up.

"Dr. Burke took him to the hospital. I think for tests," she answered.

"Thanks. I'll go right over. Want a ride?"

*

Jodi met Dr. Sobieski in the hospital lobby. He told her that Dr. Berson was undergoing a battery of tests to make sure he was well enough to fly back to the States.

"The tests should be completed in about an hour," Dr. Sobieski said, escorting her to his office where she could wait. Jeff and Simon returned earlier than she expected. She rushed to embrace Simon as Jeff wheeled him out of the examination room.

He pushed her away. "Take it easy, Jodi," he mumbled. "There was absolutely nothing wrong with me in the first place. Let's get back to the hotel and eat something."

Over the breakfast table at the hotel, Jodi announced, "Simon, you're going home. Jeff will take you back."

"You called me Simon," Dr. Berson said, breaking into a big smile. "That's the first time you called me Simon."

"Don't try to change the subject," Jodi said, repeating, "Simon, you're going back to the States."

"Whose brilliant idea is that?" Simon asked, staring at Jeff.

"Hers," Jeff replied. "And she's right."

"Come here, Jodi," Dr. Berson said. She stood up and came around to his chair. He embraced her and kissed her on the forehead. "I love you very much. If I had a daughter, I would want her to be like you. Exactly like you. Now, listen. I want to help find your parents. It's my way of making up to you for the grief I caused you when I pursued Stasha. If I don't help you, I will die a broken-hearted man. Don't send me away. Help me. Death no longer worries me. It can happen in New York or here. What I fear most is sitting and waiting for death."

He turned to Jeff. "And you, my dear Dr. Burke," he said, "you know that the two episodes I've had since we got here are nothing. I can explain them easily."

"You had the episodes, Simon. That's cause for alarm," Jeff insisted.

"Just listen. First, taking an overdose of sleeping tablets was simply a matter of my inability to adjust to jet lag," Berson said. "Second, this latest episode was a result of that damn party with Kolcharski. Too much liquor and too much food. So, from now on, Jeff, you become the drug pusher and Jodi, you become the dietician. Me, I'll be Dick Tracy, to track down your parents."

They laughed so heartily, Katya had to remind them to quiet down.

Then Jodi turned to Jeff, "You must decide whether to allow Simon to remain in Poland."

"Excuse me," Simon interrupted, "I am an adult and a physician. I will decide. Enough of that."

"Simon, I know you will make up your own mind," Jeff said. "I will tell you, however, that I believe you should return to the States, where we can give you proper care. On the other hand, I've learned a couple of lessons here. First, in New York, you probably would be sitting around waiting for death. You can no longer be active. Here in Warsaw, I see more and more the importance of Jodi's mission, important for you and for her. So, I'm going to let you hang around here and hope for the best."

"Thank you. I appreciate your permission, Doc," Dr. Berson said, with gratitude tinged by only an edge of sarcasm.

*

The next morning, they started early, hailing a cab to the Jewish Committee. The trip took a long time because Dr. Berson, acting as tour guide, ordered the taxi driver to circle the city. He craned his neck to look at the public buildings, the parks, and the wide avenues they were passing, but he could not find many of the city's old landmarks. They were gone. A new city had risen in their place. The Jewish Committee building now occupied part of what used to be the Czyste Hospital.

"Let's walk through what is left of the Czyste Hospital," Jeff said.

Only one section of the original hospital remained standing. It had become a tourist attraction. Berson told the driver to stop. Jodi and Jeff followed Simon into the empty buildings. They watched as he delicately, almost reverently touched the doors, the window sills, the walls. He looked about the rooms and then said softly, "This was the maternity building."

"I'm glad you brought us here," Jodi said to Simon. "From what Ursula told us, she was the nurse who assisted you in Franya's surgery. She remembered another coupe who gave birth to a girl in the hospital at the same time."

"Yes, yes, I remember Ursula. Testy, but a good nurse. What are you trying to tell me?"

"Simon, you remembered Franya's surgery," Jeff said, repeating Jodi's discoveries. "Ursula intimated that at about the same time, another woman gave birth in the Czyste Hospital. Do you have any recollection of that woman?"

"I'm so sorry, Jodi, I know what this new information would mean to you. But I can't help you. The maternity section, this room, was run by midwives. I rarely had occasion even to visit the ward."

"Well, I guess you can't have everything," Jodi said, trying to smile.

"Yes you can," Dr. Berson said. "We can try to find Haskel, the forger."

"OK, Dick Tracy," Jodi said, with a forced smile. "Lead us to the Jewish Committee."

"What can we do for you?" said a young woman in a Polish military uniform who greeted them at the reception desk.

Fearing a repetition of the hostile response he had received over the phone when he asked about Haskel Kornblit, Berson replied carefully, "We would like to search the committee's records for information about survivors."

"Certainly," she said and directed them to the second-floor library, where an assistant librarian showed them several journals containing thousands of names. Dr. Berson took one volume, turned several pages to the "B" section, and read, "Berson, Dr. Szymon, Stone-Winthrop Institute, New York, NY, USA."

"Now I know I survived," he remarked jokingly. "But at least we know that the information is reliable."

He then looked up Haskel Kornblit. To everyone's surprise, the name was obviously erased, and only a blank line remained where it would have appeared. Dr. Berson asked to speak to the head librarian.

"Doctor Szymon Berson, what an honor!" Chaim Grinspon, the librarian, greeted the newcomer. "I have never had the pleasure of meeting you, never thought I would, but your name is still venerated throughout Poland."

Dr. Berson introduced Jodi and Jeff and talked happily with Grinspon about the old days in Warsaw and about his work at the Czyste Hospital. When he mentioned the Warsaw Ghetto, Grinspon asked, "Did you know I was Dr. Poliakov's nephew?"

"I didn't know he had a nephew, but I knew David very well," Berson replied. "You should be very proud of him. He and I didn't agree on every decision, but I respected him. He did his utmost for the Jews in the Ghetto. But how come you and I never met?"

"My parents never registered in the Ghetto," Chaim said. "We lived with a Christian family in a small village throughout the war years."

"You were very fortunate to have found righteous Christians," Berson said, encouraging him to relate details of their success in surviving those years.

Grinspon briefly recounted his experiences as they all listened with rapt attention. Sensing that he had broken the ice with the librarian, Berson then explained why he was in Poland and asked for help with Jodi's search.

"Our only clue, our only hope, is to find Haskel Kornblit."

At the very mention of that name, Chaim's dark, brown eyes shifted from one side to the other. He looked about the room, and shook his head, stammering, "I don't know the name, never heard it."

Berson whispered, "Chaim you just said that my name is still venerated in Poland. Now, I ask you, where can we talk privately?"

The librarian hesitated, then motioned them to follow him, leading them to a coffee stand several blocks from the Jewish Committee building. Sitting in an empty restaurant, Berson again asked about Haskel Kornblit and again the librarian claimed to have no knowledge of him.

"Listen, Chaim," Dr. Burke said, "this woman is Jodi Wycliff. She's the main correspondent of Network International Corporation, America's biggest television network, and she can destroy the reputation of your Jewish Committee and your library. So stop acting like a frightened child."

"A TV correspondent!" Chaim said. "My wife is the program director for Poland's National Radio Service."

"Guta Grinspon," Jodi said, immediately making the connection. "We have exchanged several memos. "Why don't you and your wife join us for dinner at the hotel this evening."

"I'll ask her," he said.

"Let's go over to the radio station now," Jodi urged. "Anything to do with newscasting interests me. I'd love to meet her and personally invite her to have dinner with us."

By the time dinner was over, Jodi and Guta, who were nearly the same age, became fast friends, sharing reporting stories and swapping professional secrets. Jodi told her about her mission in Poland, describing her need to find her birth parents.

But, throughout the meal, Berson was like a dog restrained on a leash, seeking an opportunity to raise Haskel's name. Once, when he tried to mention Kornblit, Jodi stopped him short. After dinner, Jodi invited the Grinspons to her suite and ordered drinks and coffee from room service.

As Jeff poured the drinks, Berson heard Guta say to Jodi, "I am so impressed that you are going to get to interview Sadat again, and in Jerusalem. You'll be making history."

"She may not get to Jerusalem if she doesn't find Haskel Kornblit," Dr. Berson said bluntly. "Why is everybody here afraid to talk about him?"

Chaim Grinspon, agitated and tense, declared, "It isn't fear, Doctor. We've simply never heard of him."

Guta shot her husband a slightly scornful glance, shook her head, looked Jodi in the eye, and said, "We journalists know what 'protecting your sources' means."

Jodi replied, "It means you never told me anything. Not here, not now, never."

"Right after the war," Guta said softly, as though testifying in a legal deposition, "the Jewish Committee dealt secretly with Haskel's enterprising black market operation. He was invaluable. He provided much-needed food, clothing, and, yes, even forged documents that the committee could use to get government subsidies. He helped the committee exchange zlotys for US dollars, which was a capital offense. After a few years, Haskel broke off all contact with the Jewish Committee. He went on to bigger and better things. From being a petty forger, he graduated into the Russian Mafia and became very active in the international markets."

When Guta paused to sip her water, Jeff said, "Jodi, you remember that Glaubmann told us Haskel had made several trips to Berlin?"

"That was where he was finally apprehended – in the Russian sector of Berlin," Guta continued. "When he was interrogated by the Russian authorities, so the story goes, he blew the whistle on many high-ranking Russian officers he had dealt with, as well as the Jewish Committee."

Guta spoke freely, describing the crisis in the Jewish Committee when the authorities temporarily shut it down after Haskel's arrest.

"I can understand why Haskel's name is taboo," Jodi said. "But where is he now?"

"There are only rumors," Guta replied. "He's in a Russian prison. He was shot by a firing squad. He has escaped and is somewhere in Africa. He's joined the Mafia in Sicily. And the list goes on."

Berson slammed his fist into his palm and called out, "Another dead end."

"No," Jodi replied. "No it's not. We'll run down every one of these rumors, starting with the Russians. Thank you for what you've told me."

"Remember, Jodi, we've told you nothing," Guta said, smiling.

"About what?" Jodi grinned back.

*

When the Grinspons left, Jodi asked Berson if he had maintained any connection with the Russian authorities with whom he dealt during his postwar stay in Warsaw.

"That was more than thirty years ago," he replied.

"Bureaucrats are forever," she said.

Berson listed all the Russians he had dealt with. Major Golinkin and Major Dworin headed the list.

"Impossible," he sighed, reading the list over to Jeff and Jodi. "They were all older than me. They're probably all dead by now."

"General Kolcharski isn't," Jodi retorted.

"That's it!" Berson replied. "Do you have that letter from Kolcharski, the military orders he gave you?"

"Sure," she said, taking it out of her leather briefcase and handing it to him.

Berson took the sheet and called out, "To the army. Forward march!" He became so excited that Jeff had to quiet him. "Steady, Simon, don't get more agitated than your heart can take."

"I thought you said the EKG showed no negative signs," Jodi exclaimed.

"Jodi, anytime a person suffers several angina attacks, it indicates a heart condition," Jeff responded. "It's a warning to be extra careful, not to get too charged up…and, probably, a reminder that we all should get to bed."

*

After they had their breakfast, Berson telephoned the Madrista, Warsaw's city hall, asking for the Russian military liaison offices. After a long pause, the operator switched him to a Colonel Ivan Chablinko, who asked what business he had with the military.

Dr. Berson replied in Polish, "I have orders from General Kolcharski and I wish to know to whom to present them."

The colonel responded, "Orders from General Kolcharski? Please report to us at the Madrista in room 464, and we will act on the orders immediately. Give me your name and I will leave it at the gate with the security guard."

Before they left, Berson called General Kolcharski in Berlin to tell him about their planned meeting with Chablinko and to explain why Jodi needed to know the whereabouts of a criminal the Russian police had apprehended there.

"Is that all you want?" the general said. "I'll contact Chablinko right away. He'll be ready when you arrive. What's the man's name?"

"Haskel Kornblit."

Kolcharski repeated the name derisively and said, "I know about this Kornblit. Myself, I would kill him."

Colonel Chablinko received them graciously and handed them a report outlining Haskel's trial. Sitting in the colonel's office, Berson quickly scanned the documents.

He shook his head, "Jodi, your forger is serving a life sentence somewhere in Siberia."

Jodi did not wince. "Well, can I go there?" she asked commandingly.

"I don't think you heard him well. He's in a jail in Siberia," Jeff said, "and we're not going there. Not you, not me, and certainly not Simon."

"I intend to go myself," she replied firmly, facing the colonel.

Colonel Chablinko turned to Jodi, speaking in English, "This is most irregular. But I will have my adjutant telex Moscow, to request permission for you to visit the jail in Siberia. I will add that we are under orders from General Kolcharski to accommodate you."

Jodi was deeply grateful to the colonel, thanking him for his efforts.

The colonel poured mugs of coffee, saying, "You might as well have a hot drink while we wait to hear back from Moscow."

Minutes later, the telex machine began to clack. Colonel Chablinko read the incoming message that he ripped off the machine, and then handed it to Berson.

"Haskel Kornblit is coming to you!" he said with a smile and quickly explained that on General Kolcharski's orders, the Russian army would bring Haskel to an undisclosed location in Siberia where he would be allowed to talk to Dr. Berson on the telephone. The telex from Moscow requested Berson's phone number in Warsaw.

"When is the best time for you to get this call?" the colonel asked.

"Friday, ten o'clock in the morning," Berson replied.

"Why delay until day after tomorrow?" Jodi protested.

"There are no telephones in Russian prisons," Simon explained. "Whichever prison in Siberia Haskel is in, he'll probably need at least a day to travel to get to a working telephone."

They thanked the colonel and returned to the Grand Hotel, where Jodi prepared a list of questions for Berson to ask Haskel. She gave him the list, saying in jest, "This is how I prepare when I interview world leaders and, right now, Haskel Kornblit is more important to me than Anwar Sadat."

From that moment on, they referred to Haskel as Sadat. But it was no laughing matter when they sat in Berson's room on Friday morning, waiting for the call from Siberia. Ten o'clock came and went; so did noon. They ate lunch in the room to make sure not to miss the call. They also ate dinner there. At about 11 P.M., they went to their separate rooms, instructing the telephone operator to put any call from Russia through to Berson's room at any time. At 2 A.M., Berson's phone rang. Jodi and Jeff ran into the room almost immediately. Berson answered the call and asked Haskel for Tomasz Rynek's original name. He listened and, after about thirty seconds, said, "Thank you. Stay strong there," and hung up.

He clasped Jodi's hands and said, "Your father's name was, or is, Fenyves. Haskel could not recall his first name. He remembers only that your father was born in Budapest. As for your mother and the baby girl, he remembers taking their pictures, but that's all."

Jodi let out a cry, kissing Simon, and thanking him for coming with her. With tears streaming down her cheeks, she danced around the room calling out, "Mr. and Mrs. Fenyves, that's Mama and Papa."

Jeff whirled her around in her bathrobe and chortled, "You're dancing with me, Miss Jadwiga Fenyves."

Berson watched them celebrate for a while, then shooed them out of his room. Jodi and Jeff decided to go to a nightclub to celebrate, but in Warsaw, they found that nothing was open at nearly 3 A.M. They returned to her room, ordered champagne, and celebrated until dawn.

When Jeff left her room, he said, "Simon ordered me to be nice to you. I hope you liked my being nice."

"I loved it," she said, throwing him a kiss as he walked back down the hall.

*

Simon Berson woke up early. Still feeling exhilarated from the previous night's accomplishment, he walked out on the balcony and decided to go for a stroll in the park facing the hotel. But as soon as he walked a few steps outdoors, he felt a pain in his chest and quickly placed a nitro pill under his tongue. He returned to the hotel's coffee shop, where he found Jeff having breakfast.

"I just had a twinge of chest pain and took a nitro," he reported.

Jeff led him back to his room and ordered him to rest. After about an hour, Berson called out to Jeff, who was lying on the couch facing the bed. "Jeff, I feel fine now. Let's go back downstairs and finish breakfast."

Back in the coffee shop, Jeff brought Simon up to date. "Jodi and I stayed up all night celebrating. She says she wants to go to Israel to continue her search for her parents."

"She'll do well searching for them in Jerusalem," Dr. Berson said. "After the war, thousands of survivors from Europe emigrated to Palestine…some even before the Jewish state was declared in '48. Some had legal certificates, others made it illegally trying to break through the British blockade. When the State of Israel was declared, European DP camps and British prison camps, like the ones in Cyprus, emptied and about 200,000 Jews resettled in Israel. If her parents survived, the odds are they made their way to Israel."

"Didn't a lot of survivors come to the States?" Jeff asked.

"Yes, four years after the war. About fifty thousand Jews came to America."

"It would be a lot easier to look in America first."

"So you want Jodi to return to the US with you. You like her, don't you?" Simon said in a fatherly tone. "I don't mean to pry into your private life, but I confess, I'd be pleased."

"Yes," Jeff responded, "I like her very much. But if she goes to Israel, I'm afraid she won't come back anytime soon."

As they were speaking, Jodi came into the restaurant, strode over to their table, kissed both Berson and Jeff on their respective cheeks, and sat down humming, "Oh! What A Beautiful Morning."

"What's next?" Dr. Berson asked.

"First, I'm going to eat. I'm famished," she said, ordering her breakfast. Then she continued, "Well, I just called Mr. White, my boss at the Network."

"You're going to Jerusalem to interview Sadat," Jeff said.

"Nope, I told him to forget my interviewing Sadat," she said. "I'm going to Jerusalem to find Mr. and Mrs. Fenyves."

"Simon tells me fifty thousand Jews settled in the United States after the war," Jeff said. "Wouldn't it be wise to try to trace your parents among the survivors there, at home?"

"What are you trying to tell me?" Jodi asked Jeff.

"Remember? I have to return to the States. I'm going to head the Oncology Department at the Institute," Jeff said, haltingly. "If you go to Israel, I can't go. I mean, we won't be seeing each other."

"Jeff, it may just take a few days," she said. "Maybe a few weeks."

"But I have to go back right away. And, you know, Simon can't go with you to Israel," Jeff said. "He'd never withstand another long trip."

She looked at Berson who nodded, "I have to go back with Jeff."

"Are you sick?"

"He had a brief episode of chest pains earlier, but he's OK now," Jeff said.

"Jodi, it's not only that," Simon explained. "I can't tell you what this trip meant to me. It breathed new life into me. You know that I love you. Very much. But I have to return right away with Jeff. I've done all I can to try to make it up to you, for pursuing Stasha and causing you so much anguish."

"Simon," she interrupted, "don't apologize. Yes, I know you love me and I love you even more. And if not for your dogged attempts to hunt down Stasha, we wouldn't have gotten this far. So, in a sense, Stasha brought us together."

When Dr. Berson got up to return to his room, Jeff and Jodi followed behind. "We have to talk," Jeff said to her.

"I know we have to talk, and I know what we have to talk about. But let me first help Simon pack and make flight arrangements for you," Jodi said.

She called Chuck Knowles and asked him to arrange her flight to Jerusalem and to set up Jeff and Simon's flight back to the States. Within minutes, Knowles called back with flight information. "White is delighted that you're going to Jerusalem," he told her.

"White doesn't know half of it," she joked.

Then she called Jeff. They sat at the small table in her room, looking at each other. He finally reached over and took her hand.

"I'm afraid I won't see you for a long time," he said.

"I won't be gone long, but I'm glad it matters to you."

"You know it matters," he said. "I think you know what's happened to me."

"You'll have to tell me," she smiled.

"I'm afraid I've fallen in love with you."

"And what's so terrible about that?" she asked, reaching out to him as they both stood up, embracing each other. He took her into his arms and kissed her.

"I'm happy about the appointment at the Institute but I'm worried about losing you," he told her. "I've always been alone, until now."

"This is not an end for us," Jodi said. "This is just a delay. I'll come back to you as soon as I've found my mother. Until then, I will not be any good to you or to myself."

"I understand what you must do. I just wish I didn't have to leave. I wish I could be with you."

"You are with me."

Chapter 19

JODI ARRIVED AT BEN-GURION AIRPORT on Sunday morning. Reena Raviv, the NIC Tel Aviv bureau manager, met her and drove her to Jerusalem. On the way, Reena explained, "Sorry, I couldn't get you a room at the King David Hotel. Because of Sadat's arrival, Israeli security has closed five floors of the hotel."

"Don't worry about my hotel," Jodi said. "I have more important work here than covering Sadat."

"What could be more important than interviewing Sadat?" Reena asked.

"It's sort of a long story," Jodi said, but at Reena's urging, she recounted how she learned of her adoption and related her experiences in Berlin and in Warsaw, emphasizing the vital role Dr. Berson played in discovering her father's last name.

"My first priority in Israel is to find my parents," Jodi said.

Reena, obviously stunned, stopped the car on the shoulder of the highway and leaned over to Jodi. "Please let me help you in your search for your parents," she said, clasping Jodi's hand.

"I need your help. I am a total stranger here," Jodi replied, responding to the younger woman's warmth. "Thank you."

They arrived at the Hilton in Jerusalem just in time to watch the television set in the lobby and hear Sadat speak to the Knesset. After the speech, they went to Jodi's room, where Reena handed her Sadat's itinerary and called room service for a pot of coffee and some Danishes.

"I'm going to invite myself to come along with you in your search for your parents," Reena said, with open candor. "Your quest is the most interesting thing that I've encountered since I got married."

As they had their snack, Jodi described some of the NCI's more colorful personalities in New York, filling Reena in on a lot of company gossip.

"How did you land the job here in Tel Aviv?" Jodi asked. "I don't mean to downgrade you, but I imagined they would put in someone, well, older, with more experience, especially with the hundreds of journalists who crowd this place."

"I graduated NYU, as just another communications major. I couldn't wait to get back to Israel, but I wanted TV experience before returning there as a novice, so I hung around Network International's headquarters in New York, working as a gofer for a year. In fact, I was behind the camera when you interviewed one of our generals. At the time, I passed your instructions along in Hebrew to those you were about to interview. NCI's directors used me quite often in translating newscasts from Israel."

"I'm really sorry I don't remember you," Jodi said apologetically. "I don't usually get to the set early enough to meet with staff, though I probably should."

"Your program was my lucky break," Reena said. "When the Tel Aviv bureau manager slot opened, they selected me probably because I had demonstrated my ability to handle Israeli VIPs. Now I run the place, and the correspondents swan around being important."

"That's me!" Jodi said, laughing. "I thank my lucky stars that I have your help with the Sadat interview and with searching for my birth parents."

"So you are doing the Sadat interview?"

"Only if I get a one-on-one. I'm not going to hang around with the other correspondents waiting for Egyptian releases."

"OK, let's get down to business," Reena said, as they polished off the last pastry. "Here's Sadat's itinerary. Use whatever clout you have with the Egyptians to wangle a one-on-one. All we've got so far are tickets for you and me to attend a press conference with about three hundred other correspondents from around the globe."

Jodi studied Sadat's itinerary and checked her watch. "If your itinerary is correct, Sadat and his staff are at the King David now. Do you know anybody on his staff?"

"Mustafa Malik, Sadat's aide."

"Call him. I know him."

Reena quickly called Malik and handed Jodi the phone.

"Mustafa, this is Jodi Wycliff."

"Jodi! It's been a long time. I was expecting your call," he said. "Mr. White called to alert me that you were coming."

"It's good to hear your voice again," she said. "I only need five minutes of the president's time. Tell him you owe me one from KM 101."

"Let me clear it with Mr. Sadat," Mustafa said. "I'll call you right back."

She gave him her number. "If necessary, I'll wait all night for your call. I can come anytime."

"What was that about?" Reena asked when Jodi hung up.

"I interviewed Sadat after the Yom Kippur War at kilometer 101, where peace negotiations took place between Israel and Egypt. During that interview, I let Sadat set forth his conditions for peace at that time. The Israelis got teed off because that gave him an opportunity to set 'preconditions' to his meeting with Begin. As a matter of fact, the next day, Israel issued a seven-word statement aimed at Sadat. All it said was, 'There are no preconditions to these talks.'"

Within minutes, Mustafa called back. "Sadat will grant you five minutes when he boards his plane to return to Cairo on Monday at 2:45 P.M."

"You mean he wants me to come on the plane for the five-minute interview?" Jodi asked.

"Yep, you and your crew, no more than two other people, will be allowed on the plane at 2:15, to set up your equipment and whatever else you need for the interview." Mustafa said. "The president will get there about half an hour later."

"Thanks, Mustafa. It's lovely doing business with you."

"You too, Jodi. But now I consider my debt paid."

"Great! What a scoop!" Reena enthused, when Jodi relayed Mustafa's instructions. "Now, how will I get all that equipment in or around the Egyptian plane, and with only two crew members onboard?"

"That's why you're the station manager and I get paid just for talking into your camera," Jodi replied. "Pick me up tomorrow at noon."

Alone in her hotel room, Jodi began to work, phrasing possible questions to pose to the president. As she wrote each question, she tried to anticipate his replies, so that she would have follow-up questions ready. She erased almost as many questions as she wrote. Finally, after several tries, she was satisfied with the three key questions she had prioritized. At about midnight, her phone rang.

"Jodi, it's me," Jeff said. "I must tell you that it's lucky we brought Simon back to the States when we did. He suffered a severe heart attack as the plane landed in JFK."

"How is he?" Jodi cried out. "Where is he?"

"Fortunately, the Institute arranged for a helicopter-ambulance. He underwent a triple bypass surgery. The operation took about three hours, but he's in recovery now, in critical condition. I hope he'll pull through."

"You hope," Jodi repeated woodenly.

"That's the best I can do for now, but I'll keep you posted," she heard him say as she sat down on the bed, clutching the receiver.

Unable to sleep, she called Jeff several times during the night. Although he tried to reassure her each time, she suspected he was preparing her for the worst. She finally fell asleep as the sun began to peer over Jerusalem's hills. At ten o'clock she got the wake-up call she had placed the night before. She immediately called Jeff, but the Institute's telephone operator informed her that Dr. Burke was not answering his page. Jodi asked for the nurse at the ICU station.

"Dr. Berson's condition is still listed as critical," the nurse informed her. "Just a moment, Dr. Burke is passing by. He'll talk to you."

"Jodi, I know you're worried, but we're doing all we can. We're putting him on a respirator. I have to get to him, so I'm going to run. Talk to you soon."

Jodi felt guilt stricken. She paced around the room, crying, repeating over and over, "It's my fault. He should never have left the hospital in New York."

She looked at the clock on her bedside table, wondering whether she should keep her appointment with Mustafa or prepare to return to New York. She had trouble dressing. Her hair would not stay in place. She struggled with her makeup, but she couldn't stop crying long enough to stop smudging it. She was still a wreck when Reena called from the lobby.

"Please come up," Jodi whimpered.

Reena was stunned to see Jodi so disheveled. Amid sighs and sobs, Jodi told her about Dr. Berson's surgery.

"You'll tell me all about it on the way to the airport," Reena said. "But right now let me get you looking decent."

She fixed Jodi's hair, helped her with fresh makeup, zipped her into her fresh, pale taupe Armani suit, and in less than an hour, they were in Reena's car speeding to Ben-Gurion Airport. During the drive, Jodi tried to stay dry-eyed as she recalled Jeff's initial warning that the trip to Poland would kill Dr. Berson. She talked about her natural parents, repeating Simon's role in discovering her father's name. She kept repeating how guilty she felt, blaming herself for causing his heart attack. Reena did not interrupt her or try to console her. She listened as Jodi unburdened herself.

When they entered the airport area, Reena got out of the car and hugged Jodi, reassuring her, "You probably started worrying about Dr. Berson's condition the minute you left New York," Reena said. "But yes, he had a heart attack, and yes, he's listed as critical. But remember, he's back home, getting the best medical care. You don't mourn for someone who is still alive."

"You have good sense, Reena," Jodi said gratefully.

Reena cleared Jodi through the airport security gates. Mustafa was waiting to take her and her cameraman onto the president's plane.

"Remember the last time we did this, at KM 101?" Mustafa reminisced, but Jodi did not reply. She moved through the airport like a robot.

"Jodi," Mustafa whispered as Sadat came into sight. "Are you sick?"

She stared at Mustafa but said nothing. He quit asking questions when he saw the president's entourage on the tarmac.

The moment Sadat took his seat, Jodi came to life – much to Mustafa's astonishment. She knew she had only five minutes of Sadat's time, so she asked her three key questions: "What did your wife say when you told her you were flying to Jerusalem?…Is it true, Mr. President, that President Carter advised you against making this historic trip to Jerusalem?…Will the Palestinians agree to any peace you will make with Israel?"

Despite the advance time limit, Sadat got caught up in their conversation as he responded to her questions. He gave her almost half an hour.

Winston White called Jodi immediately after the interview feed reached New York, although it was already well into the evening on the East Coast. His voice was warm and excited, "Jodi, you really came through for us. That was the most interesting interview you've ever done. It will be seen around the world before tomorrow morning."

"Glad you're pleased. Now, don't bother me for the next three years," she said. "It may take me that long to find Mr. and Mrs. Fenyves."

"Who?"

"My father and mother."

*

On the drive back to Jerusalem with Reena, Jodi fell back into her mea culpa recitation, blaming herself for Berson's illness.

Reena said, "I don't know Jeff, but he probably knew what he was doing when he called you."

"What do you mean, 'He probably knew what he was doing?'"

"The news of Dr. Berson's surgery was broadcast on all the major networks early this morning while you were sleeping. Jeff protected you from the shock of learning about it from the television. Remember, he told you that the operation was a success. And you know everyone's condition is 'critical' after open-heart surgery."

"You're right, Reena," Jodi said with relief. "If I had heard about the surgery over the TV, I would have gone ballistic. Jeff really handled it well."

"What are his credentials?" Reena asked.

"He's a surgeon who began as Dr. Berson's assistant, protégé would be more correct," Jodi told her. "We were together for six days in Europe. He was helpful throughout the trip. And he was very considerate and warm. As soon as this search is over, I'm going home to him."

"After only six days, you're in love?" Reena asked. "Have you been in love before?"

"I just broke a long engagement." Jodi told her about her early love affairs and her recent breakup with Cal.

"I'm glad you found Jeff. I only hope you're not just on the rebound."

When Jodi did not respond, Reena quickly apologized, "I'm sorry, Jodi, I didn't mean to pry or interfere."

"Never mind, Reena," Jodi laughed. "You've been a doll, and I need all the help I can get."

"Well, let me offer some ideas on your search, then," Reena said.

"That would be great; what do you know?"

"You can do several things," Reena said. "We have to put ads in the local newspapers. We can visit the Jewish Agency, which has the most comprehensive list of survivors. And we can go to Yad Vashem, which maintains the records of the Nazi atrocities. They have lists of millions of people who succumbed to the Nazi terror in concentration camps and lists of thousands who survived."

"That sounds like a good plan," Jodi said, as they passed some of the Old City's historic sites. "Could you drop me off at the Church of the Holy Sepulchre? You can head back to Tel Aviv. I'll take a taxi to my hotel."

"Don't be silly."

Reena followed Jodi into the church, watching as she lit a thin taper and crossed herself. Walking out of the church, as evening descended on the city of Jerusalem, Jodi looked at the clear gold light of sunset. "You know, Reena, I've been to Israel a dozen times, but always on assignment, always as an observer. I was never a tourist here. I never had an emotional experience. But today it's different. For the first time, I feel a personal attachment to the city."

When they reached the hotel, Jodi thanked Reena again for being with her during her crisis. "Do you want to come back this evening and have dinner with me, now that I've stopped being hysterical?" she asked.

"I'll beg off, Jodi," Reena said. "My husband is returning tonight from his month of reserve duty with the army. It would be unfair to leave him alone."

"Fantastic. Bring him along. We'll have a special welcome home party for him right here in the hotel," Jodi said. "Truthfully, so much has happened in the last two days that I'd be glad not to be by myself."

"I'll ask Oren and call you right away," Reena replied.

*

As soon as she got to her room, Jodi called Jeff at the Institute.

"Hi. You picked a great time to call. I'm with Simon and we're very satisfied with his recovery."

"That's wonderful," Jodi said, greatly relieved.

"In fact, we're taking him off the critical list," Jeff said. "He's going to be fine."

"I'm delighted," she squealed. "And what about you?"

"First tell me how your Sadat interview went. We've already seen it on TV about four times. They're running segments of it over and over. You handled yourself beautifully."

"Thanks. I barely remember it. But now I understand why you called me to tell me about Simon's surgery. Thanks. Tell me again about your decisions. Are you still planning to stay at the Institute?"

"Yes," he said. "But we've postponed my installation as director of the Oncology Department until Simon is well enough to attend."

"I hope I'm home by then so I can come too."

"So do I," Jeff said. "I wish you could be here, Jodi. I miss you."

"I miss you too. I want to get back as soon as I can. In fact, you could do me a favor that might help move things along more quickly."

"Sure. What do you need?"

"Would you see if you can trace the name 'Fenyves' in any of the Holocaust survivors lists in the States?"

"Sure," Jeff said. "I'll get started on it as soon as I can."

*

An hour or so later, Reena called to say that she and her husband would come to dinner. "He's eager to meet the woman who interviewed Sadat," Reena explained, slightly apologetically.

"Whatever works!" Jodi laughed.

She reserved dinner for three at 7 P.M. at the hotel restaurant and ordered a cake with the words "Welcome Home." Then she undressed, drew the bath, and luxuriated in the hot suds for an hour – something she had not done in a very long time.

Promptly at seven, Reena and her husband showed up with a third man, an Israeli army officer in uniform. Reena introduced her husband, Oren, and added, "And this is his commanding officer, General Ron Shavit, who gave him a tramp from the Golan to Jerusalem."

"A tramp? What's a tramp?" Jodi asked.

"That's what you in America would call a 'hitchhike,'" the general replied. "I apologize for tagging along, but when I invited Oren and Reena to dinner at the officer's club in Tel Aviv, they told me they'd had a better offer. So I had to tag along.

"You see, Miss Wycliff," Ron added, smiling broadly, "by having me join you, you're helping Colonel Oren Raviv. After all, I'm his CO and I can make his life miserable. But if your dinner is good, I guess Colonel Raviv will escape disciplinary action."

"General, I'm always ready to do my part to help a soldier in the Israel Defense Forces," Jodi said, feigning a snappy salute.

"The name is Ron," the general said, "and if you call me General, I'll keep calling you Miss Wycliff."

As soon as they sat down to dinner, Oren and Ron badgered her with questions about the Sadat interview. She answered several of their questions, but she soon put up her hand and announced a moratorium on political talk.

"Enough with world affairs and world leaders," she said. "I want to know something about you. How come you speak such perfect English?"

"Two years at MIT and another stint as Military Attaché in the embassy in Washington, that's how come," Ron replied.

Oren and Ron complied and began swapping stories, telling jokes, and regaling her with tidbits about Israelis and Israeli life. At the end of the meal, the waiter brought out the cake Jodi had ordered. As she began to cut it, she asked, "Where's the wording I ordered? I wanted them to write 'Welcome Home' on the cake, for Oren."

"It's right there," Reena pointed out, reading the Hebrew words: "*Boachem leshalom*."

"You're pretty cute for a shiksa," Ron teased her, "but you can't read Hebrew. You need to learn the language. When in Rome do as the Romans, and when in Israel, learn Hebrew."

They laughed, but Jodi responded seriously. "I probably should learn some Hebrew," she said, "because I'm not a shiksa. I have Jewish parents."

The two men, shocked, looked at her as though seeing her for the first time.

"Oh, Jodi," Reena quickly explained, "I didn't tell Oren or Ron anything about your adoption or your search for your parents. I figured that was private."

"Thanks, Reena, but if I'm going to find my parents, I have to ask everyone I meet to help me," Jodi said, turning to Ron and Oren. "In fact, finding my birth parents is the main reason I came to Jerusalem."

"Not to interview Sadat?" Ron asked. "Weren't you scheduled to do that show before you came here?"

"Now, now, we're not talking TV or politics," she reminded him. "I just want to enjoy the evening."

"Just one little question," Ron bargained. "How did you come up with those three questions for Sadat?"

Jodi explained that it took her several hours to select her questions, from the shortlist of about five she had considered. Then she put a halt to the conversation. "Remember, no shoptalk," she said firmly.

"In that case," Oren said, reaching for Reena's hand, "let's dance. That's not shop talk."

"Fine idea," Ron said. "Jodi?"

"In the American army, a general's request is a command," Jodi smiled. "Is that what it's like in the Israeli army?"

"It is," he replied, "but I understand that Jodi Wycliff is hard to boss around. According to Reena, you're the star at NIC."

As they danced, he said he wished he had shaved, because Jodi kept pulling away from his scruffy chin. "As a matter of fact," Ron said, "it's against military regulations not to shave every day."

"So why didn't you shave?" she asked.

"I also don't listen to instructions," Ron said.

"I haven't danced for so long, I forgot how much fun it could be," Jodi said.

Ron replied, "It's not the dance, but the dancing partner."

"I see you're very humble, too," she laughed.

"It's the Sabra in me," the general replied, whirling her around the room.

They lingered a while over dessert and coffee, but at about midnight, Reena and Oren got up to leave. "We had a great evening but I'm ready to go home and collapse in my own bed," Oren said. "It's been a long month."

"Oh, I nearly forgot," Reena told Jodi as they all walked toward the door, "I'm really sorry, but I can't take you to the Jewish Agency and Yad Vashem tomorrow. It's your own doing! Your Sadat interview messed up our production schedule and I have to be at the office most of the day. Let's wait a day. Unless you want to go alone."

"No," Jodi answered, "I'd rather wait and go with you."

Jodi and Ron walked the couple out to the lobby, then they found a quiet corner table in the lounge and ordered drinks. He told her a little more about his work in the Intelligence Corps, which had temporarily stationed him in the Golan. Jodi spoke earnestly about her intense desire to find her parents and her search with Dr. Berson.

"If they were transported to Treblinka, the chance that they are alive is slight," Ron said. "You know that."

"I do know that. But if nothing turns up in Israel, I'll return to the States to question survivors there," Jodi said.

They were both surprised how quickly time had passed when the bartender announced last call and, shortly thereafter, began cleaning up.

"Thanks for a lovely evening," Jodi said. "I'm wiped out. It's been an emotionally exhausting day."

"Get a good night's sleep," he said. "And if you like, I'll take you to the Golan tomorrow. I have a staff meeting and then I can show you something you've never seen before."

"Very tempting," she said. "How long is the drive to your outpost?"

"Driving, about three hours; flying about thirty minutes. We'll fly there by helicopter," he replied. "I'll have you back in Jerusalem in time for lunch."

"Reena can't work with me tomorrow, so pick me up here. We can have breakfast and then go to the Golan."

"Sounds good," he said. "But on the Golan, you take orders: no pictures, no interviews, no stories!"

"Scout's honor," she said, giving him the Boy Scout salute.

"You should know that most Arab countries were against Sadat's visit to Israel," he noted. "They consider him a renegade, a traitor to the Arab cause. Many Arabs here in Israel will be unhappy with your interview because you described Sadat as a hero. So be careful."

"Thanks for the warning, General," she smiled. "I've been here a half a dozen times and I haven't been hauled off yet."

"Miss Wycliff," the general said, "I'm not telling you how to run your business. But as an intelligence officer, I'm telling you to be careful. There are people here in Jerusalem who do not like your views and they don't take well to people like you."

"Are you trying to frighten me?"

"Warn would be a better word."

*

They shared a hurried breakfast the next morning before Ron drove her to the Atarot Airport, where a military helicopter waited for him. She noticed that some of the flight staff and even some members of the ground crew called him by his first name. Buckling herself in, she asked about their informality.

"Is it because you're so young?" she asked. "Most generals are paunch-bellied, gray-haired oldsters."

"I've been in the army twenty-five years," Ron said. "Got in when I was seventeen and some of them have been with me all this time. I prefer it this way. We're colleagues and friends."

"Does the informality affect your military effectiveness?" she asked.

"Hey, you're not doing a story on the army," he said. "I want to show you Israel, not just Israel's military."

As the chopper flew near the Jordanian border, he pointed out places of interest, describing newly established kibbutzim, historic sites, and military installations. The helicopter finally landed atop a high hill, less than a kilometer from the Syrian border. She was dazzled by the panoply of electronic equipment around the crest of the hill and was amazed when he let her look through one of the high-powered telescopes. She could clearly see people walking in the streets of Damascus.

"If you focus it right," he quipped, "you can see them smoking. You can even see what brand of cigarettes they're smoking."

Ron's guided tour of the military installation was brief, because he had to be at his staff meeting. While he was tied up, she talked to some of the soldiers, joined them for lunch, and began planning a future TV special about the army and the Golan. Two hours after lunch, Ron reappeared, apologizing for his tardiness.

"I thought the army ran on time," Jodi said. "This has been great, but I feel a little anxious about getting to Tel Aviv to help Reena clean up from the impact of my interview."

Ron took her to the outpost's command center, where he called Reena and handed Jodi the phone. Thanking him, Jodi said, "Reena, I know we're postponing the Yad Vashem search till tomorrow, but can I help you out today?"

"Thanks, but we're OK," Reena said. "By the way, I have the staff checking on a Mr. and Mrs. Fenyves in Yad Vashem and in the Jewish Agency records. I also placed some ads in various Hebrew, Yiddish, and Polish newspapers, asking anyone with information to contact the NIC office in Tel Aviv," Reena said. "So there's nothing we can do on that front except wait for replies."

Originally, Jodi had planned to take that day off with Ron and spend the rest of the week searching. But the one day with Ron turned out to be a week – the week of his leave. Each morning, she called Reena, who told her day after day that the searches at Yad Vashem and the Jewish Agency so far had turned up nothing on the Fenyveses. "If anything comes up," Reena assured Jodi, "I'll contact you immediately."

Ron and Jodi covered Israel from the Lebanese border in the north to the shores of the Red Sea in the south. He took her out in his motorboat on the Lake of Galilee, where she enjoyed racing the boat despite the bitter cold.

"I'm glad I could get your mind off the search," he told her once.

"Ron, my mind is always on the search," Jodi said. "One of the reasons I'm enjoying the trip is that wherever I go, I imagine my parents have been there. So, in a sense, I'm walking in their footsteps."

Ron apologized for misunderstanding her and promised to take her to many other places "where your parents may have been."

When they traveled south, toward Eilat, Jodi was thrilled by the exhilarating sights of the desert, and enjoyed stopping at various kibbutzim in the Negev to share meals and meet groups of fascinating people. In Eilat they went snorkeling, spending the day on the clear beaches of the Red Sea. On their way back, Ron took her to the Command School at Tel Aviv University, where she sat in on his lecture on military intelligence. She was deeply impressed by the reception he received from the many government and military dignitaries who attended his presentation. During the question and answer period that followed, Jodi was amazed both by the audience's insightful questions and Ron's answers.

Toward the end of the session, she raised her hand. "General Shavit, I wish to ask a question," Jodi called out, startling everyone in the room. Ron acknowledged her and introduced her to the audience.

"I realize that Israel does not officially become involved in the political debate now raging in the United States between the Democratic and Republican candidates for the US presidency. My question is twofold. First – forgive me for introducing a political point to your discussion – is there a tendency among Israeli politicians favoring one candidate over the other? And second, would such favoritism indicate that Israel would be interfering in the internal affairs of the United States?"

Ron surprised both Jodi and the group when he asked members of the audience to offer their opinions. An elderly gentleman arose to answer Jodi. Ron had previously introduced him as a former prime minister, one of the signatories of Israel's Declaration of Independence.

"Miss Wycliff," said the old man, looking at Jodi, "I would turn around your question and ask you, is it interfering in Israel's internal affairs when a sitting American president not only shows favoritism but openly supports one Israeli political party over another?"

Several people immediately raised their hands, some voicing opinions without waiting to be recognized. Bitter bickering ensued among the audience, converting an academic session into a stormy political debate that Ron found difficult to control. Finally, using his gavel, he restored order.

"So much for audience participation," he said jokingly. "I'll answer Miss Wycliff's questions."

"Not too long ago, in a heated election year in Italy, the United States not only favored a candidate against his Communist opponent but encouraged Italian Americans to write, to contact their compatriots to campaign for the defeat of the Communist candidate.

"The reply to your question, then, is rather simple. If the issue between the candidates is either life threatening or diametrically opposed to democratic principals, favoring one candidate over another would not only be permitted but required. But since Israel is the only Mid-Eastern country that shares democratic ideals with the United States, it is unlikely that either of us would interfere in the political life of the other."

The audience gave Shavit rousing applause. Thanking them, he adjourned the session.

As they ate lunch in the university's cafeteria, Jodi declared, "I congratulate you on handling the hot potato I tossed at you. But you and I know that the old man was right. Too often, an American president or his cabinet members openly rebuke Israel for taking actions that we, in the States, believe to be wrong."

"Jodi, eight days ago, when we first met, you declared a moratorium on discussing your TV business. I suggest we declare a moratorium on Israeli politics. Because in Israel, politics is a burning issue with us, even more than with you in America."

"OK, no politics. So tell me what you have planned for the rest of the week."

During the next few days, they attended concerts, visited museums, and, above all, shared each other's thoughts and dreams. She even learned enough phrases in Hebrew to go shopping alone. On the last day of his leave, Ron told Jodi he had been married once, but his military career had splintered his marriage. He showed Jodi photos of his twin daughters, explaining, "I make time to be with them when I can get away from the army."

"You're away from the army now," she said. "Why don't you visit them?"

"I want to be with you."

"Don't punish them on my account. Come, I'll go with you."

Ron called his former wife, who welcomed his offer to take the girls for the day.

When Shoni and Aliza, aged twelve, romped into his car, Ron introduced Jodi. "This is my friend, Yehudit."

"That's not her name," Shoni said, ridiculing her father. "She's Jodi Wycliff. We saw her on television with Sadat."

"*BeYisrael ani Yehudit*," Jodi said to the girls, who laughed even harder as they imitated her distinct American accent.

"Miss Wycliff, we understand English," Shoni said, speaking English with an equally-distinct Israeli accent.

"I'll make a deal with you," Jodi replied. "You correct my Hebrew and I'll correct your English."

They hit if off well, as the twins bombarded her with questions about her television experiences. Ron drove to Dizengoff Square, where he dropped Jodi and the girls at a pizza parlor. He circled around until he found a parking space, and when he returned, the girls excitedly told him that Jodi had ordered the entire meal in Hebrew. Jodi made light of her accomplishment, reminding them that "pizza" and "Coke" were good English words.

"But you should hear Jodi's Israeli accent!" the girls called out, taking pride in their teaching Jodi to speak Hebrew.

"Speaking is easy," Jodi said. "It's reading that I find hard. You have no vowels. Look at the Hebrew menu. How do I know whether it's pizza or pazzo or puzzo?"

"Hebrew vowels are usually signs under or over the letters," one of the girls replied and repeated, jokingly, "It's not pazzo, puzzo, it's pizza!"

"So you have to know Hebrew before you can read Hebrew without vowels."

And for the rest of the day, whenever they passed a pizzeria along the busy avenue, they all burst into laughter, repeating, "Pazzo, puzzo, it's pizza!"

Ron took them to the newly built Luna Park, where they spent the better part of the morning. When he suggested they take in a movie, Aliza took Jodi's hand, and turned him down. "We'd rather just talk to Jodi," she said.

"Did you know she was the only woman reporter who was allowed to enter the Friendship 7 capsule – the one Armstrong landed on the moon?" one of the girls told her father.

They walked along the seashore enjoying the cold wind, but listening with rapt attention as Jodi related how she covered the negotiations between Israel and Egypt, recalling interesting tidbits about the many participants, including Kissinger. She complimented them for their intelligent questions on the political history she was describing. But, for the twins, the highlight of the day was dinner at one of the elegant hotels in Tel Aviv. They stayed excited all evening as Jodi introduced them – not that she could tell them apart – to the many Israeli and foreign dignitaries who stopped to chat with her at their table.

After dropping off the girls at their home, Ron drove Jodi back to her hotel in Jerusalem.

"The girls took to you like a fish to water," he said. "Thanks for suggesting that we go visit them."

"They're delightful," Jodi remarked. "I actually enjoyed myself. I kept trying to compare their lives to my life as a teenager growing up in Miami." She briefly recounted the problems she had growing up.

He responded, "I was probably spared a lot of those adolescent problems because I joined the military so young."

"The biggest problem I had hit me only recently, after my father died," Jodi confided. "It hit me so badly, I resorted to drugs, and without the help of a psychologist, I wouldn't have come out of it."

"You seem so self-assured," Ron said, "it's hard to believe that you would need the help of a psychologist."

Jodi described her shock when she had learned about her adoption from her dying father.

"And in addition to the usual problems facing any adoptive child, I was unable to cope with the probability of being Jewish."

"Wow!" Ron exclaimed. "You were hit with-what-do-you-call-it, a 'double whammy'. I'm sorry I called you a shiksa. I suppose it brought back that shocked feeling."

"Not at all. I even felt good when you introduced me to Aliza and Shoni by my Hebrew name."

The good feeling evaporated over the next few days when she found that her search for her parents had come to a standstill. Not only was the lack of response to the newspaper ads disappointing, but neither Yad Vashem nor the Jewish Agency had any information on their lists. Despite Reena's continued encouragement, Jodi was ready to give up, particularly with Jeff urging her to return to the States during their endless, frequent telephone calls.

"The odds are against you," Jeff told her. "There were three million Jews in Poland and fewer than fifty thousand survived. If your parents were in a concentration camp, their chance of being alive today is negligible."

"I don't want to hear that argument anymore," Jodi said.

He quickly apologized and repeated, "You would do well searching for your parents right here in the States. As a matter of fact, I already made contact with a large organization of Holocaust survivors and asked them to solicit their membership about a Fenyves family consisting of a father, mother, and a baby daughter."

A few days later, while having dinner with Ron, she told him about Jeff's suggestion that she should begin searching in the States.

"Who's Jeff?" Ron asked.

"He was with me in Berlin and Warsaw, tending to Dr. Berson."

She described her first meeting with Jeff and the subsequent help he had been in taking care of Dr. Berson and assisting in her search. Without encouragement from Ron, Jodi continued to talk about Jeff's help in Germany and Poland. She repeated his advice about returning to the United States.

"I'm thinking quite seriously about taking up his suggestion," Jodi said.

"Are you returning to the US to continue your search or are you returning to Jeff?" Ron asked.

"My experience in Israel has been another in a long series of dead ends," Jodi said, disregarding his insinuation. "I've been here two weeks and I have nothing to show for it."

They ate their meal in silence and when they finished, he asked if she would like to visit Reena and Oren.

"I'm sorry, Ron, but I'm just not in the mood for socializing. I think I'd rather start packing to go back home."

"Come anyway," he urged her. "I have an idea about a new approach to your search here, but we need Reena's advice."

She agreed to drive with him to Tel Aviv because it would also give her a chance to say good-bye to Reena and Oren. When they arrived at Reena's apartment, Ron laid out his plan.

"I thought maybe Jodi could conduct a television interview," he said to Reena. "A panel of journalists could ask her about her work. During the interview, she could talk about her adoption and her search. She could mention the name 'Fenyves' and make an appeal for help in finding them."

Neither Reena nor Jodi felt much enthusiasm for his plans. Jodi was a well-known TV personality, but she was not a national figure who merited an interview by an international panel of journalists.

"I don't know a damn thing about your end of television work, but I know Jews," he said to Reena. Turning to Jodi, he added, "We can use you and this program to find someone, somewhere, anywhere in the world, who knows the Fenyveses of Warsaw. I know this will work."

Reena thought over the details of Ron's plan and jotted down some of her own ideas. In her office with Jodi and Ron the next day, she decided to call Winston White for his opinion.

"Hello, Mr. White, this is Reena Raviv from the Tel Aviv bureau. I'm here with Jodi Wycliff and I've come up with an idea. What do you think about doing a *Jodi Wycliff Special* to cash in on her successful Sadat interview?"

"I'm not sure it would work," White said. "But I'll consult with my staff and get back to you."

"He's never given me that kind of an answer to anything before," Jodi said when Reena relayed White's reply. "When he wants something, he gets it done without consulting his staff, or anybody else."

As they were about to leave the office, the phone rang.

"The idea sounds great, Reena," White trumpeted. "Congratulations! The best part of the plan is that it will keep Jodi on the job. We'll need her back here to plan the whole program out. That's going to take at least a month." While he was raving about the plan, Reena gave Jodi and Ron a thumbs up.

"Here's the plan," Reena told White. "The program will be about Jodi. After a brief intro, we'll run a few clips of her previous successes, like the 'White House Special', the South Africa election story, and so on. Then, after the clips, our worldwide staff of correspondents will interview Jodi in several languages."

"What an idea!" White shouted. "We'll call it *Jodi Wycliff: A Self-Portrait*. Great artists like Rembrandt and Van Gogh all did self-portraits."

As White continued describing his promotional ideas, Reena cupped the mouthpiece of the telephone with her hand and whispered, "He wants you back in the States and thinks it'll take about a month to put it together."

Jodi shook her head, whispering, "No way!"

"When do we start taping?" White asked.

"That's the trouble," Reena said. "We're not taping. Jodi only agrees to do this if it's live and if we do it Wednesday."

The line went dead.

Reena covered the mouthpiece again, "I think he's fainted."

Within seconds, White bellowed, "Put Jodi on!"

"Hello, Winston," Jodi said demurely.

"A story like this we do live?" White was no longer shouting but pleading. "Only three days from now? No advance publicity? No chance to get proper timing and questions? And what will it do to our programming schedule? It could be a fiasco!"

"Have I ever let you down?" Jodi said. "Have I ever come up with an idea that ended up as a fiasco? How can you hurt me this way?"

They argued back and forth. Finally, Jodi said in her most commanding tone, "Do you want my interview or not? If yes, it's only on my conditions."

"Go ahead," White said. "Go ahead. Date? Time?"

"Wednesday, December 3. Noon-time Israel; prime time, New York," Jodi said. "And I'm staying on with NIC."

White responded with a reluctant, "OK."

Reena was eager to get started, especially since she only had two days to do preparatory work that would normally take weeks. She sat down at her phone and began calling staff members from her studio. Ron and Jodi waved good-bye to Reena and headed back to Jerusalem. They stopped at a pizza restaurant, where Jodi scanned the menu and suddenly burst out laughing.

"Pazzo, puzzo, it's pizza!" Jodi giggled. "Hebrew is amazing, particularly when your teachers are teenage twins."

Ron laughed with her, and then said, "By the way, the girls called me several times asking to go out with you again when you have time."

"As soon as we finish this dandy special you came up with, I'd love to go back out with your girls."

Ron's idea for the program was as simple as it was brilliant.

On Wednesday, December 3, at prime time in the States and at noon in Israel, NIC aired *Jodi Wycliff: A Self-Portrait*. It began with panned shots of Jodi against familiar Israeli scenes. Then an announcer articulated names as shots of great radio and television personalities flashed on-screen, ending with shots of Jodi's past accomplishments. Next, Reena ran four clips of Jodi's previous shows, followed by promos showing their high ratings and boasting millions of viewers. Jodi's interview, the highlight of the program, featured several key commentators who tossed questions at her. Most of the questions asked about her impressions of political personalities she had interviewed.

Reena Raviv, scheduled as the last interviewer, asked some personal questions she and Jodi had thoroughly rehearsed in advance.

"Jodi, why did you come to Jerusalem, other than to interview Sadat?"

"To search for my parents."

"Your parents? Stamford Wycliff died two years ago."

"I was born in Warsaw. Stasha and Franya Wojchiechowski adopted me during the war."

"Who were your birth parents?"

"A Mr. and Mrs. Fenyves. My father came to Warsaw as a student. Both he and my mother were put into the Warsaw Ghetto. They escaped and lived illegally on the Aryan side. They were arrested and sent on the death trains to Treblinka. The Wycliffs adopted me."

"Do you know where your birth parents are today?" Reena asked.

The camera then zoomed in on Jodi's pleading face. "No, I don't. Everyone tells me that they probably perished in a concentration camp. But, I now ask all my viewers in Israel and the United States if anyone knows of Mr. and Mrs. Fenyves. My father came to study in Warsaw. They lived in Warsaw under the names Irena and Tomasz Rynek. If you have any information about where the Fenyves might be now, please call me at the numbers appearing below."

Jodi remained on camera for the closing minutes, responding to follow-up questions from the other commentators. Jodi was grateful that some of the follow-up questions were also about her parents, giving her an opportunity to repeat her appeal several times.

The telephones in the studio began ringing almost immediately. There were the usual crank calls, hate calls, and calls from fans who simply wanted to speak to Jodi.

Calls came in from various parts of the world. Most of the calls were from people who knew her parents in Warsaw or in the Ghetto. One caller even remembered the young Fenyves couple on the train to Treblinka. That day, Jodi, Reena, and her staff talked to more than one hundred people.

No one had any information as to her parents' present whereabouts.

"But no one could report their deaths, either," Reena said when Jodi commiserated that the program produced little information.

Many of the calls needed follow-up attention. One caller, from the Hungarian Jewish Society in Argentina, explained that 'Fenyves' is a Hungarian name, which could be translated as 'freedom'. The caller said that many people who had that name in Hungary changed it to reflect the same meaning in the country to which they had immigrated.

"In America, for example, Fenyves became Freedman, Fried, or Freeman," the caller explained. "The same is true of those who settled in Israel. They changed their name to a Hebrew word meaning 'freedom'."

That new angle required their attention. Then, a doctor called from the Maimonides Hospital in Haifa. Reena took the call and put him on the speakerphone for Jodi to hear.

"My name is Dr. Sobel, Aron Sobel. In our psychiatric ward, we have a catatonic patient, Miriam Drori, who reacted strangely during your program. We have never had any sign of alertness from her before. This reaction was the first."

"Do you think there is some connection, Dr. Sobel?" Reena asked.

"We just don't know," he said. "But we would appreciate it if Miss Wycliff could visit the hospital."

Reena whispered to Jodi, "The name 'Drori' means freedom. It may be the Hebrew adaptation of 'Fenyves'."

"Dr. Sobel, how old is she?" Jodi asked.

"We really don't know," he said. "We couldn't extract any information from her when she was admitted. Why don't you come see her? I'll meet you any time."

"Ten tomorrow morning," Jodi suggested, and the doctor agreed.

When Jodi thanked the doctor and hung up, Reena quickly apologized, "I can't take you tomorrow morning. I have a regional hookup involving the arrival of the prime minister of South Africa."

"Reena, you've done so much. I can't thank you enough," Jodi said. "I can find my way around Israel. I'll manage to get to Haifa by myself."

Jodi called Ron, thanking him for conceiving of the *Self-Portrait* program and excitedly telling him about the call from the hospital in Haifa.

"Will Reena go with you?" Ron asked.

When Jodi sarcastically said she could travel alone "all the way to Haifa," Ron replied that he would meet her at the hospital.

The last phone call of the day came as Jodi was about to leave. The man asked whether Jodi could meet with a group of Palestinian patriots as a follow-up to her interview with Sadat. Jodi, listening in on the speakerphone, motioned to Reena to say no.

"I'm sorry, Sir, but Miss Wycliff has a full schedule and will be leaving for Haifa in the morning," Reena said, and quickly hung up the receiver.

It was 4 P.M. by the time they finished sorting out the information from the phone calls. "I've got to run," Jodi said, "I haven't eaten anything since breakfast very early this morning."

"Do you want me to go with you to the cafeteria across the street?" Reena asked.

"I know you have your own work to do, and you've already done so much for me," Jodi said. "I can find one myself and then go on back to the hotel."

She thanked Reena again for producing the TV special and walked out of the studio. Heading down Tel Aviv's King George Street, she sat down at a small table at an outdoor café and ordered a sandwich and a cup of coffee.

As she was paying her bill, a tall man walked up beside her. "Miss Wycliff," he greeted her, "I heard your program and I congratulate you and wish you success in finding your parents."

He was handsome, swarthy, neatly dressed. Jodi detected an Arabic accent.

Anticipating her concerns, the stranger said, "My name is Abdul Khalid. I represent the public relations department of the Palestine Liberation Organization."

"I did not come to Israel to become embroiled in the political turmoil facing Arabs and Jews. So excuse me, I must get back to Jerusalem," Jodi said.

"I understand and I am sorry to disturb you. I know what finding your mother means to you," Khalid said. "May I get you a taxi?"

Without waiting for her reply, he motioned to a waiting taxi and, after helping her in, he surprised her by sliding in next to her.

"The ride to Jerusalem will give me an opportunity to discuss my proposal with you," he explained. Jodi reached to open the closed car door but the driver revved the motor and the car lurched forward.

"I am truly sorry, Miss Wycliff," Abdul Khalid said. "All we want from you is for you to interview our leader, Rahman Ali."

"I'm sorry, Mr. Khalid, I will not interview him," Jodi said. "I'm not working as a correspondent anymore while I am in Israel. I'm very caught up in my personal business."

"You must understand that there are many Palestinians who do not agree with Sadat's attempt to make peace with Israel."

Jodi repeated, "I will not interview Mr. Ali. I came to Israel to trace my parents and I am not going to become involved in politics."

"But by interviewing Sadat, you're already involved."

"That's ridiculous," Jodi said, ordering the taxi driver to stop the car.

The driver paid no attention to her request. The taxi kept speeding away from Tel Aviv's business section.

"Perhaps you did not understand me," Khalid spoke with anger. "I told you, there are many who do not agree with Sadat's plans for peace with Israel."

"You mean the Hamas."

"And some of us will do everything in our power to end your search for your mother." He bluntly told her that her interview with Sadat made her an enemy of the Palestinians. He warned her that she could meet up with a serious accident.

"If you want to continue your search for your mother while you are in Israel, you really have no choice but to agree."

Jodi took a deep breath. "Let me remind you that Israeli security knows my itinerary."

"We know all about your General Shavit," Khalid said. "And we know he is up in the Golan. Is refusing to do an interview with a Palestinian leader worth throwing away your life?"

Jodi could not hide her fear. She tried to reply, but she merely muttered a few phrases.

"But this interview you will do," Khalid replied cryptically.

The taxi stopped in an alley in the Hatikvah slum section on the outskirts of Tel Aviv. Khalid told her to get out and led her up a rickety flight of stairs into a one-room, sparsely furnished apartment.

"I will leave you for an hour so I can arrange for television equipment to be set up for the interview," Khalid said. "We will frame the questions and remember, you must allow Ali fullest expression of his views."

"I don't know what plans you have, but, I repeat, Israel's top security people will be looking for me."

"I repeat, also, Miss Wycliff, we know about your friend, General Ron Shavit. He is right now up in the Golan. So don't try any tricks that will only complicate matters and endanger your welfare."

When he left, she heard the door click and lock shut. Alone in that small apartment, she recalled a news item in the *New York Times* about an American journalist who had been threatened by Palestinian gunmen ordering him to file a favorable story. She also recalled reading the article and, at the time, wondering why the *Times* had not mentioned that the article had been written under pressure.

She sat down on a low divan to consider her options. Given that Khalid belonged to a terrorist organization, she decided to follow his orders. That seemed to give her the best chance of coming out of this alive. Having made that decision, she felt less tense, more at ease. Yet she also felt she could not simply go along with their design without trying somehow to alert Ron to her predicament. She decided that in her questions, she must make some reference to Khalid.

But how?

By the time Khalid returned with the TV crew, it was already late in the evening. He boasted that the interview would be live and that both Palestinian and Israeli TV had agreed to carry it.

"Here is a list of questions," he said, handing her a typed sheet. "Stick to that text."

"Mr. Khalid," she said after reading the list, "if I am going to be forced to do this, let me do it right. Allow me to help you make this production more professional and, therefore, more newsworthy."

"Remember, no tricks," he replied.

"Let me begin with a simple introduction," she said. "Then, you make any changes you wish."

"What do you have in mind?"

"Something like this," Jodi said. "Ladies and gentlemen, because I interviewed President Anwar Sadat, I feel it is only proper for me and you to listen to other voices. As you know, I am not a politician and know little diplomacy. My questions therefore will be blunt and on target."

"I like the reference to Sadat, and I like your personal evaluation about knowing little diplomacy," Khalid said, handing her a pencil and a piece of paper. "Write it out exactly as you said it."

"I'll try to remember what I said," Jodi replied as she wrote a few words, erased others, and then handed him the written statement. "Make your corrections."

Khalid read her few sentences several times, consulted with his friends, and finally, finding no clues, approved her text.

Up in the Golan, General Ron Shavit's personal telephone rang incessantly. Finally, he answered, stating that he had little time to talk.

"Ron, this is Reena. Jodi's disappeared."

"What are you talking about?" Ron shouted into the telephone.

"She left here at about four to get something to eat at a local restaurant. I've been calling her hotel for the past hour and the reception desk tells me she hasn't come in. Then I received a cryptic message from some man who advised me to listen to Jodi on the Arab television channel. I did better. I said that Israel TV would carry her message."

"They've picked her up. I'm getting on this right away," Ron said.

"You'd better turn on your TV. She'll be interviewing Rahman Ali in about thirty minutes."

He slammed down the phone, called his team to tape the program, and asked for an immediate analysis. During the interview, several intelligence officers huddled with Ron, sharing his left-over pizza dinner.

"She's in Tel Aviv," someone said, "and there's no dubbing."

"Call headquarters there and tell them to stand by," Ron ordered.

"It's Ali, all right," another officer said, "but we haven't been able to locate him since his escape."

"The questions are not hers," Ron said. "She's reading someone's lines, so we can't get any clues from her questions."

The phone rang while the interview was being aired. Reena insisted on speaking directly to Ron. "That's the worst English Jodi ever aired," she said when Ron came on the line.

"What are you talking about? She's reading questions they've handed to her."

"Listen to her intro," Reena said. "Let others listen to the rest of the garbage."

He replayed her opening remarks and said to Reena, "What's not English?"

"I know little diplomacy...know little diplomacy! That's not Jodi talking," Reena said. "She's telling you something. There's a message in those three words. Now, you go figure it out."

On the chalkboard he wrote out the initial letters of each of the words in various forms. Nothing made sense. His team worked on the reverse lettering. Nothing.

"Anybody? Any ideas?" he asked them. "Reena says it's not good English. She knows. This is her business."

While Ali Rahman was spouting his venom against Israel and against Sadat on the big screen, Ron cleared his cluttered table, preparing to make a grid of Tel Aviv as his staff called out areas in which the Arab TV station was broadcasting. He was about to throw away the empty pizza box when he looked down at it and read the Hebrew word "pizza"...which appeared without vowels.

He suddenly bellowed, "Pazzo, puzzo, pizza! Hebrew has no vowels." He erased all the writing on the chalkboard and again wrote the initials of Know Little Diplomacy – K-L-D. "Guys, it's Khalid! He has her. Go get 'em."

A Tel Aviv police force stormed Khalid's apartment, knocked over the TV equipment, and arrested both Khalid and Ali. They swept Jodi out and put her in the back of a police car. Safe, but terribly shaken and exhausted, she anxiously waited to get back to her hotel in Jerusalem, where a twenty-four-hour guard was assigned to her room.

The receptionist gave her two messages, one from Reena and one from Ron. After she called Reena to thank her and reassure her, Jodi reached Ron and thanked him for her deliverance.

"I knew you'd get my message," she said, adding in laughter, "Pazzo, puzzo, pizza!"

"You have Reena to thank for spotting the clue, and you have to be grateful we were eating pizza and the box was staring me in the face," Ron replied. "What would you have done if pizza hadn't been on the menu tonight?"

"When I visited your soldiers' barracks, on your mountain top, I noticed that pizza boxes were everywhere, including in your headquarters," Jodi said. "I'm happy to be back in my room. That was really frightening."

"Are you sure Reena can't go with you to Haifa tomorrow?" Ron asked.

"No. She has to stay in Tel Aviv. She's got a prime minister coming in."

"This is no time for you to be alone," Ron said. "I will have a security detail escort you to Haifa. You'll need them just to get past all the reporters camped out in your hotel lobby."

"I'm not afraid of the reporters," she laughed. "I'll talk to them in a little while. I feel perfectly safe with the guard assigned to me."

"Jodi, don't put on a brave trooper act with me. I know you too well," Ron said.

"I'm not acting. I'm so excited, I feel it in my bones. This visit to the hospital in Haifa could be the biggest thing in my life."

"And if it turns out that the woman in Maimonides Hospital is not your mother, it won't be just another dead end. It'll be the end of you. This is all a tremendous emotional roller coaster."

When she did not reply, he said again, "I'll meet you there. If this isn't Mrs. Fenyves, you'll go to pieces."

"I don't think so, Ron. I'm a big girl now. But thanks for your concern. I'll see you there."

Jodi went down to the lobby, discreetly shadowed by her guard, and told her colleagues what she could about the afternoon's incident. But when she went back upstairs and got into bed, it was the hospital visit, not the near escape and the forced interview, that filled her thoughts. She was so excited she was awake all night, wondering if she was about to meet her mother.

Chapter 20

THE DRIVE TO HAIFA took about three hours but Jodi, sitting alone in the back seat, slept through it. When the taxi reached the outskirts of Haifa, the guard, sitting in the passenger seat, awakened her. She was rested and refreshed. After climbing the winding road up the Carmel slope, the taxi reached the hospital. Jodi got out and walked up the front steps to Ron, who was waiting for her at the entrance. Together, they crossed the trellised porch, where inmates of the psychiatric ward were sunning themselves.

"This is my day," she said, inordinately happy. "Even today's astrological tables said, 'Expect great happenings.'"

"You should try to settle down a little bit, Jodi," Ron cautioned. "I don't want you to be disappointed."

"You're just a party pooper," she teased.

"What does that mean?"

"It means I'm on cloud nine and I don't want to be taken down," she said as she strode into the hospital lobby just ahead of Ron.

The receptionist looked up and, recognizing Jodi, said Dr. Sobel was expecting her and asked her to wait. At first, Jodi took a seat in the lobby, but within minutes she began pacing the floor.

"You've faced excitement before," Ron said, trying to calm her.

"Never like this," she replied. "I never met my mother before."

"Jodi," Ron said quite sternly, "she may not be your mother."

The receptionist led them into Dr. Sobel's office, where he welcomed her. She introduced Ron, then they took a seat on the sofa facing the doctor.

A nurse dressed in a white uniform came in and took a chair next to Dr. Sobel's desk.

"This is Nomi Ariel, Mrs. Drori's nurse," said the doctor. "She will describe the behavior of our patient. But first let me explain about the woman you are about to meet. She has been a patient in the hospital for more than seven years. We believe she should be in her early sixties or late fifties, but that's only a guess. Thus far, neither I nor any one of our other expert practitioners have been able to find any remedy for her catatonic state."

"What exactly are the symptoms of a catatonic patient?" Jodi asked.

"Negation and resistance to all instruction," Dr. Sobel stated. "She sits for hours, staring at the blank wall, unresponsive to any stimuli and, worst of all, she suffers from extreme mutism."

"Extreme mutism?" Jodi asked.

"She has not spoken a word, literally, not a word, in the past seven years," Dr. Sobel said. "We've tried electroconvulsive therapy, the standard ten shock treatments, as well as the newest antidepressant drugs. Nothing. No reaction."

"Why do you think she may be my mother?" Jodi asked.

"It has to do with her reaction to your television program yesterday afternoon," Dr. Sobel replied. "Nomi, please describe how Mrs. Drori reacted."

"Ordinarily, she shows no interest in any television show or movie," the nurse said. "But when Miss Wycliff appeared on the screen, Mrs. Drori looked up and excitedly waved her hands toward the TV. And that wasn't all. When you emphasized the name 'Fenyves', she let out a scream that surprised and frightened the other patients in the room."

"You see, Ron," Jodi whispered, "expect great happenings!"

The nurse added that she and the attendants had tried to evoke a further response from the patient, but she had reverted to her former self.

"I reported the incident to Dr. Sobel," Nomi continued, "and he immediately called the TV station in Tel Aviv."

"Thanks, Nomi," said Dr. Sobel. Turning to Jodi, he explained, "I regret to add to Nomi's information, that since her strange reaction last night, Mrs. Drori has become more catatonic, more mute than before. Instead of being merely unresponsive, she is now showing hostility. From a medical point of view, that may be viewed as a positive reaction. At least she's showing some response, which she has not shown since her coming to us. But now she refuses to do the simple chores she's always done – feeding herself, dressing herself, and so on."

"Can you give me any background information about her?" Jodi asked.

"Yes," Dr. Sobel answered. "From her neighbors we learned that the patient's husband had been a commando in the War of Attrition."

"Sergeant David Drori!" Ron gasped and turned to Jodi, "I'll tell you later about our national hero."

"Yes, she is the widow of David Drori," the doctor said. "He was killed when a bomb exploded, tearing his body into unrecognizable shreds. At his funeral, she fainted, lost consciousness and all efforts to revive her were in vain. I should tell you that the funeral was a most somber affair. Only what remained of him, several pieces of his flesh and bones, were interred. She let out a hideous cry, then fainted. All attempts to revive her proved futile. She was brought directly from the military cemetery to this hospital."

Leading Jodi to Mrs. Drori's room, Dr. Sobel prepared her to expect the worst, warning her that she might find the woman very hostile and that she might even reject her very presence.

"She may not be your mother," Dr. Sobel added, "but we appreciate your coming to the hospital to help us unravel this mystery."

Before they entered the room, Jodi showed Dr. Sobel the picture of herself as a baby being held by her natural mother.

"Doctor," Jodi asked, "does she look anything like this?"

The doctor took the picture, gazed at it intently, and shook his head. "It's hard to tell, Miss Wycliff. You will have to judge for yourself."

Jodi and Ron walked into Mrs. Drori's room, trailing the doctor. She looked at the woman sitting in the straight-backed chair, staring out of the window. The patient showed no reaction to their entrance nor did she respond to the doctor's greeting. A photograph of a soldier in a tank corpsman's uniform stood on her night table. Jodi tiptoed ahead of the men, placing herself between the woman and the window. Mrs. Drori's face was shriveled with sagging jowls, eyebrows thickly overgrown, snow white. Her angry grimace made her appear even more aged than the doctor's estimate. To Jodi, she appeared to be closer to eighty. Jodi tried to make eye contact with the woman, but the dull, lifeless eyes of the patient were fixed in a stare, looking at nothing, seeing nothing.

"Mama?" Jodi whispered. "It's me, Jadzia. I've come from America."

No reaction. No bodily movement, not even a flick of the eye. Jodi might as well have spoken to the wall.

"Are you sure she isn't deaf?" Jodi asked Dr. Sobel.

"We don't even know the answer to that," the doctor said, explaining that they had even tried to frighten her with a sudden loud noise, but could discern no response. "Judged by her general behavior pattern she may be deaf, but more likely, her lack of reaction could be the result of her catatonic condition. Remember, we were surprised that she reacted to what she heard on your TV program. Ordinarily she shows no reaction to any program."

As they were discussing her reaction, the woman suddenly got up from her chair, wrapped her shawl about her shoulders, and lay down on her bed. She shut her eyes, as though falling asleep.

"She does that quite often when we subject her to various tests," Dr. Sobel said. "It's her way of refusing to follow any instruction."

Jodi did not give up. She approached the bed, touched the woman's bony forearm and, once again, whispered, "Mama?"

"Let me ask Nomi to join us," Dr. Sobel said. "She often speaks Polish to Mrs. Drori."

When Nomi arrived, she sat down beside the bed and stroked the woman's hair, saying in Polish, "Mrs. Drori, your daughter is here."

There was no response.

Jodi then said three words to introduce herself, words she had rehearsed in Hebrew, "*Ima zot ani, Jadwiga*. It's me, Jadwiga." She repeated it several times. The woman still showed no response.

Ron walked over to Jodi, took her by the hand, and led her out of the room. The doctor followed, asking Jodi and Ron to come to his office.

"It's another dead end," Jodi whimpered. "She didn't show even the slightest recognition."

"True, there was no response, Miss Wycliff, but that doesn't mean there was no recognition," Dr. Sobel corrected her. "She may have recognized you, but in view of her psychological condition, she is unable to respond. We're not giving up, so I hope you don't either."

"But what can you do?"

"Our team has decided to take Mrs. Drori off all of her current medications, give her body a week to adjust, and then I want to try a course of new antidepressants. Changing the medication is a common practice when a patient either shows no improvement or deteriorates altogether. Would you come back in about ten days, when the new medication takes effect?"

Jodi, still distraught, merely nodded.

"It's a trial-and-error procedure," Dr. Sobel warned. "But if she is your mother, you might be able to break through her mental barrier."

"If she is my mother," Jodi repeated.

She walked slowly out of Dr. Sobel's office and down the long corridor, hanging onto Ron's arm. He led her to his military sedan and instructed the sergeant behind the wheel to drive to Tel Aviv. For about a half an hour they rode in silence. All attempts by Ron to comfort her, to reassure her that it was not a dead end, produced no response. Jodi simply did not reply.

Trying another tack to get her to respond, Ron said, "Jodi, let me see the photograph you showed the doctor."

Again, she did not answer, remaining silent for a few moments. Then, without looking up at him, her head still drooped, staring at her knees, she quietly asked, "Why are we going back to Tel Aviv?"

"We're going away for a few days," he replied.

He expected her to question his decision to take a vacation despite her remorse and disinterest. But Jodi neither agreed nor argued. He then tried to be funny, teasing her that he preferred her feisty nature rather than submissive compliance. Again, she did not reply. He tried to lift her spirits, reminding her that the doctor was hopeful that the new medication could produce results. She raised her eyes and looked straight ahead, but said nothing.

"Now don't you become catatonic with me. I like you when you're in control." And to further arouse her, he said, feigning anger, "You journalists are always in control."

"I control the news?" she retorted, looking up at him.

"Of course you do," he replied. "You even controlled the Sadat interview."

"You, in the military, are the controllers," she argued. "We only report facts."

"Only the facts that you decide to report," he replied.

"And what does that mean?" she retorted.

"OK, you asked for it," he replied, relieved to be debating with the old Jodi Wycliff. "In your interview with Sadat, you asked the questions that would get you headlines instead of going after vital facts. Who the hell cares what Sadat's wife thought about his trip to Jerusalem? And, as for your second question, about Carter, what kind of a reply did you expect? And, your last question – would the Palestinians accept his peace? – boy, that was chutzpah. You let him spout forth his conditions for a peace treaty with Israel, conditions that would please the Palestinians but are totally unacceptable to us. You weren't reporting the facts; you were on stage, playing to your audience and looking for applause."

Jodi was incensed. She sternly explained the duties of a journalist, reminding him of a reporter's six questions, "Who, what, where, why, when, and how."

"Exactly," he replied. "First you decide which questions to ask, then you choose which replies to spotlight."

She laughed, challenging him to tell her what questions he would have asked Sadat.

"First let me tell you that every reporter is guilty, even sports writers," he said. "You're from Miami, right? The Dolphins win a football game and the reporters focus on the decisions made by the coach or the quarterback, which, according to the reporter, helped win the game. The rest of the players don't exist. The journalist selects his candidate, spotlights him, and that's the game."

She replied acidly that she was not a sports writer, and challenging him again, she asked, "What questions would you have asked if you had only five minutes for the Sadat interview?"

"I would first mention his visit to Yad Vashem, then I would ask him why there are no trees in the Grove of Righteous Gentiles for any Arab who saved Jews during the Holocaust."

"Ron, is that so important?"

"Jodi, the peace between Arabs and Jews depends on one thing only – the Arab acceptance of the Jews' right to exist as a people."

"And the second question?" she asked.

"The most obvious," he replied. "I would say, 'Mr. Sadat, when will your government stop supporting the terrorist groups in Gaza who kill innocent civilians, schoolchildren, and babies in Israel?'"

Jodi thought a while, mulled over the two questions, then said, "If I had asked him those questions, it wouldn't make good copy. Mr. White would be incensed and I wouldn't get any applause."

They were passing a roadhouse café. Ron ordered the driver to stop so they could stretch their legs. Sitting at one of the tables, she thanked him for getting her out of the doldrums she had experienced following the visit to the hospital.

"Now can I plan our next few days?" he asked. "Or do you still want to be in control?"

"You can be in control," she said. "But remember, even over the next few days, my search cannot stop for a vacation. I want to follow up on Jeff's advice to search for my parents among Holocaust survivors in the United States."

"Who's Jeff?" Ron asked, acting as though he forgot that she had spoken about Jeff earlier.

"Jeff is the doctor who accompanied us to Europe. He looked after Dr. Berson."

"That's all?" Ron asked.

"No, we got to know each other rather well," she said. "He returned to the States to assume an important position in a medical institute."

"That's all?" Ron asked.

"Jeff also suggested I return to the States and continue my search there."

"That's all?" Ron asked for the third time.

"Ron, you're impossible," Jodi snickered. "Yes, we hit it off very well while we traveled around Berlin and Warsaw."

"That's why he wants you back in the United States," Ron said. "Do you love him?"

"Don't you think that's my business?" Jodi replied.

"Jodi, it's my business too," Ron said.

"Ron, don't complicate my life any more than it is already."

Ron took her hand and held it as they sat in silence for the next few moments. She did not withdraw.

Ron said quietly, "It wouldn't be wise to go back to the States before we finalize the Drori case here in Israel. Dr. Sobel is holding out the possibility that new medication will bring Mrs. Drori around. You've promised him to come back in ten days."

They returned to the waiting car and after driving for quite a while, she asked, "So what would you do with the next ten days?"

"Well, for three or four of them, I'd like to take you with me to the Sinai. I have to go down to inspect troop deployment on the Bar-Lev Line, the border between Israel and Egypt."

"I've been to the Sinai several times, when I helped do stories on the Bar-Lev Line."

"You've seen Israel through the eyes of a reporter, Jodi," he said. "You search for headlines, not for the day-to-day sacrifices of ordinary people that don't always make headlines. You've never seen it in a proper perspective, even as a tourist."

"Come on! Human interest stories are our stock-in-trade. Journalists often write human interest stories to pinpoint the spirit of a people."

"Whose interest? What people? The poor little Arab child behind a barbed-wire fence in a refugee camp."

"Well, that child has a story too." Jodi thought a while then said, "Yes, I remember the piece the *New York Times* did on the anniversary of the Six-Day War. I thought that piece was unfair, even slanted."

"Today, when you will see the Bar-Lev Line, you will see the Sinai with fresh eyes."

"OK, I'll go with you to the Bar-Lev Line, anywhere you want," she said. "But you lay off journalists and I won't criticize your military intelligence."

When their sedan arrived at Sde Dov, the military airfield near Tel Aviv, Ron got out and asked the sergeant to drive Jodi to her hotel, give her time to pack, and bring her back safely. The driver gave an offhanded salute, pointing to the gun he had placed in readiness on the passenger seat.

She returned to the airport about four hours later, carrying only a small valise no bigger than an airline bag, and her camera case. She was dressed in a smoky blue turtleneck sweater with a matching skirt and had slung a mohair jacket over her shoulders. Ron looked at her admiringly but took away her camera case and gave it to the security chief.

"You're not on an assignment. You're coming for enjoyment, pure and simple," Ron said, and, taking her small valise, asked, "That's all you're bringing with you?"

"What else do I need in the desert?" she replied, standing there with her hair swept by the wind.

"Your mother was very beautiful. You look exactly like her. You're absolutely beautiful."

"My mother?" she asked.

"I saw her picture when you showed it to Dr. Sobel. The baby she was holding was but a smudge, but I see that you are the perfect image of your mother," he said, helping her into the cramped space of the Piper Cub.

*

The flight to the Bar-Lev Line in the Sinai took longer than usual because Ron asked the pilot to circle around several points of interest in the desert. He pointed out green patches of orchards and vegetable farms in the parched desert sand where agricultural colonies were beginning to make the desert bloom.

"Ben-Gurion's legacy to Israel was not his political or even his organizational genius," Ron said. "It was his call to the Israelis to roll back the desert, which was then about seventy percent of Israel's land."

He showed her areas in the Sinai where military battles were fought and where, during the Six-Day War, thousands of Egyptian troops were taken prisoner. At one point, he told her to sit in the copilot's seat so she would have an open view as he pointed out the Nile River and the Suez Canal.

While eating lunch in the Bar-Lev unit's mess hall, he reminisced about his military experiences. "Before the Six-Day War, the Russians supplied SAM missiles to Egypt's President Nasser. We were subjected to daily air attacks and couldn't reciprocate because of those missiles. We suffered for five years, trying to counteract the Egyptian bombardment. That was the War of Attrition. I'll show you the highlight of that era."

After lunch, he took her to the underground bunkers that formed the Bar-Lev Line, introducing her to some of the men stationed there. Then he closeted himself with the area commanding officers to discuss military affairs. About an hour later, he went out with them on an inspection tour of the entire defense line. While he was away, Jodi befriended the soldiers, who were delighted to show her around the bunkers. When he returned, he found her standing atop a tank, wearing a military helmet and with a gun slung over her shoulders. She reprimanded him for not allowing her to bring her camera.

"I told you, you're not on assignment," he said.

"I wanted you to take a few pictures of me in this outfit."

"Congratulations, Miss Wycliff," he smiled, as he helped her off the tank. "You've finally become a tourist, not a reporter!"

He led her away from the group and took her to a mound facing the Suez Canal, where he handed her a pair of binoculars, directing her to look about a kilometer beyond the canal. She kept focusing the binoculars, then said, "I see nothing but a heap of rubble and burned sand."

"That's where SAM missile launchers were placed," he said. "Because of those launchers, we couldn't stop the random bombing of cities and settlements. And that's where David Drori showed his heroism."

"David Drori," she repeated. "My father!"

"Maybe your father," he corrected her.

"Let me dream," she replied.

"It may turn out to be a nightmare," he said.

"OK," Jodi said. "Take me back to the past about the SAM missiles and this piece of burned sand in front of us."

"Military Intelligence decided to send commandos across the canal to destroy the site. After weeks of intensive training in underwater maneuvers, a commando unit headed by Sergeant David Drori was ordered to secretly cross the canal, get to the missile launchers, and blow them up. That is, all but one, which they would try to hoist over to Israel."

Jodi listened intently, looking at the sand across the canal.

"At 2 A.M., with the full moon shining, all six commandos succeeded in crossing the canal secretly, carrying blasting equipment and heavy cables. Two commandos strategically attached a cable to one of the launchers and detached it from its mooring. The others strapped plastic bombs to the remaining launchers and attached fuses. They were ready to blast on Drori's signal. David then called for a helicopter to carry off the SAM launcher. Within minutes, the tethered launcher was lifted off and carried into Israel. As the unit was returning to its base, David turned around and noticed that several fuses had become detached from one of the launchers. He realized that if it didn't detonate, the Egyptians would be left with a functioning missile launcher. He quickly returned to the launcher, where he began reattaching the fuses. Then Egyptian vehicles appeared and were speeding toward him. He continued to reconnect the fuses despite the oncoming troops and signaled for the demolition to be activated instantly.

"His body and the SAM launchers went up in flames."

Jodi kept looking through the binoculars as Ron was describing the heroic action. Then he said somberly, "We were sitting right here, as you are now, looking through the binoculars at David's work, and saw him being blown to bits."

"David Drori," she whispered the name with reverence.

"Jodi, I brought you here only to tell you about a national hero," he said, "not stories about your illusory father."

"Don't destroy my hopes, Ron," she said, annoyed. "David Drori could have been David Fenyves, Tomasz Rynek. I must now get back to my search."

"Jodi, the search is ongoing. After Dr. Sobel's first call, I asked Reena to check the name 'Drori' and any other Hebrew derivative of 'Fenyves' in all Israeli telephone directories. She sent a messenger with her report. He delivered it to me at Sde Dov, while you were in Jerusalem getting your things."

Ron reached into his attaché case and handed her seven pages photocopied from an Israeli telephone directory. "There are more than six hundred Droris and other Hebrew derivatives of Fenyves listed in the Tel Aviv phone book alone. Throughout the country, there must be thousands more."

"You're preparing me for another disappointment," Jodi said.

"I sure am," Ron replied. "Do you know what you looked like when you left the Maimonides Hospital?"

Jodi leafed through the copies of the pages from the telephone directory and nodded. "You're right. I hope I'm not setting myself up for another dead end."

"I can't promise you no dead end," Ron said emphatically. "But Reena has her whole crew checking out each of these names. If anything turns up, she'll inform you."

"Thanks," Jodi said. "Tell her to hire additional workers. Tell her not to worry about Mr. White, I'll pay for the crew of searchers."

That night they slept in one of the underground bunkers and in the morning, instead of flying back, he drove her through the desert in a military jeep, stopping at military installations, agricultural colonies, and scientific institutes, where they ate and visited. They stayed in the region several nights as part of Ron's planned three-day desert escapade. Wherever they visited, people received Jodi warmly, always relating to her as the famous American television personality.

"I hope that one day they will call me 'Jodi Drori, the daughter of David

Drori,'" Jodi told Ron when they stopped at the Desert Oasis, a popular tourist hangout.

"Stop it!" Ron glared at her. "At the hospital, Mrs. Drori showed no sign of recognizing you. What I fear most is even if they finally cure her catatonic condition, she might burst your bubble and you'll drown in your own fantasy. So, for the last time, be realistic. Accept possible failure."

"Accept failure," Jodi repeated. "That's a tough assignment."

*

They drove along the eastern border of Israel, hugging the Dead Sea. She marveled at the sheer beauty of the area, especially when they climbed up the snake path of Masada. It had been cold when they left Tel Aviv, but it was delightfully warm in the buoyant waters of the Dead Sea. When they visited the site of the Qumran caves, Ron told her about the Essenes and their dedication to preserving the ancient biblical texts. Jodi already knew most of what Ron was telling her about Israel's ancient past, but his enthusiasm gripped her.

"When you talk about the Essenes or about the massacre at Masada, you make it sound as though they're still part of you," Jodi said as they drove up the winding road.

"That's the charm of Israel," Ron said. "You're no longer just an observer in Israel's past; you're a participant in it."

"I know all about Israel's history," she said, as they sat down to eat at a coffee shop alongside the Dead Sea. "Now tell me something about yourself and about the girls."

"My twenty-five-year hitch is coming to an end and I'll have to decide whether to accept the army's offer to elevate me to the rank of major general if I sign up for another three years."

"Is that important to you?"

"If I accept the promotion, I'll be an eligible candidate to become the chief of staff of the Israel Defense Forces. Very few of my colleagues attain that level."

"That's an important promotion."

"What do you think? Should I accept the army's offer and sign up for three more years?" he asked.

"How can I give you any advice on such a personal matter?" Jodi answered.

"Jodi, you've become very personal to me."

She looked at him quite a while, but made no comment.

"Is it Jeff, the doctor with the big position in the Institute?" he asked quite seriously.

"Let's not talk about it now," she replied.

*

When they reached Jerusalem, they were too tired to continue on to Tel Aviv, so they went to Ron's small apartment in Shoresh, a former kibbutz outside of Jerusalem. Jodi showered first and then got into one of Ron's shirts. She whipped up an omelet, serving it with some odds and ends she found in his refrigerator.

"If I wrote a book about David Drori's heroism, I would call it *David Slays Goliath...Again*," Jodi said. "Now, if I could only find my parents, I might just do that."

"This is a land of miracles," Ron said, embracing her. "You deserve one. There are at least a thousand Drori families in Israel. One of them will lead you to your parents."

They watched television for a while and then turned it off and sat talking in the darkened room. At last, Jodi asked, "Ron, what have you decided about remaining in the army?"

"I have a meeting in Tel Aviv with the General Staff early this afternoon. I'm going to turn down the army's offer, promotion and all," he said. "I want to go back to civilian life. I have an offer to teach at Tel Aviv University, and I don't want the military to interfere again with my family life."

"You mean Aliza and Shoni?"

"No, I mean you."

"Ron, don't make any plans involving me."

*

In the morning, Ron asked her to accompany him back to Tel Aviv. Before she decided, she called Dr. Sobel at the Maimonides Hospital in Haifa and asked about Mrs. Drori's condition. He replied that they had cleansed her body of her old medication and were now ready to begin a new procedure.

"She should be ready for a visit in about four days," the doctor said.

As she hung up the phone, Reena called Jodi informing her that after investigating the “Drori” names in the Israeli telephone directories, they’d come up with twenty-two leads worth following up.

“I’m sorry to say that our interviewers came up with nothing,” Reena said. “But we have just received two good leads, both up in Zefat. Someone from my staff is planning a visit today to check them out.”

“Could I come along on those interviews?” Jodi asked.

“Sure. I’ll have Yitzi pick you up around noon at your hotel.”

When Jodi told Ron she was going to check out the Droris in Zefat instead of tagging along with him to Tel Aviv, he said, “I’m going with you.”

“You have a staff meeting in Tel Aviv.”

“If I don’t show up, the worst they can do is fire me,” Ron said in jest as he helped with her jacket. “So if they fire me, I’ll have more time for you.”

“You don’t give up so easily, do you?” Jodi said. “Let me call Reena and get the contact names. If you’re coming with me, let’s save her staffer a trip.”

Reena excitedly reported to Jodi. “I actually have a David Fenyves who called from the Zefat area, claiming to be a relative of the Fenyves from Hungary. The other is a Drori family also living in Zefat whose daughter sounded eager to talk to you.”

“Thanks,” Jodi joyously responded. “Ron will be the translator at the two interviews.”

Arriving in Zefat, they first met with a young woman, Dafna Drori, who greeted Jodi as if she were family. No translator was needed because Dafna spoke perfect English. She told them that her parents’ names had once been Fenyves. They had lived in Warsaw and immigrated to Israel right after World War II.

“They’re vacationing in Switzerland,” Dafna said, “but they’ll be back in a few days.”

“If they are the people I’m searching for, I’ll go meet them in Switzerland,” Jodi said. “Can you possibly get them on the phone? I’ll gladly pay for the call.”

Jodi spoke to Dafna’s parents for quite a while on the phone. She thanked them and put down the receiver.

“It’s not them,” she said to Ron and Dafna, “but they knew a Hungarian student named Fenyves who came from Budapest to study at the Warsaw

University. At the time, he was not married, so they couldn't tell me anything about his wife."

"You don't sound discouraged," Ron said.

"Well, there's more," Jodi told him. "They told me there's a circle of Hungarian Jews in Israel who had made *aliyah* and to this day, they meet regularly, like a social club. The Droris will take me to meet the club members. They were certain that someone in the group will direct me to David Fenyves, my father."

Before leaving Dafna's home, Jodi took out a hundred shekel note to pay for the call. Dafna ridiculed Jodi, saying, "If this call will help you find your father, I want to share in the joy of a family reunion."

The second interview was with a retired doctor, Daniel Fenyves, who was living in a village north of Zefat. The doctor said he had known an attorney David Fenyves in Warsaw, and although they were distantly related, they rarely saw one another. He did recall, however, that they both had registered in the Ghetto.

"But I knew that he had married his wife in the Ghetto," he said. "And when I met him in the Czyste Hospital, where he worked as a carpenter, I joked with him, wishing him a belated 'mazal tov' on his marriage, to which I wasn't invited."

"Please, please, try to remember," Jodi pleaded. "Did you ever, ever meet his wife? Can you try to recall her name?"

"All I know is that after this one meeting in the Ghetto, I lost trace of him. I think he managed to escape. But it's only a guess."

"Do you know if he was in the Israeli army?" Jodi asked. "Was he a sergeant?"

"I'm sorry, Miss Wycliff. I know what this means to you. But I don't know what happened to him or even if he ever was in Israel."

Ron realized Jodi's disillusionment. He thanked Dr. Fenyves and led her out to the waiting taxi.

She called Reena, reporting to her the results of the interviews and asked if there were any other leads.

"My people are sifting through hundreds of names. If anything comes up, you know I'll call. Where will you be?"

"As soon as I decide on our next step, I'll let you know." When she hung up the phone, she said to Ron, "I hardly know what to do with myself until I can visit the hospital again."

"Why don't you stay right here in Zefat. It's a good place to catch up with your soul," Ron suggested.

He called Reena and gave her the number of the hotel where he would register.

*

Jodi lost track of the days as they roamed the winding streets of Zefat – the artists' quarter, the ancient synagogues. Best of all, she liked the quiet evenings when she and Ron sat silently atop the mountain ridges, engulfed in the mystic silence of Zefat.

Every day during their stay in the city, she called Dr. Sobel, inquiring if there was any change in Mrs. Drori's condition.

On their third morning in Zefat, Dr. Sobel told her, "We have taken her off all medication. Physically, her condition has improved immeasurably. The side effects of years of drug use may have accelerated her physical deterioration, which you noticed," Dr. Sobel explained. "Regrettably, there's been no change in her catatonic condition. But please come to see her in a day or two."

To add to her woes, later that morning Reena called Jodi to alert her that Mr. White had called from the United States, saying he was coming to Israel with his senior staff members to produce his show, *Mama, Where Are You?*.

"So what?" Jodi said.

"He plans to use some footage from your personal show and he wants me to ask you to call him because he wants you in his show. He's my boss, Jodi, what do I do?"

"You do what you have to, but when you call him, give him this message from me: 'Jodi will not return your call.' Tell him that I will not see him under any circumstances, that his plan infuriates me, and remind him that I had quit NIC and do not intend to return."

Jodi was incensed when she told Ron about Mr. White's plans to commercialize her plight. "Can you imagine? He's going to use footage from my production!"

"He's going to use your footage in his production?" Ron thought aloud and then said, "I have an idea."

He called Reena asking if the clips from Jodi's show could be put on a cassette that could be played in a regular VCR. When Jodi heard his question, she was so enraged, she grabbed the phone from his hand.

"You're also going to commercialize that show?" Jodi asked, rebuking him. "You're playing right into White's hands."

Reena, who probably heard Jodi's reprimand, repeated Jodi's rebuke.

Taking the phone back from Jodi's hand, Ron said in a commanding tone, "Just answer my question, Reena. Can you do it? Can you take a clip or two from Jodi's show and put it on a cassette? Wait, hang on while I explain this to Jodi, she's ready to kill me. I'll get back to you right away."

He then said calmly to Jodi, "Look, that woman in the hospital, Mrs. Drori, showed some response to parts of your now-famous TV interview. Dr. Sobel suspected that there was something in that footage that triggered her reaction. Let's show her just that footage again and see what happens."

Jodi apologized and pecked Ron on his cheek. She then called Dr. Sobel to tell him of Ron's plan.

"Things are so bogged down with Mrs. Drori's case, I'm willing to try anything," he said. "I'll arrange for a VCR to be attached to her television set. Let's see…today is Monday. Wednesday noon would be the best time to come. I can't promise that our new procedures will produce any results."

She then called Reena, startling her, saying, "Get started on that cassette."

Reena nervously replied that she had already called Mr. White to relay Jodi's message to him.

"Don't worry about Mr. White. He's CEO of powerful Network International Corporation, but he's just a pussycat. I'll handle Mr. White. Don't worry about a thing."

Reena breathed a sigh of relief, then said, "I'm getting started on Ron's suggestion, but it's your show and you have a one-person-audience in mind. You'd better come here to edit it just the way you want."

"I'm on my way."

Jodi was restless and uneasy, eager to get to Reena's office to begin working on the cassette. Ron calmed her and called the local military HQ, ordering air transportation to Tel Aviv.

"Jodi, a military car will pick us up in half an hour to take us to the airport. Get your things ready, we're leaving Zefat."

"Ron, remember what you told me about your decision to leave the army?" she said, as they were flying toward Tel Aviv. "You said you didn't want the army to interfere with your family life."

"Of course. It was my way of telling you that I've fallen in love with you."

"Listen to me and listen carefully," she said. "That word, 'love', frightens me. I've fallen in and out of love so many times, I wouldn't know love if it hit me straight in my face."

"Jodi, I am willing to chuck a career that could lead me to becoming Israel's chief of staff. You're more important to me than the army, even more than the whole of Israel. And I love Israel very much."

She did not respond, but she reached for his hand and squeezed it hard. Then she released her grip and said, "Somewhere I read in one of the classic poems, 'Love is a rose.' I don't know what the poet meant, but it frightens me…a rose wilts."

He embraced and kissed her, whispering, "What the hell did the poets know about love! They never met Jodi Wycliff."

Jodi was amazed and, in a way, pleased to hear Ron's declarations of love. She realized that Israel had been Ron's mistress, during and after his marriage. She, Israel, had absorbed all the passion he had to spend. Suddenly, she, Jodi, was a new wrinkle, an unexpected path away from the military to which he had been anchored. These thoughts occupied her as she silently sat close to Ron, feeling secure in his presence.

They arrived in Tel Aviv late in the afternoon and the heavy city traffic made the ride to Reena's studio take almost as long as the flight from Zefat. Hurrying into Reena's office, they saw Oren, Reena's husband, who greeted them as they entered.

"What the hell are you doing here?" Ron asked Oren.

"Your leave was over two days ago, so officially you're AWOL. As your exec, I need to help you avoid being court-martialed."

They both laughed, but the women had no idea what the joke was all about. Reena's husband explained that when General Ron Shavit had called to report that he was not coming to the staff meeting in Tel Aviv, he also requested an extension of his leave.

"So what *are* you doing here?" Ron asked Oren.

"Reena told me of your plan. I like it and I want to help," Oren said. "So I cut myself orders to get to Tel Aviv 'officially to consult' with my commanding officer."

After a quick dinner, Reena and Jodi worked for hours, editing the *Jodi Wycliff: A Self-Portrait* tape, trying to select segments that Jodi felt would arouse Mrs. Drori's interest. They were bleary-eyed, running the tape and the selected segments over and over. At around midnight, they still could not decide which segments to include.

"It's Ron's idea," Reena finally said. "Let him decide which segments he wants."

In the darkened screening room, Ron and Oren were asked to sit and be ready to select a proper segment of the interview, with Jodi reminding them that what they choose will be the section shown to Mrs. Drori in the hospital.

"Stop," Ron called out when the second segment was shown.

"We have fourteen other segments," Reena said.

"I don't need to see any other. This is great," Ron said. "You've done a masterful job. I only hope that Mrs. Drori is alert enough to react."

"Hey, wait, isn't there some picture of Jodi as a little girl?" Oren asked. "The patient, if she is your mother, has never seen you as an adult. Would it jog her memory to see you as a child?"

"Great idea," Reena and Jodi said in chorus. "I'm calling Dr. Sobel requesting an overhead projector for Mrs. Drori's room."

As they were about to leave the studio, Reena handed the final edited cassette to Jodi and wished her luck in Haifa. Just then, Reena's private phone rang. It was Mr. White. He had just landed in Israel and was anxious to speak to them, regardless of the late hour. Somehow, he knew he'd find them in the office. Reena put him on the speaker. He informed them that he had brought both his top director and production manager to Israel to work on the show he had in mind, and he wanted both Reena and Jodi to meet him in the morning.

"Mr. White," Jodi said with feigned sweetness, "do you recall our last conversation in New York? Let me remind you. I said, 'Mr. White, I quit.' And, by the way, since you didn't pay me for my last TV appearance on your Network International Corporation, the *Jodi Wycliff Self Portrait,* the entire program, tapes and all, belong to me. I'm so sorry, Mr. White. Good night."

He began to apologize, explaining that he was wrong to suggest his scheme at the time that she was still searching for her mother.

"No, Winston, I want to thank you," Jodi said without disclosing that his plan gave birth to Ron's. "Let's have dinner tomorrow night and I'll fill you in."

The following morning, they slept in their Tel Aviv hotel rooms until noon. Jodi got up and nervously looked at her watch. She wakened Ron and reminded him they had to go to Haifa.

"Hey, Miss Wycliff, where are you going? It's Tuesday," he said, pulling his blanket over himself. "Your appointment with Dr. Sobel is for Wednesday. Anyway, you're having dinner with Mr. White tonight."

"I'm really in a dither. Can't wait to see Mrs. Drori."

Ron got up from bed, hugged Jodi, and whispered in her ear, "Congratulations. You called her 'Mrs. Drori,' not 'my mother'."

She then called the hotel operator, asking about the message light blinking on her phone.

"A Mr. White called several times to inform you that he was staying in this hotel and that dinner tonight will be in his suite at 7 P.M."

The dinner was exactly what the doctor ordered. Jodi was in no mood to celebrate or to see "Tel Aviv's nightlife." She had remained alone in her room most of the afternoon, writing up her twenty-day experience in Israel, barely mentioning the Sadat interview. Most of it centered on the unplanned and unexpected events of her search for her parents and the "miraculous" role Ron played in these. When Ron called to remind her about the dinner with Mr. White, she quickly dressed and met Ron in the lobby. Together, they took the elevator to Mr. White's suite for cocktails.

White warmly welcomed Jodi with a hug and a kiss. "I thought up all kinds of ways to apologize to you, but Reena told me about General Shavit's plan."

"It was your plan that gave me that idea," Ron said, sharing with him details of their editing clips of Jodi's show onto a cassette.

Mr. White, obviously proud that he had contributed to Jodi's search, served them a special wine he had ordered for the occasion, toasting Jodi and wishing her luck on her trip to the hospital in Haifa.

"The purpose of this dinner is for you, Jodi. I must apologize to you for what I said when you originally told me in New York of your decision to search for your birth mother."

"You said a lot of things, but why the apology?"

"At that time, I scoffed at your plan to search for someone who may have perished in Treblinka. I scorned you for trying to make an 'instant replay' of the Holocaust. For that obnoxious remark, I apologize."

"Winston, at the time I did not know why you said that. Yes, I resented your diminishing the Holocaust, equating it to a sports show. But now, having experienced the anguish, the heartache, over and over during the past half a year, I suspect you said that as a warning to me. You wanted to help me avoid that anguish. I can never forget that you went through the same pain and anguish when you were searching for your family, victims of the Holocaust."

They hugged, kissing one another, mixing smiles with tears, until Ron broke in to offer a toast, which brought on laughter and joy. "To Jodi, who is an NIC jewel and to Winston, who has yet to win an argument with Jodi!"

*

The next morning, while driving to Haifa, Ron said, "My plan of playing the cassette to Mrs. Drori may have been a good idea, but it may also lead you to a dead end. A final dead end, with her."

"I can't control my feelings. I want it to work. I want to find my mother. All I ask is, if I get shattered in the process, please pick up the pieces."

"I'll be there all the time."

When they entered the hospital at noon, the receptionist asked them to go to Dr. Sobel's office before they visited Mrs. Drori. The doctor greeted them with a worried look.

"She hasn't shown any signs of improvement," he admitted. "We're deeply concerned about our failure to help her. But, Miss Wycliff, I'm equally concerned about your ability to sustain another disappointment. Before you go in, you must understand that there has been no change, no change whatsoever, in her catatonic condition."

Leading them to the room, Dr. Sobel consoled them that Mrs. Drori's vital signs were much improved. "Since we took her off all medications, you'll find her looking a lot better."

The doctor was right. Mrs. Drori looked much better. Color had returned to her cheeks and her skin even seemed to have a luster. But she sat in the same position, at the side of her bed, staring at the window, immobile, obviously seeing nothing. Jodi approached her, straightened out the picture of her husband on the end table, and drew the curtain over the window to mute the glare from the afternoon sun.

Jodi looked straight at her, whispering, "Mama?"

The woman did not respond. Jodi nodded to the doctor, motioning to the VCR.

He put the cassette into the VCR and started the video. As soon as Jodi's image appeared on the screen, Mrs. Drori reacted in the same way the nurse had previously described, reaching both hands toward the screen.

Jodi faced her and, clasping her outstretched hands, cried out, "Mama, it's me, Jadwiga."

Mrs. Drori pulled back her hands and continued to stare blankly at the screen. Jodi repeated her cry but got no response.

When the names "Mr. and Mrs. Fenyves" appeared on the screen, the woman reached for her husband's photograph and flung it to the floor.

Jodi picked it up and handed it back to her.

Mrs. Drori startled them all by saying, raspily, angrily, "*Lo rotza. Maspik*!" Jodi knew enough Hebrew to understand what she said, "I don't want. Enough!"

Jodi reached in her purse and handed Dr. Sobel the baby picture of herself and her birth mother. The doctor quickly lit the overhead projector, focusing the image over Mrs. Drori's bed, on the white wall.

The patient sat up and stared at the projected picture for a long time. She then retreated back to her pillow. Jodi grasped her frail hand, pulled her gently into an upright position, and compelled her to look intently at the picture on the wall.

The woman turned her head to stare at Jodi, then at the picture on the wall.

Tears rolled down her face as she whispered, "My Jadzia, my little girl! *Moja Jadzia, moja dziewczynka!*"

Jodi cupped the woman's face and, with tears streaming, cried out, "Yes, Mama, I'm Jadzia, your Jadzia. Mama, oh, Mama. I am your Jadzia."

Epilogue

DR. SOBEL'S FINAL REPORT:

When Miriam and David Fenyves survived Treblinka, they made their way to Israel. They left no stone unturned in their attempts to find Jadzia. At the time, they failed because Stasha Wojchiechowski's name did not appear on any list of survivors or on any list of Polish citizens repatriated to Germany.

Frustrated and brokenhearted, Miriam blamed her husband for the death of their daughter. Her anger was so overwhelming that, for the rest of her life, she nursed a deeply suppressed wish for her husband's death.

The breakthrough in her psychological state came at one of the early sessions, when Jodi asked her what was her happiest moment. Miriam blurted out, "Becoming a widow."

This gave us a clue to pursue her relationship with her husband. It took several sessions before she could utter the death wish she had had for her husband.

When he was killed at the Suez Canal, Miriam had panicked, certain that his death was her self-fulfilling prophecy, born from her grief-stricken anger. Her catatonic condition started that day.

After six months of therapy, following her reunion with her daughter, the patient is on the road to improvement. She has begun a period of mourning over her husband's death and has even begun to feel a sense of pride at his heroism.

She now understands that had her husband not given Jadzia to Stasha and Franya, the child would have been killed instantly in Treblinka, where infants were gassed on arrival.